Welcome to the Underworld

Con Template

Also by Con Template:

Welcome to the Underworld, Book 1
The Fall of Gods, Book 2 of Welcome to the Underworld
The War of Gods, Book 3 of Welcome to the Underworld

Cover Photo by: DNL600i
http://www.officialpsds.com/Golden-Gun-PSD56366.html

Cover Illustration Design by: Dorothy Duong

Dedicated to my once-in-a-lifetime family.

Thank you for being there through every hardship and triumph.

You make everything worth it.

ACKNOWLEDGEMENTS

First and foremost, this book couldn't have been possible without the support of my family. Thank you to my mother for being a constant inspiration to me, to my father for always being my hero and to my sister for not only being my advisor in every aspect of life – but also my best friend. Thank you to the one I've always loved like a little brother as well: Kevin N. You are one of the kindest souls I've ever had the good fortune of having in my life and I just want you to know that I miss you everyday. Stay safe, stay strong and come home soon. We love you.

My gratitude also goes to "Snyderman", "The Bum," and "Hoff Hoff" for being some of the first to not only know about my publishing endeavors – but for always giving me so much encouragement in the process. Thank you to "Chief Little Fingers" and "Waddup G" for the silliness over the years as well. You all keep me sane in face of all the craziness in life.

My deepest gratitude goes to Dorothy for being a guardian over Welcome to the Underworld since its beginnings, for always watching over it and for dedicating so much time to creating such beautiful artwork for it. Your talent and genuine love for the story will never cease to amaze me.

Finally, no part of this journey could've been possible without my readers from Soompi. Thank you for not only embracing me as a young writer, but for always showering me with so much love. Words could never encapsulate how grateful I am for all your encouragement and support. This part of the writing journey is a long time coming and I thank you for being there with me every step of the way. I couldn't have come this far without you.

CONTENTS

Acknowledgments

"Our world is different from the rest."

00: Say Goodbye

"Please," the young woman pleaded, her voice quivering in anguish.

Dark clouds danced into the sky as she kneeled on the cold pavement. Apart from the discarded trash bags from a nearby restaurant, there was nothing in the alley but the two siblings.

"Please help me," she continued when her brother gave no response. A gust of wind roared through the narrow pathway, warning of an impending storm. She clenched her bloody hands with his. Hot tears streamed down her cheeks. "I— I can't live like this anymore. Please, please help me."

With his shoulders slumped and head hung low, his silence reigned. He tightened his grip on the syringe needle she had given him. It was clear that he didn't even want to hold it.

"You have to do this!" she finally screamed when his silence became unbearable for her. She wiped tears away with her bloodstained palms. When this action left a streak of blood across her face, she froze. She gazed glumly at the crimson hue covering her fingers. A haunted shadow engulfed her eyes. The blood wasn't hers.

Another pained moment passed before the young man finally peered down at his younger sister. The emotions mounting in his own brown eyes were indicative of the fact that he never once dreamed that they would find themselves in such a pitiful state.

"If I…" he began in a quiet voice. "If I do this, then I would lose you. I would never see you again." He averted his gaze away from her as bolts of lightning spilled into the sky. "There has to be another way. You *don't* want to do this."

"There's no other option for me but this. If I don't die, then I have to live with what I did." She paused, taking a moment to exhale sharply. Distant sounds of thunder bellowed overhead while she spoke. "And I can't do that."

"What about—?"

"Nothing else matters now," she interrupted firmly, her eyes seemingly lost in another world of thoughts. Holding his gaze, she made sure to eradicate any emotions from her face. She wanted to show him how resolved she was; she wanted to show him why she *needed* him to do this. "You know the bylaws that govern our world. It's either you or someone else who does this to me. Frankly, I'd rather die under your hands than someone else's."

As though her final words of conviction struck a nerve, he tipped his head back in misery. Droplets of rainwater sprinkled onto his face, the streaks of lightning reflecting in his eyes. He took another pondering moment to himself. After a few passing breaths, he returned his attention to her.

She smiled when she saw his face. She knew that look. He may have despised what she was asking of him, but he was going to do it regardless. Despite his authoritative stature in life, even his preferences took a backseat to the bylaws of their world.

He turned away from her and dug his hand into the pocket of his black jacket. He withdrew a small liquid vial. From there, everything seemed to play out in slow motion. He removed the cap and inserted the needle into the vial. Together, they watched with bated breaths as the clear liquid swam into the needle. Their breaths only returned when the needle was filled to the core.

He narrowed his solemn eyes on to her.

At this point, she had finally stopped shaking. Unable to hold his gaze and knowing what was to come, she broke eye contact. She merely lifted her right wrist to him. Things would be a lot easier if they minimized eye contact as much as possible.

"Are you completely sure about this?" he asked one last time.

"I can no longer lead life as your right-hand soldier," she replied, ready to finalize it all. "It's time to end this."

Her brother closed his eyes in pained resignation. He nodded at her words. No longer wanting to delay the inevitable, he reached for her hand. He held her wrist up and positioned the needle against her vein. The tip of the needle pierced her quickly and easily. The liquid contents flooded out of the needle and into her.

She gasped. It didn't take long for the effects to take place. Shortly after the injection, her vision blurred and her heart raced. The world around her began to spin in chaos. A throbbing migraine ensued and her vision worsened. *Everything just hurts.* Slowly, the nerves in her body felt like they were shutting down. When it became clear that the muscles in her body had stopped functioning, her body went limp. She fell backward, landing into a small puddle with a splash.

"Th-thank you," she whispered in between harsh breaths. No longer able to keep her eyes opened, she finally shut them, knowing that the world as she knew it was coming to an end.

"Goodbye, little one," she heard her brother utter before she lost all consciousness. "I'm sorry for not doing what you asked me to do."

"Some people find themselves stumbling into it..."

01: Queen of the Underworld

Three Years Later

Drawing up as if caught in a flood of waves, a startled Choi Yoori awoke with a thunderous gasp that ricocheted off the walls of her cramped bedroom. Her brown eyes enlarged from fear as her heart raced wildly. With a light layer of cold sweat glistening on her porcelain skin, it was an understatement to say that the dream she had hit a soft nerve within her.

She inhaled deeply to calm her overexcited nerves. It took only a moment for Yoori to become acclimated with her surroundings and only a moment for her to return to the confines of reality.

She squinted at the morning sun. Unable to withstand the bright rays, she lifted her hands to block out the light. She groaned, readjusting herself in her warm bed. After burrowing into that oh-so-comfortable spot, she pulled the blanket over her head and closed her eyes. Though she was awake, Yoori wanted a moment to mull over the mysterious dream she just had.

"Same damn dream again," she muttered bitterly.

A torrent of frustration washed over her. She opened her tired eyes and stared at the cover of her blanket. The rays of the morning light radiated over the comforter, making it appear as though she was hiding under a luminous blanket rather than a cheap beige comforter.

Who are they? Her aggravated mind pressed on.

It killed her that even after such a long period of time, she *still* didn't have the answer to that burning question. For the past several months, this particular recurring dream had been a cause of frustration for Yoori.

It started a year ago when her home in Taecin, a rural little town in South Korea, caught on fire. It was pure luck that Yoori survived. An hour prior, her mother had sent her out to buy some groceries. When Yoori returned, she was not only greeted with a blazing fire, but also news that her parents and her younger cousin were killed in the fire. She was told that she had missed the fire by mere minutes. If she had left a couple minutes later, she would've found herself in flames as well.

The entire situation was a daunting one for Yoori. The loss of her family should have left her in shambles, yet it didn't. If anything, as terrible as it may sound, it left her feeling more relieved than anything. It wasn't that Yoori was a heartless person who didn't care about her family. It wasn't like that at all. She cared about them very much. It was just that the predicament she found herself in left her incapable of loving them as she should.

The reason for this was that a year and a half prior to the fire, she was involved in a car accident that left her with amnesia.

Yoori could still recall the awful horror that inundated her when she opened her eyes in the hospital. She was so afraid and so frazzled. She woke up not knowing her name, who she was, who the people around her were—essentially no recollection of her life before the accident. Her mind was just blank. Only pained emptiness wallowed within it. The most frustrating part was that her family appeared more inclined to ignore her illness rather than try and help her regain her memories.

"*You ran away, hung out with a bad crowd, and made bad decisions,*" they simply told her, unwilling to go into further details. It was as though they were afraid she'd regain her memory and revert to being the bad sheep she once was.

After losing hope of ever regaining her memory (how couldn't she when her own family refused to help her?), Yoori settled into a new and very strained life with her family. She didn't know if she was ever close to them before her amnesia. Perhaps yes and perhaps no. The one thing Yoori was sure of was that throughout the entire duration with her family, she never felt the connection she felt she *should* have had with them. They were strangers and with a year and a half worth of awkward silences, they merely became her acquaintances before they passed.

After their funeral, Yoori no longer saw the point in living within the barriers of Taecin. What was the point of staying when she didn't have friends to begin with? No one knew her. For that reason alone, it wasn't hard for her to pack up and leave. The only question was: where would she move to?

The answer to that question came right after it was posed.

Yoori knew she wanted to move to Seoul. She couldn't explain her longing to move to the city, but ever since she saw a TV segment on the nightlife in Seoul, she just knew that she belonged there. So with the little money she had saved up and a strong desire to start anew, she packed up everything and left for the city.

After reaching Seoul, Yoori immediately found an apartment and a job as a waitress to help make ends meet. Although being a waitress was far from glamorous, Yoori truly enjoyed the company of the friends she made from working there. No one knew about her past, the loss of her family, or her amnesia, and she liked that. She liked that no one knew. It offered her an opportunity to start off on a clean slate, and it gave her an opportunity to be happy without having to be reminded about the unfortunate circumstances of her life. It was the first time in her life where she felt normal. It was the first time in her life where she felt like she belonged.

10

The dream came during her first night in Seoul.

The contents that played within it would always be the same. It would always be about the same people—a young woman and a young man in a dark alley. He would always possess a needle and she was always the one asking him to end her life. There was never anymore to the dream. No names, no reasons, no backstory, and most certainly no answers.

The images of the dream haunted Yoori's curiosity about her amnesia. She wrestled over the implications of the dream. Was this a memory from her past? If so, who were the two people? Did she see something she shouldn't have seen? Why did that girl want to die? What was the brother apologizing for? Question after question lingered in her mind. Was this dream a figment of her imagination or a memory from the past?

After many nights of broken sleep, Yoori tried her best to eliminate its importance from her life. However, it was difficult to ignore a recurring dream when it well, kept occurring. The problem with trying to throw it off as nothing was that the dream was becoming more and more intense. In the beginning, she was barely able to make out images and voices. Now, it was becoming clearer to her what they were doing and what they were saying. The only blurs left were the faces and of course, the reason *why* she was having this dream to begin with.

Yoori heaved a sigh when another headache threatened to commence. *Damn, I really shouldn't be so consumed with this dream…*

Resolved to not spend any more time on the matter, she threw her covers off and sat up in bed. She reached for a remote control and turned on her TV. As various colors twirled on to the 24-inch screen, her eyes bloomed at the images it displayed.

"What the hell…"

On screen was a newsreel with a slim, thirty-something anchorwoman in a white business suit. Behind her was a horde of police officers carrying numerous black body bags out of a high-rise building.

Her interest heightened, Yoori pointed the remote at the TV and turned up the volume. "…Police officers first arrived onto the horrendous crime scene early this morning. They received a call from a horrified receptionist who had reportedly walked in and was greeted with the sight of six dead men, all of whom had been shot to death on the lobby tiles."

A reel of a crying receptionist conversing with a police officer appeared on the screen. The anchorwoman's voice continued. "The police department has yet to give us any information on this matter. Our sources, however, have informed us that this is quite possibly another territorial gang war. The sources said that the cheeks of the victims had been carved into the shape of a skull, a famous branding technique of the gang who possessed the same name—*The Skulls*…"

"What a sucky way to start out the day."

Having heard enough, Yoori switched off the TV. She couldn't help but feel disturbed that she wasn't more affected by this piece of news. As tragic as it was, news like the carnage at Echo district was becoming a daily occurrence. The gang related crimes in this city was so bad that every piece of news appeared to deal, in one form or another, with gangs and their "territorial" wars.

Her morning was becoming disturbing. First a dream about a girl asking her brother to kill her and now a report about six men being shot to death in a business lobby?

What a peachy morning for me, Yoori thought sarcastically.

Mindlessly repositioning herself, her eyes involuntarily landed on her digital clock. *7:44 A.M.* Panic clutched her when she registered the time. She was going to be late for work!

"Shit! This is what I get for thinking about that goddamn dream again!"

Anxiety lacing her blood, she rocketed out of bed and flew to the bathroom like a bat out of hell. In record time, she brushed her teeth and threw on a pair of jeans and a nice green blouse for work. As she raced out of her apartment, she promised herself that she would never allow herself to be distracted with this mysterious little dream world of hers again. *Never, never again.*

Her sanity, and it appeared her job, depended on it.

■ ■ ■

"Oof! Sorry!" Yoori shouted distractedly. She ran out of the subway and fought her way through the congested sea of people. She wasn't sure if the person she bumped into replied with words of forgiveness, but she hardly cared. She was late for work and the calming, classical music on her iPod was failing miserably at tempering her anxiety. After fleeing from the cranky crowd, Yoori did the one thing she knew she had to do in order to get to work on time: she ran.

Shit! Shit, shit, shit, she chanted in her mind, irritated that her out of shape self was running slower than usual today.

After being scolded numerous times for being late, Yoori was desperate to get to work on time. The last thing she wanted to do was endure another speech about tardiness and responsibilities from her boss. Moreover, she wasn't in good standing at her position. She couldn't afford more mishaps.

Having been a waitress at Lee's Diner since her arrival in Seoul, Yoori was known to be pretty good with the regular customers. Though she received endless compliments about her amazing customer service skills from the regular patrons who frequented the diner, it didn't hold true for the new male customers who Yoori found to be repulsive, rude, and perverted. After arriving in Seoul, Yoori didn't have much luck with men. She was initially flattered when she started receiving compliments from the male customers about her beauty. Standing at 5'3" with big eyes, plump lips and a naturally toned body, Yoori had no trouble getting attention. This soon became a problem in her line of work.

In the past year alone, she had to scream at male customers for staring at her boobs and slap them across the face for touching her butt. Outbursts such as these were definitely not good for business. It was only after a formal complaint was filed from an indignant patron that her boss finally caught on to what was happening. With a lecture about responsibilities, a round of screams about politeness, and a warning about getting her ass fired, it was safe to say that Yoori was definitely on thin ice. Hence the reason for her impending aneurysm.

Her eyes snagged onto the diner at the corner of the street. "Oh God, finally!"

She glimpsed at her watch. Her brows scrunched together when it read 8:06 A.M. She was late.

"Damn it!" She switched off her iPod and tentatively pulled open the glass door to confront her fate.

Please do not let the big bad boss be here, she prayed desperately.

She peered warily at the counter. She let out a squeal when instead of catching sight of a stout little man, she spied a lean beautiful girl who was staring at her with a smile on her face.

"Chae Young! Oh my God. Hi!" Yoori exclaimed happily. She ran behind the counter, her heart elated to see her co-worker/best friend. "Hi! Good morning!"

Dressed in a simple white tank top and black jeans, Chae Young appeared glamorous even in this "mediocre" look. She regarded Yoori with playful eyes.

"Good morning to you too, little miss tardy," she said lightheartedly, side butting Yoori while she settled in behind the counter. She laughed. "Lucky you, I'm here instead of my dad."

"I know," replied Yoori, feigning a pout. "I suck for being late."

Chae Young's laugh became warmer. She waved a hand of dismissal. "I'm just playing. Don't worry about it. We don't even have any customers. No harm, no foul."

Yoori nodded appreciatively. She dug into her pocket and took out an elastic band. As she proceeded to tie her hair into a disheveled bun that resembled Chae Young's, she said, "You got back early. What happened to taking a month's worth of vacation with the boyfriend?"

Chae Young snorted upon being reminded as to why she was working that day. "I broke up with that loser."

Yoori laughed, shaking her head knowingly. She was not surprised. Chae Young was the type of girl who had the tendency to go for guys who weren't good for her. When she became "official" with her new boyfriend a week ago, she naively informed Yoori that she was sure it was going to last forever. Even though Yoori knew better than to believe that, she kept her opinion to herself because she didn't want to be a jerk and burst her friend's bubble. However, shortly after announcing that she thought her newfound relationship was going to last forever, Chae Young proceeded to also inform Yoori that she was going to take a month's worth of vacation to spend time with her "honey." Due to the fact that her father was the owner of the diner, Chae Young could afford such luxuries with little repercussions.

Unfortunately for Chae Young, the fairytale vacation was short-lived.

"What happened?" Yoori asked, stepping closer to the counter.

"He took me around Seoul and showed me all the 'nightlife' stuff," Chae Young began, bitterness encased in her taut voice. "It was fun until I caught him cheating on me with one of our hostesses. I promptly said goodbye." A sly smile appeared on her face. "But not before kicking him in the balls before I made my exit!"

"Oh man," Yoori laughed. She definitely gave props to Chae Young for doing that. She wasn't sure if she would ever have the nerve to do that. Slap perverted guys, yes. But kick them in the balls? Doubtful.

She grabbed a towel to wipe some stains off the counter. Her laughter dying down, she looked at Chae Young. "I'm sorry, Chae," she voiced sympathetically. All jokes aside, she truly felt bad for her friend. "You were so excited too."

Chae Young waved her hand as if to say, "Don't worry about it." Her eyes then flashed with excitement. There was something that overshadowed the misery of being cheated on. "Want to hear a story about gangs?"

Much like a fan girl at her favorite idol's concert, the question Chae Young posed was like music to Yoori's bored ears.

"Hmm, let me think," Yoori began, adopting a tone of reluctance. Her eyes perused the empty diner. "I have so many customers to tend to...but...*YES!*"

Hell yes!

One of the reasons why Yoori kept her opinions to herself about the new "ex" was because of his association with a gang—or so he said. Although she didn't approve of gangs, she would be a liar if she said she wasn't fascinated by the mystery cloaking this secretive society. It intrigued her endlessly. Their acts of violence were so public to the rest of the world, yet no one from the outside was privy to the inner workings of their world. It was as if they were ghosts in her world, appearing in and out, yet never leaving any trace of their identities behind. Yoori knew for a fact that Chae Young shared in this intrigue, which was more than likely the reason why she showed any real interest in the guy. Chae Young may have found him to be easy on the eyes, but his knowledge of the inner workings of the Underworld was what ultimately sealed the deal with Chae Young. Everyone liked secrets, right?

"So, what's this story about?" Yoori asked, excited to momentarily escape from her boring world and get lost in a legendary one.

"Brief history about the Queen of the Underworld. Apparently this is the juiciest story for the gang world," Chae Young exclaimed, clapping her hands together in glee.

"Ooooh," Yoori cooed, sharing in the contagious excitement. She pulled out a stool and slid onto it. She made herself comfortable by placing her elbows on the counter and resting her chin on her palms. She was ready to enjoy this story.

"Okay!" Chae Young shrieked, grabbing a stool and making herself comfortable as well. Once she was settled, she began the tale. "In the underground world three to four years ago, three gangs ruled over the Underworld like Kings. They were known as the Skulls, the Serpents, and the Scorpions."

Yoori shifted uncomfortably at the mention of the Skulls. She had forgotten, but was now instantly reminded of the news segment she saw earlier.

"The three gangs had equal power in terms of alliances with different business associates. Wars broke out for territorial and reputational gain. The black market was a lucrative business. Everyone wanted the maximum profit potential. Of the three gangs, two slowly became more powerful because of an impending merge.

As the story goes, the leader of the Skulls fell in love with the Scorpion's 'Queen.' My ex told me she was basically the crowned jewel of the Underworld. Her strong knowledge in the skills of martial arts and weaponry was what made her infamous; her breathtaking beauty was what made her unforgettable. She was the object of affection for many gang members. She only showed interest in the Skulls gang leader though. The story gets murky from there. No one really knows what happened with that relationship while it lasted."

Yoori's interest in this story was already piqued. "Tell me more about the girl."

Chae Young obliged. "My ex said that she was basically the reigning Queen of the Underworld at that time. Her older brother, who was the actual leader of the Scorpions, made her second in command. She had the protection of her older brother and the vow of loyalty from another powerful gang leader. She was virtually untouchable. I guess she was like the invisible leading hand of the Underworld society at the time. She did not have direct power, but she had the power to easily sway the Underworld any which way she liked." She eyed Yoori. "Have you heard the story about the fifteen people who were murdered in a Seoul club a couple of years ago?"

Yoori shook her head.

"That's because she was in charge of that operation. *That's* how powerful she was. She controlled everything: the legal system, the media, and all the illegal operations. They were all under the tip of her fingers. She did what she wanted and no one dared to go against her. All the crimes she committed—and it was said to have been horrific crimes—never even made the news because she had close ties to the legal authorities as well."

Sensing where the story was headed, Yoori asked, "What happened to her?"

Disappointment teemed in Chae Young's brown eyes.

"That's the sad part. She went missing for a couple of days and her body was eventually found in the back of a known gang alley. Someone had shot her point blank in the head and disfigured her face. The ones who found her said she was not even close to being recognizable. She was only later identified when her brother confirmed a birthmark on her neck or something. After her body was discovered, fingers were pointed as to who was to be blamed for her death. Some people say that she got into a fight, got her face disfigured and ended her own life because of it. I, personally, think it's someone from the Serpents gang who didn't want the Skulls and the Scorpions to merge. But it's all speculation. It could easily be some random girl who was jealous of her."

"Wow," Yoori marveled. "You have to show me a picture of her! I want to see the face of a girl that powerful."

Chae Young rolled her eyes like Yoori's request was the most ridiculous thing she had ever heard. "Don't you think I want to see it too? These underground societies are all about confidentiality. No one outside of the members of the Underworld knows what each of the leaders look like. Unless you were active in the Underworld at that time, you would not be privy to her face or her identity."

"Your ex must know then," Yoori insisted, curiosity still gnawing at her.

"Trust me, I bugged him. He only recently joined the Skulls and he doesn't want to piss anyone off. Apparently the mention of her name is frowned upon now. I guess the leader doesn't want to be reminded of the loss of his great love."

Yoori nodded in understanding. Her mind ventured elsewhere. "The Scorpions, her gang, are they still active?"

"They're still active, but not to the degree they once were. Shortly after news of her death spread, her older brother was said to have had a mental breakdown. The Scorpions eventually fell apart, now culminating to only a few active members. Some went to join the Skulls, some joined the Serpents, some formed their own gangs, and some tried to form their own gangs, but failed miserably. The ones who did stay are keeping the gang alive, but only slightly. Her brother was said to have left the country as well."

Yoori felt a tug at her heart at the mention of the older brother in the story. She could relate to him. She understood the pain of losing someone you love and the need to run away from the things that reminded you of them.

"Sad story," she muttered. She reached for the damp cloth and started wiping the counter again. Who knew such an interesting Underworld story would be *that* sad?

"Yeah," Chae Young said pensively. "Stories of a girl that beautiful with all the power and all those guys chasing after her. Kinda makes you wish you could continue on her reign, huh?"

"I don't know about that," Yoori replied candidly.

Chae Young gaped at her. "Oh come on, Yoori. You really wouldn't want that?"

"No, I mean, I'm pretty sure it's not a fairytale," Yoori clarified, catching her friend's scrutinizing gaze. She paused to correct herself. "Well, granted it's a 'duh' point that it's not a fairytale for her because she got shot in the head. But I mean, come on. She lived in a world where violence was more prevalent than peace. A girl like that must have had some serious demons."

"Yeah, but still...the part about having a hot guy chase after you must have you transfixed?"

Yoori smiled as she continued to wipe the counter. "How do you know he's hot?"

16

"Hot people have a tendency to find each other," Chae Young said in a matter-of-fact tone. Her eyes glazed over. After taking a moment to fantasize about life as the Scorpion girl, Chae Young consulted her watch. She pursed her lips when she read the time. "Anyway, I have to go to the pharmacy and pick up prescription for my dad." She grabbed her bag and flew out of her seat. Wasting no time, Chae Young waved goodbye to Yoori and ran out, slamming the door shut behind her. "Be back in thirty minutes. See ya!"

Yoori nodded obliviously, balling up the damp cloth and throwing it on the floor. The current of her thoughts had already progressed on to something else. Her curiosity piqued when she was reminded of the Skulls gang leader. Although it was incredibly silly of her, she wondered what the true story pertaining to him and the Scorpion girl was. Did he really forget about her and moved on with his life? Her state of contemplation was interrupted when the door opened.

A tall customer strode into the diner. He wore a white shirt, black pants, and a red cap that covered the upper features of his face. His head was lowered when he took a seat at one of the booths in the center of the diner.

Yoori let out an inaudible sigh.

"Time to stop wondering about what happened with other people's lives and worry about my own boring one," she said quietly, grabbing a menu and quickly making her way to the new customer. She didn't want him to wait.

If Yoori had known her meeting with this new customer would end her boring life, she probably would've made him wait just a *little* bit longer. A pleasant meeting was not awaiting her.

"Whether willing or unwillingly..."

02: Personal Assistant

"Good morning!" Yoori chirped, placing the laminated diner menu in front of the customer.

At the sound of her loud voice, the customer jumped in surprise.

Embarrassed that the deafening sound of her chipmunk voice indirectly succeeded in scaring the customer, she struggled to maintain a nervous smile. Her voice was definitely more high-pitched than she would've liked it to be. She could only imagine how annoyed the guy must be with her already.

Take a deep breath, she instructed herself. *Just smile and make it up to him by being a wonderful customer service representative.*

As silly as it may sound, Yoori was actually nervous to be this guy's server. It wasn't like he intimidated her or anything. On the contrary, positive outcomes might arise if she were to do a great job serving him. She would not only get on her boss's good side, but she would also be guaranteed job security for at least a few more months if this new customer were to become a regular because of her. Yes, if everything went according to plan and she impressed this guy, then perhaps he would sing her praises to her boss and all would be well in little Choi Yoori's world.

Pleased with herself for conjuring up such an ingenious plan, Yoori's smile widened. She continued with her much practiced line. "My name is Yoori, and I'll be your server today. May I get you something to drink as you look at our menu?"

"I don't want anything on the menu. Just coffee please, ma'am," the customer replied, not even making eye contact with her. He appeared impatient and edgy. He was also oddly fixated with staring at the table.

Although the air of arrogance exuding out of him bothered her, Yoori faked an understanding nod. "Okay, I'll bring that right out."

She turned on her heels. Her smile wilted into a frown. She rolled her eyes at the gall of this new customer. Who the hell comes to a breakfast joint to only order coffee?

"There's a coffee shop right next door," she muttered, annoyance in her voice. Another outraged thought entered her mind. And who was this guy to call her "ma'am"? They were around the same age!

She groaned inwardly. Great, now she was more pissed off. If the guy had half a brain, then he'd know very well that the last thing a man should endeavor to do was make a girl feel older than she was. Irritated with how unpleasant her day was becoming, she went into the kitchen, grabbed a tray, and placed the coffee pot and mug onto it. Reminding herself that she still needed to impress him so he'd sing her praises, she inhaled deeply to relinquish any unnecessary bitterness she was harboring for him.

"Breathe in. Breathe out. Breathe in. Breathe out..."

Ah. She felt more tranquil already. Pleased with her impressive ability to calm her temper, she returned to her guest and placed the coffee mug before him.

Uncomfortable nerves swirled within her when she became aware that he had abandoned his gaze on the table. His sharp brown eyes were now on her. Unprepared with the sudden attention, Yoori gave him a cautious smile.

"Is there anything else I can get you today?" she asked, thinking that he was staring because he wanted something else. As Yoori waited for his reply, she began to pour coffee into the mug, only stopping after it had filled to the rim.

"Yes," he said in a low and tired voice. Arrogance continued to throb within it. His eyes were still focused on her. "Now that I'm thinking about it, I'd like to order some breakfast."

"Alright then," she said with satisfaction, her annoyance with him decaying at the fact that he was now making eye contact and smiling (however forced it appeared). Ordering food at a diner and making eye contact...now that was more like it. Ecstatic that things were going according to plan, she cheerily reached into her pocket to retrieve her notepad. Her happiness died as quickly as a fruit fly. She furrowed her brows, searching her pockets for a pen. All she found was lint.

I had it just a second ago, she thought. She scanned the floor for possible signs of her pen. When the pen didn't appear in sight, she quickly turned around to face her waiting customer. Needless to say, she was feeling a bit flustered with the missing pen. Where did it go?

She laughed fretfully. "Um, heh, excuse me. I'll be right back!" She rushed back to the counter and grabbed a spare pen. Upon retrieval, Yoori hurried back to her waiting customer.

"I'm sorry about the wait!" she panted, taking huge strides back to him. She warily assessed his patience. She pouted, her hopes of getting wonderful praises and tips from him crushed. He already looked annoyed. She lifted her notepad in an effort to regain any shred of customer service dignity she had left. "What can I get for you today?"

"Well, you can start by filling up my coffee mug again," he voiced pompously, a smirk appearing on his face.

Yoori's eyes snagged on him and his empty coffee cup. Disbelief edged her. Did he really just finish the entire cup?

His smirk grew into one of irritation as he kept his pompous gaze on her. Yoori's eyes grew sharp when she caught it—his intolerably condescending and arrogant nature. *Great.* Her plans were now dashed. She was not only stuck with a jackass of a customer, but she was also positive she was going to wind up with a crappy tip. To make matters worse, she already felt her bitterness and animosity return for this guy. She didn't like how he spoke to her and she didn't like how he looked at her. Pervy customers usually started out like this before they began to shamelessly hit on her. Oh, how she wanted to slap that stupid smirk off his face.

Instead of doing that, she simply smiled apologetically. However much she wanted to physically assault him, she knew better. "Of course, I'm sorry."

Bastard, she thought angrily, picking up the coffee pot.

Still smiling, she angled the coffee pot over the mug, her blood boiling with the passing seconds. As she distractedly poured the coffee, what happened next took Yoori by utter surprise. The handle on the coffee pot suddenly broke apart. Next thing she knew, the sound of glass shattering rang in her ears before a loud male scream thundered into the diner.

"JESUS CHRIST!" She covered her mouth, watching in horror as the customer jumped up from his seat and started shaking hot coffee off his bare hands.

She had just poured steaming hot coffee all over him!

"What the hell is wrong with you?" he shouted, rubbing his hands together in agony.

"I'm—I'm so sorry!" she cried, genuinely apologetic. She grabbed a handful of napkins from the dispenser and started drying his red-hot hands with them. It was true that Yoori didn't like the guy, but she never wished to harm him like this! This was what she got for talking shit about someone in her head. Her vision became blurred with confusion as she tried to make sense of what happened. "Th—th—the handle just suddenly broke—I...oh God...are you okay?"

She looked at his hands. They were blazing red.

He glared at her, indignant that she'd be foolish enough to ask such a naïve question. "Does it look like I am?"

Her already petrified heartbeat escalated at his response. Shit. Was this real life? Was this really happening?

"I'm *so* sorry. Please, tell me what can I do to make this better? Coffee and breakfast on the house?" she asked hopefully. She couldn't afford to have this guy sue. Her boss was already at his wit's end with her customer service skills (or lack thereof).

An incredulous expression cloaked his face. "You just burned me with coffee and your reconciliation for that is breakfast and *coffee* on the house?"

Yoori raised her hands up in defeat. "Okay, okay. Good point. Perhaps free breakfast for two weeks? Or better yet, a month?"

He could barely contain his scoff. He assessed his burnt hands before casting a glance at her. For a nanosecond, she could've sworn she saw his eyes gleam with slyness.

"I suppose," he started, straightening his back. "I suppose I can sue for this."

The panic alarm blared inside Yoori. "No, no! Please! I will get fired for sure. Please, I *need* this job!"

"Why should I care about that?"

She clapped her hands together, giving the guy her most angelic face. She hoped to appeal to his humane side. "Please sir. Have a heart."

After taking several seconds to seemingly think over what he wanted to do with her, he finally nodded at her, an angelic smile of his own adorning his face.

"I guess I can do you a favor..." he trailed aimlessly, stroking his burnt hand. His anger seemed to have subsided as quickly as it came.

Yoori gratefully clasped her hands together. "Yes, please do. It would really help me out." Her mind was cheering with glee. That angelic puppy face of hers *always* did the trick.

"...If you do me a favor."

Yoori's sense of relief dispelled. A frown darkened her once angelic countenance. Her womanly instincts were working at full speed. She knew something bad was coming. Here comes the prostitution proposal...

"I need an assistant," he said, stunning her with his words.

"Eh?"

Not the most profound reply, but it was the best Yoori could do given how befuddled she was by this looney tune's proposal.

"I need a personal assistant," he repeated.

"You want me to be your *personal assistant*?" She couldn't mask the perplexity on her face. Was this a joke? Was the guy serious? She blinked at him, hoping to see a smile sweep across his face to indicate that he was joking. Her heart dropped to the lowest of lows when his face and voice remained stern and serious.

"Yeah," he confirmed, a small smile illuminating his features. "I've been meaning to look for someone to assist me in my day-to-day activities. I think you'd be a good fit."

"How'd you come to that conclusion?" Her defenses were up. This guy was officially getting creepy.

"Well, let's just say that my work is very confidential. The people I deal with and the operations I run are very...lucrative. Confidentiality is key in all of this. Basically, I don't need someone who is financially bound to me; I need someone who is legally and *ethically* bound to me." His smile broadened. He was talking to her like she had just won a free vacation as opposed to a prison sentence. "I think you can be that person."

Now it was Yoori's turn to look at him like he was a fool. Was this how recruitment for new jobs operated nowadays? Through blackmail? Did this guy really expect her to be his walking slave? Did he really think she was that stupid?

She didn't hesitate to reject his job offer. "Thanks, but no thanks."

Her bravado chipped when she saw the resolve in his eyes. It scared her briefly because it didn't appear like he was the type of guy who was used to people saying no to him. She had the uneasy feeling he wasn't going to make this rejection easy. To her surprise, instead of screaming at her, the guy smiled, taking a step closer to her. Yoori took a step back in reaction; she didn't want to be closer to him than she already was. Her sixth sense was working overtime. She had a *very* bad feeling about all of this.

"You can't say no," he said firmly. He crossed his arms in an authoritative manner. It was evident in his demeanor that he wasn't the type to give up. Not by a long shot.

Yoori jutted her chin up. She should've been intimidated by him, but she was a prideful fool. Being in the diner also made her feel more secure. This was her turf. If he wanted a fight, then he was going to get one.

"Sue me," she said irately, throwing the handful of napkins onto the table. She refused to be blackmailed into slavery.

She was prepared to walk away when he jerked her to a halt with his next statement.

"I suppose I don't have to sue you," he started, retrieving his wallet from his front pocket. He grabbed a wad of bills from it.

He threw the money onto the damp table and began to leave. Then, he did a full 360-degree turn, surveying the diner.

"Yeah, this diner must make pretty good money with waitresses like you..." He made it a point to stab her with a dirty look, a gesture that made Yoori respond with a dirty look of her own, "who feel entitled to giving customers second degree burns." He shook his head in disbelief. He placed his hands into his pockets and stared off into the distance.

Yoori eyed him cautiously, afraid of where he was taking this little speech.

He did not disappoint her expectations. "Yeah," he murmured, speaking loud enough for Yoori to hear him. "I'm doing this for the good of the other customers. This diner has to be sued. It has to be put out of business. It's only right. It's not safe here."

Yoori narrowed her eyes. This guy was truly a piece of work.

"You don't scare me. I could always find another job. I don't have very close ties to this diner."

His lips tilted upward at her smug response. "Oh yeah? Well, what about your little friend? The one you were talking to earlier?"

Yoori's demeanor softened. *Uh oh, here comes the moral dilemma.*

"Isn't this her father's restaurant?"

Damn it. She knew he was going to make this hard, but she didn't think he was going to make it this difficult.

Yoori bit her lip, truly troubled for the first time. It killed her to think that this little incident could bring any awful implications to Chae Young. She wasn't fond of the diner or her boss, but Chae Young had been a wonderful friend since her arrival to Seoul. If anything, she was Yoori's one true friend. Yoori couldn't let this guy bring Chae Young into the mix and ruin her life.

"They have nothing to do with this," she countered. She was astounded that someone could be so heartless and bring innocent people into their stupid quarrel.

Ignoring her, the cocky customer continued. "I suppose if this place shuts down, it's really their problem. Not yours. Why should *you* pay for your own mistakes when there are other people who can take the fall for you?"

The guy was masterful at being persuasive. Every word that poured from his lips, he made sure to pound them into her, knowing that the guilt was eating her alive. And eat her alive it did.

Yoori bowed her head down in disgrace. Though his tricks of trade were less than favorable to her, Yoori gave credit where it was due. The guy was smart to play the guilt card with Yoori, she'd give him that much. Even though admitting defeat was not something Yoori was used to doing, *especially* when it came down to admitting defeat to a male chauvinist pig, she also couldn't allow anyone to pay for her mistakes. In this case, her biggest mistake was existing at the same moment as this jerk.

Her shoulders slumped. *This is what I get for wanting to be a good friend and a good person...*Distress raining over her, Yoori struggled to part her lips. Words of blasphemy began to pour out of her once witty mouth.

"If I..." she began slowly, ready to give in to evil.

"Yes?"

Yoori stiffened uncomfortably, struggling to let the words out. "If I become your personal assistant, you'll forget any of this happened?"

"Yes."

"You won't come back and sue the diner?"

"Yes. Under the condition you keep your part of the deal of course."

She briefly closed her eyes in agony. "And what exactly is my part of the deal?"

A satisfied smile brightened his visage. He leaned in closer, a move that took Yoori by surprise. She involuntarily inhaled the intoxicating scent of his cologne. As he spoke, his lips were millimeters away from her earlobe. His warm breath tickled her sensitive skin. "Why don't you quit right now and we'll talk about it outside?"

Yoori pushed herself away from him, freaked out that he was invading her personal space and even more freaked out that she felt butterflies form in her tummy.

What's wrong with you, Choi Yoori? she thought distractedly.

Finding a coherent train of thought, Yoori glared at him in defense.

"We're understaffed right now," she said, still not ready to become his personal assistant quite yet. "They need me for the morning shift."

Not that she really cared about being there for the morning shift, but any excuse that would keep her from leaving with him would have to do for now. She didn't even know the guy and now she had to leave with him? Couldn't a girl have, at the very least, a day to think about the unnecessary evil that had befallen her life?

He scanned the empty diner in confusion. "I'm the only customer here though. This diner doesn't even *need* staff right now."

Yoori observed the room too. It was true. He was the only customer present at the moment. However, Chae Young wasn't going to be back for a while. Someone had to be here to watch the diner.

"Plus," he interrupted before she could say anymore, "isn't it better to have the diner be understaffed for the morning shift than have it be understaffed *forever*?"

She blanched at his statement. "Are you serious?"

He raised a brow, daring her to challenge his threat. "Get your stuff. Let's go. I have things I need to do."

"What?" she cried in outrage. "Now? No! I can't just leave! Can't you wait another twenty minutes for my friend to come back?"

"I'm going to be outside," he barreled on without mercy. "I'll wait two minutes for you. If you don't come out with your stuff in two minutes, I'll be gone. And you, along with the diner, will be hearing from my lawyers."

Her heart dropped to the ground when he was out of sight. She couldn't believe any of this was really happening to her. She abruptly pinched herself. Her eyes twitched in pain from the pinch.

Shit, she thought despondently. It wasn't a dream. All of this was *really* happening to her.

Clenching and unclenching her fists, Yoori glared at the broken glass and spilled coffee still dripping quietly onto the tiles. All of this because of crappy coffee pots. She miserably shook her head.

Fuck.

Fuck her luck.

Having the forefront to know that making her prospective boss wait any longer was a bad idea, Yoori decided that if she was going to leave, leaving right away would be a good option. She didn't want to get on his bad side—or anymore of his bad side.

Grabbing her bag from the counter, she took one last inventory of the diner.

"My life is over," she muttered before pushing the door open and jumpstarting the beginning of a dangerous new life.

What on earth does this guy have in store for me?

"How did you fall into it?"

03: The King of Serpents

"Ah, less than two minutes, I guess you're not too attached to the place after all," the cocky customer voiced upon hearing her stomping footsteps.

He stood on the street curb with his hands tucked in his pockets. He was staring off into the hectic street. He didn't even bother to turn around to look at her.

Chewing her bottom lip, Yoori kept her sharp gaze on him. "What do you want?" she asked. She folded her arms and narrowed her eyes onto his profile. Was it possible to dislike someone as much as she disliked this guy?

His eyes still on the busy street, he said, "We'll talk in the car."

Yoori was beside herself with how he was treating her. First he blackmailed her, *then* he forced her into slave labor, and now he was refusing to make eye contact while speaking to her.

Bastard, she thought furiously, glowering at him.

As if hearing the scorn in her resentful mind, Yoori's prospective boss averted his gaze from the street and settled his eyes onto her. Her body tensed up when he did this. He wasn't glaring, but his vacant stare was enough to intimidate her. It was enough to subdue any plot of murder on her part.

The pulsating motion of her blood froze when he closed the distance between them. His six-foot frame towered over her. Taking off his red cap, he fixed his disheveled hat hair and gazed upward at the sky. He sighed as though relieved to finally be able to take the damn thing off.

Despite herself, Yoori gawked as her anger gradually faded away. She was distracted. *Extremely distracted*. With all that happened in the diner, she didn't have the opportunity to get a close enough look to assess his physical traits. She figured that the guy would have a bad hair day after taking off the cap. However, she had to admit his short black hair looked good after he "fixed" it up. Yoori's breathing grew slightly shallower as her gaze on him remained transfixed. *Holy...* It hadn't occurred to her how attractive this guy was without his red cap distracting her from his face. Strong chin and jaw, full tempting lips, and beguiling eyes complemented his perfectly sculpted face. If angels existed, then this one was the arc of all angels.

She honestly had to do a double take. Was this handsome thing the same beast who blackmailed her into slavery?

Returning his attention to her, those enticing lips curved up in amusement. He wore a smile of masculine pride, one that knew without a shadow of a doubt that she was admiring his striking features.

Yoori caught herself and her eyes widened. She uncomfortably scratched the back of her head, her face growing a darker shade of pink. She attempted to look elsewhere. She was utterly mortified that she got caught gawking.

"We got off to a really bad start," he began. When he saw that she was still avoiding eye contact, he edged closer to her and tilted his head to meet her eyes.

Yoori nodded slowly, her breathing becoming unsteady again. It surprised her that she adored the sound of his voice when he was so nice and polite. She shook, vexed with herself. What was wrong with her? Wasn't she supposed to be furious with this guy?

"Yeah, forcing someone into slave labor never leaves a good first impression," she sarcastically replied, trying desperately to hold on to what was left of the sassy Yoori who wasn't infatuated with her potential boss/blackmailing customer.

"Nor is spilling blazing hot coffee on someone's hands," he retorted, his smirk morphing into a charming smile. His face glowed like an angel in the morning light.

She slowly nodded again, this time riveted by his change of behavior. He was actually being somewhat...likeable. She enjoyed their new form of interaction very much. Given the change in communication style, Yoori wondered if he was interested in her too. Was this the reason for his amicable behavior?

"Anyway, we obviously didn't meet properly," he went on. His tone was almost apologetic. "The name is Kwon Tae Hyun. Friends call me Tae Hyun."

Yoori could only blink in response. Lost in a stupor, she was forgetting why she disliked him in the first place.

The smile that brought innocence to his face soon faded into a devilish one when he said his next words. "You can call me 'boss' though, seeing as though you're only an assistant." He chuckled, roughly sticking the red cap on her head. The familiar aura of his pompous personality returned, and it left Yoori with nothing but a bad taste in her mouth.

She glowered at him. Now she remembered why she disliked him so much. She took off the red cap in irritation.

"What am I supposed to do with this?" she demanded, holding it up like he had just given her a foreign object she'd never seen before.

As her blood boiled dangerously, her face grew redder with rage. She was beside herself that she was even momentarily attracted to him. Kwon Tae Hyun was an ass. Enough said.

Clearly entertained with the death glare Yoori shot his way, Tae Hyun simply grinned as he turned away from her. He stretched his long arms into the air and yawned in boredom.

"Hold it of course, assistant," he said, referring to the red cap. He narrowed his eyes onto her. He lowered his arms, his voice turning stern. "But if you mess it up or lose it, you're dead. You hear that, assistant?"

Yoori's eyes bulged. His audacity infuriated her. Addressing her as "assistant." Who did he think he was? It enraged her how quickly he could change from being a charming guy to a complete ass in a matter of seconds. She grimaced when she came to an answer.

Typical male, she concluded with hatred. Well, she wouldn't have it! She wouldn't let this guy walk all over her.

"The name is Yoori." Hands on her hips, she took a step closer to him. "Choi Yoori," she said defiantly, killing the urge to step on his feet. She tried hard to appear intimidating under his entertained gaze. "Friends and everyone else call me Yoori, so you can do the same."

Instead of responding to her with words of dispute, Tae Hyun decided to simply stare her down. It was as if, for his own amusement, he was trying to silently intimidate her.

Being the stubborn and prideful fool that she was, Yoori puffed up her chest and glowered up at him with the same ferocity.

They stared at each other for what seemed like forever, neither blinking. The staring challenge became so intense that Yoori's eyes began to twitch non-stop, desperately begging her to blink so they could function again. A twinge of pain pricked at her eyes, making her groan. She couldn't handle it anymore. Miserably admitting defeat, Yoori dragged her gaze away, blinking in shame as her dry eyes basked in the glory of restored moisture.

Disgraced by losing, Yoori was taken by surprise when she felt him reach for her hand. He laced his fingers with hers and tugged her with him, nearly causing her to trip over her own feet.

"Car's here," he casually stated, acting as if a lethal staring contest hadn't commenced seconds prior.

Yoori distractedly followed Tae Hyun, her eyes not believing what they saw. She pointed dubiously at the black hummer limo approaching them. "You call *that* a car?"

Tae Hyun chuckled, pulling her closer once the impossibly lavish limo made a complete stop at the curb. She gaped in awe as a lean, butler-looking chauffeur ran out and glided toward them. He wore an all black suit and dark sunglasses. His white-gloved hands stretched out to open the door. He was smiling warmly at them the entire time.

Tae Hyun pulled her into the limo with him.

"Oof!" Yoori struggled to get in without falling to her face. Once she successfully planted her butt on the leather seat, the door slammed shut behind her, causing the sunlight to fade into oblivion.

She repositioned herself in the seat beside Tae Hyun. Her eyes roamed over the limo in wonderment. The interior was illuminated with white and blue lights. The black leather seats stretched out to the far corners of the limo. Beneath their feet, the carpet sparkled with a red velvet hue. Her eyes traveled the length of the bar to the side. The shot glasses that sat on it appeared to be embroidered with diamonds.

This is too rich, she thought incredulously, lost in the affluent ambiance.

"I would have figured that you were the type of girl who was used to this type of amenity," Tae Hyun observed carelessly, grabbing a bottle of Cristal and two champagne glasses. He poured the Cristal into the two glasses. He handed her a champagne glass.

"In another life, maybe." She clumsily took the champagne glass. She was very much thrown off balance with all of this. She knew Tae Hyun was not just another guy off the streets, but from the decadence of this ride, it was evident that he was far from ordinary.

"Choi Yoori."

Yoori shuddered when he addressed her by her full name. For whatever reason, it made her feel inferior to him.

"You can just call me Yoori," she corrected at once.

"Choi Yoori," he repeated, dismissing her request. "I believe it's time to talk business."

Yoori breathed in slowly, feeling more anxious than before. She was bitter that Tae Hyun was still addressing her by her full name, but she decided to let it go. She had bigger fish to concern herself with. Namely, negotiating a good employment deal.

"To start off, I run a billion dollar business. I'm a very busy man. What I need is very simple. I need someone to assist me in my day-to-day activities. My work is confidential. Once you start, you are expected to keep your mouth shut about what you see and hear. I *do not* work regular hours so you can throw the 8 A.M. to 5 P.M. concept out the window. I work with people who are known to be rough around the edges; I expect you to get along with them. I need someone who can work well under pressure and lead a group if necessary. Being in shape is crucial. It is not only for the benefit of people's eyes, but for your own benefit as well because this job will require a lot of running around. In my line of business, it is quite possible that you may get hurt while on the job. This is why I offer full health coverage."

Yoori's eyes bloomed at the possibility of needing full health coverage. What was he going to have her do?

Ignoring her dramatic reaction, Tae Hyun continued. "Your duties will range from helping me set up appointments, researching for me, making me dinner, or making me coffee — " He stopped midway and stared at his red hands. Reminded of her unimpressive track record with handling coffee, he said, "Maybe not the last part, but basically anything to help make my life better and easier. I travel a lot. I expect you to be by my side every step of the way."

He took out a Blackberry and tossed it to her. Yoori fumbled to catch it and nearly spilled her drink in the process. "Last but not least, you are now provided with the company phone. When I need you, I expect you to be there as soon as possible. You are not to disappoint me in this matter. Any questions?"

"Pay?" Yoori asked at once. It was the most important thing!

"Commission based."

"Based on what?"

"How much you make me happy." A suggestive smile touched his lips. "It can vary, depending on how good you are."

Yoori straightened, her internal alarm blaring. "Let's get one thing straight. I'm here to assist you. I'm not having sex with you."

He closed his eyes and laughed quietly, making her feel a little bit smaller than before. "I don't have sex with the help."

Yoori's teeth clenched, but she maintained her poise. She had more business arrangements to focus on. "Well, I just wanted to get that out there. I don't want you forcing me."

Tae Hyun rolled his eyes. "You will not be forced to have sex with me. Now can we move on from this topic?"

Yoori nodded. "The hours. Can I get an estimate of how many hours a day I'm working? Am I working all days of the week? Do I get sick days? Vacation days?"

Tae Hyun leaned in and leveled his gaze onto her. "You are working twenty-four hours a day, seven days a week, and 365 days a year. The only sick day you get is on Leap Year and that's the only day."

Yoori's jaw dropped upon hearing this ludicrously evil schedule. "That's slave labor!"

"That's being my assistant," he replied just as heatedly. "You literally gave me a second degree burn. You're lucky you're not in jail rotting away right now."

Yoori slapped the palm of her hand against her forehead. How crappy could this job get? "You're being unreasonable right now!"

"I'll tell you what," he pacified, edging closer to her. "We'll negotiate more once you start working. If you're an asset to have, I'll work with you on *your* terms. But for now, it's *my* terms. Do we have an agreement?"

Her eyes formed suspicious slits when another thought entered her mind. "How long will I be working for you?"

"How long do you want to stay?"

"That's the thing, I don't want to work for you at all."

Tae Hyun frowned. "Well, that obviously won't work out." Before Yoori could interject, he hurried on. "But I'll tell you what. At this point, I need you for the next couple of months. I have a lot of social events and business meetings, and it's crucial that you're there to help me. How about you start working for a couple of months and we'll just go from there?"

Yoori considered his proposition. Being his personal assistant was definitely not the ideal situation. However, she really wasn't in much of a position to further negotiate as she just met a dead-end! This guy was either going to send her to jail or force her to work for him. Given that she would at least be paid to be his assistant, there was no other choice for her.

Yoori stifled a groan. She was definitely going to regret her next words. "Where do I sign?"

Tae Hyun rewarded Yoori with a smile. "In my world, you do not sign anything. A deal is made with a shake of the hand or a clink of glasses." He held his champagne glass toward her. "Do we have a deal?"

She apprehensively glanced between Tae Hyun and his champagne glass. There was no turning back after this. It felt like she was getting ready to sign her life off to the Devil. Uneasiness clouded her body at the thought. She inhaled deeply. She was scared, but it couldn't be too hard, right?

She held up her glass, ready to seal the agreement. The glasses were about to collide before Tae Hyun pulled his away. Yoori gave him a quizzical look.

"Choi Yoori, let me reiterate this point clearly," he emphasized. "Throughout this whole process, you can completely fuck up on anything else and you will be forgiven. But the one thing I demand from you is that when I call for you, I expect you to be there. I need you to understand this. Day or night, rain or shine, when I need you, you *have* to be there."

Yoori gave him a strange look at his request. She couldn't help but think the guy was horribly high maintenance. Did he really need someone to be his slave 24/7? Not taking the request seriously and no longer wanting to prolong this "negotiation" process, she simply smiled at him and held up her champagne glass to make a bullshit promise.

"Day or night, rain or shine, when Kwon Tae Hyun needs me, I, Choi Yoori, will be right there by his side."

Satisfied with her promise, Tae Hyun nodded, clinking his glass with hers. "Deal."

The limo came to a slow stop as they drank from their respective glasses.

Placing his glass into the cup holder, Tae Hyun clapped his hands together in anticipation. He was clearly relieved that the hard part of their business relationship was over. "Alright, Choi Yoori. It's now time for you to start working. I didn't have much luck with my first assistant making it through the end of his term. I pray that you will have a different fate."

"You had another assistant?" Yoori asked.

He nodded. "I didn't make a deal with him like I did with you, but he was my right-hand man. And a good one too. It was a shame to lose him."

"Did he quit?" Yoori asked casually, taking another sip of the Cristal.

"You could say that. He couldn't handle it. He died."

"*WHAT?*" Yoori sheathed her hand over her mouth to keep from spitting out the Cristal. "Fr—from exhaustion, *right?*" she asked shakily, wanting to verify that he meant dying only as a metaphor. He couldn't possibly mean it as anything else.

Tae Hyun had an unaffected look on his face. "No, he died," he repeated simply.

"From *exhaustion?*" she inquired again, unease seeping into her.

"No, he took a bullet for me."

"Uh, in what sense?" she stuttered, hoping desperately that Tae Hyun was horrible at using metaphors. The thumping in her heart escalated. Her sixth sense was working again and it wasn't giving her good news.

He leveled his gaze with hers, bored that she still didn't get the point. "In the sense that someone shot at me, missed, and killed him instead."

Yoori gaped at him in horror. She reawakened when she realized that her Cristal was about to spill all over the carpet. She held it upright and gazed at him, finally comprehending the hazardous situation she was in.

"What business are you in?" she screamed, inching away from him. If this was his idea of a sick joke, it wasn't funny.

The sound of the door opening permeated the limo. Tae Hyun stared back at Yoori. His face glowed under the rays of the natural light, giving him a divine appearance. Further elongating Yoori's anticipation and the burning silence gnawing away at her, he purposely made things worse by reaching for a black blazer on the other side of the seat. Tae Hyun kept his gaze on her the whole time he put on the blazer. Yoori gulped in the deafening silence. Why did Tae Hyun somehow appeared more intimidating than before?

Once her anxiety reached its precipice, he finally decided it was time to enlighten her.

"I am one of the leading entrepreneurs of the Underworld," he explained coolly. "Some people know me as Kwon Tae Hyun, but most know me as the King of Serpents, the leader of one of the most notorious gangs in this country."

He extended his hand out to her, the same amused smile layering his striking face.

"Choi Yoori, welcome to *my* world."

"I was born into it."

04: Kiss from the Serpent

"You got PUNK'D!" Was what Yoori was hoping to hear as she blinked fearfully at Tae Hyun. One minute, he was a customer service representative's nightmare and the next moment, he was the leader of one of the most violent gangs in South Korea—a human being's nightmare.

Yoori gulped, staring at his outstretched hand. Death definitely appeared more imminent now. Not wanting to piss him off by making him wait, she downed her drink and grabbed his hand, allowing him to help her out.

When she stepped foot outside, Yoori scanned her surroundings with hopeful eyes. She was praying for Ashton Kutcher to come running out of the corner, laughing at her for being stupid and pointing a camera in her face. She desperately hoped that she was on some hidden camera show and that this was all fake. Sadly for Choi Yoori, Ashton Kutcher was nowhere to be found. She squeezed the red hat in magnified fear. All of this was real. She was really in the company of an infamous crime lord.

"You don't strike me as the type of girl who would be afraid of all this," Tae Hyun observed, gesturing goodbye to the driver. As the limo drove away, he turned and strode toward the building where they had been dropped off.

Purposely sealing her lips to keep from responding, Yoori followed Tae Hyun quietly. She didn't want to get on his bad side. Being the combative hothead she was, this meant she could never open her mouth again.

Her lack of verbal response did not sit well with her new boss. "Choi Yoori," Tae Hyun called with irritation, obviously not enjoying the fact that she wasn't responding to him. "What has gotten into you? Why aren't you replying?"

Yoori jumped at the sound of his roaring voice. Feeling his eyes on her, she made it a self-presevational priority to keep her head lowered to better avoid eye contact.

Hear no evil, see no evil, she chanted in her head. *He can't hurt me if I don't make eye contact…*

"My God, are you kidding?" There was utter disbelief in his voice. When they passed through the revolving door, he said, "Assistant, please tell me you're joking right now."

When she didn't reply or meet his incredulous gaze, Tae Hyun shook his head.

"Choi Yoori, don't be like this," he coaxed, his tone more lenient. His expression softened. He was addressing her as he would a fragile child. He took his eyes off her for a fleeting second when he sensed company. He smiled, nodding courteously at a group of people in the lobby. Once they ambled past the group, Tae Hyun returned his full attention to her.

At this instance, she almost tripped after feeling a tinge of pain in her neck. *The woes of keeping your head lowered for so long*, she thought. Ignoring the pain, Yoori decided it was best to continue to avoid eye contact and eliminate any verbal communication between herself and Tae Hyun. She did not want him to put a bullet in her mouth for saying something wrong to him. She shuddered at the thought. *Damn gang bangers and the danger that comes from being around them...*

"When did you become such a chicken?" Tae Hyun finally asked. He was befuddled with her behavior. "Choi Yoori…" He nudged her in an attempt to shake some life back to her. It was quite obvious that Tae Hyun wasn't the type who appreciated being ignored. "What happened to that spunk you had?"

Yoori flinched at his touch, but continued to keep her chin tucked in and lips sealed.

Spunk died when I realized I could leave this world at any moment, she thought stiffly. Though her head was still lowered, she could tell that the building was an apartment complex and with the gold plated tiles, it was an impressive apartment complex at that.

"I don't believe this," uttered Tae Hyun. With no warning, Yoori felt him grab her wrist as they went further into the building. It surprised her that it wasn't fear that ran through her when their skins made contact, but electricity. The nice kind that glided through your body and made you warm all over.

Thrown by the unexpected reaction she received from it, Yoori followed obediently when Tae Hyun herded her into an elevator. She could hear him sigh when he pressed a floor button. After the button illumed, the doors slid closed and the elevator started to ascend.

Awkward silence reigned.

Though Yoori felt compelled to break the tense silence, she vetoed that idea as quickly as it materialized. The truth was that she really had nothing to say. Nothing to say that was worth dying for anyway.

"Look," Tae Hyun began understandably, gently pulling her closer. His lethargic eyes studied the reflection of himself and a cowering Yoori on the gold surface of the door. "I know that this caught you off guard..."

She mentally scoffed at the casualness of his statement. *No kidding.*

"But you're not making matters better by not talking to me."

Matters don't matter if I die.

Their reflections parted ways when the elevator stopped and the doors slid open. Yoori waited for Tae Hyun to step out of the elevator. She almost yelped in surprise when she felt him pull her along with him.

"I know that first days are hard," he continued, still trying to breach the silence.

Oh God, thanks for reminding me that there are more days like this to follow.

"You're worried about making a good impression."

That's because guns are a big motivator.

"You meet some intimidating people."

Murderers, she corrected in her mind. Her attention shifted to the hall they were in. She was impressed with the extravagant décor that embellished the hall, which was lined with gorgeous white carpeting. On the ceiling, a string of stunning chandeliers lit up the breathtaking landscape paintings that sat on the walls. The air of affluence was palpable. Lost in observation, Yoori was brought back to reality when Tae Hyun's soothing voice invaded her mind.

"And I know it's worse because I'm a demanding boss."

No shit. My life is now hanging in the balance.

"But I have a feeling you can handle it." He smiled after he stopped in front of a metal door. It didn't take a genius to conclude that they'd finally reached his apartment.

Oh goody, he can murder me without anyone around now.

He pulled a key card from his pocket and slid it into a card reader. The door automatically clicked open. Yoori followed him in, her head still hanging low. Judging from the decadence of the hall leading to this apartment, Tae Hyun's apartment was just as expected. It was amazingly picturesque.

A massive chandelier hung from the center of the ceiling, lighting up the rest of the apartment. Black tiles with dashes of silver lined the base of the apartment while black leather couches and sofas were spread out in the center of the living room. Half moon shaped glass shelves protruded from the walls, holding up various collectible weapons that ranged from ancient swords, to crossbows, to butterfly knives, and to various guns. This final (albeit dangerous) decor brought the whole "King of Serpents" ambiance together.

To add to all of that magnificence, the apartment had a spectacular view of the city as well. Yoori glanced at the huge balcony that stood outside the glass sliding doors. She could only imagine how nice it would be to just sit out there and enjoy the panoramic view.

"How long do you plan on keeping the silence going?" said Tae Hyun, drawing her out of her observation. His voice contained suppressed irritation.

As long as I can, she stubbornly answered in her head.

"Choi Yoori, come on!" he said disbelievingly. "I'm not going to kill you! I *just* hired you!"

Yoori squeezed the red cap in fear. *You killed the other guy!*

He expelled a weary sigh. Then, after taking in a deep inhalation, his voice grew inflexible. "Choi Yoori. Hold your head up high and look at me while I am speaking to you."

Yoori flinched at the steel in his voice. She knew she couldn't avoid looking at him anymore. With trepidation, she gradually lifted her head. Her eyes rested upon him. Although he did not look scary, she knew there was more than what met the eyes. He did not become the undisputed King of a notorious crime syndicate by being a nice guy.

"Please say something," he said wearily, crossing his arms with impatience. His face said it all: he was getting tired of this game.

Yoori merely blinked at his request.

Frustrated with her stubbornness, Tae Hyun uncrossed his arms. "Wow, you really are something."

He shook his head, turning his eyes away from her. After pacing back and forth for a few seconds, he stopped.

Yoori could've sworn she saw his eyes glimmer deviously when he laid his gaze back on her. She suddenly found herself becoming very uneasy. What was he up to?

He began toward her, his eyes on her every step of the way. He only stopped when he found himself an inch away from her. He was so close that she could inhale his alluring cologne. She was surprised that she was actually becoming a big fan of the scent.

"I suppose I can work with this," he murmured, reaching up and stroking her hair, his eyes glimmering with seduction when he did this.

Yoori's eyes grew huge at his unexpected actions. Her mind was skittering with confusion. What the hell was this guy doing?

"Tell me, Choi Yoori...are your lips as soft as they look?"

Huh? Before she could utter a reply, she felt his hand reach behind her head. At the touch, she instinctively closed her eyes. What happened next threw her into a whirlwind. He pulled her head forward and without preface, pressed his supple lips against hers.

"*Oh my God*!" she finally screamed, her voice muffled by his kiss. Yoori was gobsmacked by the emotions that assailed her—the primary one being that of pleasure. Though it was inappropriate, Yoori couldn't deny that the kiss actually felt...nice? It was so strange. A part of her wanted to wrap her arms around his neck so they could prolong the kiss. Yet the bigger part of her knew that it was wrong. Prolonging the kiss was most certainly not an option. Given her state of affairs, Yoori went with choice number two. She started slapping and punching his chest, attempting to free herself from his grasp.

Amused by her violent actions, Tae Hyun only pulled her closer and continued to interlock her lips with his. The grin on his face was a telltale sign that he enjoyed this immensely.

"*TAE HYUN*!" Yoori shouted desperately, her lips still pressed against his. The heat of her blood was scorching beyond all measure. This was her first kiss and it wasn't supposed to be like this. Distressed, she did the only thing she could do at that moment: she went crazy.

"Tae Hyun, you bastard! Let me go!" she hollered at the top of her lungs.

Tae Hyun released her from his hold as if her indignant scream was the only thing he was yearning for. Sporting a satiated smile on his face, he took a step away from her. Nothing but delight adorned his handsome face.

Yoori touched her former virgin lips. Fury rushed through her as she gave him the most venomous glare she could muster up. "What the hell is wrong with you?"

Tae Hyun chuckled, utterly guiltless. "You were being rude. I asked you a question and you ignored me. So I did the only thing I could do, I had to find out the answer myself." He touched his own lips and grinned. "In any case, glad to hear your voice again, assistant."

Yoori gawked at the childish idiot before her. Really? This was the gang leader? And not just any gang leader at that, but the gang leader of one of the most powerful gangs in the country. How was it possible that someone of his authoritative stature just kissed her because she gave him the silent treatment?

She shook her head. What a strange world.

"You're an idiot," she said simply, her sassy personality returning. Gang leader or not, this guy was a fool and he was pissing her off royally. She pointed a warning finger at him. "If you ever pull another stunt like that again, I'm going to kill you."

She was pretty sure the threat was worthless, but she felt powerful saying it anyway. The anger in her voice became intermixed with bitterness and curiosity. She was angry, but also curious. Now that he kissed her...what did he think?

His arms still crossed, he approached her with that familiar smirk. He made it no secret that he was staring at her lips while he was speaking. "Then don't give me a reason to do it again."

He then sighed, a bit more dramatically than Yoori would've liked. It made her stomach drop in anticipation. He had that playful, mischievous glint in his eyes again. With no filter, he said, "I thought it would have been softer. It was kinda salty..."

Yoori stopped breathing. Salty? What the hell? She had never felt so small and embarrassed in her life. Judging by the good-natured tone in his voice, Tae Hyun could very well be joking. However, it didn't matter to Yoori. She already took the critique to heart and she was pissed.

"You're *salty*, you jerk!" she retorted. Her face was red. Not from the anger, but from being mortified.

Openly pleased with her reaction, Tae Hyun patted her on the shoulder. Yoori shook his hand off.

"Glad to see your spunk is back," he approved. He took a step away from her, but then returned a second later. Steel present in his voice, he said, "But if you talk to me like that again, you're dead. You hear me?" He walked away, only to return again. "And also, if you ignore me again, you're dead. When I talk to you, you better talk back. But when you talk back, you better not 'talk back' to me. Just reply, but watch your mouth. You got that?"

Yoori folded her arms in disbelief. Even though he was her boss and there was nothing she could do about that, Yoori knew it would be really difficult for her to speak civilly to him. It was obviously best to watch her mouth, but she had the feeling it wasn't going to do much good. She was a hothead by nature and even the threat of death would do little to stop her from expressing her thoughts—especially if she was provoked.

"I'll..." *try to*, she added in her mind, "watch my mouth, your highness," she sneered, doing her best not to sound too evil.

Tae Hyun ignored the sneering tone in her voice and nodded. "Good. Now let's get down to business."

He reached for a brown briefcase on the sofa. He held it toward Yoori.

A fearful expression frozen on her face, Yoori only stared at the mysterious looking briefcase in dread. What the hell was in it?

When she didn't take hold of it, Tae Hyun shook the briefcase with impatience. The scowl on his face convinced Yoori to grab the briefcase by the handle, her whole body shaking.

"What's in here?" she asked with a quivering voice. She stood motionless, worried that a bomb might go off from inside the briefcase if she moved the wrong way.

"Don't concern yourself with it. Just guard it and hand it to me when I ask for it."

He made his way to a desk and pulled out the top drawer. Chills traveled down her spinal column when she saw that he was taking out a silver gun.

Uh oh.

Concealing the gun in the space behind his back and under his blazer, he eyed her with a smile that resembled the mischievousness of a child. "Let's go have some fun."

Yoori's whole body froze when Tae Hyun eagerly grabbed her hand.

"In my line of business, it is quite possible that you may get hurt while on the job. This is why I offer full health coverage."

His words replayed over and over again in her head as he pulled her along.

Yoori struggled to peel herself from his grip. It didn't take a trained investigator to deduce the danger Yoori was about to be placed in.

"No, wait!" she shrieked, struggling against Tae Hyun's hold. "Can't I stay here? DON'T YOU WANT ME TO COOK?"

Tae Hyun laughed, effortlessly dragging her to the doorway. "Don't worry, you'll get to do that soon enough. Well..." he trailed off, "assuming nothing happens to you of course."

He laughed at his own joke.

Yoori stared in dismay as he pushed her out the door. She didn't find it funny.

"Don't worry," he cajoled, herding a terrified Yoori into the elevator. "If they shoot, just duck. It's *that* easy."

Yoori gulped in the purest of agony. "Shit. Holy shit."

"That's why I'm here right now."

05: Boss

Yoori clutched the mystery briefcase and red cap close to her chest, frightfully dragging her feet after Tae Hyun. Her heart galloped so fast that she thought she was going into cardiac arrest. She stole a bitter glance at him. He walked a few feet in front of her, hands in his pockets, strutting his stuff like he was on a runway. She glanced lower and stared at his back. Although she couldn't see the gun, it was obviously there and he was obviously planning to use it.

Tightening her grasp on the briefcase and cap, she peered up at the clear blue skies in utter despair. It had only been a little over an hour since she woke up and left for work. How was it possible that her life could change so drastically within such a short period of time?

"I want to go home," she murmured, lowering her head to keep from losing her balance. She flickered another look at Tae Hyun, who appeared to be quickening his already brisk pace.

"Why are we walking so fast? Shouldn't we wait for your men?" Yoori inquired, quickening her pace after him. Death was far less likely when you had more numbers by your side.

"I don't need any men to take care of this," Tae Hyun answered like she had just insulted his capabilities. He stole a glimpse at her and caught sight of the worry on her face. Softening his stern expression, he added, "Two of them are already there," before he turned back and continued down the street.

Yoori glared at his back. She felt better that they had back up, but she was appalled with his nonchalant behavior. She couldn't believe the guy. There she was, shaking in fear and he was walking around like he was getting ready to go gallivanting around the mall. Yoori shook her head. Apparently shooting people was normal for the guy. Shortly after making this observation, she scoffed at herself for stating the obvious. He was a crime lord. Of course all of this was a normal occurrence for him.

The walk toward impending fatality did not take as long as Yoori would've hoped for. After turning the corner, she noticed that Tae Hyun had stopped walking. She closed her eyes in dread. Stopping only meant that they have arrived at their destination. Her eyes snagged on the dark alley before her. Another torrent of anxiety washed over her.

Of course.

Of course this meeting was going to take place in an alley. Where else could stereotypical gang members shoot each other to their heart's content?

Tae Hyun turned to face her. A grim mask marked his face. "When we walk through it, stay close to me, but stay hidden in the shadows, alright?"

Yoori nodded obediently. Maybe it was because he had a gun. Maybe it was because he was the leader of a gang. Maybe it was because he had reinforcement in the alley already. Or maybe it was because of the lack of fear that he showed. Whatever the reason, the words from Tae Hyun's lips made Yoori feel less afraid, but only marginally.

"And try not to gawk too much when I beat all those guys." He chuckled softly. He turned around and advanced into the alley.

Yoori gaped at him, watching as he disappeared into the alley. She felt the uncertainty cultivate. Was this guy for real? Was he really joking with her at a time like this? Paranoia struck her at full speed. Would he be able to protect her if the situation called for it? Would he be able to keep her safe or would she end up like the other assistant? Dead and only to be talked about when he recruited another assistant? She groaned at the horrible thoughts cycling in her mind. She mumbled something unintelligible and ran after Tae Hyun, hoping and praying they would make it out alive.

Deep in the alley, she could hear faint sounds of screams emitting from the further end of the narrow pathway. Her fears came back at full throttle when the sounds of bones cracking disturbed the air. She craned her neck to get a better view of what was happening. Straight ahead was a group of ten shadows beating up two other shadows.

A sinkhole formed in her stomach. She knew her luck. She knew it all too well. She knew who those two men were. She knew right away they were Tae Hyun's men.

Oh my God! I'm going to die! Yoori thought, coming to an abrupt halt. Her survival instincts kicked into gear. Still holding on to the briefcase and the red cap, she turned toward the entrance of the alley, wanting to make a run for it. The rays of light illuminating from the entrance made it seem like a passageway to heaven. Suddenly, she whirled around. Her eyes locked onto Tae Hyun's back. He was still walking down the life-threatening side of the alley. His nonchalant demeanor remained and, if anything, his arrogance radiated a bit more clearly in the looming darkness.

She debated on taking off and leaving him, but couldn't bring herself to do so. Although the jerk blackmailed her into servitude, she had an unexplained attachment for him. They came into this alley together and for reasons she couldn't explain, it felt wrong to leave him.

"Leave no one behind," a distant voice whispered in her thoughts. She had not the slightest idea where she heard that statement before, but at that precise second, it couldn't have rung truer. She couldn't leave him behind — not yet.

Damn moral obligations. Mentally chastising herself at the stupidity she was about to partake in, Yoori threw all caution out the window and continued to follow Tae Hyun.

A loud voice rang through the alley, causing Tae Hyun and Yoori to stop.

"Ah, Tae Hyun. You made it."

The beating ceased after the voice swam through the confined space. The ten dark silhouettes drew away, leaving two dark figures to lie on the pavement, twitching and groaning in pain. Though it was dark, Yoori could tell they were bleeding profusely. A shortness of breath assailed her. She was positive she was going to pass out from all the anxiety. This was all too scary and real for her.

From the crowd emerged a young man who appeared to be in his early twenties. He was dressed in a handsome dark suit and was smoking a cigar. He was tall and lean, his facial features reminiscent of an aristocrat who got into too many fights in his lifetime. He wasn't the typical handsome guy, but he was attractive nonetheless. He claimed her attention, not because of his appearance, but how he presented himself. He was easily the youngest in the crowd, yet it was clear that he was the leader.

Unease rummaged through her. Yoori blended further into the darkness when she observed that she wasn't the only one doing the staring.

"Good job picking out your toys, Tae Hyun," the other gang leader said mockingly, craning his neck to get a better view of her.

He laughed once he noted that Yoori moved further out of sight. Sensing her fear, his chuckles grew more pronounced. He took another whiff of his cigar. "Though I can't see that pretty little face, you can tell from the rack on her that this one seems like a lot of fun to play with in bed."

The men in the background roared in agreement.

"I'd want some of that tonight," one of them jeered.

"Where you headed later tonight, baby?"

"Does that pretty little ass of yours need a good spanking?"

Yoori clenched her fists. Anger throbbed inside her. It wasn't right. Chauvinistic pigs were taunting her, and it made her blood simmer. Her eyes seared. She was tempted to propel out of the darkness to give those jackasses a piece of her mind. However, knowing better, she kept her mouth shut and her face out of sight. Despite being a force to be reckoned with when she was enraged, she knew her odds of even being able to slap one of them were slim. She had to pick her battles and this one definitely wasn't one of them.

"Let them go, Jae Won," Tae Hyun instructed the other leader, his voice hard as steel.

"Let me remind you, Tae Hyun," began Jae Won. His expression was lined with irritation. Smoke exuded from his mouth and evaporated into the wind. "You have no power here."

For a tense second, silence occupied the alley. Much like an introduction for the stream of events to come, a big gust of wind flew into the narrow alley, pulling up the curtains for the show to come. All eyes watched with anticipation as Tae Hyun bent down and picked up a metal pipe on the pavement beside him. Upon retrieving it, he stood up.

"Let go of my men," he repeated. His hand clenched on to the pipe in lethal warning.

The crowd of men stiffened up. It was then that Yoori saw what an intimidating and powerful person Tae Hyun was. Even in the presence of enemies who outnumbered him, he exuded such confidence and fearlessness that it was hard to see Tae Hyun as anything but a God in human form.

For that fleeting instant, when everyone watched Tae Hyun with understandable fear, Yoori herself felt envious of him. It was a foreign and perplexing feeling for her. She was not envious because she longed to have the power he had. No. She was envious because, for some reason or the other, it felt like she was yearning for a power that she *used* to have. Halting her train of unnatural thoughts, Yoori swiftly disregarded such feelings and returned her attention to the crowd of men lingering behind Jae Won.

As if everyone felt the enviable power that Tae Hyun displayed, fear subsided for the time being as sounds of knuckles cracking surged up in the form of echoes. Although power was intimidating, it was also a desirable trait that all humans yearned for. All the men standing parallel to Tae Hyun knew that they could easily take that power from him. The odds were in their favor. After all, Tae Hyun was only one man in the presence of eleven others. If the Gods wanted to be entertained, then this was the perfect moment.

Yoori had the strongest urge to tug at Tae Hyun's arm and haul his ass out of the alley. The resolve on his face confounded her. Instead of exhibiting fear like a sensible human being, he was actually watching them with anticipation. If anything, he was entertained with the crowd in front of him. She was tempted to scream at him for being a fool. Given the severity of the situation, she was unable to say anything. Truth be told, Tae Hyun intimidated her too.

"Who do you think you are giving orders around here?" Jae Won screamed out, incensed with Tae Hyun's cocky disposition.

"You know who I am," he answered, unaffected by the rage flooding from the other gang leader.

"Oh yes, the King of Serpents," Jae Won mocked, taking another puff of his cigar. He laughed derisively. "The God who is here to save the day, right?"

Tae Hyun smirked. "Yes, Jae Won. Unlike you, I do not turn my back on my brothers. We stay through the tough and good times. From what I hear, this is an attribute that you, *very famously*, lack."

Any sense of humor fled from Jae Won.

"You know nothing about me," Jae Won growled. It was clear that Tae Hyun's comment hit a sensitive nerve within him.

The curving smirk on Tae Hyun's mouth remained. Jae Won's reaction was the one he wanted. Utilizing the break in Jae Won's composure, he continued to pick at the wound.

"You turned your back on your gang and pathetically tried to form a new one." He measured the crowd of men behind Jae Won. He was not impressed. "And the best you can come up with are these pitiful fools? I know you well enough. You are a failure and you will always be a failure."

The alley thundered with fury.

Yoori slapped her forehead with the palm of her hand. She was flabbergasted with the idiocy Tae Hyun displayed. Why was he insulting a group of men who outnumbered him? Did he have a death wish?

Jae Won spat his cigar out and stepped on it. "Tae Hyun," he prompted with a small smile. "Congratulations, you have just signed your own death certificate."

Behind him, a group of five men stepped forward from the crowd. They grinned uncontrollably. Each well-built gang members possessed weapons that ranged from a pipe, baseball bat, rope, and knives. After the round of insults from Tae Hyun, they now appeared fired up to take him down.

Shit! Shit! Shit! Unable to keep her mouth shut, Yoori tugged at Tae Hyun's arm. Maybe if she could convince him to run, then there would be a chance they could still make it out of this alive.

"Are you seriously going to fight them by yourself? There's one of you and five of them. Can you not do the math? Are you that stupid?"

Ignoring her observations, Tae Hyun peeled off his blazer and tossed it in her direction. Yoori caught the blazer in resignation. She knew it was Tae Hyun's bizarre way of telling her that he'd be fine. Unconvinced, Yoori watched painfully as Tae Hyun stepped forward to face those five men.

"Last chance to back off," Tae Hyun said to them. He bounced the pipe up and down on his left palm. There was no fear in his stance, only anticipation.

When all they did was laugh at his statement, Yoori's fears worsened. It was traitorous of her to admit it, but if she weren't on his side, she would've laughed as well. Did he really think he was going to win?

"Let's play, King of Serpents," one of the men said boldly. He wasted no time in charging toward Tae Hyun. The knife he held up was pointed straight at Tae Hyun's stomach.

"No!" Yoori gasped when the gang member attempted to take jabs at Tae Hyun. The sharp knife glowed under the slits of light coming through the alley, its glowing blade hungry for Tae Hyun's blood.

This is it. The idiot is going to die right now, she concluded morbidly. Her hopes for his survival diminished with every attack that flew in his direction.

She couldn't have anticipated the next sequence of events.

Tae Hyun easily dodged each strike and used one of the alley walls as a prop to perform a spin kick that inevitably left the knife man on the floor. A collective gasp issued when the gang member accidentally stabbed himself in the stomach.

"That was for your lack of manners," Tae Hyun stated simply, a triumphant smile illuminating his features.

With the sound of pained groans lingering in the background, Tae Hyun reached his hand out to the remaining men. He motioned them forward. He wasn't done teaching them their lessons.

Like bulls on command, they came stampeding toward him with vindictive speed.

As another out-of-the-world performance, Yoori watched in amazement as Tae Hyun threw men who were twice his size against the walls like they were rag dolls. One by one, as they came charging for him, they all went down, never lasting more than several seconds with him. Did she need to mention that throughout this entire ordeal, he had yet to use his pipe?

"Damn," Yoori uttered, marveling at what she just witnessed. He told her not to gawk, but it was really difficult. To her credit, she wasn't the only one gawking. The audience in their company also reciprocated this particular feeling of awe.

Jae Won's nostrils flared. Annoyed with the wonder his men found in Tae Hyun, Jae Won shot them a glare that spoke of nothing but fury. "What are you idiots waiting for?" he bellowed at the top of his lungs. "Get him!"

On Jae Won's command, the remaining men snapped out of their stupor and went on the attack.

"TAE HYUN!" Yoori screamed when he became engulfed by a horde of gang members.

Her confused eyes lingered on his back. She didn't understand why he wasn't using his gun. It was baffling. If only he took it out, then he wouldn't have to deal with all of this. He wouldn't be at such a disadvantage.

She shook in worry. All she could hear was the sound of men grunting as they kicked and punched Tae Hyun. She stared helplessly at the sight before her. Frustration mounted over her. Why wasn't he using his gun? She held her breath and closed her eyes in anguish. There was no way he could make it out of that crowd alive. There was just no way. She was sure of it.

Well, she thought she was sure of it until she heard something that revitalized her hope.

"What the fuck!" one of the men shrieked.

Yoori opened her eyes, its core brimming with hope and excitement. Sounds of metal hitting bones ran rampant in the air, and she spotted him.

Tae Hyun was beating each gang member to a pulp with his pipe. He was very much alive. It didn't take too long for Tae Hyun to knock each and every one of them down. Pretty soon, it was just Yoori, Tae Hyun, and Jae Won left standing. Everyone else was on the floor, groaning in pain. Apart from the bloody lip he was sporting, Tae Hyun looked totally fine.

Yoori smiled stupidly at him. This unreal bastard was absolutely mind-boggling.

Clapping emitted from the hands of Jae Won. "Very impressive, Tae Hyun," he said, taking the words right out of her mouth.

Stripping off his jacket, Jae Won approached Tae Hyun. As his shoes echoed with every progressing step, Jae Won started to roll up his white sleeves, preparing himself to go into battle.

"Now I know why they call you the King of Serpents. Your fighting skills are impressive." He tossed his jacket on the ground. "But I must tell you that I was trained by the best fighter in the Underworld. So with that said, you, my friend, are going down."

All eyes watched in anticipatory silence as Jae Won clenched his fists and raised them up, positioning himself into a fighting stance. He was ready to take on Tae Hyun.

Tae Hyun's lips bent into an amused smile. He wiped the blood away from his mouth and flung the pipe aside. He rolled up his own sleeves. "Let's have some fun then, kid."

Like a gun signifying the start of a race, Jae Won rocketed toward Tae Hyun. He swung a punch at Tae Hyun but missed, enabling Tae Hyun to punch him in the face while following that with a brute kick to the stomach. Jae Won stumbled back after Tae Hyun's steel-like foot made contact with his abdomen. He gasped for air when he slammed against the brick wall.

Wiping the blood from his mouth, he stood up again. If the expression on Jae Won's face gave any indication, he was extremely pissed off.

Soon after standing up, he rounded onto the lid of a lone trashcan. With amazing dexterity, he projected himself up and bequeathed Tae Hyun with a kick to the side of the face. As Tae Hyun fell backward, Jae Won, who wasn't done with his attack, grabbed him by the collar. Instead of allowing him to fall to the ground, Jae Won delivered a powerful punch across Tae Hyun's face. The assault had him falling straight for the wall. Colliding into the brick foundation back first, Tae Hyun managed to sneak a couple more strikes on to Jae Won, his punches as hard as the next. Despite such retaliation, Yoori could tell the fight with the other gang members had taken a toll on Tae Hyun. He simply did not have enough energy to fight Jae Won. He may have been fighting, but he was slowly losing.

Using one of his fallen men as an added prop, Jae Won jumped onto him and flew into the air, his legs pointing straight at Tae Hyun. Yoori watched in horror as Jae Won delivered the final spin kick that left Tae Hyun spitting coagulated blood into the air. Weakened, Tae Hyun slid down the wall from the assault. He didn't allow the strike to keep him down for long though. Struggling, he surged to his feet once more. Though he was up, his balance wavered.

"Well done, kid," Tae Hyun breathed with a mocking smirk. "It only took several of your minions to fight me beforehand for you to get this far."

Jae Won chuckled, unfazed by how he got to this point. The only relevance was the victory awaiting him. "Now," he began expectantly, a victorious grin already forming on his face. "It's time to kill the snake."

The concern for Tae Hyun's safety amplified within Yoori. As her unblinking eyes remained on Jae Won, her gaze, for whatever reason, was suddenly analyzing Jae Won for a particular weakness in his stance. She noticed something in the way he walked. It was so subtle, but she finally caught it…a weakness that would save Tae Hyun. Her eyes bulged. Before she could stop herself, she announced her finding to Tae Hyun.

"TAE HYUN!" she shouted at the top of her lungs.

The next words that came from her mouth took her by utter surprise. "TAE HYUN! HE HAS WEAK LEGS! GO FOR THE LOWER LEGS!"

As if finding familiarity with her voice, Jae Won turned his attention to Yoori.

44

He squinted his eyes, attempting to make her out in the darkness. Distracted with Yoori, Jae Won failed to see that Tae Hyun had begun toward him. Jumping slightly off the pavement, Tae Hyun served a lower spin kick that left an unsuspecting Jae Won on the floor. A pained grunt emitted from him when Tae Hyun proceeded to perform various punches and kicks to Jae Won's lower legs. This beating eventually left Jae Won groaning on the floor in agony.

Slightly huffing and puffing, Tae Hyun ceased with the assaults. He stood before the war zone in triumph. Though he had trouble balancing, he managed to keep his head up high as he addressed the gang members, all of whom were writhing on the pavement in pain.

"You all have just witnessed first hand what the repercussions for going against a Serpent consists of." He stood up high. The pride in his voice grew. "Death...as of now...should be imminent in your futures." He scrutinized them intently. "But I have another proposal in mind."

All the gang members listened with shallowed breathing, their attentive eyes on Tae Hyun. The only one not looking at Tae Hyun was Jae Won. His eyes were instead locked on a faceless Yoori. She was still hiding in the darkness. After several passing seconds, he turned his eyes from her and peered at Tae Hyun. "Who is she?"

"It doesn't matter right now who she is," Tae Hyun dismissed. He went back to the business at hand. "My proposal is for a merging of gangs."

His eyes went over each of the men. "Members of the Dragons gang. You all have precisely sixty days to decide whether or not you want to join the Serpents or spend the rest of your days in hiding from us. You will be provided with a briefcase filled with forms and documents that will essentially consist of you giving up your bank accounts, among other things, to the Serpents if you should choose to merge."

He turned to Yoori with an outstretched hand. "Briefcase."

Initially, Yoori hesitated to come out of the darkness. She didn't want any of those gang members to see her face, just in case they ever wanted to seek revenge. However, she knew that if she didn't come out, Tae Hyun would more than likely drag her out instead. Sighing, she decided to come out on her own accord.

Finally stepping out of the shadows with the briefcase firmly gripped between her fingers, Yoori watched with puzzlement as Jae Won's eyes grew huge upon seeing her face for the first time. She hesitantly handed the briefcase to Tae Hyun. He tossed it onto the pavement. The briefcase landed beside Jae Won with a thud.

"Look closely at what I have just given you," Tae Hyun said purposely, only speaking to Jae Won at this point.

Jae Won, instead of paying attention to the briefcase, kept his gaze on her. His expression spoke of shock, confusion, and fear.

Yoori felt a strange feeling wash over her as she returned his gaze.

Given the chance to get a closer look at him, he somehow appeared really familiar to her. Mystification flooded over her as her mind pondered the unthinkable…why did he seem so familiar? Yoori wanted so much to ask him if they had met before. Yet, as her mouth became glued in apprehension, she couldn't bring herself to even part her lips. Of course it wasn't possible that they had met before. How could they have met before?

Tae Hyun spared a glance at Yoori.

She was still staring uncomfortably at Jae Won.

"This is just the tip of the iceberg. Take a long and hard look at everything. Realize who is on our side and why we are the best."

Jae Won averted his attention to Tae Hyun when he said, "realize who is on our side."

"I expect to hear from you soon, Jae Won," Tae Hyun concluded, grabbing hold of Yoori's hand. To his men, he said, "Let's go."

Before Yoori even had a chance to soak in Tae Hyun's speech, or think about Jae Won and the strange way he was acting toward her, she already felt Tae Hyun's tug as he pulled her toward the exit.

On cue, Tae Hyun's men slowly rose up. Their soft groans reverberated in the dense air. Holding on to one another, it became clear that every cell in their body hurt as they limped after Tae Hyun and Yoori.

"Thanks boss," one of the men said while he helped the other one stand a little taller.

"Yeah, thanks boss," the other said, coughing as they followed Tae Hyun.

"Anytime," Tae Hyun said coolly, his hand encircled around Yoori's wrist.

Yoori rolled her eyes at his lax response. After all that, Tae Hyun still acted like it was nothing. *How annoying.*

As they made their way out, Yoori heard something that made her stop dead in her tracks. It was strange because it was such a soft whisper she heard. It was so soft that she was sure no one else heard but her. It sounded more like the murmur of the wind than anything.

She whirled around. She saw that all the Dragons gang members were still groaning on the pavement from the aftermath of fighting with Tae Hyun. However, much like the rest of the scenes before them, there was also one person that stood out from the crowd.

Her inquisitive eyes fixated upon Jae Won. He had his gaze on them, or her to be precise. A look of fear and confusion washed all over his now pale face. He continued to stare at her with a mixture of doubt and certainty.

Yoori wasn't sure whether or not she heard right.

She wasn't sure if the voice came from the two men speaking with Tae Hyun or if it actually came from Jae Won. Against her better judgment, she could have sworn she heard Jae Won say something directed to her, but it didn't make sense at all.

Though it was impossibly absurd, Yoori could've sworn she heard him say, "*Boss.*"

"That's why I have this much power."

06: I Quit

Instead of being given the chance to absorb the supposed words that came from Jae Won's mouth, Yoori was sidetracked when she felt a pair of hands grab her shoulders and spin her around.

"What do you think you're doing?" she asked, glowering at Tae Hyun.

In lieu of answering, Tae Hyun merely pushed her ahead of him with impatience. "Do you think we have all day here or something?"

"Don't!" she protested, nearly tripping over when he pushed his weight against her back. "I can walk by myself!" she shouted, quickening her pace to avoid being mowed to the ground by Tae Hyun. Why was he in such a hurry?

After reaching the end of the alley, Yoori took one look at his men and shuddered. The faces of both men were barely recognizable as humans. Their noses and mouths were bashed in and their eyes were so swollen that they could hardly open them.

When she saw that they had trouble balancing, she thought it was best if she helped them maintain their equilibrium. After making a move to help them balance themselves, she was mystified to find that both men had backed away in fear. She gaped at them. Both huddled closer to one another while cowering away from her.

She was bewildered with their behavior. Was she really in the presence of gang members? Why were they acting like she was the Devil?

Tae Hyun brushed past her, disrupting her string of thoughts. He moved close to the two men. When he reached them, he whispered something into their ears. They regarded her briefly and then hastily averted their eyes. Both nodded at him, confirming their understanding of what Tae Hyun explained to them. Once Tae Hyun took care of business, he took a few more steps into the street to hail a cab. A silver cab stopped at his call. He opened the back door for his men.

Yoori watched as he carefully helped his men into the cab. She shook her head in amazement. Even though she had already categorized him as a complete ass, he certainly had his moments where you could clearly see that he was human. At least he had *some* compassion for other people in physical pain.

"Get them to the hospital in less than three minutes," Tae Hyun said firmly, throwing a wad of cash at the driver.

The cab driver's eyes twinkled in delight. After counting through the wad of money, he nodded in glee. He put the cab into gear, slammed on the accelerator, and peeled away, leaving a cloud of dust in his greedy wake.

"What was wrong with them?" Yoori found herself asking. She was unable to hold back her confusion. Nothing made sense. How Jae Won looked at her, what he called her, and how those two men looked at her. They all acted like she was going to kill them.

Tae Hyun sighed, approaching her. He grabbed his blazer from her. "They're not feeling well," he said simply, putting on his jacket. His tone of voice made it appear as if that should put an end to the conversation.

Unsatisfied with his answer and certain that there had to be more to it, she continued to probe. "Why were they so afraid of me?"

Much to her mounting disappointment, his blank expression remained. "Choi Yoori, put yourself in their position," he went on nonchalantly. "They were beaten to a pulp for God knows how long. You were getting ready to touch them. Did you not expect them to flinch the way they did?"

Yoori pondered the question. What he said made sense. If she had gotten beaten up like that, she wouldn't be too keen on any strange person touching her either. Then, something more pressing occurred to her. She abruptly shot her head up. She glared at him, unforgiving fire brimming in her eyes. She *just* realized something much more important.

"You stupid idiot!" she suddenly screamed out. Catching sight of the red cap she was still holding since her meeting with him, she looked at it in disbelief. "Why the hell am I still holding this?" She threw the red cap at him.

Tae Hyun gaped at her when the cap smacked him on the chest. He caught it before it fell to the ground. His expression said it all: he was appalled by the drastic change in her personality. "What the hell has gotten into you, woman?"

"Put yourself in their shoes, *huh*?" she fumed. She lifted a leg up and ripped off her black flip-flop. She threw it at him with full force. Bitterness and anger multiplied within her. "Well, I was almost in their shoes!"

The flip-flop missed him by a mere inch when he dodged it. She shook, backing away from him. Her heart pounded nonstop. Her life was really and truly in danger and it was all because of him.

"Do you realize what just happened?" she shouted, feeling the overwhelming urge to claw his eyes out. He was staring at her like she was some unreasonable lunatic. "It was a miracle we made it out alive! You could've lost and they could've killed you! And then what would they have done to me? Oh my God..." She placed both hands on her chest and began to hyperventilate. "I could've wound up like those two guys! OR WORSE!" She rolled up her sleeves in horror. This really wasn't her day.

"Okay, *now* you're overreacting," Tae Hyun said calmly, attempting to get closer to her.

She retreated away from him.

"It wasn't a miracle we made it out," he continued tactfully. "Don't you realize that? They couldn't beat me. They all lost the moment I stepped foot into that alley."

Yoori snorted. This guy was unbelievable. "What about the fight with Jae Won?" She pointed an accusing finger at him. "Don't lie! You were about to lose!"

He laughed as though she had told him an outlandish joke. "I admit. I underestimated Jae Won and his fighting skills. I was more exhausted from fighting his gang than I thought I would be. He caught me off guard, but he wouldn't have beaten me. He hasn't had the training I've had. Few individuals in this world could ever beat me."

"I helped you!" she interjected. "You wouldn't have won if I didn't tell you about his legs."

Tae Hyun waved his hand like it was no big deal. "Anyone could see he has weak legs. You merely distracted him for me."

She rolled her eyes. Guys and their stupid egos. She shook her head, reminding herself why the conversation started in the first place. "No, I can't do this anymore. You can sue me, you can sue the diner, you can even sue the homeless shelter down the street for all I care. I'm done. Nothing is worth all of this."

Yoori watched Tae Hyun's expression turn grim. "Do you realize what you're doing?"

"YES! I'M QUITTING!" she declared, feeling a strange burst of bravery propel through her.

"You've only been on the clock for two hours!" he screamed, not believing someone could have such a horrible work ethic.

Yoori's mind raced. It had only been two hours? Holy crap! It felt like two years were taken from her.

She jabbed a furious finger at him. She would not allow him to make it appear as if she was overreacting. "Don't make this sound like an office job where I'm sitting on my ass all day!"

Clearly having lost his composure as well, Tae Hyun combated Yoori's fighting words with comebacks of his own. "You might as well be! What the hell were you doing back there? You held a goddamn briefcase while I did all the dirty work."

"I WAS FEARING FOR MY LIFE!"

"*Exactly*! You weren't doing anything!"

Shock stamped her face. Yoori placed her hands on her hips as a response. His last comment did not even merit a reply.

As soon as the words escaped his lips, Tae Hyun's stern expression morphed into one of regret. It seemed as if he was chastising himself for blurting out that insensitive comment. The softening expression on his face did little to reassure Yoori of the severity of her situation. If anything, it vindicated her fears. Life would only get harder if she stuck around as his assistant.

Her resolve solidified, she continued to retreat from Tae Hyun. "I'm done," she said with finality.

Instead of nodding in understanding as Yoori hoped, Tae Hyun's somber gaze hardened into a death glare. He didn't want to let her go.

"You made a deal with me," he cautioned solemnly. "I will see to it that you keep your end of the bargain."

"Are you kidding me?" She was at her wit's end. It was as if this guy's ultimate mission in life was to drive her over the brink of sanity. "Look at me!"

She stopped retreating and extended her unsteady hand toward him.

He gaped at her shaking hand and then looked at her strangely.

"What the hell are you doing?" he asked, not amused with her bizarre behavior.

"Look at me!" she commanded again, her quivering hand still outstretched. "I'm *shaking*! I'm twenty-three-years-old and I'm shaking in fear! I think I'm about to have a heart attack!"

Tae Hyun snorted, waving a hand of dismissal. "Oh come on, assistant. Something small like that and you're already affected? Nothing even happened."

Her jaw sagged. Was this guy serious? Steam started to burst out of her ears. That was *definitely* the last straw.

"Hey listen up, psycho!" she finally screamed. "When I signed up for this, I didn't know I was making a deal with a *killer*!"

His eyes flared. It surprised her, the anger, disbelief, and offense that burned in his gaze. It was apparent that he had lost any shred of patience with her.

"Choi Yoori, do you realize the repercussions of backing out on a deal with me?"

Yoori gulped at the grave question. How did he expect her to answer that?

At her silence, Tae Hyun's face smoothed into a calm expression. He bent down and picked up Yoori's flip-flop. He held it out to her. A small smile appeared across his bruised face. "I wouldn't have brought you here if I thought for a second something bad was going to happen to you. You *have* to believe that."

Yoori narrowed her eyes in suspicious slits. If she didn't know better, she would've thought that he was actually sincere with his last statement. He was a good actor. She knew she had to be careful with this one. Kwon Tae Hyun had the uncanny ability to be the world's biggest jerk and then change into the world's most charming man within a matter of seconds. If she were any other girl, then the very vision of him smiling would have completely thrown her over the edge. He looked damn seductive, standing there like he was her knight in shining armor.

She stole another glance at him before eyeing her flip-flop. Luckily for her, she wasn't just any other girl. She was his assistant, and after only two hours on the job, she already knew him better. Weighing her options, Yoori nodded to herself, her mind set on her decision. She sighed loudly, resting her lethargic gaze on him. Slowly, she approached him, dramatically hanging her head down low as if admitting defeat.

Tae Hyun smirked in triumph at her defeated posture. He held out the flip-flop a little further for her, thinking he won. "See? I knew you could handle this. A couple more rounds and you'll be a seasoned pro. You won't even worry about any of this anymo—*what the fuck?*"

Yoori, with all her strength and courage, snatched the flip-flop right out of his grasp and ran. She *literally* ran for her life.

His roaring voice thundered behind her. "Choi Yoori! Do you have a death wish? Come back here *right now*!"

50

Disregarding Tae Hyun's last words, Yoori continued sprinting. Adrenaline pumped through her body like foreign electricity. She was huffing and puffing so incessantly that she was sure she was going to cough out hairballs in the near future.

She had never been much of a runner, but when your life hangs in the balance, your limitations in life take a backseat. She was determined to put an end to her misery; she was determined to live to see another day.

Frantically turning at a corner and picking up speed, she ran far away from the threats of danger, far away from her new job, and far away from the King of Serpents.

"That's why I can do whatever I want."

07: The Other Part of the Punishment

It had been precisely eight days since Choi Yoori was introduced to Kwon Tae Hyun. It had also been precisely eight days since she made her abrupt escape from the murderous gang leader. Everything that took place that fateful day replayed ominously in her head.

It started out like any other day. She was working and then somehow, she spilled coffee on a stranger and he threatened to sue her friend's diner if she didn't become his assistant. To be a good friend, Yoori reluctantly agreed to the terms under the pretenses that it couldn't be *that* bad.

How could she have been so wrong? The guy just happened to be Kwon Tae Hyun—the leader of one of the most well known gangs in South Korea. This revelation was where the damnation of her life became apparent. After being thrown into a situation where she was surrounded by senseless violence, Yoori turned in her two seconds notice and made a run for it.

And now, here in her apartment, she miserably waited for judgment day.

Yoori lay on the sofa with the baseball bat next to her. Boredom was written all over her face. She had waited eight days for the King of Serpents to return to finish her off, thinking he was going to appear at any moment.

She thought back to her journey to this moment.

On the first day, after making the mad dash away from him, she was certain she had signed her death warrant. What was she thinking running away from him? Did she really think she could get away?

Locking the door in absolute fear, Yoori whispered a silent prayer. She didn't think she'd survive the night. How could she? She angered a powerful crime lord and revealed her face to another one who lost in combat. If Tae Hyun didn't come to take care of her, then Jae Won surely would.

Having spent the entire day sitting in front of her door with a baseball bat in hand, Yoori was positive that one of the gang leaders would send his goons after her with machine guns. In response to the threat of imminent death, her grip on the bat grew stronger. Whoever it may be, she wasn't going to go down without a fight.

Then came the second day of awaiting judgment...

The goons had yet to arrive. Yoori reasoned that Jae Won probably wouldn't waste his time with her. It wasn't like she was the one who defeated him in combat. Regardless of the eliminations of threats, there was still a threat big enough to keep Yoori awake at night. The goons hadn't shown their faces, but she knew that Tae Hyun was bidding his time, enjoying his power over her life.

Throughout the night, Yoori jumped at every sound she heard in her apartment, thinking every squeak meant Tae Hyun was coming to get her. Before falling into a deep sleep that night, she heard a soft knock that left her panting in fear. Instinctively, she jumped off the sofa with her baseball bat in hand. She proceeded toward the banging door with surprise bravery. She was ready to fight.

She curled her fingers over the door handle. She turned it ever so slightly, preparing herself for the assault ahead. She pulled the door open while simultaneously raising the baseball bat high in the air.

"You will die—*oh my gawd*!" she gasped.

"Ahhhh! Mommy! Mommy!"

Yoori gaped in dismay as two young girls ran down the hall, screaming and crying for their mothers. She just threatened two little girls selling cookies for their school!

"Wait!" Yoori shouted, utterly horrified at what she had done. She held up several boxes of the cookies splattered across the hall. "You forgot your cookies!"

They never came back and needless to say, Tae Hyun never came that night either.

On the third day, Yoori moved from sitting in front of the door to sitting on her bed with a laptop in front of her and the baseball bat by her side. As she opened her second box of unpaid cookies, doubt overcame her. She was beginning to think that Tae Hyun had used up all his resources to try and find her. He probably failed miserably in trying to locate her whereabouts.

She suppressed a hopeful smile. She shouldn't be rash in thinking that going outside her apartment would be safe. Tae Hyun could be anywhere. If anything, she could never go outside again. In a desperate attempt to ensure some form of income, Yoori started searching for online jobs in hopes of being able to work from home. She posted her resumé everywhere. Sadly for Yoori, none of the jobs turned out to be legit.

On the remaining four days to follow, as Yoori lay on her bed with her head hanging upside down, frustration began to mount over her.

As the hours ticked by, she wanted desperately to call Chae Young. She had so much to tell her and she was going crazy with the lack of human interaction.

Her rationality got the best of her though.

She reasoned it was safer for Chae Young to not be involved in the gang activities that Yoori got roped into. To quell her friend's worry, she sent Chae Young a text message telling her that she had a family emergency and that she was going to be out of town for an unknown period of time. Apart from leaving worried voicemails, Chae Young, much to Yoori's relief, did not stop by the apartment to make sure Yoori wasn't lying. What jerk would doubt someone when they said they had to leave because of a family emergency?

Dressed in her pink floral pajamas, Yoori expelled a huge breath while she stared at the clock. Her entire body was stiff from the lack of physical activities. She was bored like hell and was beginning to doubt Tae Hyun would ever show up. Had he forgotten about her? Could she finally move on with her life? Her stomach growled when she finished her last batch of cookies. She hadn't been out of the apartment for a week and she was not only running low on food supply, but she was also running low on her sanity. At this point, even imminent doom appeared more entertaining than staring at the clock.

Where the hell was this crime lord? Was he coming or not?

Finally, on the eighth and present night, as she rummaged through her handbag, Yoori took out the Blackberry Tae Hyun gave her. There were no missed calls. She gasped in disbelief and took a speculative glance around her apartment. It had been more than a week since she ran away from Tae Hyun and he had not even called to scream at her.

A small smile graced her face. Could it be possible that he really didn't give a damn?

Convinced of her safety and finally relieved, she threw the Blackberry onto her bed in glee and promptly grabbed the towel beside it. She waited all week for a showdown and her neck and entire body ached from the anticipation of something that would apparently never take place. Unexpected happiness aside, she needed a warm shower to massage her tense muscles and she needed one immediately.

"Can't believe I wasted a week of my life fearing a gang leader who didn't even want to be bothered by me," she mumbled sourly, grabbing a face wash and squeezing the soap out. She massaged her face with it.

An uncertain and troubling thought hit her.

This was all too easy.

Though she had only known Tae Hyun for a few hours, he didn't strike her as the type of guy who would let her run off without chasing after her to get her back. Judging from the tone of his voice when he screamed at her, it didn't seem as if he would let go of the situation that easily. However, as much as she was beginning to doubt he would ever appear in her apartment, a big part of her believed he would come when she least expected it. She should be on her guard at all times, at least for the next few days.

As she massaged her face, her fingers stroked her lips.

Yoori's thoughts ventured on to the stolen kiss she shared with Tae Hyun. Yoori recalled the softness of his lips when he pressed them against hers. As much as she hated to acknowledge it, Tae Hyun was a gorgeous bastard. One couldn't complain too much when he gave you your first kiss.

Yoori grimaced upon remembering his observational review after kissing her. *"It was kinda salty."*

Her face turned red again. Was there any worse insult? She chastised herself for wasting time with this. Did all of this really matter now? The way she figured it, if Tae Hyun hadn't arrived by now, then he more than likely wouldn't ever show up.

After completely freeing her face of soap, Yoori plunged her head into the deluging warm water. She switched the shower off and gathered her hair, twisting the water out of it. Thoughts of relaxing in bed for the remainder of the night entered her mind. Excited for that prospect, she slid the shower door open and was greeted with a wad of steam. She struggled to see against the fog of steam and reached out for her towel.

As the sensation of soft cotton grazed her fingers, Yoori grabbed the towel that was extended to her and started to mindlessly dab her body with it. When she was done drying herself, Yoori ended the sequence of actions by wrapping the towel across her chest. She was ready to step out of the shower when it occurred to her...who the hell handed her the towel?

A jolt of shock electrocuted her body. Goose bumps materialized on her skin at the possible answer.

Squinting her eyes, Yoori tried hard to acclimate her vision against the wad of steam in the air. Once the fog evaporated and her line of vision returned, panic sliced into Yoori. To her dismay, someone sat on the toilet seat cover.

Gazing at her with a hand to his chin and a smirk on his face, the invader was none other than the infamous Kwon Tae Hyun.

"Hi," he greeted casually, waving at her as if he was just passing by her through the streets.

"Ahhhhhh!" Yoori screamed at the top of her lungs, struggling to the corner of the shower. She shook, not in fear, but from plain shock.

"What are you doing in here?" she shouted irately, sitting down on one of the railings. She held on tightly to her towel. Questions hammered in her mind: How did he get in? How long had he been sitting there? And more importantly, how much did he see?

Tae Hyun rose to his full height. He reached over and casually grabbed a pink bathrobe that hung off the railing of the shower door. He fixed the dark business suit he was sporting and took a huge stride into the shower. He lowered himself to her level and gazed at her with a bored expression on his face.

Yoori's heart raced a thousand miles per minute. Normally a bored expression would be a good thing, but when it was Kwon Tae Hyun who was bored, then you know you're in deep shit.

Yoori felt her throat grow dry as she tried to gulp her anxiety away. This was not going to end well.

After observing the anxiousness in her frightful eyes, Tae Hyun finally parted his lips as he tossed the bathrobe at her. When he spoke, his voice was as smooth and enticing as death itself.

"Get dressed. You...Choi Yoori, are in big trouble."

■ ■ ■

Sitting there on her living room sofa, her hands clenched tightly on the fabric of her pink bathrobe, Yoori realized Tae Hyun had not uttered a single word since he spoke to her in the bathroom. She was astounded. She had anticipated that she would be convulsing in pain, bleeding incessantly from a brutal beating, or shot to death by now.

Her eyes shadowed him when he returned to the living room with a suitcase in hand. After making his exit from the bathroom, Tae Hyun welcomed himself into her room to do God knows what. She sneaked a quick glance at the suitcase in his possession before averting her attention back to him. Tae Hyun's calm demeanor disconcerted her greatly. Yoori wasn't sure whether she should be afraid or relieved. It was uncharacteristic of him to keep the silence going for so long. It troubled her that she had no idea what he had in store for her.

As if sensing her anxiety, a small grin edged his lips. He threw the suitcase on the floor and took a seat on the couch beside the sofa. He measured the apartment. She could tell by the boredom in his eyes that he was not impressed.

"Choi Yoori, I need your advice," he managed at last. He turned his full attention back to her. His poignant eyes locked on hers, ready to get down to business.

She looked at him in surprise, not expecting to hear that. What did he need advice for?

"You see, I recently hired this girl to be my assistant. As the Underworld Kings before me did it, we clinked our glasses to have this employee-employer relationship. It was my understanding that the deal consisted of her promising me that she would be there for me when I called for her. That is of course what her position as my assistant entails. After roughly two hours on the job, however, I found her telling me that she was quitting. She appeared to change her mind about resigning as my assistant, but then she proceeded to grab her belongings and essentially ran for it."

Yoori played with her fingers uncomfortably. This story sounded dangerously familiar.

He continued idly. "It is an understatement to say that I am upset. I mean, who has work ethics like that? Better yet, who has ethics like that? Backing out on your word after you made a deal with your boss. It's…disgusting." He faced her, a hint of fire scorching in his eyes. "So…Choi Yoori, I am asking for your advice. This girl has to be punished. How do *you* suggest I punish her?"

No longer keen on participating in this shenanigan, Yoori decided to get straight to the point. She hated beating around the bush. "You can't really blame me!" she argued petulantly.

He raised a challenging brow. "Oh, I can't?"

"Look." She repositioned herself on the sofa to face him directly. "I'm sorry, okay? Unlike you, we're not all born with superhuman powers. And unlike you, I happen to fear death. *A lot*."

"I told you that I would make sure nothing happens to you."

"I'm sorry," she said decisively. "But that's not good enough."

Yoori could've sworn she saw a dash of disappointment appear on his face after hearing her last comment. A tinge of guilt surfaced inside her. She promptly shook it off. She may have been too blunt, but she hardly knew the guy. How could she trust that he'd make good on his words?

As a response, Tae Hyun stood up from the couch and sat down on the sofa, right beside her. Yoori tried to scoot to the further end of the sofa to avoid sitting too close to him. The plan backfired when the edge of the sofa blocked any future escape route. It also didn't help her situation when Tae Hyun drew closer, blocking her in from his end as well.

"Look," he started, staring into her eyes while he slid a bit closer to make peace. "I'm ready to get past this. Can you come back to work?"

Yoori gawked at him. After all that happened, he still wanted her back? Mystification assailed her. Did this guy need an assistant *that* badly?

He stared at her expectantly, those enticing brown eyes holding her gaze. "Please?"

"What is wrong with you?" she asked incredulously. "You still want me to be your assistant? I broke the most important rule. I wasn't there when you called for me."

He gaped at her like she was crazy. "What are you talking about? I never called you."

Yoori paused. That was true. He never did.

"Why didn't you call me?" she demanded. After hearing her own voice, Yoori instantly regretted what she said. She sounded like a high maintenance girlfriend rather than his unwilling assistant.

"I figured—"

"Probably figured I wouldn't pick up the phone, huh?" she interjected absentmindedly, empathizing with the pain and disappointment Tae Hyun must've felt when she left him. "You probably ran out of resources when you couldn't track me down those first seven days, right?"

Tae Hyun flashed her a "what-the-hell-have-you-been-smoking?" look. "Choi Yoori, don't flatter yourself. I didn't come get you sooner because I was away on business. I'm not going to spend the manpower on having people search for you for seven days. Give me a break."

Her cheeks burned with humiliation. Was she not worth using manpower? Was she that insignificant? She mentally reprimanded herself for thinking about these silly things. Why did she care so much about whether or not he used manpower to try and find her?

"How did you find me then?" she inquired quickly.

"I googled you."

Her face went blank. Seriously?

"Found your resumé floating around the internet with your address on it." His smile grew wider when he recited what she wrote. "'Objective: To find a job where I can work from the safety of my home.'" He laughed, patting her head, obviously amused with her innocence—or stupidity—whichever came first.

Yoori remained silent.

This whole time, she assumed Tae Hyun had men searching the city for her and all he used was the internet highway? She started to get angry. She wasn't sure if she was angry because he didn't put more effort into finding her or angry because of the entire situation. She didn't know the cause for her bout of anger, but she knew she was pissed. Pissed at him to be precise. Who did he think he was, waltzing into her apartment and demanding that she return to her role as his assistant? What kind of medication was this guy on?

"What makes you think I'll go back with you?"

Tae Hyun hid a smile. He measured the apartment again. "Judging from the state of the dump you're living in and the resumé that I found, I get the feeling that you're low on cash..." He consulted his Blackberry and then glanced up at her, his eyes turning diabolical. "And on the account that you have just been blacklisted, I think you're low on options."

Yoori's brows bunched together. "Blacklisted from what?"

"That's right." He held up his Blackberry in triumph. "You have been blacklisted from being able to work in this city. My men sent the word out. If anyone hires you, they will find their business in flames within a day."

Yoori gasped. "Tae Hyun, you have gone too far!"

"Did I not tell you that you would regret taking off on me?"

Yoori kept silent. The truth was, she did hear it. She knew something like this was going to happen. She shouldn't have taken off the way that she did. If she could go back, she wouldn't have ran. Yoori closed her eyes in agony. Now that she thought about it, if she could actually turn back time, she'd avoid being his waitress altogether.

Tae Hyun stood up and buttoned his jacket. "I'm leaving now, assistant. If you're smart, you'll follow."

Yoori eyed him with hatred. Resentfully, she stood up with him. Was there anything left to say in this matter? She'd been backed into a corner. She lost to Kwon Tae Hyun and his illegal, scheming ways.

He extended the suitcase to her, and she held it apprehensively. She irritably wondered if it was necessary for him to pack for her.

He headed for the door, but stopped when he heard something. He craned his neck in the direction of her bedroom. "I think your phone is ringing."

Yoori also craned her neck. Though barely audible, the phone was indeed ringing.

"Be right back," she said, taking off in the direction of her room. She pushed the door open, placed her suitcase down and searched for her phone. It was buried beneath the waves of her blanket. When she found the phone, she gazed oddly at the screen.

Caller unknown.

Yoori flipped the phone open. "Hello?"

A hoarse voice came from the other line. The voice was so soft, she could scarcely hear it.

"Hello?" she prompted again. "*Hello?*"

She turned to the doorway. Tae Hyun was there, pointing impatiently at his watch. He mouthed, "*It's time to go!*"

She gave Tae Hyun a pleading look. Covering the mouthpiece of her phone, she said, "I'll be done in a bit."

He nodded edgily. "Fine."

"Is this a prank call?" she asked again, getting irritated with the caller. "Hurry and talk clearly before I hang up."

"Boss?" the person on the other line finally whispered.

Yoori stood up straight. She recognized the voice. Jae Won? So it really was him who called her "boss" in the alley. She looked around worriedly. How on earth did he get her number?

"Boss! Boss, don't react to anything I'm about to say. Just keep smiling."

A smile appeared on Yoori's face as she looked at Tae Hyun. She then turned away in astonishment. Why was she listening to Jae Won? More importantly, why did he keep calling her "boss"? Did she miss the part where she became his boss?

"Why are you calling me?" she asked nicely, smiling to keep up appearances with Tae Hyun.

"Boss! Listen to me! Whatever you do, do not go anywhere with him. I repeat, do not go anywhere with him. He's dangerous."

Yoori rolled her eyes. Did he take her for a fool? Of course Tae Hyun was dangerous. He was the leader of the Serpents for Christ's sake. Jae Won really did get punched too hard during his fight with Tae Hyun. She couldn't believe he had the nerve to call her with such urgency to only state the obvious. She was too tired to deal with another gang leader who appeared to have mental problems. Crazy. All these gang leaders were crazy.

"Well, thanks for calling. Bye," she concluded brusquely. She could hear Jae Won protesting hoarsely when she switched off her phone.

She feigned a reassuring smile at Tae Hyun, who was looking at her curiously. "Who was that?"

"Telemarketer," she answered at once, the fake smile never leaving her face.

It was possibly a better idea to tell him that it was Jae Won who called. However, she didn't feel like it was necessary at the moment. Tae Hyun would probably use all his manpower to track Jae Won down and kick the crap out of him. All of this would only lead Yoori down another life or death situation. It was unnecessary drama at best, and she planned on doing everything she could to avoid it.

Tae Hyun regarded her with suspicion. She could tell he found her behavior peculiar. She could also tell by his tired expression that it was too late in the night. He was exhausted and didn't want to deal with whatever she was hiding either. "Are you ready then?"

Yoori bobbed her head. She bent down and picked up her suitcase. She actually wasn't ready to leave her apartment, but it wasn't like she had a choice. She might as well pretend that she was leaving on her own accord as opposed to getting dragged out kicking and screaming. She followed his lead toward the door. She stopped when he came to a sudden halt.

"Oh and also...Choi Yoori, we have not decided on the formalities of your punishment."

She looked at him, the weight of the suitcase heavy in her hand. "Well, isn't having me be your full-time servant good enough?"

"Assistant," he corrected as though the politically correct term would make her feel better.

"Crumbs to the peasant," she dismissed. She held her chin up. "That said, I think forcing me to move in with you is punishment enough."

"Who says you're moving in?"

Annoyance knitted her brows. "Why am I holding my suitcase then?"

"You're staying over as part of your punishment for running away. I can't trust you right now. Think of it as your probation. I need you where I can easily find you."

Again, Yoori did not like his choice of words. *"Part of your punishment..."* What else could he punish her with? Wasn't the torture of being around him 24/7 enough of a punishment?

"Okay..." she trailed off uncertainly. "What do you have in mind for the rest of my punishment?"

He lifted his powerful shoulders up and shrugged. "I'll think of something."

Her spine stiffened. He seemed *too* happy, like he already had something diabolical in mind...

"Choi Yoori," he said, diverting her thoughts to the living room. "I think I left my wallet on your coffee table. Please go grab it for me."

She sighed at his request. *My first official duty as a walking slave...*She dragged her feet and went into the living room. She didn't like how he commanded her as opposed to asking her nicely, but she felt no energy to argue. She was absolutely exhausted. As she drew closer to the coffee table, she belatedly realized that she was still dressed in her bathrobe.

"Before we go, give me a few minutes to change out of this bathrobe — *What the hell?*"

When she felt something cold encircle her left wrist, Yoori whipped her head back like a snake.

Her gaze lowered to her wrist in horror. Every muscle in her body froze at the sight of the ghastly device. *It couldn't be what she thought it was...*

Yoori's nightmare became reality when she concluded that she had just been handcuffed! And if the horrific sight before her wasn't bad enough, Tae Hyun decided to sprinkle a bit more disaster on to Yoori's already crappy life.

The flow of her blood slowed when she watched as Tae Hyun encircled his right wrist with the other cuff. He fixed the collar of his shirt, inadvertently causing Yoori's left wrist to dangle about with his actions. Tae Hyun then purposefully tugged at her wrist, leading her to the door.

Lost in disbelief, Yoori gawked at a smug Tae Hyun as they exited her apartment. She was stupefied beyond words. It was bad enough that she was handcuffed like a common criminal, but to be handcuffed to the Devil himself?

"Choi Yoori," he began, extremely pleased with himself. A roguish grin crept upon his handsome face. "If you haven't already figured it out, I've decided on the other part of your punishment."

"To be the leading hand in this world..."

08: Chained to You

It could not have looked more wrong.

Being dragged out of her apartment complex with a handcuff on her wrist could not have looked more wrong. Things could not have looked worse, but they did. They looked worse because she was not only dragged around in handcuffs, but she was also dragged around while wearing a pink bathrobe. Could this make her look anymore like a common prostitute?

In the purest of shame, Yoori lowered her head while she exited her apartment with Tae Hyun. She couldn't have hated him more.

"Is this really necessary?" she hissed, hiding her face behind his back when she passed several of her neighbors.

"Was it really necessary for you to run off?" he asked, relentlessly pulling her out into the cold streets.

"Yes!" she screamed through gritted teeth. Her body shuddered when the cool air speared through the fabric of her bathrobe and grazed her skin. It definitely didn't help that she had just showered. Her hair was still damp and she was getting a headache from the cold.

"Then it's necessary that I do this as well," he countered, speeding up.

Struggling to keep up, she glared at his profile. "How is *this* necessary?"

He kept his attention on the sidewalk ahead. "You show absolutely no remorse for what you did. You don't think what you did was wrong. How can I trust that you won't run away again? I can't trust you. Not right now. This is the only way to make sure that you will never run again."

"Okay, okay, okay. Lesson learned," she lied, already formulating a plot to take off again. "Can you please un-cuff me? My wrist hurts."

"Choi Yoori, this is not a lesson. This is a punishment. It doesn't matter if you 'learned your lesson.' This punishment will ensure that you will never forget it."

She glared at his wickedly witty answer. "You are pure evil."

He hid a crooked smile. "I prefer to see myself as strict."

Yoori's attention veered when she took inventory of the unfamiliar scenery around her.

It was darker now.

The unnatural silence of this new neighborhood scared her. Her eyes scanned the streets again. It looked empty, but she somehow knew that wasn't the case. Akin to a scary movie playing in her mind, Yoori jumped after hearing a twig snap. She was sure of it now. They were definitely not alone. Fear alive and well in her body, Yoori sped up to be closer to Tae Hyun. At least one of them appeared unaffected by the sudden change in their environment.

"I run everything around here," he calmly reassured her, his eyes focused on the sidewalk ahead. "Nothing is going to happen."

Yoori remained alert. His territory or not, the area they were in was too scary for her. It didn't help that she couldn't really defend herself by making a run for it because she was handcuffed. It also didn't help that she was still wearing her bathrobe. She cursed the fated world for this horrible karma. Everything was going against her.

As if the ominous silence wasn't enough to scare her, an unexpected murmur in the darkness caused Yoori's heart to race faster.

"*Is that really her*?" a voice asked.

"*What's she doing with boss?*" another voice asked.

"*Shit,*" the third one stated. "*She's back.*"

A rock lodged in her throat. Yoori turned in the direction of the voices. She spotted four shadows standing near a tree. They froze upon noticing her attention on them. As they continued to walk, Yoori glanced at Tae Hyun, who remained unaffected by the entire situation.

"Did…Did you hear that?" she stuttered, speeding to catch up with him. "What did they mean when they said I'm back?" She looked around, trying to spot more hidden shadows in the darkness. To her relief, she didn't find anymore—none that she could spot at least. She swallowed uneasily. Was it her or was something odd happening around here?

Tae Hyun shrugged his indifference. "They know you as the assistant who ran away. Word gets around."

Yoori nodded, staring around vacantly. His answer made sense. They *always* made sense, but they never seemed to quench her curiosity. Her intuition told her that there was more than what he was telling her however, her rationality told her to stop being overly paranoid. For that night, Yoori decided it was best to be rational.

"Are we there yet?" she whispered. It no longer mattered where they were headed. She just wanted to get off the streets.

She was surprised when he actually said yes.

She stared up at his apartment complex in disbelief. After what appeared to be the longest journey of her life, they finally arrived at the doorsteps of Tae Hyun's apartment. She was finally out of the scrutiny of the public eye.

Tae Hyun yawned before closing the door behind him. He switched on the lights.

"Well, I'm ready for bed," he announced, fatigue present in his quiet voice.

Yoori nodded absentmindedly, following him into his bedroom. She was ready for bed too.

When they walked into his bedroom, Yoori's stunned eyes perused the room. The room was a *very* spacious one. A handsome mahogany desk sat in the room with various cabinets surrounding the area. The king sized bed, which was ordained with black silk, caught her eye. It was absolutely breathtaking. The decadence of the bedroom appeared as if it was a room specifically built for royalty.

All hail the King of Serpents, she marveled stupidly. Oh how she wanted to sleep on that bed for the rest of her lif—*wait a second*!

She looked at their cuffed wrists in dread. The prude within her emerged. "Um, Tae Hyun?" she began shyly.

Loosening his tie, he regarded her. "Yeah?"

"There's only one bed..." she trailed off, hoping Tae Hyun would catch her drift. Didn't he realize what an honorable girl she was? She couldn't share a bed with him.

He stared at her blankly, his expression not comprehending her subtle words. "Yeah?"

Yoori blinked slowly. She didn't know if he was playing dumb or if he was serious. "There's two of us..." she continued, trailing off again. She prayed he would catch the drift this time.

His blank stare remained. "*Yeah*?"

Yoori gawked at him. Wow, he really sucked at picking up subtleties. "Should. I. Move. The. Couch. In. Here?" she said slowly, enunciating every word.

He frowned in response to her speaking to him like he was a child. "I don't like people moving my stuff."

Her exasperation with him elevated. He was really being a pain in the ass. It wasn't like she was moving his couch out to the park or something. She just wanted to move it into his room so she didn't have to share a bed with him!

"Well, should you un-cuff me then?" she suggested, preferring this option anyway. "I'll go sleep outside in the living room."

He appraised her like she was the most untrustworthy criminal in the world. He shook his head. "I don't trust you. You'll probably take off again."

She sputtered in outrage. "Where the hell am I going to sleep then?"

He took off his tie and began to unbutton his shirt. "You can sleep on the floor next to my bed or you can sleep on the bed." He yawned, approaching the bed with Yoori in tow. "Whatever you decide is fine with me."

Yoori followed with a grimace, her cuffed wrist leading the way. "You're *serious*? My only options are the floor or the bed?"

He flopped himself onto his bed, a move that caused her cuffed hand to be outstretched. He sighed as though relieved to finally be in the comfort of his own bed. Though it could never be proven, she was sure that it was his subtle way of telling her that she should choose the bed.

Her eyes gradually fell upon his chest. He had unbuttoned his shirt and his perfectly tanned chest was now peeking out at her...not to mention a hint of his six-pack abs.

Wow.

Was she drooling? No, of course not. Gawking yes, but *not* drooling.

Yoori broke out of her momentary gawking phase when she saw that he opened his eyes.

"Bed feels nice," he crooned in a hushed voice. He motioned her to the bed by patting the mattress.

Yoori stared at him incredulously. What had gotten into him? Was he really flirting or just screwing around? She heaved a bitter breath, positive that he was screwing around with her. She cursed and angrily grabbed a pillow from his bed. She couldn't believe she allowed his handsome physique to get the best of her...*again*.

Determined to not allow herself to be hypnotized by Tae Hyun's physical attractiveness, she tossed the pillow on the floor. She would not, under any circumstances, share the same bed as him. It wasn't right. For one, he was her boss and second, he was an evil crime lord. That fact in and of itself was a powerful deterrent.

Yoori scowled when she heard Tae Hyun chuckle, his eyes on her as she kneeled on the floor. As soon as her bare knees touched the cold tiles, goose bumps ran up and down her skin, causing her to shiver under the pricking cold. With her left wrist dangling from his right wrist, she laid down. She groaned softly. The floor was cold, uncomfortable, and unforgiving.

Tae Hyun poked his head out from above the bed. "There's enough room on the bed, you know."

Yoori stared up. She felt her heart grow warmer at the sight before her. It amazed her that he was still smiling. Kwon Tae Hyun didn't strike her as the type to be smiley for such a long period of time. It surprised her. Not so much that there was a genuinely happy smile on his face, but that seeing him happy made her smile too. It was one of those weird contagious things.

Catching herself, Yoori cast her attention to her pillow. She didn't want to be caught staring for too long again. God knows the teasing he would put her through if he caught her gawking.

"There's enough room down here too," she countered, repositioning her pillow in distress. It broke her heart. No matter how much she repositioned it, the pillow would never be comfortable enough for her.

"Alright then," she heard him say. She watched his head vanish from the bed. Her resentment amplified. The fool could try and convince her to sleep on the bed. She wasn't planning on taking him up on his offer, but wasn't it the gentlemanly thing to do? At least offer a couple more times before you actually stopped!

There was a slight tug on her cuffed wrist before the flash of a comforter gliding over the bed soared into her vision.

As pricks of the gnawing cold jumped from the tiles and onto her skin, she was reminded of the importance of being warm. "Hey, do you have another blanket?"

"Nope."

Her jaw slackened. "You really only have one?"

Without deigning to stick his head out to speak to her, he said, "Yup."

"Well, can you throw half of your comforter down here so I can use it too?" The tiles were alarmingly cold.

"Sorry. No can do. I don't like having my blanket on the floor."

She sputtered in disbelief.

"It's freezing down here!" she snapped, wanting to rip the comforter away from him instead of asking for permission. Though the alternative was tempting, Yoori resisted the urge to start any unnecessary drama.

"You can come up on the bed at any time," he offered offhandedly.

Although she couldn't see him, she detected a huge grin on his face when he said that last sentence. What a jerk!

"Ugh! Forget it!" She grudgingly turned to her side. She tried to cross her arms to shelter herself from the cold. The anchor of the cuffs made it impossible. She shut her eyes, forcing herself to fall asleep so she wouldn't have to suffer any longer.

"Choi Yoori," she heard his voice again.

Her lids lifted. His head reappeared above the bed. He lay on his chest, resting his chin against the edge of the bed. He smiled down at her.

"What?" she answered impatiently.

"Tell me about yourself," he prompted casually, staring down at her with interest.

She gave him a skeptical look. After all that happened, he decided it was best to get to know her *now*? She eyed him suspiciously, wondering what he had up his sleeves. Tae Hyun's smile grew wider in response to her suspicious stare.

Feeling that there was no harm in having this conversation, she sighed. "What do you want to know?" she asked, growing uncomfortable upon remembering the loss of her family and her amnesia. She was determined not to get into that part of the story. The last thing she wanted to do was share with a gang leader her sob story.

"What do you *want* me to know?" he answered courteously, reading her uncomfortable body language.

She relaxed fractionally, relieved that he posed the question in a way that made it easier for her to answer. "I'm originally from Taecin," she began lively. "I first moved to Seoul about a year and a half ago. I've been here ever since."

Tae Hyun kept his gaze on her, expecting her to go further into details. When all she did was blink at him, he chuckled. "Wow. That's really all you're going to tell me?"

Yoori bounced her head smugly, feeling proud that she had the upper hand in the information-withholding department. "There's really not much to tell. That's the gist of it."

Minus the amnesia and the part where her family died in a fire, of course. But again, Tae Hyun didn't need to know any of that.

He nodded, accepting that she wasn't going to give him more details.

Yoori jutted her chin up. "Your turn. Tell me about yourself."

He laughed, thoroughly amused at the ball being bounced in his court. "Well, to start, what do you *think* you know about me?"

She was taken aback by how he posed the question. Interesting how he was supposed to answer, but he somehow made it about her. She had no complaints though. She wanted to answer this one.

"The King of Serpents," she launched, examining him with a critical eye. *The stereotypical hot and evil gang leader…* She shook her head, unable to think of anything else to say aside from the obvious. "There's not too much room for imagination here, boss. Unfortunately, you're every unpleasant thing I would expect a gang leader to be."

She had expected him to cuss her out for being so blunt. Instead, he just nodded, appreciating the straightforwardness of her answer. "You're right. There's definitely not a lot of room for imagination here. Whatever you think you know about me, it's probably true."

Yoori got excited. Ooh, a chance to give him a low blow!

"What if I told you that I think you're a monster?" she asked quickly, scanning his face for a reaction. She was surprised to find that he smiled pleasantly.

"Then I would say that you're probably right on the dot. God knows I'm no angel."

Her critical stare still on him, it threw her off her smug course when it felt like *she* was the one who received the low blow. She couldn't help but feel dispirited with how nonchalant he acted. It disturbed her immensely. "You sound so proud of that fact."

"I wouldn't be where I am today if I didn't embrace it."

Her interest peaked. "So you're telling me that regardless of all that charm you throw around at times, all those tiny moments of kindness that you show…beneath it all, you're completely free of morality? You really are a monster?"

He stiffened his jaw, struck by the severity of what she said. He, however, remained collected. "I'm telling you that it's in your best interest to always think the worst of me. If I'm nice and playful with you then enjoy it, but don't form any attachment to it. I'm one of the Royals in the Underworld for a reason, and I don't want you to forget that."

"He's dangerous." Jae Won's warning words replayed in her mind as she kept her gaze on Tae Hyun. Of course he was dangerous. She had always known that. She didn't need Jae Won or Tae Hyun, himself, to tell her that. She already knew it.

"Why are you telling me all this?" she asked, growing curious of his motives.

"To get you ready for what's ahead of you. I'm a tough person to work for. I'm trying to prepare you for it the best that I can."

Silence surrounded Yoori. She found herself strangely disheartened by his answer. She didn't know what she was hoping to hear, but that wasn't the answer she wanted from him. She broke eye contact and stared absentmindedly at the tiles. When you put rationale in the equation, Tae Hyun, with how he treated her, was horrible beyond words. He not only fit the role of the overly possessive and inhumane gang leader well, but he did it with so much pride that you couldn't help but feel justified calling him "evil."

Her focus on the outlining of the tiles became stronger as her contemplative mind sailed on. Regardless though, was he really evil? A big part of her refused to believe that he should be categorized as a monster. *No*, she reasoned. There was definitely more to Tae Hyun. Her instincts burned in certainty. She was sure of it. There was more to Tae Hyun—he wasn't as he portrayed himself to be.

Yoori's breathing grew a bit unsteady when she allowed the next few words to flow out of her apprehensive mouth. "What if," she began, slowly returning her gaze to him, "I was to say that I think there's more to you than what meets the eye?"

She watched Tae Hyun freeze, his gaze on her uncomfortable. Silence enveloped him. It was only a brief moment, but she caught it—that flicker of light in his eyes. It was so minute, but in that split second, vulnerability within his eyes shined through.

"Then I would say that you're an optimistic one," he noted emotionlessly, avoiding her gaze. "And that you're probably setting yourself up for disappointment, but that's just me."

"You're a pessimistic one, aren't you?"

"I guess we learned a little bit more about one another, right?" He lifted his chin off the edge of the bed and let out a somewhat forced yawn. She could tell he didn't like where the conversation was headed and was ready to put an end to it.

"Alright," he uttered, clapping his hands together in triumph. "That's my boss-and-assistant bonding moment for the night. I'm sleeping now." Avoiding any further eye contact with her, his head moved out of sight. She felt her cuffed wrist move when he repositioned himself on the bed. "Good night, assistant."

"Night," she replied, crestfallen that their conversation had to end so soon when it was actually making progress.

As she repositioned her pillow, she found her eyes peering at the edge of the bed where Tae Hyun rested his chin moments before. A glimmer of hope appeared before her eyes. Was it possible that Kwon Tae Hyun, the glorified Underworld King, was not the monster he made himself out to be? It was a foolish thought that Yoori embraced. She liked to think the best of people. It gave her hope, gave her something to smile about.

The same thought replayed in her mind as she drifted off to sleep, her mood elated.

Perhaps Kwon Tae Hyun wasn't as dark as the Underworld he ruled over.

Perhaps he wasn't a monster and perhaps somewhere deep down, he was truly human after all.

"You have to be flexible with your morals."

09: Make Things Right

"Why do you have to do this?" The tall shadow asked, his voice filled with grief and outrage. He grabbed the other shadow's hand and pulled her closer to him.

The woman pushed him away in exasperation. She didn't understand why he made this so much harder than it had to be.

"Can't you understand that I can't live like this anymore?" she shouted for the hundredth time, not understanding why he couldn't get the big picture.

His voice was equally angry. "Can't you understand that I don't want you to live like this either?" He clapped his hands together and brought them to his lips, a gesture to appease his growing frustration. "But there has to be another way to go about this," he reasoned, taking another step closer to her.

She shook her head. He didn't get it. He didn't understand that this was her only option. "There's no other way. I have to do this."

"Do you realize how ridiculous you sound? Out of all people, you want your *brother* to do this?"

She remained unfazed by the disbelief in his voice. "He's the only one who can make things right."

"He's not going to help you kill yourself."

"If he's the person I know he is...he will."

"Baby, don't do this," he pleaded, grabbing her arms to prevent her from retreating. "We'll figure out another way to make things right. You can't risk your life like this."

Her impatience with him growing, she pushed him away with all her might. "You don't understand what I'm going through!" Pain, indignation, guilt, and shame were all present in her elevated voice. "I can barely breathe without getting sick to my stomach. I can't eat. I can't sleep...I can barely even look at my brother! All I can do is think about it...what happened...what should've happened and what I can do to make things right. I can't go on pretending that everything is fine. I can't. I can't live like this anymore."

She began to retreat again, her pace quickening by the second. She knew he would have a hard time accepting what she had to do, but she didn't think he'd put up such a fight.

Her pace was matched by her significant other's pace. He raced to her. "Do you realize how selfish you're being right now? Do I really have no say in this matter?"

"If you're not going to support me, then that's fine," she uttered, stopping abruptly. She gazed at him unblinkingly, her determination never faltering on what she had to do. "But do not think for one second that you can change my mind!"

She breathed heavily, gazing at his frozen countenance. "Tonight is the night where he helps me make things right," she continued, her voice breaking. She held back the tears that were ready to stream out of her eyes. "Tonight is the night where I make things right. If you love me, then you'll help me make things right as well."

She watched in anticipation as he took a step closer. He pulled her into an embrace, breaking the silence they were getting ready to drown in. "I love you, more than you will ever know. Know that whatever happens, I'll be right here by your side. I love you. I always will."

She smiled sadly, her embrace on him tightening. She believed him. Every word he said, she believed him. She knew that he really did love her that much. Tears brimming in her eyes, she buried her face into his chest. She loved him so much.

"Don't forget..." she whispered before pulling out of the embrace and leaving his side. "Don't forget what you have to do..."

Yoori's eyes sprang open once she felt the golden rays of the morning sun flow over her face. With her bare arms lying above the comforter, it didn't take long for Yoori to feel the morning chills creep up her skin. Yoori instinctively tucked her arms underneath the haven of warmth from her blanket. Wanting to take the necessary precautions to further protect herself from the cold, Yoori pulled the comforter up to her exposed neck. Tickles of pleasurable warmth replaced the iciness that once pricked her body. Satisfied with her victory against the cold, Yoori's sleepy mind traveled back to her bittersweet dream.

Ah, yes.

A small, bemused smile waltzed across her lips at the recollection of her dream. This was a new dream for Yoori. Funny how the other one somehow stopped reoccurring and this one appeared in its place. Not that she was complaining. She much preferred this dream to the other one. Albeit it was another sad dream, she admitted that she loved it more. At least this one had *some* romance to it (as opposed to the depressing, assisted suicide content of the other one). And of course, the romantic guy in the dream was a big catalyst for her favoritism.

Another drop of happiness poured into her as she mulled over this—the sweet boyfriend in the dream. Although he was a figment of her imagination, she felt a small crush form for him. Even through the dream, she could feel his love for his girlfriend and it warmed her little heart. Her smile grew slightly wider at the thought of the embrace they shared.

Ah yes, she was definitely living vicariously through the female protagonist in her dream.

As she replayed the scenes of the bittersweet dream in her mind, Yoori found herself growing envious of the girl in her dreams.

Strange how these two dreams, the one in the alley and the one she just had, completely interrelated with one another. It was the same girl. Yoori bit her lower lip, her curiosity for the mystery girl heightened with every breath. Why did she want to die? How could the girl choose to leave when she had such a great guy in her life? What did she want to make right? What did she do? What on earth happened?

Oy, get a grip, Choi Yoori, her inner self scolded.

She laughed at herself for bearing such stupidity. The only way to truly find out answers was to sleep and *hope* that another dream appeared with the answer to her questions.

She rolled her eyes.

Good luck with that happening, she thought sarcastically.

Yoori was prepared to get lost in another bout of introspection—that was until she felt something that froze every warm nerve in her body.

She felt *movement*.

A hail of dread ravaged her stomach. Her eyes widened slowly. She stared cautiously at the comforter covering her, alertness returning to her awakened mind. If memory served her correctly, she was sure Tae Hyun said that this comforter was *not* going to touch the floor.

Awkwardness shafted through her.

Timidly, Yoori carefully depressed her shaking fingers. She silently prayed that she was still sleeping on the floor. Like a tipsy drunk losing her fight with gravity, Yoori's heart sank into the nearest abyss when she realized that the "floor" was soft enough to be pushed down.

"Oh no," she thought, horrified.

This was Kwon Tae Hyun's bed.

Yoori painstakingly turned her gaze to the other side of the bed. She whispered words of prayer. "Please don't let Tae Hyun be on the other side of the bed. Please? Plea—oh crap."

And there the Devil himself laid.

If she was falling into the abyss before, then the abyss somehow led into the depths of hell. This was *exactly* where Yoori felt she landed when she saw that the unthinkable happened.

There was Tae Hyun, on the other side of the bed, merely inches away from her, sleeping like an angel. A Devil in the form of an angel anyway. Her heart hammered at the sight of him in such a state. A barrage of questions inundated her mind. Why was she on the bed? How long had she been sleeping next to him? And more importantly, what the hell happened last night?

Her merciless glare rested on an unconscious Tae Hyun. She was determined to get her answers.

"Wake up!" she screamed, shaking him with her hands. "What happened last night? What'd you do to me?"

Though his eyes were still closed, she saw a smile creep on to Tae Hyun's face. He ignored her screams and covered himself with the comforter, murmuring as he did this. She watched him shift his body to the further end of the bed.

"Go back to sleep," he responded lazily.

She was livid. She could *hear* the smile on his face. How could he behave in such a lax manner? Her mind was a vortex of confusion. What happened?

She irritably shook her cuffed hand, leaving Tae Hyun's cuffed hand to waver lifelessly. He continued to ignore her. His indifferent attitude taunted Yoori. Frustrated, she ripped the comforter off the bed, leaving him suddenly without a blanket.

"Tae Hyun! If you don't tell me what happened, I am going to choke you with my bare hands. I don't care if you're the leader of a gang. I will kill you!"

She was past the realm of fury. And to think that she actually thought there was more to him than being an evil gang leader.

"You have got to be kidding," he whispered with exasperation. Finally sitting up in bed, he turned to her and leaned against the headboard. Tae Hyun's unbuttoned shirt flew apart, exposing the length of his bare chest and his rock hard abs. His amused eyes smiled at her as they acclimated with the morning sun.

At the sight of him in such a seductive position, Yoori turned away in annoyance. She hated that her eyes immediately lowered to his naked abs as soon as they came into view. How perverted could she be?

"You're really not a morning person," he observed tiredly.

Yoori's eyes went back to his tired face. Perversion aside, she had business to get down to. "Cut the crap. What happened last night? How'd I end up on your bed?"

She was certain he would admit that he was a pervert and that he lifted her into bed himself. His unexpected answer horrified her.

"You got on yourself." The indifference in his monotonous voice remained when he closed his eyes. He obviously wanted more sleep.

She glared, bewildered. Her womanly pride made it hard for her to believe the verity of his words. "I did not!"

His indifference and closed eyes remained. "Yeah, you did."

"I did not!"

He opened his eyes and looked at her with a bothered countenance. His patience with her was wearing thin. "Yeah, you did. You muttered something about being cold, got up from the floor, and basically pushed me to the other side of the bed as you got on." He scrutinized her. "You don't remember *any* of that?"

Yoori shook her head, doubt swarming her. Although she didn't want to believe him, the likelihood of something like this happening was too great. She had always been a heavy sleeper. She knew that. However, she didn't realize she was also a sleepwalker. Was it really possible that she had been freezing and got onto the bed because of pure survival instincts?

Anything was possible.

She eyed him cautiously, reluctantly believing him. "Did anything else happen?"

"Yeah. You snored...*very* loudly."

Blood rushed to her enflamed cheeks. That wasn't what she meant.

Despite the reddening of her embarrassed face, he went on like the energizer bunny. "It was so loud, I thought my eardrums were going to burst. I couldn't sleep all throughout the night. I only managed to get some shut eye an hour ago."

Yoori stayed quiet, her pride deflated and her face now crimson red. Why oh why did Tae Hyun always make it his personal mission to make her flush like a goddamn tomato?

"Your snoring stopped when you started murmuring something. I assume you were having a dream?"

Yoori nodded, feeling guilty about overreacting the way that she did. Granted, her guilt was minimized by the simple fact that Tae Hyun was a mean jerk. As she nodded, she began to recall the dream. Apparently it was the only pleasant thing that occurred to her this eventful morning.

Sensing the beam exuding out of her, an entertained smirk edged Tae Hyun's lips. "A dream about me I suppose..." he teased, inching closer to her.

"That would be called a nightmare," she countered, pushing him to stop him from coming any closer.

She was irritated that he was being so flirty. She couldn't tell if he was joking or if he was seriously flirting with her. Under typical circumstances, she could usually tell with other guys what their intentions with her were. Tae Hyun on the other hand was a big fat question mark. She swallowed hard, trying to assess him for some answers. Knowing Tae Hyun, Yoori would put money on the first option, which was the joking around option. He enjoyed toying with her. If she didn't know better, she would think her blushes were his fuel for a good and productive day.

He chuckled warmly when she pushed him away. Once he settled back on his side of the bed, he rested his head on the headboard. His alluring chest and abs glowed as they basked under the golden rays of the sun.

"What'd you dream about?" he asked. Though he feigned disinterest, Yoori could tell by the look in his eyes that he was curious.

"A guy...that I like," she said without thinking. She contorted her face in embarrassment. Doh! He didn't have to know that!

Her eyes sliced into him like daggers when she heard him laugh. Even though she had expected him to do that, it wasn't a nice feeling to be made fun of.

"Aw, my little assistant dreaming about her future husband when she's lying in bed with her boss," he cooed with hilarity. "Man, that's just classic."

Yoori's twitching eye glowered at him intensely. She thought back to her deep contemplation the night before about him having a heart. At the moment, she was having second thoughts about that.

His laughter subsiding, he eyed her idly. "Is he better looking than me?"

"You're an idiot," she responded, smacking him across the shoulder.

Though she didn't verbally answer him, Yoori pondered his question nonetheless. Was the dream guy better looking? She stole a glimpse at Tae Hyun. He was leaning over to get a better view of his alarm clock. Given the level of physical attractiveness that he so easily commanded, it was difficult to visualize any guy being better looking than Tae Hyun. However, she had the distinct feeling that this dream guy was probably just *as* good looking. Plus, from what she could remember, he was a really sweet and romantic guy. This already gave him extra points in her book.

Yoori shook off the glee of her illogical reasoning. Why was she spending so much time thinking about this dream guy? He didn't even exist!

"It's too damn early," she heard Tae Hyun complain.

Yoori glanced over at the alarm clock. It read 1:06 P.M.

It's not early at all, she thought incredulously, turning her attention to Tae Hyun. He looked like he could use a couple more hours of sleep. Guilt hounded her. Well, they *did* get back pretty late last night and if he only got the hour of sleep because of her snoring then...

Well, it's his fault! Yoori thought stubbornly, her guilt coming to a standstill. Even though she may have been the reason for his fatigue, she refused to feel guilty. If he allowed her to sleep outside on the couch, then he wouldn't have been this tired. He brought all of this on himself.

Tae Hyun cleared his throat, pulling her from her reverie. He reached his left hand into his pocket and fished out something that lifted Yoori's solemn mood.

Her eyes sparkled.

Freedom, she thought thankfully, extending her left wrist out.

A small silver key dangled from his fingers. The key gleamed in the sunlight, making it appear magical, mythical even. For a paranoid second, she had expected him to torture her by putting the key back in his pocket. She was delighted to find that he actually moved to un-cuff her.

She watched as he struggled to wake up while attempting to unlock the cuffs. Her impatience getting the best of her, she reached for the keys to unlock the cuffs herself. She was deterred when Tae Hyun gently smacked her hand away.

She pouted. She just wanted to help.

"I'll get it done," he muttered firmly, his eyes now awake. He pulled the cuffs closer and finally rammed the key into them.

Yoori's world brightened when the cuffs fell from her wrist. She had never felt so free in her life. She wanted to spring up and twirl around the room. Punishment was over!

Free! Free! Fre—

"You have twenty minutes," Tae Hyun declared loudly, raining on her parade.

Yoori felt herself stumble off cloud nine. "What?"

"You have twenty minutes to change, brush your teeth, and shower. Do whatever you have to do before you get the cuffs again."

"*What?* We're not done?"

Tae Hyun simply smirked at her before he climbed out of bed to undress.

She fumed. Of course her punishment wasn't over. Tae Hyun, the Devil here, would never let her off that easily.

She lowered her eyes when he stripped off his shirt. She didn't need to see his naked upper body right now.

Tae Hyun chuckled when she lowered her eyes. "You can look if you want, assistant."

"I don't want to," she said sharply. Even though she did, *slightly*, want to. But no! She had more self-control than that. She was not a pervert.

He laughed, grabbing a clean towel from the drawer. "I'll leave the bathroom door unlocked if you want to come in and brush your teeth." He presented her with a heart-stopping smile that was enticing enough to weaken the knees of nuns. "You can come join me in the shower too, if you want."

She hurled him a death glare.

He laughed again. "Kidding!" he shouted as he strolled into the bathroom. "Oh man, your expressions are classic."

She frowned as he disappeared into the bathroom, wondering how he would fare if she were to suddenly attack him.

Her ears perked up when she heard the sound of water spraying. Her eyes journeyed to the door in the living room. Running away would definitely be a good idea right now. Almost instantly, Yoori shook her head, vetoing the idea as soon as it came into consideration. She wanted to run, but she knew better now. If she ran, Tae Hyun would find her again. She didn't have many places to go other than her apartment. Moreover, she could only imagine what his next punishment for her might be if she hauled ass again. He would probably lock her up in a dungeon for months on end if she were lucky.

Acknowledging that she would have to do her time, she retrieved her suitcase and withdrew her clothes. She stripped off her bathrobe and threw on a pair of black jeans and a nice satin red top. She grabbed a toothbrush and toothpaste from her suitcase. Instead of heading into the bathroom, she went straight for the sink in the kitchen. She did not want to be around Tae Hyun while he was naked.

After brushing her teeth, she found herself eyeing his apartment cautiously. She stared at the dirty dishes in the sink, the mountain of dirty clothes on the laundry machine, and the dirty floor in the kitchen. She wondered if she should start the morning off right by cleaning. She nodded. Regardless of whether or not she wanted to be here, she was officially his assistant and she was bound and determined to be a good one—especially since it was commission-based and all.

When she was about to wash the dirty dishes, the doorbell rang.

Her gaze shifted to the bathroom. She could hear that Tae Hyun was still in the shower. *He must be expecting someone*. Without giving it a second thought, Yoori opened the door. Her eyes enlarged at the sight of five men standing before her. She had expected one or two, but definitely not five.

Her surprised gaze roamed over them.

All covered in the decadence of designer suits, expensive looking haircuts, and standing with perfect posture, they all looked like they were worth a million bucks. All looked the same with the exception of the one who stood up front. He was dressed much like the rest; the difference was that he sported a pair of sunglasses that made him stand out from the pack.

The reason why he caught her eye was because as soon as his eyes fell on her, his sunglasses immediately came off. His brown eyes inspected her, his curious gaze morphing into one of disbelief. He gazed at her like she was merely a figment of his imagination.

Her eyes fastened on the four men behind him. Much like the one up front, the four men in the back had their eyes firmly solidified on her. The difference was that their gaze was much more hostile. If looks could kill, then Yoori would already be in an early grave.

Anxiety struck her like a lightning bolt.

Why did she have a feeling something bad was about to go down?

Tae Hyun. Get out of the fucking shower, she thought worriedly. She had the distinct feeling that she was going to need his help.

Her fears were realized when the four men, with their eyes tightly set on her, reached behind their backs. Her throat grew drier than the Sahara desert.

They couldn't be pulling out what she thought they were getting ready to pull out...

Her suspicions were confirmed when one by one, the four men pulled out their guns and promptly aimed them at her head. Their guns cocked and fingers firmly placed on the triggers, they were ready to shoot.

"You can never let them forget who you are."

10: Apologies

Yoori's entire body trembled in feverish fear. Her eyes locked on the four barrels of guns pointed at her.

So it's true, Yoori thought dejectedly. Your life does flash before your eyes when you're staring death in the face. Granted, she only had three years' worth of memories, but it was still her short life flashing before her eyes nonetheless.

"What are you doing here?" one of them demanded, leveling the gun onto her forehead.

Light layers of cold sweat coated her forehead. The rock in her throat grew so huge that she was sure she was going to choke on it.

I'm Tae Hyun's assistant, she wanted to scream out to them. Instead of screaming, the words lodged in her throat. She was too scared to even speak. Were they in Tae Hyun's gang or were they rival gang members? Her mind spun relentlessly. It didn't matter whose side they were on. The only thing that mattered was that they were getting ready to shoot her and Tae Hyun was nowhere close to finishing his damn shower.

She shuddered. This was just her luck. Her luck was *this* horrible. What did she do in a past life to deserve this?

"What the hell are you guys doing?" the guy with the sunglasses screamed, pushing one of the men back to his senses. "She is boss's girl! He brought her here last night!"

Yoori nodded fervently, counting her blessings that this angel, disguised as a gang member, appeared to save her. Her hope for survival resurrected.

Yes. Yes, lower your guns, she pleaded in her mind.

Unsatisfied with the explanation, the rest of the men kept their guns pointed at her. They weren't convinced that she wasn't a threat.

Intensity blared in his eyes. "Listen to me," he began gravely. "If you value your lives, then you will lower your guns right now. Boss will kill each and every one of you if you so much as touch her."

That was what did it.

The four men exchanged apprehensive glances. Then, they gazed at her with caution. Hostility still embedded in their eyes, they lowered their guns, each keeping their eyes on her like hawks.

Yoori stood frozen, the aftershocks of fear pulsating in her veins. Could you really start functioning right after having four guns pointed at you? She was only able to make the slight progress of moving her head toward the direction of the guy with the sunglasses.

He spoke to her, his voice warm and gentle. "Sorry about that," he said, smiling at her. He scratched the back of his head in uneasiness. "You can't be too careful when you see a stranger in your boss's home, right?" he added, trying to make it seem like they pointed guns at people all the time. She thought about it again. They probably did do that often.

He elbowed the man standing beside him to the right. That guy eyed her suspiciously. "Right?" he prompted with the leading question.

The glaring man nodded, now avoiding eye contact with her. "Yeah, reflexes," he answered quickly, not meaning it at all.

The other three men said the same thing, reluctantly easing up on the hostility they once harbored for her.

In the midst of this, Yoori was baffled. She was one girl. What were they threatened about? She was still a little shaken up from what occurred and couldn't even think straight. What would happen now? Should she hug it out with them and let it go? Who on earth points a gun at someone and tells them that it was just "reflexes"?

"Uh, is boss here?" the one with the sunglasses asked, purposely veering the discussion elsewhere.

Yoori nodded, grateful for the change of subject. She stepped aside to allow room for them to come in.

The four men piled in, each avoiding her gaze. They took their places on the sofa and couches in the living room. In other situations, Yoori would have been angered that they didn't personally apologize for what happened. But, in this case, when the sight of their stern faces gave her chills, she was satisfied with not having any further interaction with them.

"Hi," Sunglasses-guy greeted her again. He wore a kind look on his face.

She spared him a reluctant smile. Yoori didn't want to talk to the rest of the men, but speaking to him was fine, since he saved her life and all.

"Hi," she replied, looking at him guardedly.

He gave her a nervous smile. Judging by the look on his face, her instincts told her that he was about to ask her for a favor. And, judging by what took place, she knew what this favor was.

"It would be greatly appreciated if you didn't talk about what happened with boss," he requested softly. He had an apologetic expression on his face as he went on. "It was bad reflexes on their part, but he'd really flip out if he knew."

Though Yoori was confused as to why he would make a request like this when it was the other four idiots who scared the hell out of her, she didn't want to venture too far into contemplation about it. She wasn't in the right mindset to deal with anything right now.

Instead of verbally replying to him, Yoori simply nodded at his request, not really thinking it over. The shock had yet to leave her. She would've agreed to anything to get some peace of mind.

"Thank you, Yoori," he said delicately, giving her a small bow.

As she watched him take a seat in the living room, she also caught a glimpse of herself in one of the mirrors on the wall. She shuddered at the ghostly sight. Her face was sickeningly pale.

"I look like a ghost," she uttered, pinching her cheeks in a desperate attempt to reclaim some color to her face. She felt like she had woken up from a nightmare.

"Oh. Hey guys."

Everyone, including herself, turned their heads in the direction of the voice. Reprieve overcame her when Tae Hyun came into frame. He made his way out of the bathroom. He wore a white bathrobe and his hair was wet. Residual mist covered some parts of his face, making it appear as if he was glowing. In light of what took place, Tae Hyun couldn't have looked more like her knight in shining armor. She already felt safer with his presence. Her relief soon faded into one of resentment. Four gang members held her at gunpoint and all he had to say was, *"Oh. Hey guys"*?

Tae Hyun looked around, surprised to see his men in the living room. "I forgot that you guys were coming."

She clenched her fists at his casual statement. How irresponsible could he be? A little heads up for either party would've been nice. A little, "Hey Yoori, don't open the door, you might get shot" or "Hey boys, I have a new assistant. Don't shoot her when she opens the door." If he had given *anyone* notice, then it would have worked out in her favor. But no. No, he *forgot*. Anger revved through her. It was an understatement to say that Yoori was livid.

"Hey boss," she heard a couple of them greet, bowing their heads as they straightened up in their seats.

"Hey, you alright?" Tae Hyun asked, drawing close to her when he took inventory of her troubled expression.

She flinched in surprise when he touched her forehead to feel her temperature, misinterpreting her paleness for illness. The warmth from his touch caused a horde of butterflies to float about in her tummy.

"What's wrong?" he asked again, concern reveling on his face. "Why are you so pale?"

Yoori stared at him silently. She could see from the corner of her eyes that his men were watching them. They held their breaths, praying she wouldn't say anything. They were afraid. The King of Serpents was here and they were afraid of his wrath should he find out what they did to her.

She was tempted to tell Tae Hyun that those bastards sitting on the couch pointed their guns at her. She wanted to tell him that she hated him and all the bad luck that came from being around him. She wanted to tell him how pissed she was and that she was quitting, *again*.

Her mind was reeling. She had so much she wanted to say. Instead, she resentfully said, "I'm fine."

She could hear the four men exhale in relief after hearing her answer.

Unconvinced, Tae Hyun divided his attention between Yoori and his men. "Did something happen?"

"I'm fine," she repeated impatiently, folding her arms and turning away from him. She no longer wanted to talk about this.

Tae Hyun's look of concern dissolved into one of annoyance. It was apparent he didn't enjoy being brushed off when he was actually showing some semblance of concern. He shook his head like he shouldn't have acted so concerned and drew away from her. He diverted his attention to the living room.

"Hey," he said distractedly, forgetting that he already greeted them. He took a seat on the chair that stood a little higher than the rest in the room. In this scene, he looked like a modern day King.

"Hey boss," they said again in unison, their voices resonating across the room.

Getting back to business, Tae Hyun looked between his men and Yoori. "I take it you all have met?"

Everyone gave a reluctant nod.

"Well, I'll make it official." He turned to Yoori. "Choi Yoori, these are the boys." He turned to his gang members. "Boys, this is Choi Yoori. She's my new assistant."

Yoori and the "boys" awkwardly acknowledged one another again.

"She will be assisting me in my daily operations. You will be seeing a lot of her. Please inform the others."

Yes. Please inform the others, she thought desperately. She really didn't want to find herself in a similar predicament. Having death stare you in the face takes a lot of energy out of you.

"Choi Yoori," Tae Hyun continued, "aside from myself, these five hold the highest positions in our gang. They are in charge of the various territories that the Serpents have taken over. They basically keep me updated on the happenings of our various businesses and help make sure that our operations are running smoothly."

The tone of his voice and how he explained their positions gave her the impression that he was still a little bit annoyed with her dismissive attitude toward him. She felt a twinge of guilt, but not enough to make her feel bad. If she had her way, she'd smack him upside the head. Whether directly or indirectly, it was all his fault that she was traumatized.

He turned to his men. "Am I missing anything else?"

They shook their heads, keeping their eyes solely focused on him and avoiding Yoori.

Satisfied, Tae Hyun shifted his attention back to her. "Now that introductions are done, please grab a notebook, pull up a seat, and start taking down some notes."

On his command, Yoori immediately grabbed a notebook and pen from the counter. She was surprised that she was willing to do anything to distract herself. As long as it didn't require her to stand there and think about what took place, she was a happy camper.

She pulled up a chair from the dining table and placed it beside Tae Hyun's seat. She capped off the red pen and held it above her notebook. She was ready to start her secretarial duty.

Tae Hyun addressed the guy with the sunglasses. "Kang Min, please start."

Kang Min nodded, casting a quick glance at Yoori before beginning.

As their meeting progressed, Yoori found herself scribbling frivolously. She took notes about particular dates and times of different gang wars, prices of the illegal merchandises they were selling, and names of people on their hit lists. It bothered her that they were so indifferent about all of this. They made it appear standard. Killing people and breaking the law was really no big deal to these people.

After about an hour of sitting through their meeting, she also found herself staring at Tae Hyun. She recalled the conversation they had the night before. *He's really fitting the role of the heartless gang leader right now*, she thought despondently. Gradually but surely, Yoori started to doubt her own belief that he wasn't the cold-hearted gang leader he made himself to be. It was hard to vouch for someone and say they *might* have a heart when they could be this unattached to people's lives.

"Boss."

Yoori peered up when she heard Kang Min's voice. She looked at him anxiously, wondering what he had to say to her.

She grew curious when no words came out of his mouth. He looked uneasy as he flickered his eyes from Tae Hyun to her. She curiously turned to Tae Hyun. He had his eyes on her for a transitory moment before turning his attention back to Kang Min.

Oh crap.

Finally realizing that Kang Min was referring to Tae Hyun when he said "boss," she slumped in her seat. She mentally chastised herself for being so dense. She didn't understand why she thought Kang Min was talking to her. Tae Hyun was *obviously* the boss around here.

"Stupid Jae Won," she muttered under her breath. Jae Won calling her "boss" all the time was screwing her up royally. Now her big subconscious head must think she was everyone's boss!

Kang Min remained silent. He kept his worried gaze on Yoori.

"Kang Min?" Tae Hyun inquired firmly, interrupting Kang Min's daze. "How is the operation dealing with the Skulls?"

Yoori raised her head upon the mention of the Skulls. She had been so immersed in the Serpents world that she completely forgot that another powerful gang existed. She cast her thoughts back to the news segment about them and how they made a show of murdering those men in the business district.

To her horror, she began to think that there was another gang out there that was more ruthless than Tae Hyun's.

Kang Min returned his attention to Tae Hyun. "Good. We're making good progress. They are ahead of us in terms of numbers though. We just need something to shake people—to get them on our side. We need to be a bit more persuasive."

Tae Hyun nodded. "I'm in the process of formulating a strategy for that. I need to run some things by you though."

"Okay, boss," Kang Min said absentmindedly. His mind appeared to be elsewhere.

Stretching his arms out in exhaustion, Tae Hyun nodded tiredly at them. "That concludes our meeting." He rose up from the couch. "Alright boys, thanks for coming. Please keep your eyes out and make sure things run smoothly. I'll see you all soon." And with a simple wave of the hand, Tae Hyun made his exit from the living room and back into his room.

Having received their cue to leave, each of the men stood up from their seat and bowed their heads at Yoori before exiting the apartment. Yoori uneasily bowed her head too. They appeared less hostile toward her, but only slightly. She then frowned when she stood up to close the door behind them. They could've at least said, "thank you" to her for not ratting them out. But, then again, she was just glad they were gone.

She was prepared to close the door on the awkward situation when a hand pushed the metal door open.

The hand belonged to Kang Min.

"What is it?" she inquired, feeling nervous with the way Kang Min was looking at her. Now that she had a better view of him without the guns pointed at her, she realized that he looked a lot younger. The perplexed gaze on his face bore a strong resemblance to that of a child's. He was handsome, but in more of a cute, little brother way to her.

"I wanted to personally apologize for the rest of the guys about what happened earlier," he began quietly, looking almost too nervous to talk to her. "You must've been terrified."

"There's no need for you to apologize," she said genuinely. "You were the one who made it better."

"Regardless, it shouldn't have happened. And again, I'm sorry I couldn't prevent the situation from occurring altogether."

She nodded, leaning against the door. She could deduce from his voice how guilty he felt. However, she wondered if he even knew what he was apologizing for. He appeared so...*out of it*. Despite how strange Kang Min was acting, the smile remained on her face. She couldn't bring herself to be that intimidated by him. He was too sweet of a guy.

"Apology accepted," she said, patting his shoulder. He didn't have to apologize, but she also knew he wouldn't let the matter go if she didn't utter the words of forgiveness. It troubled her to witness such a sight. Poor thing seemed to be feeling horrible about what happened. It wasn't like it was his fault.

"Good," he uttered, relieved.

His eyes wavered every which way but toward her.

Yoori watched him in curiosity. Why was he so hesitant to make eye contact with her?

"Did you need something else, Kang Min?" She heard a voice ask from behind her.

Yoori turned to see Tae Hyun approaching them. He was dressed in a less formal manner today. No suits. Just a simple white shirt and khaki pants. The shirt molded perfectly to his body, accentuating hard muscles that corded beneath it. Yoori felt her breathing intensify. She bit her lips and turned away before another round of gawking ensued. Damn, he still looked hot.

Tae Hyun stopped behind her. His big arms crossed over his chest. He gazed at Kang Min expectantly.

Kang Min's nervous countenance changed to a more serious one. He shook his head and cleared his throat. "I just wanted to have a couple of words with Yoori here."

Tae Hyun smiled. "Welcoming her into the family, I see."

Kang Min nodded absently. As an awkward stillness threatened to rain upon them, Kang Min shifted his eyes from Tae Hyun to Yoori, and then he bowed his head. "Well, I'd best be going now."

His eyes fell on Tae Hyun. "Have a good day, boss."

Tae Hyun silently nodded as a response.

Kang Min then turned to Yoori. "It was nice meeting you, Yoori. If you ever need anything, please don't hesitate to come to me."

Yoori smiled gratefully. Could this guy be any sweeter to her? "It was nice meeting you too. And *thank you,"* she emphasized, truly grateful for being able to meet him.

Yoori waved goodbye as Kang Min proceeded down the hall and disappeared into the elevator. A swell of sadness hit her in response to his absence. It was a perplexing feeling, but she already felt an unusual attachment for Kang Min.

"Stop gawking," Tae Hyun commented playfully, gently pulling her aside. He closed the door, smiling. "He's too young for you."

"I was *not* gawking!" she huffed, following Tae Hyun into the living room. She already forgot that she was supposed to be upset with her irresponsible boss. She halted when she digested Tae Hyun's words. "Wait, how old is he?"

"He just turned eighteen."

Her chin dropped. "*What*? Oh my God, he's a baby!"

Tae Hyun laughed, reaching down and messing up her hair. "Yes grandma, so don't think about doing anything with him."

"I'm not interested in him like that!" she countered, using her fingers to comb her hair back into place. Fully realizing how old he was, she found herself smacking Tae Hyun across his shoulder. "What the hell is wrong with you? He's one of the top leaders in your gang already? How old was he when he joined?"

"Fifteen," he answered indifferently.

She shook her head in disappointment. She was appalled with Tae Hyun. Why was this guy out recruiting kids?

Sensing her criticism, Tae Hyun didn't miss a beat in defending himself. "Hey, he was in the Underworld long before he joined my gang, alright? People in our world start off young. Plus, he was taught well. He's better than ninety-percent of the guys who have been doing this longer than him."

Yoori nodded vigorously, her mind detouring on to another topic. "How did you find him?"

"He found us."

"What do you mean?"

"He was initially in another gang."

"What gang was he in?"

"Some random one. I don't remember the name."

Yoori eyed him suspiciously. "He just came up to you and said he wanted to join?"

"Yeah, pretty much."

"It's *that* easy to get a leadership position in your gang?" She scrutinized him with a critical eye. His answer verified her beliefs that he was quite possibly the most irresponsible gang leader in existence. There went the glamour of thinking that the Underworld was such a cool place with masterminds as their leaders.

Tae Hyun frowned, catching on to her insinuation. "Kang Min is an asset to have. No Underworld King would pass up someone like him."

"He's *that* good?"

"He's one of the best I've seen so far. Definitely an asset to have on your side."

"Yeah," Yoori agreed offhandedly. She recalled what happened earlier. Kang Min was definitely a good person to have on your side. "He saved me."

"What?"

Yoori wanted to smack herself when she realized she blurted out a string of no-no words.

"Nothing," she lied, smiling in hopes of appeasing the situation. The curve of her smiling lips quivered under Tae Hyun's hardened gaze. He was inspecting her for a lie. He might have caught on to what happened.

"What do you mean 'saved' you?" he asked, folding his arms again in curiosity. The muscles in his biceps became all the more pronounced when he did this. By the way he stared at her, she could tell he wasn't going to let it go.

The words of blasphemy bubbled in her throat. They were waiting to come out. That was the thing with Yoori. If you bugged her enough, then she would be more than happy to spill the beans. It was so hard for her. In other circumstances, she would've spilt the beans already, but she promised Kang Min that she wouldn't say anything. Confliction swirled within her.

Damn moral dilemmas.

She was only fully convinced when Tae Hyun gave her the "I'm-going-to-kill-you-if-you-don't-speak-soon" look.

To hell with it, she thought firmly, the weight of the guilt gliding off her chest. Since she accidentally let it out already, she might as well let it all out. And that was what she did. She let it *all* out...

84

"So he said, '...Boss will kill each and every one of you if you so much as touch her,'" she concluded dramatically. She looked at Tae Hyun anxiously, pleased with the "what-the-hell" look on his face.

Yeah, they'll be in trouble now, she thought haughtily. Perhaps he'd have them come back and beg her for forgiveness. Or perhaps he'd even have them become her assistants? The possibilities were endless.

"He said, 'he brought her here last night'?" Tae Hyun asked, completely dismissing everything else Yoori told him and crushing her dreams of having those guys beg for her forgiveness.

"Eh?" Yoori lifted her eyebrow at him, dumbfounded by his peculiar interest in that insignificant part of the story. The part that mattered was when they pointed their guns at her and when Kang Min saved her. Why did he care about the trivial fact that Kang Min knew?

"Yeah. He said that," Yoori confirmed, a little bit annoyed that he didn't seem too bothered that they held her at gunpoint.

"Huh..." Tae Hyun murmured, seemingly perturbed with the new piece of information she presented him.

Yoori eyed him oddly. A prickle of uneasiness gripped her. "What is it?" He was acting especially bizarre.

He looked at her, clearly debating about whether or not he should share what was on his mind. When Yoori gave him the "you-better-tell-me-what's-going-on" glare, he gave in.

"It's just that...they all just got in from being out of town this morning. None of them could've known about me bringing you over here last night. How could he have known?"

In that chilling instant, goose bumps appeared on her body.

"Maybe someone else told him?" she reasoned, trying to make the situation appear less freaky. "Maybe those guys who saw me last night told him. Like you said, 'word gets around,' right?"

Tae Hyun nodded at her, smiling as though to mollify the seriousness of the situation. "That's probably it."

She could tell he felt uneasy. She felt uneasy too. Now that her thoughts were aligned together, there *was* something peculiar about Kang Min and his behavior.

"Anyway," Tae Hyun said boisterously, waving his hand slightly to change the subject. "I've decided you won't be cuffed to me for the next few hours."

Yoori's face brightened prematurely. Could it be that there was some good in him after all? Was her theory correct? The evil Kwon Tae Hyun was human after all?

He threw himself onto his sofa and lazily switched on his 55-inch, flat screen TV. "Please clean my apartment well. It's been a couple of days since I last got around to tidying up around here."

Yoori's bitter face darkened. Of course, he was not *that* kind. She looked around the room and grimaced. It seemed more like it had been a couple of months than just days since he last got around to "tidying" up.

"Jerk," she muttered.

Dejectedly pouring soap into the sponge, Yoori began to clean the dirty dishes piled up in the sink. Because of the repetitive nature of the activity, Yoori found herself reliving what occurred earlier. Everything from the moment the guns were pointed at her, to Kang Min saving her, to Kang Min's apology before he left.

Then something occurred to Yoori. The way he acted around her and the way he looked at her...

She suddenly shot her head up, dropping the dish she was cleaning. The dish clinked loudly when it collided with the sink. Chills bolted up her spine when she recalled Kang Min saying, "Thank you, Yoori" before Tae Hyun even appeared from the shower.

Something was definitely off.

How on earth did Kang Min know her name before he was even introduced to her?

"You can't allow yourself to be weak."

11: Out of Character

As the next couple of weeks crept by, it didn't take Yoori long to forget about Kang Min and the "something-is-off-about-him" fiasco. Though the confusion was never really cleared up, Yoori came to the conclusion that gang members were freakishly weird. There was really no other way to put it. There was no point in trying to figure out what was wrong with them when in truth, everything was wrong with them. After all those life, death, and morally questionable situations they placed themselves in, at the end of the day, they were paranoid and awkwardly strange people. This was just something that Yoori, for the sake of her own sanity, accepted.

Unfortunately for Yoori, she soon found herself immersed with another fiasco: the pain of being Kwon Tae Hyun's personal assistant.

Being tired was an understatement. Yoori was completely, painfully, and utterly exhausted. In the span of the last couple weeks, Tae Hyun had her perform various tasks that ranged from the believable (washing dishes, cleaning the apartment, and ordering food) to the unbelievable (taking notes at meetings with his fellow gang members, calling and confirming meeting times with crime lords, making excel sheets of hit lists, and bribing dirty cops to help get his men out of jail).

The cuffs came off, but only during the times she was in the apartment with him. The cuffs came back to prevent her from making any quickie escapes when they went to sleep. Tae Hyun got the bed and Yoori got the floor. Cuffs or no cuffs, Yoori was always by Tae Hyun's side, ready and unhappily servicing his every unreasonable demand.

And, as if the menial tasks she had to perform for Tae Hyun weren't making her exhausted enough, she was also not getting enough sleep. After the dramatic incident of waking up in his bed that first morning, Yoori kept herself awake to make sure such a disaster would never occur again. Sadly for Yoori, keeping herself awake at night might have kept her from climbing onto Tae Hyun's bed, but it wasn't stopping her from sleeping anywhere else.

"Choi Yoori," she heard a faint voice call out her name as she fluttered in and out of consciousness.

She was a feather. She felt herself wavering in her seat, her balance sublimely challenged by gravity. She should open her eyes to avoid collision with the floor, but her eyelids were so heavy. The sensation of resting her eyes was too euphoric. If only she could have a couple more seconds to rest—

"CHOI YOORI!"

Her arms flailed up when Tae Hyun's roaring voice breached her once peaceful state. In the process of returning to the land of consciousness, she accidentally knocked something off the table. Yoori brought her hands to her ears and closed her eyes, attempting to block out the inevitable sound of shattering glass. No matter how hard she pressed her hands against her ears, Yoori could still hear the deafening impact as the glass shattered into a million pieces. She gave a nervous smile, slowly lifting the lids of her eyes.

The image was just as she remembered it before she drifted off to sleep. She was in one of Tae Hyun's many nightclubs in the middle of the afternoon and surrounded by his men. She was sitting right beside him, her hand cuffed to him while facing a group of new gang associates being interrogated for perjury. He was still wearing a white dress shirt and dark pants, looking as striking as ever. The only new image was the sight of everyone staring at her. Not to mention the worst sight of all: Tae Hyun glowering at her in annoyance.

"Sorry," she voiced meekly. She peeked at the shattered champagne glass being swept away by one of the Serpents.

Tae Hyun grounded his teeth. She could tell he was trying very, very hard to remain composed.

"As I was saying," he began tightly, doing an awful job of hiding his irritation with her. "Min and his friends here are telling me that they've given me all of the money from the drugs they sold at their university. All $10,000 of it. I'm thinking otherwise. Can you verify what they're saying is true?"

By the tone of his voice, what he asked was more of a command than a request.

"Oh yes," Yoori mumbled, taking out a pink notebook from her white purse. She was relieved that the embarrassment brought on by the shattering glass was looked over. She flipped through the pages. Her finger scanned through the list of sellers and expected profit for Tae Hyun's drug business.

"Let's see, Min and friends," she muttered, skimming her fingers down the page. When she found their names, she stopped and stared at them warily.

They were supposed to have $12,000.

Sure enough, Min and friends looked at her with tears welling up in their eyes. They knew they were about to be called out for their lies. She glanced cautiously at Tae Hyun.

His expectant eyes were on her.

Dread besieged her. She didn't want to be the one to tell him that they lied to him.

She fidgeted uneasily.

Her fears did not come because she was afraid of Tae Hyun. They came at full speed because she didn't want to see him bash in the skulls of Min and friends. She looked at them. In a sea of Serpents dressed like corporate CEO's, Min and friends looked young and pitiful in their t-shirts and jeans. Her eyes moved to Min. From her hire date until now, Yoori had chatted with Min on several occasions. From these exchanges, she found him to be charming. She didn't want to be responsible for any ill deed that may be bestowed on to him and his friends.

"Choi Yoori?" Tae Hyun prompted, staring at her with piercing eyes.

"They were actually supposed to make $6,000," Yoori said brightly, determined to save them from getting their asses kicked. "They made $4,000 more for you."

Min and friends looked up, stunned that Yoori was protecting them.

Tae Hyun's head shot up too.

"What?" he practically shouted. He went for the notebook. "Let me see."

She slapped his hand away and tried to run off. She was reminded that she couldn't get too far with the anchoring of their mutual cuffs. She groaned and sat back down in exasperation. She glared at him.

"Don't you trust me?" she asked sternly, her breath growing unsteady. Yoori could feel beads of sweat form on her forehead. She was nervously bluffing. She had never been too good of a fibber. She doubted Tae Hyun would fall for her lies.

As anticipated, Tae Hyun eyed her skeptically and shook his head.

Crap.

She tried to keep the stern expression firmly solidified on her face.

Tae Hyun took his scowling eyes off of her. He turned to Min and friends. He pointed a threatening finger at a cowering Min. A murderous inferno rippled in the irises of Tae Hyun's brown eyes. He looked like he was ready to rip Min's eyes out.

"Thank you for the profitable sales," he said in a mild voice, surprising everyone in the room.

Min and friends, as well as Yoori, gawked at him with openmouthed confusion.

Yoori was mystified.

Did Tae Hyun really believe her?

Min breathed out, visibly relieved that he dodged impending death. He wiped the beads of sweat off his forehead. "Of course, sir. Any time."

Tae Hyun nodded, smiling as a tiger would at its prey. "But in the future," he said, his calm voice vibrating with an undercurrent of admonition, "it'd be better if you came up with the *exact* amount to prevent any future misunderstandings."

Yoori regarded Tae Hyun with amazement. That was the nicest threat she had ever heard.

Min and friends bounced their heads in understanding. They rose up from their seats and started bowing incessantly. "Won't happen again, sir!"

"For your sake, I hope not." He waved his hand as a gesture for them to leave before he changed his mind and actually killed them. "You can go."

At record pace, Min and friends flew out of the nightclub, leaving Yoori, Tae Hyun, and the rest of the Serpents in their wake.

Yoori exhaled gustily. She wished she could run off with them. Now that they were off the hook for lying to one of the Underworld's chosen Kings, it was her turn to face the music.

She faced Tae Hyun nervously.

He rose from his seat. "Let's go."

Yoori reluctantly followed him, receiving bows as they made their way out of the nightclub. Passing the last remaining Serpents by the exit, Yoori noticed that they all had a small, but highly entertained, smile on their faces. It seemed as though they were amused to see Tae Hyun acting the way he did with Yoori.

Yoori wasn't the only one who noticed these smiles.

"What are you guys smiling about?" Tae Hyun suddenly roared.

All smiles evaporated like water under the sun.

They lowered their heads at once. "Nothing, boss."

Satisfied with their quick reaction, Tae Hyun grabbed Yoori's wrist and exited the club.

"Choi Yoori! That was the sixth group you gave a free pass to!" Tae Hyun screamed as they trudged back to his apartment.

"They learned their lessons," Yoori replied, her ears hurting from listening to Tae Hyun lecture her about the importance of being a responsible worker. After leaving the club, he wasted no time in reprimanding her for messing with the positive "cash flows" of his lucrative business.

"That's not the point. They lied. I should've made an example out of them."

"Well, why didn't you?" she countered, getting tired of listening to Tae Hyun. "You obviously knew they were lying. What was stopping you?"

Tae Hyun gaped down at her. He was flabbergasted that she didn't see the logic behind his actions. "You realized that *you* were lying to me as well, right?"

Yoori sighed. "Yes."

What was his point?

"Well, if I punish them, then I would have to punish *you* as well."

"Well then, why didn't you?" she snapped. She was aware of how annoying she sounded, but she was on her last shred of patience with Tae Hyun. Could she help that she had a moral conscience? Could she help that she wanted to save some college kids from certain death?

"My God, woman," he grated. He looked like he was about to retort with more angry words. Instead, he closed his eyes and said, "You drive me crazy."

"Look. If you want the money so badly, then I'll pay what they owe you."

"Well, aren't you the personification of morality?"

Yoori glared. "Do you want the money or not?"

Plunging his left hand into his pant pocket, he turned away. His pace quickened while he quietly said, "Keep your money."

She stared up at his profile in astonishment. Was the fight over? Did she win? Yoori was bewildered. She at least expected Tae Hyun to argue with her until one of them gave up—herself being the likely candidate. It was out of character for him to let her win. However, as she watched silence cloak over his lips, she knew that she "won." She wasn't too smug about it though. He was probably tired of talking to her.

For the next few blocks, a quiet stillness accompanied them as they trudged along with their wrists linked together by the handcuffs. Since their last interaction, Tae Hyun had yet to utter a word to Yoori and Yoori was not inclined to be the first to breach the silence. Still bitter about how he treated her outside the club, Yoori was not keen on being the bigger person in this work relationship. The silence could go on like the energizer bunny for all she cared.

"Tae Hyun!"

The silence was disturbed when from across the street, Yoori caught sight of the girl who called out to Tae Hyun ever so affectionately.

The girl came over to them, performing a perfect runway walk. This girl was tall with flawless porcelain skin, long silky black hair, and a short black dress that hugged every part of her pretty body in the right way. There didn't appear to be an ounce of fat on her. In short, this girl was the epitome of a beautiful supermodel.

And boy, did she make Yoori, who was simply dressed in a white shirt and jeans, feel physically inferior.

The only thing that threw off her runway model status was the fact that there were two men, both dressed in beige hoodies and black jeans, trailing closely behind her. Yoori deduced that they must've been her bodyguards. What grown men would follow a girl around like that? Well, none that she knew of anyway.

She watched as Tae Hyun laid his eyes on the girl. Instead of gazing with interest, his eyes were unfazed. If anything, he looked somewhat annoyed.

"Tae Hyun," the girl whispered seductively, stopping in front of them. Just as her two bodyguards stopped behind her, Yoori made awkward eye contact with the girl. The girl gave Yoori a quick glare before turning to give Tae Hyun another one of her comely smiles.

Yoori returned the glare. So it was like that, huh?

"Hey Jin Ae," Tae Hyun greeted with a bored expression on his face. There was no disguising that this girl had fallen out of favor with the Underworld King. He didn't want to talk to her, but for appearances sake, he was civil. Yoori surmised that the girl must have been his ex-fling. Or, knowing Tae Hyun and his sneakiness, a current fling.

"I haven't seen you in so long," she crooned, running her index finger down his arm. She fluttered her long eyelashes, giving him bedroom eyes and completely dismissing Yoori's obvious existence. "I've missed you."

Yoori wanted to vomit at the pathetic sight before her. Did the girl have to act like this in public?

She shuddered.

She hated girls who threw themselves at guys like that. She glanced up at Tae Hyun, bitterness in her critical gaze. Of course, *this* would be his type of girl.

Tae Hyun casually pulled her finger away from his arm, and after doing so, quirked a patronizing brow. "You didn't seem to miss me too much when you slept with Ji Hoon last week, did you?"

Ooh, burn, Yoori thought, feeling a small wave of satisfaction flood through her. Yeah! She liked that the snobby and feisty Tae Hyun was not showing any interest in Jin Ae. Her wave of satisfaction was overshadowed when she saw that Tae Hyun's face turned grim when he said the name "Ji Hoon."

Who's Ji Hoon? She wanted to ask as she watched the rest of the scene play out between the ex-flings.

The bedroom eyes Jin Ae bestowed to Tae Hyun faded. Her smile, however, remained. "Baby, that didn't mean anything. You know I love only you."

Yoori cringed. Jin Ae's voice was like nails on a chalkboard.

Tae Hyun nodded at Jin Ae. "That's nice," he said disinterestedly, suddenly interlocking his cuffed hand with Yoori's.

Yoori looked at him in surprise.

"I'll take you home in a bit, babe," he said affectionately, giving Yoori a peck on the nose.

Yoori, after feeling the slight impact of his lips on the tip of her nose, thrashed her head back in response.

What the hell?

She gave him a quizzical look, thunderstruck by his public display of affection. What the hell was he doing?

At her bewildered reaction, his striking smile remained intact, if not widening larger than ever. His next words threw her into a twister of mystification.

"Aw, baby, you're being shy again."

Yoori felt the urge to strangle herself in disbelief. What was he up to?

No longer able to ignore Yoori's presence, given how much attention Tae Hyun was showering her, Jin Ae pursed her lips together and leveled her eyes on Yoori.

"And who is this?" she asked idly, the happy glow waning from her face.

"This is Choi Yoori," Tae Hyun introduced proudly. He yanked her closer to him. "My girlfriend."

"WHAT?" The absurdity of Tae Hyun's reply scandalized Yoori. She was unable to restrain her outrage. It was just too preposterous. *She* was Tae Hyun's girlfriend? Yeah, maybe when hell froze over.

"Baby," he said again, smiling through clenched teeth. "Another shy outburst like that, I swear I'm going to make out with you nonstop when we get home."

It was a threat.

He was smiling, but it was a threat. Yoori understood by the sternness in his eyes. It was literally screaming, "Play along or you'll regret it."

Putting aside her shock, Yoori nodded, quietly fulfilling his unspoken request.

Damn being a personal assistant and being there whenever your boss needed you!

92

At this point, Jin Ae was already huffing and puffing in anger. The cuffs encircling their wrists were the only things that distracted her. Her brows creased. She pointed at the silver chain anchoring Tae Hyun and Yoori to one another.

"Wait, why are you guys handcuffed together?"

At her observation, her two bodyguards craned their necks to get a view of the handcuffs.

Yoori and Tae Hyun gaped at each other. They laughed tensely, unable to come up with a reasonable answer.

After several seconds, where panic began to drown Yoori, Tae Hyun said, "It's a couples' bracelet."

"What?" Jin Ae asked, understandably baffled by his ludicrous answer.

"Yeah, it's the new trend," Yoori hastily added, impressed with Tae Hyun's ability to think quickly on his feet. She gave Jin Ae a proud smile to add some flavor to the lie. The proud smile thawed when it was met with Jin Ae's piercing glare. Pretty or not, this girl scared the living daylights out of Yoori.

"Anyway," Tae Hyun said impatiently, no longer keen on being around Jin Ae. "We have to go. Bye Jin Ae."

Tae Hyun managed to walk past Jin Ae unharmed.

Yoori, however, was not as fortunate.

"Listen up, you little bitch," Jin Ae hissed through clenched teeth. Talons dug into Yoori's arm when Jin Ae yanked her closer. "I don't know who the fuck you think you are, but I am one of the top female bosses around here. You're fucking with the wrong person. Stay away from Tae Hyun, or I'll make you live to regret it."

"Jin Ae!" Tae Hyun screamed. "What the hell are you doing?"

Taking a second to further squeeze her razor like nails in Yoori's arms, Jin Ae released Yoori and flashed Tae Hyun another innocent smile. "Properly introducing myself to your new girlfriend."

She turned back to face Yoori. "Nice to meet you," Jin Ae mouthed before turning to Tae Hyun. Her voice was exponentially brighter when addressing him. "Bye baby. I'll see you around."

She favored Tae Hyun with a wink and an even bigger smile before taking off with her bodyguards in tow.

Yoori fumed. She watched Jin Ae prance away like she was God's gift to men. The blood simmered in her veins, boiling like the lavas of hell. She was livid. No one had ever disrespected her as much as Jin Ae. It was out of character for Yoori, but she was besieged with an overwhelming hatred for Jin Ae. Gang leader or not, Yoori felt the irresistible need to teach the girl a lesson. She wanted to pick up a pipe and bash Jin Ae's head with it. Then, she wanted to have Jin Ae kneel before her and beg for her life. After that, she wanted to rip the limbs off Jin Ae's body.

Yoori clenched her hands together, her heart thumping fervently. She couldn't wait. One day, she would teach Jin Ae a lesson she would never forget—

HONK!

Yoori snapped back to reality when the sound of a random blaring horn roared in the street.

She looked around, astounded by what was going on inside her. Never in her life had she wanted to hurt someone as badly as she wanted to hurt Jin Ae. And so violently at that.

Yoori swallowed uneasily. What had gotten into her?

It was out of character for her, but in that split second, she felt as though someone else entered her body and envisioned those horrible thoughts.

For that brief moment, she turned into someone else.

"You have to be able to punish people without fear."

12: The Dawning of a New Era

"So, is she always that peachy?" Yoori asked sullenly, referring to Jin Ae.

They had been walking in silence for the last few blocks and her mind was reeling.

Her equivalent of an exorcist moment was driving her nuts and her curiosity about Tae Hyun's relationship with Jin Ae was at its peak. She might as well quench her curiosity with an answer from the source himself.

Tae Hyun laughed. He was amused with her choice of words. "I suppose she is always that 'peachy' with other girls." His eyes migrated to hers. "I take it you received little words of warning from her?"

"Oh yeah," Yoori replied automatically. Residual fury laced her voice. "She uttered little words of warning alright." It occurred to her that this must be a norm for Tae Hyun if he knew about the threat. She turned to him. "I take it this happens quite often to your new 'girlfriends'?"

A sheepish smile appeared on Tae Hyun's face. He shifted his eyes away from Yoori. He had the face of a kid who got caught with his hand in the cookie jar—or several cookie jars.

"I wouldn't call them *girlfriends*," he said as if it would make things sound better.

Yoori laughed incredulously. Judging by his attractive physique, she concluded the guy had no problems getting girls. It was only after the meeting with Jin Ae did the obvious became apparent. Tae Hyun, aside from being the King of Serpents, was also a player.

She creased her brows, a bout of annoyance with Tae Hyun and his womanizing ways befalling her. She turned away, having no more appetite to talk to him. Her eyes firmly focused on the street ahead, she quickened her pace, trying to stem away from him as far as the cuffs would allow.

"Don't tell me you're jealous," he called after her, quickening his pace to match with hers. There was a broad smile on his face that conveyed he was amused with Yoori's behavior. He seemed to enjoy seeing this reaction from her.

She stopped walking. She was bothered that Tae Hyun was basically insinuating that she liked him.

"Don't mistake my annoyance with jealousy," she said firmly, though she wasn't too certain of her own words. She went on, wanting to squash the insinuation before it grew any larger. "I just don't like being used, alright?" He was about to reply when she pressed on. "Look, it's fine that you have a lot of girls on the side. I really don't care. What I *don't* like is being used as a pawn to get girls that you're tired of off your back."

"Hey, that's not fair," Tae Hyun retorted. "It's not like I planned to meet her. You saw how it happened. The girl appeared out of nowhere. I had to think on my feet about the best way to get rid of her. Introducing you as my girlfriend was probably not the best tactic, but it yielded the same results."

"So the end justifies the means?" She was beside herself. How dare he use her like that? Wasn't forcing her to be his walking slave enough? What more could he possibly want from her?

Taking stock of her overt frustration, Tae Hyun expelled a tired breath. "If you're worried about her coming after you, then don't concern yourself with that. As long as I'm with you, she can't touch you."

"Oh, that's comforting," she said sarcastically.

Tae Hyun frowned.

She frowned as well.

"And what makes you think I'm afraid of her?" she hastened to add, offended by Tae Hyun's low opinion of her bravery. "I'm annoyed. There's a big difference."

Tae Hyun stared at her. "You're acting really strange."

"I'm annoyed," she emphasized again, irritated that he was looking at her like she was a looney tune.

"What's the big deal?" he asked in an exasperated voice. "So what if I told her you're my girlfriend? We *both* know it's a lie. *She's* the only one who has to believe that it's true."

After absorbing his words, Yoori froze when a train of rationale speared through her. They must've had some long, sordid history if he had to lie like that. Being one of those people with a horribly short, and easily distracted, attention span, Yoori could hardly care about being pissed off with Tae Hyun. She wanted to learn more about their relationship.

"Was she your girlfriend?"

"I wouldn't call her a girlfriend," he said before he began to walk again. It was clear he didn't want to talk about any of this with her. "Just some girl I had fun with."

Yoori rolled her eyes. Of course that was his answer. She anticipated this reply, but she was surprised when she felt a small sense of relief upon hearing that their relationship wasn't *that* serious. She then recalled the scene where he subtly scolded Jin Ae for being with another guy.

"You sounded jealous enough to be her boyfriend when you talked about her being with that guy," she casually instigated.

Tae Hyun regarded her with hardened eyes. "Girlfriend or not, I don't like my girl sleeping around with other guys...especially with *that* particular bastard."

"Well, aren't we possessive?"

"I prefer territorial."

Yoori snorted at his amendment. Though it was fairly entertaining to see him riled up, it also troubled her that he was so sensitive with this topic. Why was he so angry?

She wanted to know more.

"Who is this guy?" she asked earnestly. "Why don't you like him? His name is Ji Hoon, right?"

The simple act of voicing Ji Hoon's name brought Tae Hyun's stride to an abrupt halt. He turned to her with fiery eyes. He did not like her saying Ji Hoon's name.

"Wow," she found herself uttering bravely. "He's *that* bad where I can't even say his name without pissing you off?"

Tae Hyun allowed his eyes to fall on her for a few seconds before softening his grim expression. He managed to suppress his anger—but only slightly.

"He's another gang leader," he said simply. Although his tone of voice was calm, he looked like he was ready to annihilate something.

Yoori nodded. Of course it was another gang leader.

"Small-time or big-time?" she continued to probe.

A brief period of silence settled upon them as Tae Hyun turned away from her, aggravation seemingly rippling in every fiber of his being. She noted the muscles tightening dangerously in his jaw. If this wasn't a clear sign of a human being hating another without filter, then Yoori didn't know what was.

As a small stream of wind gushed past them, Tae Hyun slowly returned his gaze to Yoori.

"Ever heard of the Skulls?" he finally said.

Yoori stood up straighter when she heard the recognizable name. Why was it that every time the Skulls were mentioned, she *always* felt a knot form in her stomach?

She nodded. Yes, of course she had heard of the Skulls.

"Lee Ji Hoon," Tae Hyun began, carefully studying her expression, "is the leader of the Skulls. The other powerful gang in South Korea and my biggest enemy."

Yoori inhaled slowly. Lee Ji Hoon, the leader of the Skulls and Kwon Tae Hyun's biggest enemy. Of course, he was Tae Hyun's biggest enemy—as a rival gang leader, that part made sense. The only part that didn't make sense to her was Lee Ji Hoon and Jin Ae.

An unexplained jealousy sparked inside her.

The love story pertaining to Ji Hoon and the Scorpion girl came stampeding back into her mind. This whole time she was under the impression that he was the brokenhearted prince mourning the loss of his great love. Yoori didn't understand why it felt like someone had kicked her in the stomach after hearing that Ji Hoon had moved on. Was it that easy for him to move on to another girl? And not just any other girl, but a girl like Jin Ae? The fury rose inside her. Yoori may not have known him personally, but she still felt resentful for the Scorpion girl.

Yoori lifted her face and laid her gaze on Tae Hyun. He stared at her with a blank expression on his face. She couldn't tell what he was thinking, but she didn't give it too much thought. There was another burning question she had to get an answer for.

"Tae Hyun," she prompted hesitantly, mentally chastising herself for not asking him about this earlier.

"Yeah?"

"Did you know that Scorpion girl?"

Yoori attempted to suppress the newfound excitement in her body. She had been such a fool. All this time, she had been so curious about the mysterious Scorpion girl, and she failed to realize that Tae Hyun was another gang leader. He had to have known her.

Tae Hyun tilted his head, intrigued by her question. His eyes scrutinized her cautiously. It was as if he was debating about whether or not he should speak to her about this. After a moment, he shook his head and said words that crushed every excited fiber in Yoori's body. "I've actually never met her."

Yoori could have sworn she heard tires screeching. That was certainly not the answer she expected. Yoori gave him a quizzical look. "But aren't the leaders supposed to know—?"

"I wasn't a leader during the years she was alive in the Underworld," he interjected.

Yoori gaped at him, confounded.

Reading her mind, he repeated the statement. "I wasn't the leader."

The curiosity on her face remained. What the hell? If he wasn't leading the Serpents, then who was?

Tae Hyun sighed, looking rather uncomfortable. Almost begrudgingly, he answered her unspoken question. "My older brother was the leader of the Serpents during the years she was alive in the Underworld. I took on the reign three years ago."

A look of confusion flashed on Yoori's face as she processed this. This entire time, she assumed that he had been a crime lord his whole life. She couldn't believe he had only been the King of Serpents for three years.

Her eyes urged him to continue with the story. It was getting too interesting. She was all ears.

Tae Hyun, at the sight of her earnest gaze, remained silent.

She gently nudged his shoulder with her hand, determined to get the knowledge she sought.

"Kwon Tae Hyun," she cajoled, her voice soft and sweet as sugar. "I'm curious now. Give me a history lesson. What was going on in your world before you took on the reign as the King of Serpents?"

He lifted a brow. He was amused, both at her sudden sweet voice and at her extreme interest in all of this. "Do I look like I have time to give you a history lesson?"

Her sugary-self turned bitter. "Well, being your assistant and all, I seem to recall that you're actually free all day."

A stubborn aura emitted from his stern gaze. He wasn't planning on giving in. "Why should I waste my breath? I already know what happened."

"You owe me."

He smirked, studying her like she was the most entertaining thing he had ever laid eyes on. "What do I owe you, my disrespectful assistant?"

"Let's see," she began, feigning deep contemplation. She snapped her fingers. "Oh yeah, remember when your goddam gang members held me up at *gunpoint*?"

That was how Yoori successfully persuaded Tae Hyun to see it her way.

He chuckled, nodding courteously at her. He was impressed with her crafty persuasion skills. "Point taken."

Yoori curtsied, gracefully accepting victory. She stared at him expectantly, her eyes unblinking. "Please begin."

"Where do you want me to start?"

"What do you mean?"

"The Underworld goes back several long decades. Do you want a history lesson on what occurred fifty years ago...forty years?"

"The part that matters," she answered without missing a beat. No matter how rich the history, there was always an era that stood out from the rest.

Tae Hyun nodded, knowing exactly where to begin. "The important part started five years ago." He heaved a sigh of uncertainty. "But to be perfectly honest, I really don't want to tell you because I don't think you can handle it. Some parts are really...disturbing, even for me."

"Just tell me," she pressed, annoyed with his low opinion of her bravery. How could he say that he didn't think she could handle it? She had been in the Underworld for a long time now; dangerous things had happened to her. She could handle it.

"Fine," he said with resignation. "But don't say I didn't warn you."

She tapped her foot impatiently. "Just start."

Smirking, he began the tale. "Five years ago, it all began with my brother—Kwon Ho Young, Lee Ji Hoon, and An Young Jae."

A nerve jumped within her at the vocalization of a particular name.

"An Young Jae?" Yoori parroted. A strange interest with this third person percolated inside her. Why did his name sound familiar?

"An Young Jae," Tae Hyun said again, looking at her attentively. "The King of Scorpions."

She nodded. Oh yes, the older brother of the Scorpion girl.

Tae Hyun continued. "It was Lee Ji Hoon, An Young Jae, and my older brother who ruled the three respective gangs. People called that period 'the dawning of a new era.' It was basically the new filling in for the old. They all took over for their fathers, all of whom were the previous Kings. It was a big deal because they were all so young at the time. It was the first time in history the Underworld was ruled over by a group of Kings so young."

"How old were they?"

"Lee Ji Hoon was twenty. My brother and An Young Jae were twenty-one."

"And they all became leaders? Just like that?"

Tae Hyun shook his head. "There's an unwritten clause in our world. To even be remotely respected as the leader of a gang, you have to mark your status with blood."

"You have to kill someone," Yoori added instinctively.

"And not just anyone. In your career as a gang member, you'll kill plenty of people. But to be the leader of a gang, you have to kill the one who holds the same stature in life."

"Another King."

He nodded, faintly impressed that Yoori followed along with the story so well. "It all began with Ji Hoon's father. A foreign, rival King shot him down while he was traveling in China. Ji Hoon was the next to lead the Skulls. However, in order to do so, he had to kill someone." Tae Hyun's mood grew solemn. "My father's life paved the way for Lee Ji Hoon's current standing in life."

Yoori nodded apprehensively. This was why Tae Hyun hated Ji Hoon so much. She grew uneasy as she stared at his vacant expression. She debated whether or not she should utter words of condolences to him. Before she was able to make a decision, Tae Hyun already continued with the story. It was apparent that he didn't want to spend any time on this delicate matter.

"After my father's death, it was my older brother's turn to lead. My brother chose to kill An Young Jae's father before his succession to the throne."

It happened for a split second that didn't merit much of Yoori's attention, but she felt her eye twitch after hearing about the death of An Young Jae's father.

"And finally for Young Jae, he did what others could only dream of. There was a fourth bigger gang in the picture five years ago. For his blood marking, he went after them. In the dead of the night, he exterminated the entire bloodline of that gang and took the Scorpions' throne." Tae Hyun smirked at Yoori. "Supposedly it was a very entertaining year for the Underworld."

Yoori looked at him disbelievingly. "It all happened in a year?"

He nodded. "The biggest change in power the Underworld has ever known. Lots of bloodshed and lots of pandemonium."

"Where were you throughout all of this?"

"I was in America." He gave a nonchalant shrug. "College."

A dubious smile curved Yoori's lips. "College?"

He grinned. "I don't look like the type?"

Yoori shook her head, charmed with this interesting revelation. Apparently crime lords went to college, and not just any college, college in America. That one was a curveball.

"My father firmly believed that there's a correlation between being successful and being thoroughly educated. As much as many would hate to admit it, the Underworld, as unlawful as it may be, is still a lucrative empire to be managed like a business."

"There are other businesses that you could've gotten into," Yoori countered quickly.

His smile remained. "This is a family business. I'm doing my part to keep my family's legacy alive and well." He laughed. "That and power is a big motivator."

"How honorable of you."

He pleasantly dismissed her sarcasm. "I'd like to think so."

Yoori sighed, this time falling into another stupor of contemplation. She absorbed all the new information. There were many aspects of the story that left her feeling more curious. She was disappointed that she didn't hear much about the Scorpion girl. Out of bias for notorious female figures alone, she cared about her story more than the rest.

"That's why you never met her," she said mindlessly, her hope crushed of learning more about the Scorpion girl from Tae Hyun.

"By the time I came back to Korea three years ago, she had already died." He laughed wearily. "I would have loved to have met the girl though."

Yoori turned to him with renewed interest. "Why is that?"

It was a thoughtless question. The truth was she would've loved to meet the girl too. The Scorpion girl seemed like a celebrity in this unlawful society—a faceless one anyway. There was just something so fascinating about the girl that once you'd heard of the legends behind her, you could never stop wondering about her story.

"I hear she was easy on the eyes."

Yoori rolled her eyes. "Glad to see you're not as superficial and shallow as you appear."

Tae Hyun laughed, unfazed by her caustic remark. "Well, that and the fact that she's well-known for being cruel and heartless. I want to know why the girl left such a lasting impression on my men and the rest of the Underworld during her reign."

That caught her attention.

Yoori looked at him intently, her eyes urging him to further elaborate.

He obliged. "To start off, my men are very powerful and brave men. It is profoundly remarkable to see them shaken up. The mere mention of her sends chills up their spines."

"She was that scary?" Yoori knew the girl was powerful, but she didn't think she was someone to be so incredibly feared.

Tae Hyun smiled, his expression mirroring Yoori's. He couldn't believe it either. "You see, that's what I wonder too. But as they tell it, the girl looked like an angel, yet had the morals of the Devil. She wasn't known so much for killing people, even though she did a lot of that. She was known more for her survivors. If that's what you want to call them."

A gust of wind deluged past them, acting like a prelude to what was to come. It could have been the breeze or it could have been the anticipation of where the story was headed, but she began to feel uneasy.

"What do you mean?" Why did she have the feeling that her Cinderella was about to become the evil witch?

"The Scorpion girl was said to have enjoyed fighting very much. She loved challenging people. The thing with her was that for every round that she beat you in combat, she got to torture you."

Revulsion rained over her face. "Torture?"

"Imagine the worst possible things you can do to torture someone, and she probably did it."

Shock and horror running through her, Yoori remained silent as Tae Hyun continued.

"She was a huge fan of psychological warfare, as well as hand-to-hand combat. She was known for leaving three types of victims: dead ones, amputated ones, and the ones left unharmed—physically anyway. She left the survivors to spread the word about her power, and I suppose to continuously torture them by allowing them to breathe and relive what she did to them. She targeted other gang members in the Underworld, but the brunt of her fury was bequeathed upon the Serpents be—"

"Because of her father's death," Yoori absently finished for him.

Tae Hyun nodded.

Her mind was running. That was a lot of new information to absorb. She glanced at Tae Hyun, intrigued. She had to get clarification for another thing.

"Do you know about the love story?"

Tae Hyun wore an apathetic expression. "The one between her and Ji Hoon?"

Yoori nodded, surprised by his less than positive reaction to her question. "I mean, I've heard about it, but—"

"People outside our world hear the censored version, as I would put it," he interjected in a somewhat bored tone. "From what I hear, they fed off each other in terms of the violence they committed. They were both cold-hearted murderers who sought out power. That combination in anyone is dangerous, but that combination in two people is horrific. I was away in America and I still heard about all the repulsive things they did. You know that their crimes are horrendous when it sends shockwaves throughout the Underworld."

"Wh-what did they do?"

"A lot. But there was one incident that made them infamous."

Yoori kept her silent eyes on Tae Hyun, waiting with bated breath.

It was like someone had just completely rewritten her Cinderella story. Tae Hyun's version of the love story between the Skulls leader and the Scorpion girl opened Yoori's eyes to the darker side of their story. It was definitely a disturbing side and she was beginning to regret ever asking Tae Hyun to share his version with her.

Tae Hyun was about to further darken the story. "Three years ago, at a club here in Seoul, the Scorpion girl and Ji Hoon did the unthinkable. In the middle of the night, they somehow managed to lure an entire family to the club. No one's sure how they did it and why they chose that particular family, but what happened next is inhumane...even for our world."

Fear undulated in Yoori's eyes. She knew what was to come. "Sh-she killed them all?"

He nodded, looking equally disturbed. "They were in that club for five to six hours. She tortured and executed all of them. The youngest were twin boys. They were shot execution style in front of their mother." Tae Hyun paused for a moment before continuing. "They were five-years-old."

"Oh God!" Yoori yelped, covering her mouth.

She took an unsteady step back, horror spreading through her. Her heart grew heavy as she envisioned the faces of the young children who were executed. How could someone be that much of a monster? Executing an *entire* family and killing five-year-old children?

She was sick to her stomach with disgust and…guilt?

For whatever reason, the story affected her immensely.

Soon, she found herself wavering to keep balance. Her heart raced and her breathing became uneven. She closed her eyes as an impending migraine ensued in her head. It may have been from lack of sleep or the shock of the new piece of information, but she was no longer able to keep herself balanced. Darkness clouded her vision.

"Yoori!" she heard Tae Hyun scream, catching her before she fell to the ground.

She felt him shake her, urging her to stay awake.

Yoori gradually opened her eyes. She groaned when she realized that her vision was extremely blurred. She wavered in and out of consciousness.

"Damn it, Choi Yoori," Tae Hyun muttered as he struggled to grab hold of her left wrist.

Seconds later, she felt the cold cuffs disappear from her wrist. She then felt Tae Hyun position his hand behind her back and legs. A breath later, her hands were around his neck and he was carrying her down the street.

"Put me down," she said softly, trying hard to open her heavy eyelids, but to no avail. Her mind was swirling. "I can…I can walk."

"I'm taking you home," he assured, racing down the street. "Just rest."

"I can walk," she repeated breathlessly.

He wasn't listening.

"I knew telling you that story was a bad idea," he grunted. He tightened his hold on her. "Choi Yoori, that story is all in the past. Don't worry about it so much."

"She's a horrible person," Yoori whispered, swallowing past her disappointment. She tightened her hold around his neck and buried her face into his chest. She felt horrible for the family and those two kids. How could someone do something so horrific?

"At least she's dead, right?" Tae Hyun offered, trying to appease the situation. He sounded like he was out of breath.

Yoori nodded thankfully.

"At least she's dead," she agreed before slowly losing consciousness.

"Wrong or right..."

13: The Night Before

The dream came again for Yoori.

The alley, the siblings, and the heartbreaking scene replayed perfectly in her mind.

She could feel the pain and anger the girl felt as she begged her brother to end her life. She could feel the girl's desperation to make things right—to do what she dreaded. This time, the content played in vivid colors, sounds, and emotions. She could feel nearly every emotion the girl felt and the truth was, she was overwhelmed. She was so overwhelmed in fact that it became hard for her to breathe.

"Help," she wanted to call out, feeling her heart pound without any signs of slowing down. "Someone help..."

As if hearing her desperate pleas, something cool grazed her face, causing Yoori to stir from her dream.

Alarmed by the cool breeze, Yoori abruptly woke up.

She looked around, slowly acclimating herself with reality. When it was clear that she was no longer dreaming, the constriction in her chest diminished. She exhaled, bringing her hands up to massage the sides of her head. The dream played again in her mind, causing her head to pound even harder. It felt like she had woken up from a hangover. She was mulling over how crappy she felt when she became aware of something.

Wait a second.

What was she sleeping on?

Her shock filled eyes rested on the mattress she was laying on. "My God," she whispered, realizing that she was, yet again, on Tae Hyun's bed.

Her face turned a crimson hue. It wasn't always healthy to get into a guy's bed when you're conscious; the fact that she did it so frequently when she was unconscious disturbed the hell out of Yoori.

After mentally scolding herself for her inability to be chained to the ground, she steadily sat upright.

Her eyes skimmed over the room. Her brows inverted when she saw no one else. It was just her in the room. Tae Hyun was nowhere to be seen.

Curious, she threw off the comforter and inspected her left wrist. Wonder suspended over her when she observed that the cuffs were no longer there to hold her captive. She lowered her wrist and narrowed her eyes to the floor. She took stock of the pillow and rumpled blanket below.

The memories of the day before came gushing back into her mind. She remembered that they were talking on the street. Tae Hyun was giving her a history lesson on the Underworld and the next thing she knew, a migraine ensued in her head. Then, she remembered feeling incredibly faint and woozy. The last thing she remembered was Tae Hyun carrying her down the street.

She stared at the unmade blanket on the floor again. If memory served her correctly, she could've sworn she had woken in the middle of the night and saw someone sleeping on the floor...

She froze. Was it possible Tae Hyun slept on the floor last night? She glanced at the empty spot on the bed and then moved her eyes to the floor once more. Was Tae Hyun on the floor last night or was it her? Was he that considerate? Her mind churned. She looked around the room. Where was Tae Hyun when she needed answers?

As if on cue, her question was answered by a muffled sound in the near distance.

Her head lifted when she heard some clattering on the other side of the door. What was he doing out there?

She jumped off the bed. Her hand found the cold doorknob. When she poked her head out the doorway, Yoori was surprised to be greeted with the delicious smell of eggs and bacon in the morning. Like a sleepwalker, she followed the delicious scent down the hall. What she witnessed next threw her into a tornado of shock—the good kind of shock.

She stood there, amazed at the scene in front of her.

Tae Hyun, dressed in a white shirt and white drawstring pants, was running around in the kitchen, cooking what suspiciously looked like a hearty breakfast. She was not only amazed that he was cooking—she was also amazed at how domestically sexy he looked.

Strong arms moved over pots and pans with purpose, bringing her attention to the light sheen of sweat that clung lovingly to his well-muscled body. When those long, powerful hands cracked those eggs and scraped those sausages off the pan, she wondered how he made such a normal human duty appear so godsend. She also wondered how in the midst of such delicious looking food, he could look like the most scrumptious thing on the menu.

Her breath hitched.

Waking up to see a hot guy cooking a hearty breakfast. What could be more appetizing?

Why does he always have to look so good, she thought distractedly, not realizing that her headache had gradually subsided. It was probably the food, but she was already in a better mood.

"I see that your lazy ass is finally up," he said loudly, giving her a side-glance while he scraped the eggs off the pan and onto the plate.

Yoori frowned. Just like that, the morning hunk suddenly looked less attractive. She shook her head reprovingly. Would it kill him to say, "Good morning"?

Instead of telling him off for being rude, she decided it was best to be civil. She owed him for carrying her home and letting her have the bed.

"Smells good," she commented cheerily, sweeping her bitterness from his less than warm greeting aside. She craned her neck to get a better view of the assortment of breakfast food. Breakfast was not only limited to eggs and bacons, it also included pancakes, sausages, rice, and freshly squeezed orange juice.

Her mouth started to water.

Turning off the stove and throwing the pans in the sink, Tae Hyun grabbed the plate filled with eggs and proceeded toward the dining table.

Yoori kept her gaze on Tae Hyun. His face was unusually red, but in a very attractive way. It was probably from cooking in the kitchen, but she had to let him know because he did look somewhat awkward.

"Your face is red," she blurted out, not thinking twice that it may have been a bad idea to be so informative.

"I've been cooking all morning," he answered briskly. He set the plate on the table. He looked at her and smiled. "I didn't get to sleep in all day like someone else I know."

Now it was Yoori's face that turned red. She felt slightly guilty and ashamed that she slept for so long. She also felt bad that he had to sleep on the floor because of her. Well, actually scratch that assumption. She wasn't sure if he slept on the floor or not. Rest assured, Yoori was determined to find that out later.

"Aren't you going to eat?" he asked. He settled at the dining table, gazing at her expectantly.

Relieved that he was no longer keen on bashing her for sleeping in all day, Yoori smiled. Nodding vigorously, she flew to the cabinet and quickly reached for a clean bowl and a pair of chopsticks. Tae Hyun was unusually kind today and she was going to milk it for all it was worth.

She sat across from Tae Hyun and rubbed her hands in delight. She was so hungry!

"Everything looks delicious!"

"Yeah?" Tae Hyun asked, beaming like a kid. He seemed proud.

Yoori was impressed. Tae Hyun was cooking and better yet, he cooked for her too. Boy oh boy was he on her good side today.

"You are amazing," she squealed, focusing her eyes on the plate of sausages.

Tae Hyun nodded. "I *am* pretty amazing," he concurred wistfully, pushing the plate of eggs and sausages closer to her. He seemed to be in a really good mood.

"Is this an experiment or something?" she added enthusiastically, not thinking that she may have been too blunt with her question. The truth was, she really wasn't thinking. The only thing on her mind was food.

The warmness on Tae Hyun's face cooled. "What do you mean?" he asked, his tone calm, but his eyes staring at her attentively.

Oblivious to the change in Tae Hyun's once positive air, Yoori laughed, overly excited to get a chance to eat. "Are you testing your cooking on me before you use this method with other girls?"

Though it was a joke, she was also half serious with the comment. Tae Hyun, that sly womanizer. She knew he couldn't be that nice to her. There had to be an alternative reason why he cooked for her. But nice or not, Yoori always welcomed delicious food in her life.

Tae Hyun frowned. "Is your opinion of me really that low?"

Yoori shook her head, waving her hand in the air. "Of course not! I'm giving you a compliment. It's smart to test your food on me. I'm a good tester. I'll let you know what works and what doesn't work. Then we'll make sure you get lots of girls. We'll just have to make sure I'm out of the apartment before you..." She cleared her throat. "You know...'put them to bed.'"

She smiled sheepishly at him. If Tae Hyun could put his cockiness aside and give her the bed, then she could put her judgment aside and help him get more girls. It was definitely a win-win situation. She stared hungrily at the sausages again. The only loser in this game was the food that was going to be devoured by her.

Yoori, so completely lost with the mouthwatering food surrounding her, did not notice that Tae Hyun was fuming in silence.

Her oblivious eyes grew wide. She did not know what to eat first. Deciding on her first victim of the morning, Yoori's chopsticks earnestly reached for the sausage. Her quest for sustenance was deterred when another pair of chopsticks slapped hers away.

"Who says you can eat this, assistant?" Tae Hyun asked, reaching for the sausages with his chopsticks. He no longer looked like he was in a good mood.

Yoori watched in dismay as Tae Hyun bit into the sausage. "Why can't I eat this?" she asked, mournfully taking inventory of the decadent feast before her. What had gotten into him? He was so nice a second ago.

"You said it yourself. I would only cook like this for girls I want to get into bed with." He stuffed himself with eggs and drank it all down with orange juice. "What makes you think you'll get to eat this?"

Yoori blinked at the seductive breakfast in outrage. First he got her hopes up about getting a chance to eat this wonderful food and now, he was taking all of it away from her? Was he really that cruel? She scrutinized him, hoping to see that he was merely joking. As he ruthlessly polished off his breakfast in front of her, she soon realized that he was not going to show her any mercy.

Her chin trembled. "What am I going to eat then?"

He stabbed his chopsticks into another sausage. "There's cereal on the counter."

"Ce-cereal?" she stammered, pointing at all the food. He couldn't be serious. There was enough food here to feed several third world countries.

"Cereal," he said unyieldingly, glaring at her before taking a sip of his orange juice. Needless to say, if glares could pinch, Yoori would be yelping in pain.

"Ugh!" Knowing all too well that she wasn't going to win this argument, she angrily slammed her chopsticks on the dining table.

Tae Hyun ignored such a tantrum and continued to eat in silence.

She scowled at his reaction, or lack thereof.

"Fine!" She stood up and retrieved the frosted flakes cereal box. Before returning to the dining table, she made her way to the fridge to get milk. Much to her dismay, she found that there was no carton of milk in the fridge. Her stomach growled.

"We're out of milk!" she whined, closing the fridge door. How was she going to eat this horribly cold breakfast without milk?

"Oh yeah, I used all of it to make pancakes," he said, eating the pancakes as if to taunt her.

Yoori closed her eyes to soothe her ruffled feathers. She restrained the temptation of physically assaulting her evil boss. Instead, she bit her inner lip and took her seat across from him.

The next few minutes were torture for Yoori.

She crankily munched on her frosted flakes, avoiding eye contact with the delicious breakfast. She couldn't understand why he was so mad at her all of a sudden. Was it something she said? Was it because she called him out for being a player? It wasn't like she was being judgmental. If anything, she was actually being supportive. What was his problem?

Grabbing another handful of cereal, her eyes on him softened. She was reminded of last night. All anger aside, she owed him for the night before. Or at least she owed him for what she thought he did for her.

"So...about yesterday," she began, throwing the handful of cereal back into the box. She allowed her gaze to settle on him. "What exactly happened last night?"

"You weren't feeling well," he said casually, taking his eyes off of her while sipping orange juice. "I carried you home and you pretty much slept the entire day afterward."

Yoori nodded silently, recalling the story Tae Hyun told her about the Scorpion girl. She felt obligated to explain what happened. Her reaction wasn't normal and she felt like she had to say something to address it.

"The girl was like the Cinderella version of this world to me," she said quietly, grabbing a frosted flake. She mindlessly broke each flake into little pieces and began to throw them on the dining table.

She knew it was stupid to get emotional over someone, worry about who they were and what they did in their past life, especially if it was over a girl who she didn't even know. However, Yoori couldn't suppress the disappointment when she thought about the Scorpion girl. Killing other gang members was one thing, but an entire family? That was despicable.

"I was so captivated by her story." She laughed wearily, not realizing that she probably shouldn't have ventured off on to that touchy subject. "It was stupid of me, but she was like a fairytale protagonist in a way. It was a big shock to find out she was actually the villain."

Tae Hyun nodded. To her surprise, he actually looked like he empathized with her disappointment. "The thing is that sometimes, to get into a position of power, some actions are unavoidable."

She measured him. Was he defending the Scorpion girl?

"She executed an entire family," she voiced firmly.

"I'm not saying it's right. But sometimes, with the circumstances you are given, you have to do whatever is necessary."

Yoori shook her head decisively. "There is never a necessary circumstance to kill like that."

Tae Hyun nodded quietly. He had nothing more to say.

"Anyway," she began, changing the topic. The mood of the morning had grown a bit too solemn for her taste. She no longer wanted to dwell on the Scorpion girl and the evil deeds she committed.

Yoori's short attention span became swamped by another topic. "Did you sleep—?"

"Don't worry," he assured automatically, taking his eyes off her. He grabbed another sausage with his chopsticks. "I slept on the floor."

"Yeah, I know," she said, trailing off as she kept her eyes on him. She waited awkwardly for him to look up while he ate. It was better to thank someone when they were looking at you and Yoori wanted to make sure she had Tae Hyun's full attention before she uttered those simple words of thanks.

As the seconds passed and his attention (and eyes) remained on his food, Yoori frowned. Realizing that he wasn't planning on looking up anytime soon, she decided to let it out. "Thanks for that."

She watched him carefully, hoping for a reaction.

He simply nodded, taking another sip from his cup.

Wow, he's really making this whole thanking ordeal hard, she thought with frustration.

There was a moment of silence before he spoke up again. "You know you got down on the floor and slept with me, right?"

WHAT? Yoori began to cough incessantly when the frosted flakes became momentarily lodged in her throat. Her eyes enlarged, mainly from shock. She was horrified by the new piece of information Tae Hyun so casually shared.

"Whoa, whoa, whoa. What?" she finally breathed past her coughs.

He observed her with a playful expression on his face. "Wow, assistant. You're either lying or you have terrible control of yourself when you're sleeping. Either way, I'm worried for you."

Yoori gritted her teeth. To think she actually thought the guy wasn't *that* bad. Now he decided to lie about something that happened last night? She might not have had a crystal clear memory of the night before, but she was sure she would never get down on the floor and sleep with Tae Hyun.

That shameless liar!

"Okay, look. You're probably bitter that you had to carry me home, but joking about something like this isn't funny for a girl like me, okay? So I'd appreciate it if you just told the truth."

Tae Hyun looked at her, offended that she essentially called him a liar. His eyes grew serious as he stared at her intently. "You want the truth?"

Yoori nodded, digging into the cereal box and grabbing a handful of flakes. "Yes, of course."

"Okay." Taking a moment to inhale and exhale, he looked at her and said, "The truth is..."

You lied, she supplied in her mind.

"I'm *not* lying."

Yoori glared at him in disbelief.

"I think we should talk about this," he continued.

"I think you should shut up," she countered, her irritation with him intensifying by the second.

Undeterred by her hostile tone, he spurred forward. "You really don't remember what happened last night? God, you're such a little—" He stopped as though realizing that he shouldn't finish his sentence.

Fire blazed in Yoori's eyes. "Little what?" she asked sharply.

That insufferably charming smile embellished his lips before he turned away from her. "Tease," he said quietly.

Yoori scoffed again. If she had the guts, she would've thrown a handful of cereal at him. She turned away. He was being a complete jackass and she didn't want to deal with it anymore.

"Can we get past this?" she said with agitation.

He obviously wasn't telling the truth. Why on earth would she voluntarily get on the ground and sleep next to him? Tease? Images of a girl giving a guy a lap dance popped into her mind. What tease? Yoori and "tease" should not be put into the same sentence. She didn't even freaking know how to tease!

Tae Hyun smirked, throwing another piece of egg in his mouth. "Fine. We'll stop talking about that. I have something else I want to bring up. We have to talk about your sudden bout with exhaustion." He eyed her seriously. "I know you haven't been getting enough sleep because you're afraid of jumping into bed with me again."

Yoori bobbed her head in agreement. "Got that right," she said grouchily, grabbing another handful of frosted flakes and throwing them into her mouth. Would a tease go through that much trouble to *not* get into a guy's bed? That was what she thought. Of course she wasn't a tease.

"That said, you can have the bed. I'll take the floor."

Yoori found herself coughing incessantly again. She pounded her chest profusely.

"Excuse me?" she managed to sputter out before she took a huge gulp of water. Did he say what she thought he said? She knew Tae Hyun was being nice last night by letting her have the bed, but she didn't think he was going to make it an everyday occurrence.

"I said, 'you can have the bed. I'll take the floor,'" he repeated, not looking at her.

110

She saw it in his demeanor. He didn't want to sleep on the floor (who in their right mind would?), but he was willing to do it for her. Despite her mood swings with him, she was touched.

"Kwon Tae Hyun!" she uttered happily, letting go of all hostility she held for him. "Am I to believe that you have a heart?"

Tae Hyun's face turned serious at her smiling countenance. He pointed a steady finger at her. "I'm only doing this because I can't have my assistant fainting at the corner of every block. Do you realize how heavy you are? My arms are sore! You will never make me work that hard again."

The smile evaporated from Yoori's mortified face. Sweetheart stage for Kwon Tae Hyun vanished again. She bit her bottom lip, suppressing the urge to flip him off. Heavy? *Heavy?*

"Fine!" she screamed out. Who was she to complain? She got the bed and he got the floor. It all worked out. It all worked out, but she wasn't satisfied. There was a better alternative to this whole dilemma. He was just being an ass and ignoring it.

"That's why you should un-cuff me permanently and let me sleep outside," she countered, shedding light on an option he steadily ignored.

Tae Hyun snorted. "Nice try, sprinter."

"I'm not going to run off!"

"And I'll make sure of that."

Yoori stared at him incredulously. She didn't understand him. He'd rather sleep on the floor than un-cuff her?

"You're a character, you know that?" she stated decisively.

"Touché," he retorted, finishing his last bite of bacon. He grabbed a napkin and cleaned off the sides of his mouth. "Anyway, glad we could come to an agreement." He rose from the seat and tossed the napkin onto the empty plate. "Now clean up."

Yoori's jaw sagged as she watched him take a seat in the living room. He lazily picked up his Blackberry and began to check his voicemails, ignoring her as he chilled in "relaxation" land.

Yoori discarded the cereal box in bitterness. Muttering to herself, she gathered the dirty dishes. She had lost her appetite and was beginning to regret thanking him for his "kindness." She dragged her feet to the sink and tossed the plates in.

"Could the volume be any louder?" she whispered as she started wiping down the plates.

Tae Hyun was checking his voicemails. And they were loud. Very loud.

A couple of the voicemails were from Tae Hyun's Serpents updating him on the happenings of the Underworld. She rolled her eyes when she heard the giggling voices of girls calling him to "hang out." *They* were the girls she was talking about earlier. She couldn't comprehend why he took so much offense to her stating the truth.

Once she was done with cleaning up, she went inside the bathroom to brush her teeth and change. She was surprised to find that he was still checking his voicemails when she came out in her jeans and a black top.

How many voicemails does this guy have, she wondered in amazement. She took a seat on the couch. She grabbed a newspaper from the coffee table and began to read from it, or at least tried to. She was much more interested in eavesdropping on his voicemails.

"Last voicemail," she heard the lady's voice announce through his phone.

As she flipped through the newspaper, Yoori looked up in disgust when she heard the sounds that emitted from Tae Hyun's Blackberry. It was the sound of a girl moaning.

Yoori was dumbfounded. Was the girl having an orgasm over the phone?

"Who…Who are you calling?" The girl in the voicemail asked, her voice breathless. "Hang up right now!"

Yoori heard a guy laughing before he hung up.

"End of message. To delete press—" Tae Hyun interrupted the machine by immediately pressing a tab. "Message deleted," the automated message said before he hung up.

Oh man...

Yoori stared awkwardly at Tae Hyun. He was breathing hard. His eyes were boiling with fury as he stared off into space. He looked like he was ready to kill someone.

Questions started thrashing in her mind. Who was the girl? Who was the guy? Was it Jin Ae? It didn't sound like Jin Ae, but she could easily be wrong. Judging by the angry look on Tae Hyun's face, Yoori was sure the girl wasn't just a friend.

Her thoughts were interrupted when she became aware of his eyes on her.

Grabbing a hooded black jacket that was on the couch, Tae Hyun threw it on. She hated to admit it, but in that moment, he really scared her.

"Choi Yoori," he said, irritably grabbing his Blackberry. "Let's go. I need to go bash some skulls against the wall."

Yoori sat frozen in her seat, dismay prevailing over her.

Why did she have the uneasy feeling he was talking about bashing the skulls of the *other* infamous gang in South Korea?

"You have to stick by your decisions."

14: The King of Skulls

"Please…Please help us," the bloodied man begged in distress. He made an attempt to reach for Yoori's hand. His efforts proved fruitless when he was pulled away by one of Tae Hyun's men.

Yoori's ears burned as she listened to him and three other men scream in pain. She retreated further into the corner of the room, closing her eyes in anguish.

Shortly after leaving Tae Hyun's apartment, his limo took them to a desolate warehouse on the other side of town. As soon as she stepped out of the limo, she knew it wasn't going to be good. Her ears were instantly greeted with sounds of men screaming in agony. She was horrified to find that there were a dozen of Tae Hyun's men pummeling four men to a pulp.

As Tae Hyun took a seat on the only available chair in the center of the warehouse, Yoori found herself standing in the dark corner of the room, unable to move.

Moments prior, Tae Hyun had such vibrancy and color to his character but now, his mood was so *cold*. She knew it was because of the voicemail he received earlier…the one with the girl over the phone. The voicemail left Tae Hyun livid, and it left Yoori with much to wonder about. Who was this girl that had Tae Hyun all worked up? She had never seen him so angry.

Yoori looked at Tae Hyun. His eyes were unforgiving as he stared at the four men before him.

He must really care for her, she reasoned. No guy would get this angry if it wasn't for a girl he really cared about. A tinge of jealousy erupted within her after she silently acknowledged such a fact.

After taking a moment to revel at the scene before him, Tae Hyun finally cleared his throat. His men ceased with the violent attacks on the four men and retreated to the dark corners of the warehouse, leaving the stage for their King to venture on.

The four men sat up in pain. Their bloody and bruised faces stared at Tae Hyun with much trepidation.

Tae Hyun rose from his seat and approached them.

"Where's your King?" he asked casually, circling the men like a shark in the night. "Isn't the Skulls leader coming to save the day?"

Yoori shifted her attention from the four men to Tae Hyun. So it really was Ji Hoon who called and left the voicemail. She suspected it was him, but she didn't have the nerve to confirm it with Tae Hyun. He wasn't too keen on being conversational after receiving that voicemail and she wasn't too keen on provoking him. But now, it was official. Lee Ji Hoon, the notorious King of Skulls, was most certainly the one they were all waiting for.

At the mention of Lee Ji Hoon, her heart rate quickened. It was much like meeting a celebrity. She had heard so much about him and yet she knew nothing about him. She cast her mind to the news segment she saw a while back. The one about the Skulls leaving a pile of branded, dead bodies in a business building. The story about him and the Scorpion girl torturing that family in the club also came to mind. The only thing she could properly surmise was that he wasn't someone to mess with.

Yoori fixed her eyes on Tae Hyun. The concern for his safety swam inside her. She didn't need to be a gang member to guess the aftermath that might play out if two powerful crime lords were to meet—especially ones who possessed enormous hatred for one another. Her eyes grew more concerned. And judging from Tae Hyun's temper, she was sure it could very well end in a bloodbath.

Tae Hyun continued to encircle the four men. While he did so, each of the men huddled closer to one another, anxious to avoid being closer to Tae Hyun than they had to be.

Yet, despite how beaten up he was, one still had the conviction to say, "He'll be here soon."

Tae Hyun chuckled. "I don't doubt that he'll show up. The only question is *when*?" His amused expression melted into agitation. He stopped circling them. "I'm starting to lose my patience here, boys."

It could very well be that they had finally realized that they were truly at the mercy of Kwon Tae Hyun because it was like the calm before the storm. They knew that Tae Hyun was not a storm to be reckoned with. No one dared to say another word to him.

The silence was only broken when Tae Hyun said, "Choi Yoori."

His eyes scanned the warehouse, searching for her.

Yoori took a tentative step out of the shadows and approached him.

"Yes?" she croaked, stopping before him with her hands behind her back. She kept her eyes firmly on the ground. She did not want to look at Tae Hyun or the four bloody men.

"My head is killing me," he began, closing his eyes in overt aggravation. "There's medicine in the glove compartment of the limo. Please go get it."

Yoori nodded without complaint. "Okay."

She needed any excuse to get out of the warehouse. Tae Hyun's headache couldn't have come at a better time. She was about to make her exit when Tae Hyun called after her again. He gently grabbed her wrist and pulled her back to him.

"Did you need something else?" she asked, unsure as to why he looked at her so uncertainly.

Tae Hyun shook his head. He looked as though he didn't know what to say to her. Then, he delicately pulled her closer to him. He whispered loud enough so that only she could hear. "Once you get inside, stay in the limo."

Stay inside the limo? Her eyes flew to him. An uneasy sensation pulsated inside her when she processed what he was doing. "But—"

He released his grip on her wrist, his face grim. It appeared as if he regretted making the decision to have her come in the first place.

"Go," he repeated.

"Tae Hyun, what—?"

"Choi Yoori." His unyielding eyes prohibited her from finishing her sentence. "Please leave before my headache gets worse."

Yoori cast a cautious glance at the audience in the room. They were all staring at them. She had to watch her words. Tae Hyun was vague for a reason.

Realizing that any further retorts with Tae Hyun were futile, she nodded slowly. "Alright then, boss." What was there left to say? A war was about to break out and if she was given the opportunity to avoid being a casualty, she'd take it.

"Show them the consequences of going against a Serpent." Yoori heard Tae Hyun command his men before her hands reached the doorknob of the exit. She forcefully pushed it open. Like a bat out of hell, she bolted out of the warehouse, leaving Tae Hyun, the agonizing screams of the four men, and the warehouse behind.

She opened the passenger side of the limo and threw herself in. She shut the door behind her, her heart palpitating wildly. Yoori took a moment to stare at her surroundings from the safety of the limo. Her breathing quickened after she closed her eyes and attempted to make sense of what happened.

"*I told you that I will make sure nothing happens to you.*" Tae Hyun's words from one of their first encounters resounded in her head.

"Tae Hyun, how stupid can you be?" she whispered hoarsely, pounding the back of her head against her seat.

She didn't understand why he was in that warehouse when he knew that nothing but a bloodbath would commence. She didn't understand why he brought her here, only to seemingly regret it later. She didn't understand why he was acting concerned for her when nothing in their relationship would merit such concerns. She didn't understand him at all. She sighed. But more importantly, she didn't understand herself. Here she was being critical of him for fearing for her safety when, in truth, she feared for his safety as well.

Her gut wrenched as she stared at the warehouse before her. Regardless of his less than delightful temperament, there was something about Tae Hyun that made her grow fond of him. She thought about it further and realized that despite how much they argued, he had truly become something like a...like a friend to her. *My friend*. Yoori didn't have very many friends and with the few she did have (Chae Young and apparently now Tae Hyun), how could she abandon one? How could she abandon a friend?

She thought about the possibility of a war breaking out in that warehouse.

He should be fine, right? This was Tae Hyun, the guy who took on all of Jae Won's men with ease. Of course he would be fine. She paused. But what about Lee Ji Hoon who had an equally powerful reputation? Both didn't seem like the types to go down without a massacre ensuing.

"Crap," she uttered. In the midst of trying to organize her thoughts, Yoori was interrupted when she heard car doors slamming in the distance.

Instinctively, she lowered her head and peered at the rearview mirror. Her eyes grew massive when they caught sight of over two dozen men in business casual attires walking in the direction of the warehouse. They were all led by one leader. It was clear the King of Skulls and his men had arrived.

"Shit." She recalled the mere twelve guys Tae Hyun had and the twenty-plus men that Ji Hoon brought. Tae Hyun did not have a snowball's chance in hell of winning.

She struggled to get a good view of the infamous King of Skulls. Such an effort was fruitless when all she could see was his back. He wore a blue dress shirt and black pants. He was very tall and from how he walked, he was enraged.

She watched in a frenzy as the new gang barged their way into the warehouse. She knew at this point that she should either stay in the limo or make a mad dash back into the city. With either choice, her safety would be guaranteed. Yet, as she sat frozen in her seat, the two rational choices didn't make sense to her. However, there was an irrational choice that *did* make sense to her.

"Unbelievable." Muttering an incoherent cuss for the idiocy that she was about to embark on, Yoori pushed the limo door open. She ran as fast as she could to the back of the warehouse. Yoori didn't know what she was about to do, but whatever it was, she was determined to help Tae Hyun.

She cautiously stepped over the pile of decaying wood and moved closer to the backdoor of the warehouse. She pushed the door open ever so slightly to avoid being noticed. She tiptoed in. The silence was music to her ears. She was relieved to find that violence hadn't broken out, *yet*.

She strategically hid behind a pillar in the warehouse and peeked her eyes out.

In the center of the room stood Tae Hyun and the Skulls gang leader. Behind their respective sides were their gang members. Standing at comparable heights, Tae Hyun and Ji Hoon glared at each other in silence.

A soft gasp issued from Yoori's lips when she finally got a better view of the other King of the Underworld. Yoori was surprised to see how young and handsome he was. For a moment, she forgot about the intensity of the situation.

What the hell is up with these gang leaders being so good-looking, she thought with curiosity.

She squinted to focus her eyes on Ji Hoon. There was a familiarity about him. Where had she seen him before?

"Finally," said Tae Hyun, cutting her thoughts short. He tilted his head, displaying no fear even in the presence of enemies who outnumbered him. "It took you long enough."

"You have some nerve taking my men hostage," Ji Hoon replied coolly. He looked calm, but the minutest tone in his voice told a different story. He was livid.

Yoori froze upon finally hearing Ji Hoon's voice. Seriously. Where had she heard that voice before?

Ji Hoon turned to his men and nodded. Four of his men emerged from the crowd. They raced to the four fallen men. They helped them up and took them back into the crowd.

"I was welcoming them to the Underworld," Tae Hyun responded with a smirk. He locked eyes with one of the bloodied men. "How fortunate you are to be here today. Thousands of Underworld soldiers go lifetimes without meeting me and here you are, being personally welcomed by the King of Serpents himself."

"Since when did you become the Underworld's new welcoming wagon?" Ji Hoon inquired.

"I see you've brought a lot of new faces today," said Tae Hyun, ignoring Ji Hoon's retort. "Congratulations on the new recruits. You're going to need them for what's coming up."

Ji Hoon smiled. He glanced at Tae Hyun's men. He was not impressed. "A lot of new faces on your side as well. But the numbers are a little low, aren't they?"

Tae Hyun's cool smile remained. "You definitely have more new recruits, but I'm not too sure they possess the same qualities as my men." His eyes settled upon the four men being nursed by several other Skulls members. "They were so quick to beg and scream for mercy."

Ji Hoon was unfazed by Tae Hyun's comment. A sneer appeared on his face. He had something else in mind to retort.

"Speaking of screaming and begging," he began with much amusement. "Some girl I was with last night was also screaming and begging." His smirk grew. "But for totally different reasons."

Tae Hyun continued to remain silent, yet the subtle fury exuding out of him was palpable. His jaw tightened dangerously.

Oh no. This is it, Yoori thought. Tae Hyun was at his breaking point.

"Tae Hyun." Ji Hoon masqueraded a look of shock. "I'm sorry, but I must have mistakenly called you last night." He laughed. "Sorry about that man, I was checking my voicemail. I must have misdialed." He patted Tae Hyun's shoulder. "At least you heard a good show, right?"

Tae Hyun swatted Ji Hoon's hand away. "Stay away from her," he said simply.

A mocking astonishment dawned on Ji Hoon's face. "Wait a second." He pointed at Tae Hyun. "That girl...you know her?"

Tae Hyun didn't reply. He was too busy fuming. He looked like he was ready to rip Ji Hoon's face off.

"Yeah, what was her name again?" Ji Hoon took a moment to think about it before saying, "Oh yes. Hae Jin...*Kwon* Hae Jin."

Yoori's eyes rounded. It couldn't be!

Ji Hoon pretended to be surprised with this piece of information. "Could it be that you two are related? Isn't that your younger sister?"

"You know who she is," Tae Hyun said icily, maintaining his composure. He stepped closer to Ji Hoon. "Stay away from her."

Yoori's jaw dropped. This was what it was all about. Tae Hyun baited Ji Hoon here to warn him to stay away from his younger sister. All along, he wanted to protect his younger sister.

Ji Hoon smirked, unaffected by the obvious anger rising within Tae Hyun.

"You're damn right I know who she is." He leaned closer to Tae Hyun, whispering loud enough for everyone in the warehouse to hear. "She's the horniest piece of ass I've ever had."

And that was it.

That was all Tae Hyun needed to hear before he slammed Ji Hoon to the ground and started to savagely punch him. And that was the only cue the gang members needed before they started attacking one another as well. In mere seconds, a war broke out before Yoori's eyes. In this chaos, all she could focus on was Tae Hyun and Ji Hoon. They were beating each other to a pulp.

The warehouse soon housed a sea of violence as men threw ruthless kicks and punches at one another. Yoori stood frozen in her stance. She craned her neck out to get a better view of the two gang leaders.

Tae Hyun managed to throw another punch that left Ji Hoon spurting blood out of his mouth. Forcefully grabbing the collar of Ji Hoon's shirt, he threw him against one of the pillars in the warehouse. Ji Hoon's impact against the pillar was so hard that it caused the dust from the ceiling to come deluging down. Distracted by the wave of dust that clouded his vision, Tae Hyun was unable to anticipate the forceful kick that Ji Hoon bequeathed upon him. He immediately fell to the floor.

"Tae Hyun!" Yoori whispered, feeling the urge to run over to help him.

She expelled a thankful breath when Tae Hyun quickly regained his balance. He rocketed toward Ji Hoon with full force. When he reached him, he swept the floor with his right leg, stealing the ground from Ji Hoon's feet. Ji Hoon fell, but not before Tae Hyun delivered an uppercut that had Ji Hoon crashing into the pillar again.

As they fought, she saw Ji Hoon struggle to get something behind his back. Alarm blared through her when she saw that he was reaching for his gun. It occurred to her that Tae Hyun neglected to bring his gun with him. She covered her mouth to muffle a scream when Ji Hoon produced a black gun from behind his back. He pointed it at Tae Hyun.

Tae Hyun, amused with the weapon, stopped fighting with a scoff of disbelief.

Afraid that a wrong move would cause their King's head to be blown off, Tae Hyun's men followed suit and stopped fighting.

Ji Hoon's men took the opportunity to follow their leader's example by taking out guns of their own. They aimed at each member of the Serpents. A victorious sneer appeared on their faces.

Silence descended upon the warehouse.

It was only disturbed by Tae Hyun's cool voice.

"Come on, Ji Hoon. I was having so much fun beating your ass. You were that desperate that you had to resort to taking weapons out?" A challenging light played in his eyes. "Put the gun down and fight me like the Underworld Kings we were raised to be."

"I promised Ju Won I wouldn't kill you before his 65th birthday party," Ji Hoon said instead, ignoring Tae Hyun's proposition to fight one on one.

Ju Won? Yoori's mind was reeling. Who was Ju Won?

Annoyance pierced through Ji Hoon's eyes. "I was going to let you live a little bit longer to see me take over the Underworld." Ji Hoon wiped the blood from the side of his mouth. He glared at Tae Hyun who stood there, undaunted by the gun aimed at him. "But you've proven time and time again that you're irritating to have around." Yoori held her breath when Ji Hoon centered his gun onto Tae Hyun's head. "Give me one good reason why I shouldn't shoot you right now."

Tae Hyun smiled, finding hilarity with the state Ji Hoon was in. "Seeing as that I'm close to taking over the Underworld as my own, I can't see any other reason why you shouldn't shoot me right now."

He glared at Ji Hoon, daring him to pull the trigger.

"This is your only chance, Ji Hoon. We all know that Ju Won favors giving his empire to me. You also know that the majority of the Underworld favors me as their King. If you don't kill me now, you will never get the chance again. And trust me, in the future, there will be *a lot* more reasons why you should shoot me."

What the fuck? If Yoori had a gun of her own, she'd probably bash it against Tae Hyun's dense head. Daring Ji Hoon to shoot him? What was he thinking?

"But I can understand your hesitation." Tae Hyun smiled widely at Ji Hoon. It was clear Ji Hoon was apprehensive with pulling the trigger. "You'd never stand a chance of getting his fortune if you kill me. You know that."

Ji Hoon nodded, his eyes burning. Much to Yoori's relief, he started to lower his gun. But such an action was short-lived when a smile lit his face. A light bulb went off in his head.

"He doesn't have to know that it was me who killed you," he mused, centering the gun on Tae Hyun's head once more. There was no more hesitancy on his part. Slowly, he began to pull the trigger.

"Nooooo!" Without thinking, Yoori found herself making a mad dash toward Tae Hyun and Ji Hoon. Her safety no longer mattered. The only thing that mattered was helping Tae Hyun.

Her rationality only returned when she saw that all of the guns went from being aimed at the Serpents to being aimed at her.

She stopped in the darker corner of the warehouse, her heart pounding ruthlessly. One would think that by now, Yoori might've gotten used to having guns point at her. But as she stared at the barrel of Ji Hoon's gun and the guns of his men, she knew that she had made the biggest mistake of her life.

Crap.

She really should've thought this plan through.

Tae Hyun finally lost his composure once he saw that it was now Yoori's life that was in danger. "YOORI! WHAT THE HELL ARE YOU DOING? GET THE HELL OUT OF HERE!"

He didn't have to tell her twice. What was she thinking running to Tae Hyun and Ji Hoon like that? Did she really think she could've stopped Ji Hoon from killing Tae Hyun?

A wave of common sense engulfing her, she decided to abort her plan, *or lack of a plan*, altogether. With the utmost velocity, she attempted to head out in the direction from which she snuck in. She barely made it halfway before she felt a pair of hands latch on to her shoulders.

One of the Skulls threw her like a rag doll into the center of the room. She yelped when her knees made an agonizing impact against the floor. With her head hanging down in exhaustion, she stared at the two legs standing before her. Trepidation struck her. Why did she have the feeling that those legs belonged to a certain Skulls leader?

She heard a soft chuckle that made her breathe heavier in fear.

"Tae Hyun, you fucking bastard," she heard Ji Hoon say in between laughs. "I can't believe you brought your girlfriend here."

"Leave her out of this," Tae Hyun commanded. His voice was tight with worry. Not for himself, but for Yoori.

"She's a new one, right?"

"Let her go," Tae Hyun commanded once more.

Yoori closed her eyes in distress. She continued to kneel on the floor of the warehouse, her head hanging down. Her legs throbbed and she did not want to look at Ji Hoon. She was afraid if she made eye contact, she'd be shot to death right then and there.

Ji Hoon laughed once more before squatting down beside her. She felt his eyes lay upon her. "Tae Hyun, you and I always seem to have the same taste in girls…" Ji Hoon allowed his gun to trace the outlining of her left cheek. "I wonder if I'll like this one too."

Yoori snapped her head further to the side when she felt the cold gun graze her face. She shook like a leaf in the wind.

"Ji Hoon," she heard Tae Hyun warn. "*Don't* fucking touch her." She could hear him struggling to run to her, but Ji Hoon's men must have held him back because he was nowhere near her and Ji Hoon.

Terror reached an all-time high for Yoori. What was this guy going to do with her?

"Wow Tae Hyun, look at you," Ji Hoon observed. "Replacing Jin Ae already, huh?"

"Ji Hoon," Tae Hyun seethed gravely. "If you so much as hurt a strand of her hair, I will slice your head off."

Yoori had no courage to look up. Under any other circumstance, she would be touched by Tae Hyun's overt concern for her. Having mentioned that, this was not the time for her to dwell on the uncharacteristic side that Tae Hyun showed. She was a little bit more preoccupied with fearing for her life, *again*.

Ji Hoon said nothing to Tae Hyun. He averted his attention back to a quivering Yoori. "You must be something, you know that?" he said delicately, this time allowing his fingers to trace the side of her left cheek. "The King of Serpents doesn't get worked up like this over just any girl."

Yoori recoiled when she felt his fingers trace her face. She didn't want him to touch her.

Ji Hoon laughed, unoffended by Yoori's actions. He slid closer to her. "I'll tell you what," he whispered softly so that only she could hear. "If you lift your head and let me see how beautiful you are, I'll consider letting you and Tae Hyun go."

His delivery was mocking. Yoori was positive that even if she obliged with his request, it might not give her and Tae Hyun a free pass to leave the warehouse. Ji Hoon, from the looks of it, did not appear to be the type of person to let anyone go that easily.

However, regardless of her lack of trust for this particular gang leader, she was really backed into a corner. If there was a small chance that she and Tae Hyun could get out of this situation unscathed, then she should take it.

And that was what she did.

She took the chance.

"Good girl," Ji Hoon said approvingly, satisfied as the dim lighting of the warehouse gradually revealed Yoori's face. Her blank eyes fell onto Ji Hoon's smiling countenance and she stared at him in silence.

The ball was in his court now. Whatever he chose to do with her was up to him.

She had expected him to mockingly smirk at her when she made eye contact with him. What happened next threw Yoori into a whirlwind of confusion.

As the full features of her face became unveiled, Ji Hoon's smile evaporated. His eyes soon grew huge as he scanned her face in disbelief. The vibrancy that he once possessed vanished. His breathing quickened while the intensity in his eyes grew. Yoori couldn't make sense of what was happening. Why did he look so…confused?

Silence monopolized the warehouse as Ji Hoon shook his head in disbelief, his eyes firmly set on an equally confused Yoori. To her, he no longer appeared like a demonic gang leader who was ready to take her life at any moment. *No.* He appeared utterly dumbfounded, lost, and vulnerable.

He was looking at Yoori like she was a ghost.

During the moment of silence, Ji Hoon's lips parted more than once, but no words came out. Nothing was making sense to him. He didn't seem to understand what was happening. Despite his bewilderment, his unblinking gaze on her remained. It was as if he was afraid that if he closed his eyes, even for a second...she'd disappear.

Disturbed by what was happening, Yoori made an effort to part her lips to attempt to break the silence. Much like Ji Hoon, she found that no words came out.

The simple act of parting her lips, however, was all that Ji Hoon needed to break out of his trance. He held his breath and finally lifted his hand toward her. Apprehensively grazing her face with his shaking fingers, Ji Hoon's eyes glistened in happiness. It was as if he finally realized that she was *real*.

The next words out of his mouth echoed through the warehouse, leading Yoori further into bewilderment. "...Soo Jin?"

"Because if you don't . . ."

15: The Meeting

If there was ever a moment in time that allotted Yoori the opportunity to crumple her face in confusion, this was that moment.

Soo Jin?

Words could not properly describe how gobsmacked Yoori was. A migraine began to plague her after being witness to such a psychotic episode. Ji Hoon had lost his mind. He had officially lost his mind.

Terror cloaked her eyes as she gazed at him. She had to get away from this guy.

She slapped his fingers away from her face and attempted to stand up. Pained nerve endings exploded in her legs, causing her to instantly fall back down. She hadn't realized that the impact of the fall made such a lasting impression on her kneecaps. The pain was so acute that she was sure she would black out at any moment.

"Soo Jin!" Ji Hoon uttered, reaching out with the intention of helping her regain her equilibrium.

"No," Yoori said warningly, her hands outstretched to prevent him from coming any closer. Rallying all the effort she had left, she managed to prop herself up with her own hands.

Ji Hoon froze when Yoori backed away from him.

"Soo Jin, please." He gazed at her. He didn't understand why she was hostile toward him. His focus flickered to her knees. "Your legs...are you okay?"

Yoori gawked at him, utterly mind-boggled with his behavior. This was quite possibly the strangest situation she had ever found herself in. Were the lights in this warehouse that dim? Did he need glasses? Lee Ji Hoon must've had too many girlfriends if he couldn't even keep track of the faces of girls he'd been with.

"Look," she said, ignoring his query about the welfare of her legs. She wanted to get straight to the point. As vulnerable as Ji Hoon appeared, the gun he held was a big motivator for her fear—that and the sole fact that he was acting like a crazy person wasn't helping his cause either. "All of this is a mistake. I don't know you. We've never met."

Ji Hoon inhaled deeply, not listening to the actual words that flowed from her mouth. "Why are you acting like this?" He took a step forward and tried to reach out for her. "Baby, please..."

Yoori limped backward in a panic. "Stop it!" she screamed, nearly tripping over herself. Her legs and head throbbed with exacerbated pain. She continued to retreat from Ji Hoon.

"Ji Hoon! Get away from her!"

No longer having the patience to watch the scene before him, Tae Hyun managed to fight off the Skulls that held him back. He took off like a missile and sped to Yoori like there was no tomorrow.

Yoori glanced at Ji Hoon, who had his back turned to her. With Tae Hyun distracting Ji Hoon's focus, Yoori knew that this was her moment to make her escape. It was more than likely the adrenaline pumping in her body, but as she took off in Tae Hyun's direction, she no longer felt the pain entrenched in her legs.

"Soo Jin!" Ji Hoon screamed when she zoomed past him. He attempted to seize her hand. His fingers grazed her wrist, failing to form any grip on her.

Bewilderment covered his face while he watched Yoori take off toward Tae Hyun. It was as though he was beginning to realize that she wasn't the girl he thought she was.

"Soo Jin?" he asked softly, this time uncertain if the girl before him actually answered to that name.

"Yoori!" Tae Hyun screamed, speeding up in her direction.

Yoori sped up as a response, surprised that her legs could run that fast. If she weren't so out of shape and panting ruthlessly, she probably would've screamed out his name as well. It felt like forever, but reprieve spilled over her when she finally reached Tae Hyun. Without saying a word, Tae Hyun grabbed Yoori and pulled her behind him, effectively becoming her shield. Cautiously retreating backward, Tae Hyun positioned Yoori in an angle that protected her from any incoming bullets.

They both panted in exhaustion. Yoori's panting was a little bit more aggressive than Tae Hyun's. She made a mental note to work out more often in the future—that was if she ever made it out of this warehouse alive.

Her blood ran cold when she saw that one member of the Skulls had his gun aimed in their direction. His finger grazed the trigger.

"Oh no."

This was it. This was where the story ended.

Yoori closed her eyes in anticipation of the incoming bullet. Her heart galloped to a stop when she heard the fatal gunshot. The earsplitting sound howled throughout the vicinity of the warehouse, bouncing off every possible wall and ceiling. Panic ensued when she registered that nothing penetrated her body. She warily opened her eyes. If she wasn't hit, then it meant that Tae Hyun was.

Her eyes landed on Tae Hyun. He was still standing in front of her, his breathing intact.

Yoori gasped when she observed that Tae Hyun wasn't shot either. Had the bullet missed them? Her eyes prowled the warehouse. She didn't understand what happened. The guy had a direct aim. How could he miss?

She craned her neck over Tae Hyun's shoulder. She peered in the direction of the shooter. Yoori made a strangled noise when she took in the scene around her. Instead of finding the shooter standing before them as she had anticipated, his body was instead sprawled across the floor. There was a pool of blood around him.

Her eyes focused on Ji Hoon's men. The Skulls gang members still had their guns pointed at them, but their attention appeared to be elsewhere. Shock and dismay sprawled across each of their faces. She followed their gaze and her eyes fastened on Ji Hoon. Her face soon mirrored the expressions of Ji Hoon's men.

The image of Ji Hoon standing before her with his gun outstretched in the direction of the fallen shooter caused her to cover her mouth in shock.

He just saved them.

Ji Hoon's furious eyes remained on his horrified gang members. Lowering his gun, he said, "Lower your guns."

Yoori was stupefied. Lee Ji Hoon was actually helping them.

One of his gang members doubtfully spoke up. "But boss—"

"I said lower your guns!" Ji Hoon thundered, cutting off his confused gang member.

Sounds of shuffling could be heard as each man swiftly lowered his gun. The look on their faces said it all: what had gotten into Ji Hoon?

He kept his murderous expression on them. "Never point a gun in her direction again," he enunciated dangerously, every word threaded with ire. "If I ever catch any of you pointing a gun at her again, I will make sure each and every one of you eat a bullet. Understand?"

His men nodded quickly, fear spreading throughout each of their eyes.

Ji Hoon returned his attention to Yoori and Tae Hyun. His eyes grew guarded when they focused on Yoori. He was finally piecing everything together.

"Who are you?" he managed at last.

Yoori turned to Tae Hyun, her eyes questioning whether she should answer Ji Hoon.

Tae Hyun nodded guardedly. He looked unsure as well. He repositioned his stance in front of her, as if telling her that whatever occurred next, she would still be under his protection.

She turned back to Ji Hoon cautiously. He was staring at her with a small ounce of hope in his dimly lit eyes.

"Choi Yoori," she finally answered.

Upon hearing her answer, the small ounce of hope vanished from Ji Hoon's eyes. He took an unsteady step back. He looked like he had the wind knocked out of him.

"Choi Yoori," Ji Hoon repeated faintly, staring at her with a wounded visage.

After what seemed like forever, Ji Hoon finally inhaled deeply. It occurred so fast that Yoori was almost uncertain of what was happening. He finally took his eyes off her.

Within a matter of seconds, his demeanor changed. He no longer looked pained or agonized. The once vulnerable countenance on his face was replaced with a powerful one. The vulnerable Lee Ji Hoon had made his exit and the King of Skulls had returned in his place.

His potent gaze landed on Yoori once more.

"I'm sorry, Yoori," said Ji Hoon, the air of his charm and vibrancy racing back into him. "I thought you were someone else."

Confusion worsened the pain pulsating in her head. Yoori wondered what triggered the abrupt change in Ji Hoon's behavior. One moment he was this vulnerable, confused guy who had mistaken her to be someone else and now, he was this emotionless gang leader apologizing for his mistake. Something wasn't right.

Tae Hyun laughed disbelievingly. "You've been with that many girls to mistake her for someone else?"

Ji Hoon swiveled his attention to Tae Hyun. Though the vibrancy was still present within him, he was a little less charming to Tae Hyun than he was to Yoori.

"This is a new one for you, Tae Hyun," Ji Hoon said unexpectedly, ignoring his retort. He flickered his gaze to Yoori and shook his head. "Using a pretty girl to distract me."

"She's not here for you," Tae Hyun replied darkly.

"She's not here for me? That's a shame..." Ji Hoon stared at Yoori adoringly. "I told you that if you lifted up your head and let me see how beautiful you were, I'd let you and Tae Hyun go." He repositioned his gun behind his back. His smile grew. "You really are beautiful beyond words. Since you did your part, it's time I did mine." His eyes landed on Tae Hyun. "For her, I'll keep my word. You may go."

Tae Hyun chuckled insultingly. "Don't make it appear as if anything drastic would've happened if she wasn't here. You know you wouldn't have had the balls to do anything. Ju Won's favor is a good motivator."

Ji Hoon's smile remained. "You're right. I probably wouldn't have done anything. Ju Won's favor really is a big motivator." His eyes locked onto Yoori for a second. He returned a challenging gaze to Tae Hyun. "But I'm afraid I'm after something else now."

Yoori held her breath. So that was his new plan. He wanted *her*.

She watched uneasily as Tae Hyun's body hardened upon hearing Ji Hoon's second remark. When it appeared as if Tae Hyun was ready to bash Ji Hoon's head in, Yoori took possession of his hand.

"Tae Hyun." She gently formed a grip with his hand, silently telling him to not overreact. It was obvious that Ji Hoon wasn't going to hurt her, but she knew he was waiting for a reason to hurt Tae Hyun.

She stiffened when she saw that Ji Hoon had his eyes lowered to where her hand held Tae Hyun's. A muscle twitched in his blank face. It was clear he didn't like her touching Tae Hyun like that.

The tenseness in Tae Hyun vanished when Yoori's hand held his. Though she couldn't see his face, she knew he had suppressed his urge to pummel the living hell out of Ji Hoon. She released her hold, silently praying that Tae Hyun would be calm and sensible. The only important thing now was to get out of this warehouse alive.

Although Tae Hyun's grim expression remained, he soothed his need for violence. "The only reason why you're breathing right now is because of Ju Won," he began calmly. "Heed my warning, Ji Hoon. If you don't stay away from her, I will make your life a living hell when the time comes."

An amused expression overtook Ji Hoon's face. "Your sister is out of the picture." His eyes locked with Tae Hyun. "And it is not because I'm afraid of you."

Yoori only stared at him in response. As handsome as Ji Hoon may be, she was actually getting more and more irritated with him. He was definitely not the prince she once thought he was. He had no respect for his dead girlfriend. This was the guy who slept with Jin Ae, slept with Tae Hyun's sister and left a voicemail about it. This was the guy who had mistaken her to be another one of his many girlfriends. Her gaze graduated into a glare. She didn't like him already.

Her glare was fleeting when she started to become lightheaded. The pain throughout her body was gradually becoming worse.

"I wasn't just talking about her," Tae Hyun countered. He appeared more angry and protective this time.

At this point, Yoori was no longer listening. The throbbing state of her body stole her attention. The room felt like it was spinning. She tried desperately to keep from blacking out. All she needed to do was hold out for a little bit longer.

"Of course you weren't." His eyes shifted to Yoori for a succinct second before returning to Tae Hyun. He, like Tae Hyun, was oblivious to what was happening to Yoori. "You have no idea what you're getting yourself into. I always get what I want."

Tae Hyun smiled challengingly. "We'll see how true that is. I always get what I want as well."

Ji Hoon nodded, accepting that challenge.

If Yoori wasn't so pre-occupied with her bout of pain, then she probably would have taken into account what—or who—these two gang leaders were challenging each other for.

She steadied herself to keep from falling backward.

From her head to her toe, everything was hurting. She was only able to take her mind off the pain when she became aware of Ji Hoon raising his hand in the air, a gesture to his men to make their exit.

Taking a couple steps back, Ji Hoon kept his firm gaze on Tae Hyun. "Take good care of her for me."

Yoori stared at him questionably. What? Was he talking about her? Or Tae Hyun's sister? Or Jin Ae? Who's *her*?

Another small smile outlined Ji Hoon's face when his eyes held Yoori's. "It was nice meeting you, Yoori. I look forward to seeing more of you in the future."

Slightly bowing his head, he finally made his exit with his men in tow.

A shortness of breath assailed Yoori after she watched Ji Hoon disappear out of the warehouse. No longer being able to withstand the horrible pain she was experiencing, she started to shake as a spell of faintness poured through her.

Oh no, she thought. *Not again...*

She felt Tae Hyun grab her before she stumbled to the ground.

"Yoori!" he called, lightly shaking her. "Are you okay?"

He gently brushed her bangs away from her eyes. Yoori's heartbeat escalated as she stared off into the distance.

"Wh–where," she stuttered, regaining her balance and pushing him away from her. She found it hard to breathe normally. Everything in this warehouse was suffocating her. "Where's the bathroom?"

"In the back," he answered dubiously. He stared at her pale visage. His face was full of concern.

Yoori nodded absentmindedly, making her way to the back of the warehouse. She stopped when she felt him grab her wrist.

"Choi Yoori, do you need me to help you walk—?"

"I can walk by myself," she answered quickly, releasing herself from his grip. This was all too much. She had to get away from him. She had to get away from this warehouse. She had to be alone so she could think. "I'll be right back."

Before giving him a chance to say anything else, she rushed to the back of the warehouse. She pushed the bathroom door open, stumbled in, and closed the door at once.

Breathing harshly, she leaned against the wall of the bathroom. She took a moment to stare at her reflection in the mirror. She brought her hand to her chest. Her heart thumped rapidly. She felt another shortness of breath when she raked her fingers through her hair. It felt like a bomb had went off inside her head. The pain was killing her.

She looked around the bathroom. Anxiety inundated her senses. The walls of this warehouse felt like they were closing in on her. She had to get out. Her eyes rocketed up to the window in the bathroom. She stared at it pleadingly. The nausea was becoming unbearable. She was literally suffocating. She had to leave.

Making up her mind, she strategically used the bathroom sink as a foundation to thrust herself up to the window. She carefully climbed out of the window and jumped onto the ground outside. Then, Yoori felt her legs take off.

She wasn't too sure what she planned to do after she was done running, but none of it mattered at that moment.

She ran faster.

All that mattered was that she had to get away.

She had to get far away.

"You'd end up destroying yourself."

16: The Bad Guy

The journey back into the city was a long one for Yoori. Her adrenaline wore off and she began to feel the drawbacks of running on injured legs. While limping through the streets, she couldn't refrain from cursing her current predicament.

"Why the hell is this happening to me?" she whispered, exhausted.

Yoori inhaled deeply, taking in the fresh air. However aggravated she was with the pain shooting up and down her legs, she was actually more grateful for the walk. The escape allowed her time to recollect her thoughts. Her mind drifted back to what took place at the warehouse. The constant concern and protection Tae Hyun gave her...the strange interest Ji Hoon showed her...the unexplainable emotions that roiled inside her when she was around them... She didn't understand it nor could she explain it. Everything that happened at that warehouse was just so crazy and *weird*.

She turned the corner of a familiar street. Yoori's traffic of thoughts took a backseat when her eyes shot up in relief. A couple more blocks and she would be back at her apartment. *Home sweet home*. Her relief was fleeting when Tae Hyun drifted into her mind. She grimaced to herself. He must have been searching for her now. She felt awful for leaving the way she did, but she couldn't handle being in that warehouse any longer. It was just so…suffocating.

She peered at the street ahead of her. She knew that Tae Hyun would search for her at her apartment before going anywhere else. This thought made her feel a little bit better. He'd find her. He'd eventually find her here and when he found her, she'd explain why she left and then she'd return with him to his apartment. After returning to his apartment, they could talk about what happened in that warehouse, because in all honesty, what happened between them was damn strange—considering their normal, bickering interaction and all.

It confounded her.

Yoori wanted to pick his brain. Maybe if she understood what happened from his point of view, then perhaps she could understand what happened from her own perspective as well.

She came to a stop when she detected footsteps behind her. From the corner of her eye, she spied the silhouette of a tall shadow. She closed her eyes in relief. She thought right away that it must've been Tae Hyun following her. Having the forefront to anticipate his temper (especially when this was her second big "escape") she turned around in haste. She was ready to explain herself.

"Look, I—" Her words jammed in her throat when she observed that the person she addressed wasn't Tae Hyun.

The air vacated from her as she stared at the person before her. No. It definitely *wasn't* Tae Hyun. The person standing before her was the exact polar opposite of Tae Hyun.

"Hi Yoori, " Ji Hoon began gently, a ghost of a smile materializing on his handsome face.

Butterflies began to form in her stomach as she stared at him silently. She wasn't too sure if it was good or bad butterflies. She was about to find out.

"We didn't get to really talk earlier. Can I have a moment with you?"

Yoori clamped her mouth shut.

"No, Lee Ji Hoon, you cannot have a moment with me. Who do you think you are following me and requesting such a favor?" This was what Yoori wanted to say to him as he awaited her reply. Much to her dismay, her lack of a spine did a wonderful job of preventing her from saying such a retort. Instead, she blinked at the Skulls leader with trepidation.

If she had more energy and her legs weren't so cramped up, then she would have left him. Tragically for Yoori, she had no leftover energy. She had no option but to stand there and awkwardly stare at him.

Her eyes appraised his smiling face for the first time in broad daylight.

The dim lighting in the warehouse really didn't do justice to the perfect features that he possessed. Yoori was almost sure that Tae Hyun had fast become one of the most handsome guys she had met in her life. Now, with a distinct adversary standing in front of her, Yoori admitted that Ji Hoon really did rival Tae Hyun in terms of looks. These crime lords were quite possibly two of the most handsome men she had seen in her life. They were close to perfect. The only deterrent being that they were both crime lords, of course. That mentality in mind, her cautious stare on him remained.

Ji Hoon promptly raised his hands up in midair. "I'm unarmed," he said affably, the smile never leaving his face. "In case you're worried."

"You don't have to be armed to be a threat," she uttered without thinking. She mentally slapped herself for being such a smart aleck. Who did she think she was talking to him like that? Did she have a death wish?

Laughter issued from his lips. He lowered his hands. He didn't seem to mind her less than filtered retort. "You're right. Being unarmed really doesn't eliminate any threat." He took a step closer to her, his gentle brown eyes holding their gaze on her like she was the most fascinating thing he had ever seen. "Trust me when I say this though, I will *never* be a threat to you."

"How comforting," she said, taking a step back.

Judging by how he looked at her, she was positive that he would probably abduct her at any given moment. Hot or not, being kidnapped by someone was no fun.

"If I wanted to take you home, then I wouldn't be wasting my time with small talk," he replied, reading her mind. A devilish smirk manifested on his face. It appeared as though he may have caught himself in a little white lie. "Granted," he continued slickly, "I *do* want to take you home, but I'll muster up some self-control."

The temperature rose inside Yoori. She tried hard to quell the warmth that rolled over her. She really did. She hated to admit that Ji Hoon's charismatic personality was really magnetic. Something about him attracted her. There was an air of arrogance about him that she found to be aggravating and simultaneously appealing. The simple truth was, regardless of her ill-feelings for him in terms of all the things he had done, he was still that "prince" in the story that had her fascinated with the Underworld. This meeting was much like meeting a celebrity. It was not only a surreal moment—it was also an intoxicating one.

She steadied her breathing, determined to not allow her fascination with Ji Hoon to cloud her judgment. There was a part of her that told her he was harmless, that he would never hurt her. However such a part was overturned with the common sense pounding away in her mind. *Trust is foolish*. Especially with someone like Lee Ji Hoon who was a glorified crime lord and someone she hardly knew.

"How long have you been following me?" she inquired sternly, trying to sound stronger than she was. She didn't want Ji Hoon to know that he was getting to her. It was best to have her guard up at all times with this guy.

"Since the warehouse. Pretty girl like you shouldn't be walking alone."

Yoori scoffed, ignoring the added compliment at the end. "An offer for a ride back into the city would've been nice. That was a long walk, you know?"

"I would have offered, but knowing you, I knew you wouldn't have accepted."

Yoori lifted a suspicious brow. "Knowing me? What are you talking about? You know nothing about me."

"Hence the reason why I'm here. I don't like having a question mark next to a pretty face."

Yoori grimaced after the recent round of flattery Ji Hoon threw in her direction.

"Okay, this is really inappropriate." She surveyed her surroundings, expecting Tae Hyun to pop out at any moment. All expected punishment from her quick-tempered boss aside, she felt a bit guilty. Being around Ji Hoon made her feel like she was cheating on Tae Hyun. They weren't romantically linked, but it still felt like she was betraying Tae Hyun. He was her, albeit at times insufferable, friend after all.

"I just want to talk to you," Ji Hoon added, his voice sincere.

"I don't want to talk to you."

"Why not?"

"Because." She couldn't think of a fast enough answer.

"I just want to get to know you."

"I don't want to get to know you," she repeated with annoyance. She was tired of this game. She wanted to leave.

"That's too bad. I'm an interesting person."

"My loss, I suppose," she said sarcastically, turning on her heels to leave.

Ji Hoon appeared enough like a gentleman for her to think that she could easily leave. She had hoped that simply walking away would merit a graceful exodus. Her hopes were shattered when he caught her wrist. She nearly tripped over when he pulled her back to him.

She fixed him with hardened eyes, oblivious that the trepidation she had for him had dissolved.

"Are you a threat now?" she asked critically.

Ji Hoon let go of her wrist. She assumed he was letting her go until his hands found the back of her waist. In a matter of seconds, he pulled her closer against his body. Yoori gulped when she processed that their bodies were touching.

"What do you think you're doing?" she asked in a panic.

"I'm not going to do anything to you," he said softly, tucking her stray bangs behind her ear. His face was angelic as it could be. "Just give me ten minutes. Give a love-sick puppy a break?"

The sensation of his fingers grazing her face reminded her of the warehouse and his out of character mode (which involved him calling her by another name). Her face grew unyielding. She had no intention of being someone's replacement.

"I know you're only doing this because I remind you of someone," she said quickly, trying to break away from his grasp.

Ji Hoon effortlessly held on to her. "I told you already that I made a mistake. The lights were dim and I was disoriented from the fight. Now that we're out in broad daylight, you actually bear no resemblance to her."

"Really?"

Relief. Relief was what Yoori felt when she heard his answer. Though the better part of her knew that there was more to what he told her, at that particular point in time, she chose to ignore her instincts and believe him.

She sighed. "And you're here now because?"

She shook when he pulled her closer. They were so close that she could feel his heart pounding against his chest. She struggled to free herself, but to no avail.

"We met on a bad note. I want our first meeting to end on better terms."

"Well, to be perfectly honest, if you haven't noticed, I really don't want to be around you right now."

Ji Hoon smiled, his eyes twinkling a little more as he delicately stroked her face. "Believe me when I say that under any other circumstances, I'd be more than happy to oblige with what you want. But right now, with my interest for you at its apex, I really must say that your needs take a backseat to mine."

"Forward much?"

"I hate beating around the bushes."

"This is all about you, isn't it?"

"No. This is all about you."

Her mind went blank. Why did he have such good comebacks?

"Just ten minutes," he repeated, his eyes gazing at her adoringly.

"What are you planning to do in ten minutes?"

"Convince you that I'm not the bad guy."

Yoori scoffed. "You're going to need more than ten minutes."

He feigned disappointment as he stared at her lips. "Have I done something to deserve such hostility?"

"Were you not in the same warehouse?" she asked in disbelief. She angled her face away to remove her lips from his gaze.

His focus returned to her eyes. "Tae Hyun was the one who set the ball in motion. I just went onto the court and joined the game." His voice stiffened upon the mention of Tae Hyun. He didn't seem to enjoy talking about him either.

"Yeah, you definitely didn't provoke him by sleeping with his sister and leaving a voicemail chronicling the entire ordeal."

Ji Hoon's face went blank. A blanket of guilt overtook his countenance. He strained to keep a weak smile on his face. His hold on her softened. "It didn't mean anything."

The arrogant air that once surrounded Ji Hoon vacated, leaving him to uncomfortably turn away from her. It was apparently difficult for him to look at Yoori without feeling guilty. After several seconds, his eyes returned to her. His voice darker than before, he said, "What is your relationship with Tae Hyun?"

"That's none of your business."

"Isn't it?"

"Why would it be your business?"

"Because I've taken a liking to you as well."

It took all her might to prevent any more blood from rushing to her cheeks. Summoning all the strength at her disposal, she toughened her gaze on him.

"You're only interested because you think I'm his girlfriend," she said without thinking.

"Think?" Ji Hoon arched his eyebrow in interest. "Are you not?"

Yoori paused. She probably shouldn't have said that.

"It's complicated," she hastened to add.

Funny, it really *was* complicated.

He smirked knowingly. "Should I help make it less complicated?"

"Don't even think about it."

"I'd be a good boyfriend."

"I'm sure your ten girlfriends in the picture right now would agree to that."

"Other girls don't exist when I'm with you."

"Who's Soo Jin then?" she asked casually.

In the short amount of time that she had known Ji Hoon, if Yoori would give him credit for one thing, it was his ability to keep his composure. He was able to keep the smile firmly solidified on his face with every insult she threw at him and he did it well. The only times he ever really lost composure were when she called him out for sleeping with Tae Hyun's sister and whenever the name "Soo Jin" was brought up. True to form, Ji Hoon didn't disappoint this expectation. His eyes softened upon the mention of the familiar name. He appeared lost in contemplation as he stared at her silently.

"A one-night stand," he finally answered, his face now an impenetrable mask.

"What?" She had expected him to say that she was a long-term girlfriend—or even a short-term girlfriend. But a one-night stand? Yoori glanced up unfavorably. "A one-night stand? You scared the hell out of me because of a one-night stand?"

"She was a mesmerizing one," he chimed in with charm.

Yoori scoffed again. So this was the big secret. The girl she reminded him of was a one-night stand. Her opinion of him dropped to an all-time low. This guy was really something.

"I think your ten minutes are up," Yoori said impatiently. Though she was sure, with her luck, that there was probably another minute or two left before that fact became true.

"I actually have five minutes left."

"I gotta tell you, I'm really not fond of you. I think we should cut this meeting short."

"What do you see in him?"

"Excuse me?"

"Tae Hyun. What do you see in him?"

Yoori froze, floored by the question. She studied his expression with uncertainty. The truth was that she didn't really know what she saw in Tae Hyun either. She wasn't even sure that she saw anything in Tae Hyun.

Tae Hyun. Tae Hyun. Tae Hyun.

Images of Tae Hyun began to circulate in her head, ruthlessly reminding her that she shouldn't be standing here with Ji Hoon. Tae Hyun, regardless of his less than calm demeanor, was still someone that she surprisingly cared for. No matter how hard she tried to deny that fact, she knew that it was true.

"He's a good guy," she replied, the unexpected verity in her statement surprising her. Though his recent actions and his current status as a crime lord would refute that statement, she really did believe that there was more to Tae Hyun than the surface layer.

Ji Hoon's eyes sharpened on Yoori. He caught the brief warmness that shined through her eyes when she thought about Tae Hyun.

"Do you even know him?" he began tersely, his eyes critical. "The type of person he really is?"

The warm feeling she had pertaining to Tae Hyun vanished slightly. She eyed Ji Hoon distrustfully. Wow, she really didn't think Ji Hoon would result to bringing up piles of dirt to make her lower her opinion of Tae Hyun.

"Don't try to bring up stuff to make him look bad," she said warningly, her anger spiking up. "I know that you killed his father. I know all about what you and the Scorpion girl did in that club." Her eyes bred hatred for him when she recalled the five-year-old kids who were shot to death. Finally being able to push herself away from his clutches, she shot him a disgusted look. "You're despicable."

"You know nothing about what happened that night," he said, taking a dangerous tone with her.

"I know enough."

Tense lines outlined his face. "No, you don't."

"I know that she tortured and killed that family and that you were there to help. You're both heartless killers."

What happened next startled Yoori. Ji Hoon grasped her shoulders and held her tight. He leveled his gaze with her, his eyes dark and angry.

"It *wasn't* her fault!" he roared.

Yoori gaped at him, horrified with the sudden change in his behavior.

The severity in his eyes mitigated when he saw the fear in her eyes. He steadied his breathing. "She wasn't that type of person," he repeated quietly, his eyes boring into hers. He released her. "And don't you ever forget that."

After being released from Ji Hoon's grasp, Yoori retreated in fear. She chastised herself for getting too comfortable with Ji Hoon. What was she thinking bringing up the Scorpion girl?

Ji Hoon allowed a soft sigh to escape from him. The darkness that once inhabited his eyes faded. He looked at her apologetically, his eyes expressing regret for acting the way that he did. The regret, however, vanished almost as soon as it appeared.

"Was Tae Hyun the one who fed you all of this hearsay crap?" he inquired. Although his voice was calm, it was also filled with subtle anger.

"Hearsay crap?" she asked defensively, oblivious to the fact that she always forgot to watch her mouth whenever Ji Hoon brought up Tae Hyun. "Fine, the club one might be hearsay crap. But are you saying you didn't kill his father?"

"I did."

Yoori shook her head. There was nothing he could say to make himself look any better.

The frustration was prevalent in Ji Hoon's eyes. He didn't enjoy the fact that Tae Hyun was in a better position than he was. He looked determined to change that fact. "Did Tae Hyun share with you who he killed in order to sit on his current throne?"

Yoori felt a lost of air upon hearing Ji Hoon's question. She never once thought to ask Tae Hyun about who he had to kill.

Silence claimed her vocal chords.

Ji Hoon scoffed, taking her silence as an answer. "I figured. Bastard probably made himself sound like an angel in comparison to me, right?"

Yoori's spine stiffened. She refused to allow Ji Hoon to put the Devil's horns above Tae Hyun's head. "I know all about your unwritten rule about killing other gang leaders to be deemed the new leader. Whoever it is he killed, I really don't care—"

"Ho Young," he interjected.

Yoori's entire body went still. That name sounded dreadfully familiar.

"*Kwon* Ho Young," Ji Hoon repeated, feeding on her reaction.

Punched. At that point, it felt like Ji Hoon had punched the living hell out of her. Every ounce of warmth left in her vanquished.

"Tae Hyun killed his older brother and stole the Serpents throne," he continued slowly. "That's how good of a guy Tae Hyun is. I killed an enemy. He killed his own brother. *That's* the Tae Hyun you know."

Yoori took a step back, finding it harder to maintain her balance. Pain, distraught, disgust, disbelief...all of it percolated within her. Tae Hyun killed his own brother to assume the Serpents throne? She breathed in roughly. What kind of monster kills their own family member?

Her anger getting the best of her, she glared at Ji Hoon. "You just really had to bring that up, didn't you?"

"He shouldn't have the upper hand because of information he withheld. He doesn't deserve you."

She looked at him disparagingly. They had only just met, but she was already sick of being around Ji Hoon. "And you do?"

It seemed like he wanted to answer, but he kept his mouth shut. His face grew impatient though. He couldn't let that question go unanswered. "In time, you'll see why I'm better than him."

"He's still better than you," she added, even though she heavily doubted the truth in that statement.

A wounded expression fell over Ji Hoon's face. He closed his eyes and regained his poise, determined to appear unruffled by what she said.

They're as bad as each other, she thought, aggravated.

"Can I go now?" she asked suddenly. She knew that five minutes had long passed.

"When can I see you again?"

Yoori looked at him incredulously. Was this guy really still at it? "Why? So we can have more moments like this? I think I'll pass."

"The next time will be better. I promise."

There wouldn't be a next time if she could help it. "Don't count on it."

Turning on her heels, she power walked home without any sign of slowing down.

"Yoori, remember that you're better than him," he called after her. "He doesn't deserve you."

"Don't come near me again!" Yoori shouted, quickening her pace.

She was resolved on getting away from Ji Hoon, Tae Hyun, and everything related to this screwed up Underworld.

"You can never forgive the ones who betrayed you."

17: The Attack

Yoori breathed in exhaustion after she stopped a block away from her apartment complex.

"Finally," she muttered in the greatest of relief. At long last, she would be able to relax at home. Her adrenaline running dry, she decided it was best to limp home. Anymore unnecessary pressure on her knees would screw her over more.

Memories of her encounters with Tae Hyun and Ji Hoon replayed in her mind when she neared her apartment. Today was quite possibly one of the most horrible days of her "new" life by far. First, she got dragged to a warehouse where Tae Hyun decided to wage war with Ji Hoon. Then, her stupidity got the best of her and she tried to save Tae Hyun from getting shot by Ji Hoon. After that, she was held at gunpoint, *again*. Such a scene was immediately followed by Ji Hoon having a psychotic episode where he had mistaken her to be someone else. And if the events that took place at the warehouse weren't enough, she soon found herself stalked by Ji Hoon, who conveniently chose to tell her that Tae Hyun really was the monster he portrayed himself to be. He executed his own brother to become the Serpents' King.

She raked an agitated hand through her hair. "This day couldn't get any worse," she verbalized begrudgingly.

Unfortunately for Yoori, the universe was intent on throwing a couple more curveballs her way.

Her horrible day was *just* getting started.

"My, my, my, look at Tae Hyun's new girlfriend walking down the street alone," said a voice that sounded menacingly familiar. "Doesn't she realize how dangerous the streets are?"

The fine hairs on the back of Yoori's neck stood up. She stopped dead in her tracks and shot her head up toward the direction of the voice. She was horrified to find that the owner of the voice was exactly who she anticipated it to be: Jin Ae.

Standing a few feet away from Yoori, dressed in a pair of denim blue jeans and a simple black tank top, Jin Ae didn't look intimidating in appearance. Yet, the fact that she stood with three heavily muscled bodyguards behind her and a knife twirling in her hand rendered Yoori speechless.

"You don't know who you're fucking with," Jin Ae said calmly, her eyes heavily focused on the knife she was playing with. "I told you to stay away from Tae Hyun. You obviously didn't listen. And now I find that you're flirting with Ji Hoon out in the open? You have some nerve going after the guys I've been with. I'll give you that much."

Terror waltzed all throughout Yoori's body.

"You have no idea how wrong you've got all this," Yoori replied cautiously. Her eyes darted from the knife in Jin Ae's possession to the bodyguards looming behind her. She'd be a fool if she didn't think bodily harm lurked around the corner for her.

She swallowed tightly.

Bodily harm and quite possibly death.

"Don't talk back to me, bitch," Jin Ae growled, finally raising her eyes to meet Yoori's. A sardonic smile played on her lips. She stopped twirling the knife. Her critical eyes scanned Yoori from top to bottom.

"I wonder what Tae Hyun will think of you when I'm done with you," she said idly, hints of excitement in her voice.

"He'll kill you," Yoori said at once, already anticipating what Jin Ae had planned for her. Even though she highly doubted the validity of her own statement, she hoped Jin Ae wouldn't catch her bluff. As she watched a sneer take over Jin Ae's countenance, she knew her bluff was caught.

"We'll see about that," Jin Ae said nonchalantly. She turned to the three men standing behind her. "Beat the fuck out of her."

Her bodyguards started cracking their knuckles in anticipation.

Jin Ae narrowed her vindictive eyes. "Since she's such a slut, do what comes natural after you're done beating the hell out of her."

The three men smiled knowingly, their perverted gaze settling on Yoori with pleasure. They were happy to oblige with Jin Ae's orders. As if already undressing her with their eyes, they began to approach her, each staring at her hungrily.

"Choi Yoori, right?" Jin Ae yelled out while her men drew closer to Yoori. "Enjoy what's to come. Because after they're done with you..." She held up the knife smugly. "Your face will no longer merit lustful stares. Tae Hyun and Ji Hoon will never look at you again."

"You are fucking crazy," Yoori croaked.

She turned around in a panic, ready to make her escape. Her efforts were hindered when she saw that there was another heavily built figure—another one of Jin Ae's bodyguards—blocking her path. She was trapped.

"Crazy, huh? You have some nerve saying that to me." Jin Ae smirked. "After they're done with you, I'll cut off your tongue. Then we'll see how much nerve you have left." Her venomous eyes landed on the three men. "Start."

Yoori glared at the men approaching her. "You have no idea the hell you're going to be in for if you touch me," she said warningly, desperately hoping that they wouldn't catch her bluff and that they would recoil in fear.

Terror flooded through her when all they did was exchanged smiles and increased their pace.

"When we're done, I get to screw her first," the one in the middle stated, moving to her with heightened speed.

Yoori cursed, her heart pounding wildly. She attempted to run. Such an escape was thwarted when a powerful kick slammed into her stomach. Yoori fell roughly onto the pavement. An explosion of pain pulsed through her. She pressed the back of her head against the cement, finding it hard to breathe. As if the pain throbbing in her stomach wasn't enough, another brute kick to the side of her head left her gasping for air.

"Woo, you stupid idiot," the second guy said to the one who assaulted her. "Don't kick so close to her face. I want to screw this beautiful little thing in all her glory before boss slices her face open."

The one who answered to the name "Woo" laughed.

"My bad," he sneered unapologetically. He reached his hand out and firmly clutched her chin. He centered her face to meet his eyes. "I'll avoid hitting this beautiful face from now on."

After taking a moment to reflect on her pain, Woo imparted Yoori with two slaps across each side of her face. He laughed heartily, enjoying that his handprint left a mark on both sides of her face.

"My bad," he mocked once more.

Yoori took in a shaky breath when she felt the painful sting of the slaps. Her vision blackened for a moment as she wiped the blood escaping from her mouth. With the little strength that remained, she attempted to stand up. She struggled to get away.

She didn't get far.

A pair of hands wrapped themselves around her ankles, causing her to fall back down.

"God, baby, you have no idea how excited you're making us," the third guy groaned. He tugged her to him. He grabbed a fistful of her hair and roughly pulled her closer to him. His perverted hands found their way onto her legs.

"This is going to be fun," he whispered hoarsely, his fingers violently groping her thighs.

Rage whipped through Yoori like a tornado.

No one touches her like that.

"Don't fucking touch me!" she shrieked, her hand suddenly reaching out for anything she could use as a weapon. She managed to secure a discarded glass bottle in her hand. Rallying all the strength within her, she roughly slammed the bottle against the guy's skull, causing the side of his head to bleed profusely.

"Fucking bitch!" Pain morphed on to his face. His hands clamped over his head. He applied pressure against the wound, loudly cursing at Yoori.

With the broken tip of the bottle in hand, Yoori managed to get up and point the broken fragment at the two who still stood there. Maybe it was because of the pain throbbing within her, maybe it was because of how they touched her, or maybe it was the adrenaline pumping through her body, but as she stared at the two men, her eyes poisoned with an elevated level of hatred, she turned into someone else.

Rage consumed her body.

Blood.

She wanted their blood.

Kill them. All of them, her newfound devilish conscience whispered from inside her head.

She was happy to oblige.

Though the number of opponents outweighed her, she knew victory was possible. As her strategic eyes fell onto each of their necks, she knew that one slice was all it took to leave them knocking on death's door. She stood there, waiting like she had done it so many times before. All they had to do was come a little bit closer and she'd be ready to strike. She'd be ready for the kill.

"You truly do not know who you're fucking with," Yoori whispered dangerously, steadying her grasp on the bottle. And she would show them. She would show all of them who they were fucking with. "I am going to kill all of you."

Woo laughed in response. "I am going to have so much fun screwing you."

He advanced, ready to put her in her place.

Just a couple more steps, Yoori thought in fervor, her tactical eyes following his advancement. Her heart beat impatiently. She raised the tip of the bottle in anticipation. Just three more steps and she'd be able to slice his throat open. Just three more steps and this sorry piece of shit would understand what hell was.

Three...

Her focus on him heightened.

Two...

Her grasp on her weapon tightened.

One...

She *froze*.

He was exactly where she wanted him to be. He was standing at the exact position where death was imminent. All she had to do was run the shattered bottle against his throat and he'd be spurting out blood. All she had to do was act. It was that simple. Yet as he stood there, oblivious to the fact that his life was truly at her mercy, Yoori couldn't find the courage, or the heart, to kill him in such a manner.

The hunger for blood evaporated from her eyes.

She couldn't.

No.

Choi Yoori was not a killer.

No matter how strong the urge was, she just couldn't.

And that was all it took to have that violent alter ego leave her side.

She dropped the bottle to the floor. It shattered, obliterating any future protection it may offer her.

That was all it took for her to stand there, vulnerability raining over her. That was all it took for her to become a prey...*once more*.

"I knew you wouldn't have the guts," Woo said darkly, standing dangerously close to her. "Now it's time to show you the consequences of going against my boss." He produced a pocketknife from his back pocket. "Scream really loud as I slice off your face, alright beautiful?"

It all happened in slow motion. Woo raised his knife in the air and before she knew it, the knife was flying at her, the sharpness of its blade hungry for her blood. It was so close. It was merely centimeters away from cutting into her skin when she realized that the knife had contracted backward. Her eyes bloomed. She watched Woo contort his face in pain as he sagged forward.

Someone had pulled him away from her.

Someone had saved her.

To avoid getting pummeled by Woo's fall, Yoori stumbled backward. Her shock filled eyes fell upon her unexpected savior. Her eyes stretched when she made out the face of her rescuer.

"Jae Won?" she uttered, watching in disbelief as he took on the rest of Jin Ae's men.

Jae Won resembled a ninja dressed in all black business casual clothing. The punches and kicks he imparted unto them appeared effortless. One by one, they all crumpled to the floor. When he was done, he stood in between her and Jin Ae's fallen men. Jae Won had a taut smirk on his face that indicated he was annoyed with the situation at hand.

"Jae Won!" Jin Ae screamed. Her eyes went from Jae Won to her fallen men, all of whom were groaning in agony. "What do you think you're doing?"

"You fuckers." Jae Won's enraged eyes settled on Jin Ae and her fallen men. "You have some nerve touching her like that."

"Nerve? What the fuck are you talking about? What is your relation to that bitch? Is she screwing you too?"

"You watch your mouth, Jin Ae!" He pointed a threatening finger at her. "The only reason why you're not convulsing on the floor right now is because of your relation to Ju Won! If you dare to talk about her like that again, I swear I'm going to rip your tongue out!"

Relation...to Ju Won? Yoori thought curiously. Her mind ran amuck. Who was this man that everyone kept bringing up?

"Jae Won! Do you have a death wish?" Woo hollered upon hearing Jae Won speak to his boss in such a manner. He attempted to stand up, but failed miserably. Jae Won's assault left him in shambles. In other words, he had the shit beat out of him and he wasn't going to stand properly for a long time.

"I should ask you the same thing. Speaking to her like that... Do you have any idea what she can do to you?" Jae Won paused, his anger amplifying. "You know what? Fuck it!" His fury prevailing over him, Jae Won could no longer resist the urge to impart another round of kicks to Woo, who was now whimpering in pain. "You're such a tough guy, huh? Hitting her like she's nothing?"

Stopping midway, his breathing relentless in speed, Jae Won managed to pull himself away from a terrified and bloodied Woo.

Yoori was mystified. She couldn't believe her eyes. Why was Jae Won so protective over her?

"Yoori, are you okay?" a gentle voice asked behind her. A pair of hands reached behind her and helped her up. When she stood upright and turned her head, another familiar face greeted her.

"Kang Min?" she asked with uncertainty, looking him up and down. Were her eyes playing tricks on her? Did she get beat too hard? Why was he here?

"Get the hell out of here before I kill all of you!" Jae Won roared at Jin Ae's fallen men.

"One second, Yoori," Kang Min said smiling. He left Yoori's side to join Jae Won.

"Kang Min! Are you with Jae Won? Did you already switch sides?" Jin Ae screamed, obviously unhappy with the new players and their cameo in her arena.

Good job, Jin Ae, Yoori thought dazedly, watching the scene unfold. She was painfully curious too. Why were Jae Won and Kang Min together? What was the meaning of this?

Ignoring the questions Jin Ae posed, a very pissed off Kang Min whipped a black gun from his black leather jacket and promptly aimed it at Jin Ae. A look of fear danced over the once pompous girl's face.

"You have five seconds to leave before I blow your heads off," he warned gravely. His eyes fastened on the fallen men before him, all of whom had turned to each other in fear. His finger tightened around the trigger. The conviction in his gaze conveyed that his threats were not to be taken lightly.

Jin Ae's men didn't hesitate to crawl up with unmatchable speed and skitter off like cockroaches. During his grand exodus, Woo hastily grabbed Jin Ae's arm. She was screaming words of protests when he dragged her away.

"What the hell are you doing, you spineless piece of crap?" Jin Ae screamed, slapping Woo across the face. "Die if you have to! I want her blood!"

"We'll finish her off next time," Woo said pleadingly, his face red from the merciless slaps.

"Choi Yoori! This is not over!" Jin Ae screamed at the top of her lungs before her men threw her into a black SUV and drove off. "I'm going to kill you if it's the last thing I do!"

The car screeched off, leaving Yoori, Jae Won, and Kang Min alone at the scene of the crime. Yoori faced her two unexpected rescuers. She noticed that their demeanors had changed since their exchange with Jin Ae.

Jae Won's face resembled a kid's as he ran toward her in eagerness.

Placing his gun back behind his back, Kang Min followed closely behind Jae Won. His face was more stern and wary.

"You two..." she began when they stopped in front of her. She was at a loss for words. What were they doing together? Why was Kang Min with Jae Won? Did he betray Tae Hyun and joined forces with Jae Won? And Jae Won, had he been following her since that day in the alley?

They saved her, but what were they going to do with her?

As her curious eyes bore into them, Yoori began to notice the subtle similarities in their faces. The features were so subtle that one wouldn't be able to figure out the resemblance if they stood any further apart. They were related, she was sure of that much. She just wasn't sure of what they wanted with her.

She anticipated Kang Min would answer her un-verbalized questions when he opened his mouth. To her bewilderment, his next words did not answer any of her questions. Instead, it brought up more.

"It's been—" he said almost absentmindedly, his eyes scanning her face. He closed his mouth, unsure if he should finish his sentence. His face remained puzzled; he seemed uncertain of what was happening as well.

Jae Won, however, gazed at her with the utmost happiness and certainty.

"It's been a while," he said without reluctance, finishing Kang Min's string of thoughts for him. He reached behind his back and pulled out a gold gun.

Her body went rigid when she took inventory of the gun. Did he save her just to execute her in the end?

Her question was answered when Jae Won reached for her hand and raised it palm up. He placed the gun in her hand.

Yoori studied the gun in awe. For some strange reason, it felt like a pet had been returned to her. The beauty of its craftsmanship was amazing and the familiarity of its presence mesmerized her.

She looked at Kang Min and Jae Won questioningly. What was happening? What was the meaning of all of this? What was she supposed to do with the gun?

Jae Won only smiled as a response. His hand met hers and he gently folded her fingers so she would have a better grasp of the gun.

"We've missed you," he said simply, his eyes hopeful and eager. He looked at the gun and then at her. "Welcome back, boss."

"You have to make an example of them..."

18: The Lost Scorpions

Welcome back, *boss*?

Needless to say, it took Yoori more than a few breaths to fully soak up the ridiculousness of the statement.

Her flabbergasted eyes went from Jae Won and to Kang Min. Jae Won still had a hopeful smile spread across his face. Kang Min, on the other hand, was still looking at her with uncertainty. Regardless of the dissimilarities in the expressions they held, she knew they were both anxiously waiting for her reply.

She stood in stoned silence, a cloud of confusion hovering over her. Question after question pounded in her head. If her mind was racing before, then it was racing tenfold now.

Welcome back, *boss*?

That whole statement didn't make sense. She paused briefly. Well, the "boss" part she could absorb quickly. Jae Won had called her that since he saw her in the alley. However, what about the gun?

The weight of it seemed to have increased in her hand. She didn't understand why he gave her the gun. Why *they* gave her the gun. More importantly, she didn't understand why it felt natural for her to be holding it. Was it possible that she had been in this world for so long that even holding a weapon felt natural now? She grimaced. She would have to come back to that question again.

She cast her thoughts to the most troubling part of the statement.

Welcome back.

That was probably the most riveting question and the only one she truly cared enough to dissect. Welcome back from what? Welcome back to the apartment? Welcome back from the fight with Jin Ae's men?

Her rationality told her that Jae Won had to be referring to those two options. It couldn't be possible that he'd be welcoming her back from anything but those things. Her intuition, however, told her there was definitely another meaning to that statement. She didn't want to push it though. It was a strange gut feeling, but she was almost too afraid to know. In addition to that cautious gut feeling, she was also exhausted. Probably not too exhausted to not care about the confusion these boys had thrown her into, but definitely too exhausted to exert any real energy to try and find out what was going on. Her entire body was in pain and all she wanted to do at that precise instant was to get away from everything.

Intent on making her much-needed exit, Yoori's gaze on them grew firm.

"I'm sorry," she finally managed, breaking the thick silence.

She flattened her hand out and extended the gun back to Jae Won. "I honestly don't know how I became your 'boss,' but all of this is a mistake. I am quite possibly the most spineless girl you'd ever meet. I'm in no position to even be holding this gun. I would never be able to use it."

She extended it closer to him, hoping that he would nod in understanding and release it from her grasp.

Please just take it and let me leave, she thought, gazing at him intently. Her face started to twitch in pain. Her legs were ready to give out.

Unfazed by her behavior, Jae Won gave her a knowing smile that caused her to delve deeper into perplexity. He leaned in closer to her. Without so much as looking at the gun she was extending to him, he whispered, "Boss...Kang Min and I already checked. There's no one else here. You don't have to pretend you don't know us anymore."

Pretend?

The hell?

Yoori looked at him hesitantly. "I know who both of you are," she said with certainty, stealing a quick glance at Kang Min. He was still quiet.

Jae Won beamed prematurely.

"I just don't know what the hell is going on," she added punctually.

His expression fell.

With the weight of the gun prominent in her hand, she no longer had the patience to hold on to it. The familiarity and attachment she was forming with it scared her. She had to get rid of it.

She hastily grabbed Jae Won's hand and returned the gun.

She backed away.

Jae Won's face grew dim.

"Please tell me you're joking," he said hoarsely, becoming as pale as Kang Min. "Boss, if you're acting right now, then you're starting to look believable."

Her heart grew heavy at the crestfallen look on his face. Her entire body then tensed up in realization. This particular dialogue felt too similar to the one she had with Ji Hoon in the warehouse. Too damn similar.

"Jae Won," Kang Min finally spoke up, his voice shaking vaguely.

Yoori and Jae Won turned their attention to the sudden active role Kang Min took in the conversation. Though the look of uncertainty had since left his face, his pale expression remained.

"It's not her," he finished with pained conviction.

His words were simple, but it was enough to hit a nerve within her.

"Not her," Yoori repeated, furrowing her brows.

Not her. Not her—

Realization paralyzed her.

Eyes enlarging, she divided her focus between the gun and each of their faces.

That was when all the puzzle pieces aligned.

Soo Jin.

The girl that Ji Hoon had mistaken her to be in the warehouse...Ji Hoon's one-night stand.

She looked at Jae Won and Kang Min, her heart beating a little faster than she'd like it to. Apparently Ji Hoon's one-night stand was also a gang leader. Jae Won and Kang Min's gang leader to be exact. Annoyance brewed within her. She didn't know who this Soo Jin was, but she was getting pretty annoyed with everyone mistaking her to be this girl.

"I'm not your boss," she declared in a resolved voice.

She was curious though. She would love to meet the girl who everyone was confusing her with. Where did this mystery girl go?

Kang Min remained quiet, his face unfazed by her answer. Jae Won, however, had a less than graceful reaction.

"Are you fucking serious?" he roared, causing her to jump in fright.

Attempting to steady her rapid breathing, she merely stared at him. What was she supposed to say to that? *"Yeah, you crazy person with a gold gun. I am fucking serious?"*

Yeah, she reasoned, her mouth glued shut. It was definitely better to not say anything.

"Fuck!" He looked at her and then looked at Kang Min. Comprehension finally dawned on him. "Fuck, it's true. Boss would never let anyone slap her around like that."

Yoori frowned. Though she was pleased that the kid finally came to his senses, she was also offended. What was wrong with him? It wasn't like she voluntarily ran up to Woo and told him to slap her.

"I told you," Kang Min stated, every word spoken with deepening bitterness.

While Jae Won rolled his eyes at Kang Min's remark, Yoori's eyes sharpened like daggers once she processed what they said.

"Slap around?" She looked at Kang Min and then returned her gaze to Jae Won. She finally realized an important fact. "The slaps happened early on," she began slowly. "Were you watching the entire thing before you decided it was due time to help me?"

The boys grew stiff.

Caught.

Kang Min regarded her uncomfortably. He wore an apologetic smile. "I wanted to help you before the bastard even had a chance to touch you, but"—He glared hatefully at Jae Won—"this idiot here wanted to see if you were truly who he thought you were."

Yoori scoffed, momentarily forgetting that her first priority was to make a quit exit. Priorities aside, she was pissed. Who the hell stood around and watched as a guy beat a girl? Well, Jin Ae and apparently Yoori's two "saviors."

Jae Won's distressed eyes latched onto her. "You were supposed to slice his throat," he said dejectedly. His eyes focused on the dried blood on the side of her lips. She sensed that he was beginning to realize that slicing someone's throat wasn't something Yoori was capable of. He groaned. "This shit is crazy."

No shit, Yoori thought. This day was getting stranger and stranger.

Kang Min glared at Jae Won. "Idiot," he mumbled, showing an uncharacteristically immature side.

Jae Won turned and pointed a threatening finger at Kang Min. "Do you want to fucking die? At least I ran my ass out there before the knife slashed her face. What the hell were you doing? Coming out at the end and pointing that stupid little gun of yours?"

"It worked, didn't it? They ran their asses out."

Her blood boiled while she watched them bicker like ten-year-olds. She was already infuriated with them for standing by and allowing some asshole to assault her. Now they had the gall to choose this time to bicker like idiots? Were these two serious?

"Chicken shit," Jae Won said venomously, his right fist rolling up into a ball.

"Dumb shit," Kang Min retorted, his chest rising up without fear.

Yoori groaned inwardly. They really were this immature. She resisted the urge to pound her head against the wall. Why did she suddenly feel like a mother?

"That's it," Jae Won continued angrily, taking a dangerous step forward. "I'm going to fucking teach you some respect."

"Don't hurt your brain cells while you're at it," Kang Min yelled, taking a step forward as well.

"Why you little—"

"SHUT UP!" Yoori bellowed, her irritation at the bickering couple reaching an all-time high. As soon as the deafening words poured from her mouth, she covered her lips in horror.

Why was she yelling at them? They had *guns*! Did she have a death wish?

Startled by the thunderous scream that emitted from Yoori's petite frame, the two gang members jumped in shock. Both fell silent at once.

Yoori gulped uneasily at the unexpected spotlight thrust onto her. She was also taken aback at the newfound authoritative tone she took with them. She nervously tucked her bangs behind her ears. Yelling at them was probably not the best tactic—regardless of how annoying they were being. She concealed a small smile. Even though it *was* slightly amusing to see them obey her command the way they did. Her small smile wilted when the pain within her body worsened, reminding Yoori that she still needed to make her exit before her body completely gave out on her.

"Well," she began, her voice trembling. "I'm glad we've come to the conclusion that I'm not your boss. Thank you for saving my life and all, but I've got to go now."

Her right foot leading the way, Yoori began to stagger her way back toward her apartment, silently hoping that they wouldn't object to her leaving.

Her prayer was not answered.

"Wait, wait, wait!" Jae Won and Kang Min yelled concurrently, trailing after her like shadows. Each seized her hand and stopped her in her tracks.

"It doesn't matter who you are," Jae Won reasoned, anchoring her from her exit. "It's not safe for you to be alone."

She groaned, managing to free her hands from each of their grips. She twirled around and faced them. She clapped her hands together and looked at them pleadingly. "This has been a really fucked up day and you two are not making it better. Please just leave me alone."

"Yoori, boss will kill me if he finds out that I've let you out of my sight," Kang Min added desperately.

Yoori didn't know if it was even remotely possible to be happy and extremely angry at the same time. The mere mention of Tae Hyun did an impressive job of easing her mind while simultaneously pissing her off. She hadn't forgotten about the tidbit of information Ji Hoon shared about her quick-tempered boss. The faint happiness was overshadowed by the anger wallowing within her. To think she thought there was some good in the guy. To think she thought he was like any other human being...

She scowled at Kang Min for even bringing up the existence of Tae Hyun.

"Do you hear how pathetic you sound?" commented Jae Won. He glared at Kang Min, visibly displeased with the obedience Kang Min displayed for Tae Hyun.

"Not as pathetic as you when he gets here and pummels your face in," Kang Min replied heatedly.

She gasped and pointed at them. It was all starting to make sense. From the sound of Kang Min's voice, he made it seem like Tae Hyun *knew* that they were already here.

"He knows that you're both here together...with me?"

Kang Min froze to look at Jae Won, worried. Jae Won, in response, gave him the "just-tell-her" look.

Slowly, Kang Min bounced his head in confirmation.

Her eyes grew wider. "He knows everything?"

Kang Min smiled nervously. "Well, he knows we're here. But he doesn't know about the gold gun and this imbecile calling you 'boss.'"

"Hey," Jae Won voiced sharply, slicing Kang Min with a death glare.

"So he's coming?" she inquired quickly, wanting to keep them on topic.

Kang Min nodded. "He should actually be here soon." Another nervous look canvassed his face. "Which brings me to what I wanted to ask of you. We'd appreciate if you kept what happened after the assault from Jin Ae's gang...you know...between us."

She gawked at him. If she recalled correctly, he had requested that once before already (not that she kept her end of the deal for that request).

"Why should I?" she challenged, growing comfortable around them now.

Kang Min smiled perceptively. "Well, we did save your life and all. Surely you won't throw your rescuers under a bus?"

Jae Won nodded, concurring with Kang Min's line of reasoning. "He has a good point."

Yeah, but you watched a good round of beating before your asses came out, she thought grudgingly.

Regardless, it was true. They did save her and for that, she couldn't throw them under a bus. Or in this case, throw them under Tae Hyun's merciless temper.

She held her gaze on them.

Maybe it was because she was too pissed at Tae Hyun to even be remotely loyal to him and inform him that he may have traitors in his midst. Maybe it was because the pain in her body was clouding her judgment. Maybe it was because she already felt safe around them. Or maybe it was because she had already begun to form a bond with these two gang members, but against better rationale, the innate part of her trusted that they had her best interest at heart. It was a big leap of faith (which could conversely be seen as stupidity) on her part, but she trusted them—wholly.

Before verbally agreeing though, she wanted to fully confirm some things. "Tae Hyun knows I'm here?"

Kang Min nodded. "He called me and told me to get to your apartment right away."

Yoori flicked her attention to Jae Won. "And he knows that you're here?"

Jae Won nodded. "I switched sides today."

"And you were ordered to come here for me?"

"Well, I would've come regardless, but yeah, those were his orders."

"But you switched sides for me?"

Jae Won nodded.

"But you know I'm not her," she continued.

Jae Won nodded, disappointment forming on his face again.

"So why are you still here for me?"

"To watch over you."

She wasn't satisfied with his answer. "What if your boss comes back? Won't that be a conflict of interest?"

"It—"

Jae Won never completed his sentence. The sound of a slamming car door in the near distance stole their unwavering attention. Yoori didn't turn. She could tell by how Jae Won and Kang Min stiffened up that there was only one possibility of who the person coming into their midst could be.

They studied her, their eyes urging her to give them a sign that she was ready to accept the requested favor.

She nodded as a gesture of her agreement. "But we will continue this conversation," she whispered. She was looking at both of them, but her attention was focused more on Jae Won. She sensed she'd find out the most information from him.

Jae Won nodded briefly before turning his full attention to the new guest that was about to accompany them.

Yoori sighed. Now that one conversation had been set aside, another complicated one was about to begin.

"Boss," Kang Min respectfully greeted over her shoulder.

The anticipation was a ruthless one for Yoori. All anger and frustration aside, she was surprised that she actually missed him. It had only been a couple of hours since she last saw Tae Hyun, but it felt longer to her.

148

Taking a step to the side, Jae Won and Kang Min made room for the long awaited King.

Yoori's breathing became shallow when she felt him brush past her, the familiarity of his cologne making its way through her nostrils. Lowering her head to avoid eye contact, she felt herself stiffen up with his near presence.

In a funny way, she was filled with mixed emotions. She was upset by what she learned about him—she didn't really want to look at the guy. At the same time, she yearned for the familiarity of his company. In light of all the crazy things happening, it was astonishing that Tae Hyun had become her constant in this new world.

"Hey sprinter," he said coolly, his tall figure towering over her. Though his voice was calm, Yoori could tell that he was quelling the urge to scream at her.

She could feel his eyes on her.

No longer wanting to delay the inevitable rounds of screams that were her fate, Yoori gradually lifted her face and allowed her eyes to meet his.

She paused upon seeing him after what felt like so long. He still looked the same. He wore the same black hoodie and white drawstring pants from earlier in the morning. His soft brown eyes still spoke of annoyance for her and her unwarranted getaways. Even that tightening of the jaw, the one he appeared to always give out when he was unsure of what to start lecturing her on, was the same. Everything about him was the same. Everything was the same...except she knew better now.

To her, Kwon Tae Hyun was no longer that questionable gang leader hiding the fact that he may have a heart. No. She had resided to the fact that he was actually a cold-hearted person—the very same cold-hearted gang leader he had always portrayed himself to be. A person with a heart would never kill his own brother. A person with a heart would never do anything that disgusting. And for this, she would treat him as he should be treated: less than human.

Her gaze on him sharpened. As difficult as it may be, she planned to be careful around him now. If she had to work with him, then so be it. That in no way, shape, or form meant she had to be friendly with the guy.

Knowing fairly well that if this silence continued, then their inevitable argument would worsen, she decided it was best to give her defense about her untimely "escape" from the warehouse. Better to do it now than give Tae Hyun the chance to berate her.

"Look I—" She was prepared to explain why she left the way she did when she observed that his anger had since dissolved into concern. He had just taken stock of the full features of her face.

She looked at him awkwardly, her eyes questioning why he was assessing her in that manner. His face was a mixture of concern and anger. Why was he looking at her like she had been ran over by a car—*oh*. It was then that she realized how screwed up her face must've been after the assault. Two puffy red cheeks from the slaps and a dried up bloody mouth *did* merit this type of attention.

With no preface for his actions, Tae Hyun reached for her hand and pulled her toward him. It felt like déjà vu with what occurred with Ji Hoon. She yelped in surprise when she felt their bodies collide. She looked at Tae Hyun, her face growing red. His eyes roamed over her face.

Against her better command, her body, as opposed to fighting to be out of his grasp—the way that she did with Ji Hoon—instead grew comfortable within Tae Hyun's hold. Lost in a slight trance, she momentarily forgot about the hostility she was supposed to harbor for him.

Tae Hyun, Tae Hyun, Tae Hyun.

Tae Hyun always had a tendency to make her forget what was going on in the world around her. He *always* had a tendency to make her lose all rationale. What was it about this guy and his ability to do all this to her?

With his left hand resting on the back of her waist, he brought up his right hand and positioned it closer to her mouth. His finger merely grazed the tip of her bloody lip before he contracted his hand in hesitation. It was as if he was afraid the slight touch would hurt her. His breathing grew heavier while he examined each bruise. After counting all the maladies that were present on her face, his eyes teemed with indignation.

Holding her close, Tae Hyun turned to Kang Min and Jae Won. He looked like he was ready to burn an entire city.

"Who touched her?" he finally spoke out, his voice deep and dangerous.

They answered immediately. "Woo."

After being reminded of the boys' presence, Yoori slipped out of her trance. She stared at the profile of Tae Hyun's furious face with renewed displeasure. Why was he trying to act like he had a heart?

Unaware of Yoori's glare, Tae Hyun's eyes grew wide after hearing their answer. "Jin Ae's Woo?"

Kang Min and Jae Won nodded.

If it was even possible, his face grew angrier. Turning to Kang Min, he said, "Send out the word. I want those responsible on their knees in front of my doorstep before the week is over."

"But what about Ju—?"

"I'll deal with Ju Won. Do as I say."

Kang Min nodded, satisfied with the order.

Tae Hyun's attention returned to Yoori. The fire relinquishing from his eyes, he said, "You just *had* to take off, didn't you?"

"I wasn't feeling well," she replied, dimly hoping the answer would appease the impending argument.

"Well, do you feel a lot better now?"

Yoori bit her lower lip, unable to answer his patronizing question. The truth was he should have slapped her instead. It would've stung less than his sarcasm.

"I got my punishment, didn't I?" she snapped back, releasing herself from his grasp and breaking eye contact. It was difficult to look at him with Ji Hoon's blasphemous words lingering in her mind.

He toned down the censure. "I'll take care of them," he reassured, misinterpreting her cold treatment for him as anger from getting assaulted.

She kept quiet and turned around.

Tae Hyun didn't know. He didn't know that Yoori despised him more than she ever should. She despised him because he was a disappointment to her. She despised him because she had such high hopes for him as a person. But now, with the truth present in her mind, she hated him for not being the better person she thought he could be.

The late afternoon wind gushed past them, ferociously hitting Yoori's bare arms. It not only caused her to shiver, but it also broke her out of her reverie.

"Choi Yoori," she heard Tae Hyun's voice call out from behind her.

She kept her back turned to him and pretended to not hear him.

His footsteps were so light that she didn't even hear him approach her. He gently spun her around to face him.

She was annoyed. She was ready to blow up at him when she realized his intention for spinning her around. Tae Hyun had removed his black hoodie and was offering it to her. His hands parting the bottom fold of the black hoodie, he waited patiently to help her put it on.

"No, thank you," she said, taken aback by the display of kindness.

"Hurry and put it on before you get sick," he replied with a tired voice, already helping slip her right hand through the gap in the hoodie.

"No, I'm seriously fine. I don't need— "

"Choi Yoori," he said sternly.

Resigned to the fact that any further objections would be futile, she closed her eyes and lifted her arms, allowing Tae Hyun the ease of slipping the black hoodie over her head and onto her body. She held her breath when she felt his hand graze her neck. Hating him was becoming more and more difficult.

Tae Hyun gathered the hair devoured by the inner part of the hoodie and lifted it free. He inched it onto one side of her shoulder. He lifted the hood and covered the upper part of her head with it. The hoodie hung a little bigger on her, but it did its job at warming her up.

She kept her silent eyes on him, the pain in her head exacerbating, reminding her of the hostility she was supposed to bear for him. It didn't matter to her how nice he was being. She couldn't bring herself to return the civilized favor. She hated (or wanted to hate) his guts and wasn't too keen on hiding it.

"Are you ready to go?" he asked, his eyes satisfied that she was now sheltered from the cold.

He reached his right hand out and stepped forward, ready to help her walk back to the limo.

She retreated from his reach, her legs staggering, but her face holding firm.

"I need to get some stuff from my apartment," she said at once, her face showing no remorse for her overt cold treatment of him. She wasn't too sure what she needed from her apartment, but she'd figure it out when she got inside. Her main priority right now was to delay any further interaction with him.

Tae Hyun, in response to her reaction, slowly lowered his outstretched hand.

Yoori softened her firm gaze when she noted a hint of disappointment within his eyes as he stared at her questioningly. As his gaze went from her semi-shaking legs to her stern face, she couldn't decipher whether or not he was concerned about her falling to the ground or confused as to why she was treating him so poorly. It could very well be a combination of both.

Releasing a barely audible breath, he turned away from her and faced Kang Min.

"Go with her," he commanded, his tone defeated. "Make sure you help get everything she needs."

Kang Min nodded. "Okay, boss."

Jae Won was ready to follow Kang Min to Yoori. He was stopped by Tae Hyun's stern voice. "You can stay for a little while longer. We have some things we need to discuss."

Yoori, Kang Min and Jac Won exchanged worried glances before looking at Tae Hyun expectantly. What was he up to?

Tae Hyun's eyes settled on Yoori. He raised a questioning brow. "Do you not need to get stuff from your apartment anymore?"

"I do," she said slowly.

"Then please do it soon. I'd like to get you home before it gets dark."

Worry set in. As strange as it may sound, she had already formed an attachment to Jae Won. She didn't want anything to happen to him. Tae Hyun appeared to not like him very much. It was safer for Jae Won if he went with her.

"Can Jae Won come and help me to—?"

Tae Hyun cut her off. "Kang Min will be enough help. Please go before I change my mind."

Knowing that she couldn't save Jae Won from the inevitable nightmare of having a one-on-one conversation with Tae Hyun, she decided it was best to get her stuff without delay. Tae Hyun might really change his mind. She didn't want to test him. Moreover, Jae Won should be fine. Right?

"Let's go, Yoori." Allowing her to lead the way, Kang Min shadowed her closely as she staggered by Tae Hyun. The pain throughout her body worsened with each step. However, she tried to keep her poker-face on.

"Kang Min," Tae Hyun called out when they began to move away.

"Yeah, boss?"

"Make sure she doesn't carry anything," he commanded, his soft eyes on her for a fleeting moment before turning around to face Jae Won.

Kang Min bowed his head before falling into step with Yoori.

Limping along with him, Yoori turned her head to the side. She caught sight of Tae Hyun and Jae Won, both of whom had their arms crossed while speaking in hushed tones. She was extremely curious as to what Tae Hyun wanted to discuss with Jae Won.

Truthfully, she didn't want either of them to get hurt. She hoped that Jae Won would be smart enough to know how to handle Tae Hyun. She hoped that Tae Hyun would be smart enough to control his temper. She hoped that they'd both be smart enough to not do anything stupid.

She turned to face Kang Min. His attention was focused on the destination ahead. Her eyes grew marginally brighter when she realized that she would be able to have some alone time with Kang Min.

The worry for Tae Hyun and Jae Won's one-on-one conversation aside, this was the perfect chance to privately extract some information from the mysterious Kang Min.

"By reminding them what you're capable of."

19: Lookalike

Yoori knew that Kang Min, excluding his interaction with Jae Won, was very skilled at keeping his composure. In the span of the past twenty minutes, as he ran around her room helping her pack up, the only topic of conversations he initiated were ones that consisted of him asking her if she wanted to pack a particular article of clothing. Never once did he bring up anything that pertained to what occurred earlier.

It wasn't like Yoori didn't try to initiate the conversation either. She was anxious to bring up that burning topic, but each time she made the attempt, she was shot down when he very blatantly pretended he didn't hear her.

It was only when he kneeled down to zip up the luggage that she knew she couldn't allow the moment to pass. She couldn't wait any longer to get her answers. It was now or never.

"Are you going to tell me about your part in this whole thing or am I going to get all of my information from Jae Won?" she asked casually, repositioning her seat on the edge of her bed.

He froze. Midway finished with zipping up the last suitcase, he looked up at her cautiously.

Yoori tilted her head. It didn't matter if he planned on making this harder; she was bound and determined to get enough information out of him.

"You two have been in this together since I first met you, right?" she prompted, hoping he would take the leading question and start running with it.

Much to her disappointment (and annoyance), his silence prevailed.

She persisted. "I knew there was something off about you when you knew my name before you were even introduced to me. I knew there was something wrong when you knew that Tae Hyun had brought me to his apartment the night before. I received a call from Jae Won that night before I left with Tae Hyun. Were you following me that night as well?"

"No," he finally answered, no longer able to keep the silence going.

"What is your part in all of this?"

"I have no part in any of this," he said quietly, his cautious gaze diminishing into a soft one. "I was thrown into all of this...thrown in by Jae Won."

Her eyes urged him to continue.

He took a moment's pause. "As I was preparing for my flight for Seoul, I received an unexpected call from Jae Won. We separated from our mutual gang years ago; I never thought I'd hear from him again. But the content of his topic was enough to draw me back in." He swallowed tightly. "He told me that our boss had returned and for whatever reason, she was with the King of Serpents and she went by the name 'Choi Yoori.' I told him that he had gone crazy, but he urged me to see for myself."

He took a second to inhale deeply before continuing. "That morning, when I went to Tae Hyun's apartment, I had expected to see someone who resembled her in only the slightest of ways." His gaze connected with Yoori's. "I couldn't believe my eyes when I saw you. Physically, everything about you mirrored her. But I knew right off the bat that you couldn't be her. Looks aside, you possess none of the qualities that she had."

Yoori's brows inverted. She wasn't sure if he insulted her or not.

He smiled gently at her reaction. "I don't mean anything by it. My boss had a very strong personality. It could never be duplicated by anyone." His voice grew sterner. "And I emphasized that to Jae Won. But Jae Won, being the hopeful that he is, was sure that our boss had returned—that she was only pretending to be someone else. Believing this, he called up Tae Hyun and agreed to formally switch sides. I was with him when he did it. When we received our orders from Tae Hyun to come and find you, I was ready to run to your rescue before Woo even laid his hands on you."

He stood up as if reliving the dramatic incident. His face looked regretful. "But Jae Won...Jae Won said that we should wait. Wait so he could prove to me that you could handle yourself – to prove to me that you really are our boss. So we both watched as Woo assaulted you. It was wrong on my part, but at that moment, I was in the same hopeful mindset as Jae Won. When we saw you raise that broken bottle, I was almost sure that you were her. You were standing in the same fighting stance as she always did. All you had to do was slice his throat. That was all you had to do. But when you allowed the moment to pass, I knew once again that you couldn't be her. Before I even had a chance to take off, Jae Won had pushed me aside and ran to you already."

She nodded, processing the new information. So that was how it all went down. Her eyes became scrutinizing when she was reminded of the last scene where they handed her the gun.

"You still thought I was her when he handed me that gun," she began, wanting to know their intentions after that scene. What if it was really their boss? Her concern for Tae Hyun was sparked. "What was going on in your minds? Were you planning on betraying Tae Hyun and taking over the Underworld with your boss or something? What were you thinking?"

Kang Min raked an aggravated hand through his hair. "I could've strangled Jae Won for his stupidity when he handed you that gun. Jae Won's loyalty, as admirable as it may be at times, will be his death one day."

"And where does your loyalty lie?" As much as she didn't want to show that she cared about Tae Hyun's well-being, she was still worked up about it. She condemned what he did to his own brother, but she didn't want him to get hurt either.

Kang Min's eyes became foggy. "At a young age, I swore my life to my boss. When it comes down to it, she will always have my loyalty. But now that she's gone, I have since moved on." He held her gaze. "I know what you're thinking and yes, my loyalty lies with Tae Hyun. What happened with Jae Won was unexpected, something I couldn't control."

Kang Min looked certain that he would never betray Tae Hyun, but Yoori wasn't satisfied. There were too many loopholes in his statement. One of the loopholes was obviously Jae Won. She was confident of that.

"If you gave Jae Won's motives up to Tae Hyun, then it'll be in your control," she instigated, trying to see how far Kang Min's loyalties went for Jae Won.

A bitter smiled appeared on his face. "I could never do that."

"Why are you so adamant with protecting Jae Won?"

Kang Min's smile grew. "It's kinda hard to turn your back on your older brother."

Yoori leaned back, flabbergasted. "Older brother?"

He nodded.

She stared, openmouthed. Brothers? It was an odd mixture. Their subtle resemblance to one another was enough to have her infer that they were related, but it wasn't enough to have her assume that they were brothers. Things kept getting stranger and stranger.

"How old are you again?" she asked, her curiosity mounting.

"Eighteen."

"And how old is Jae Won?"

"Twenty."

She blinked in surprise. She knew that Kang Min was younger than her, but she didn't realize that Jae Won was also younger than her. Now that she thought about it, they had an interesting dynamic between them. The brothers appeared close enough to each other, but there was one thing that didn't make sense. Why would two brothers split off and join different gangs? Why didn't they stay with their boss if they were so loyal to her? Why would they leave?

"Why did you two part ways and joined different gangs?" she asked, finding it hard to keep this question to herself.

Before Kang Min could even think to answer, he was punctually interrupted by a familiar voice.

"Kang Min," the voice called out from Yoori's living room.

Yoori's eyes snagged on the owner of the voice.

Speak of the Devil, she thought ironically, watching as Jae Won made his way into her bedroom. She looked him up and down. No bloodied up face, no bruises, no dislocated jaw, no broken bones. The conversation with Tae Hyun must have gone well.

Jae Won stopped in front of Kang Min. "He's waiting for you outside."

Yoori raised a speculative brow. Why was Tae Hyun having a solo session with each of the brothers?

She watched the two brothers exchange knowing glances before turning their attention to her.

"I'll see you out there," Kang Min said before vacating the room. He seemed relieved to be free of her and her interrogations.

Under any other circumstances, she would've been upset with him for leaving during such a crucial part of the conversation. However, Jae Won's presence more than made up for Kang Min's absence. Since she was done interrogating one brother, she'd go after the other.

Her eyes darted over to Jae Won when Kang Min made his exit. The reminiscence of a child's smile brightened Jae Won's face as he edged closer to her. She couldn't help but adore the guy. He looked so cute whenever he smiled like that.

"Hey boss," he said happily.

She glowered. She suddenly adored him less.

"Haven't we established that I'm not your boss?" she said grimly, annoyed that he'd even dare to start calling her that name again.

"Actually you are. It's been confirmed by Tae Hyun."

Yoori was dumbfounded. "What?"

"The almighty King of Serpents," he began in a somewhat mocking, but playful tone, "has made me his assistant's personal bodyguard. So again, hello boss."

"How did this happen?" she inquired, forgetting that she wanted to learn more about him and his past. Screw that for now. Her future was more important. "What did you guys talk about?"

Jae Won shook his head. "A lot of what we talked about is confidential, but he basically asked me what it would take for me to be loyal to the Serpents. I told him I wanted to work with you. And as in work with you, I mean watch over you."

Yoori scoffed disbelievingly. "And he agreed to it?"

"He's a smart guy. He can't always be there to watch you, which is where I come in."

"You're both off your hinges. I don't need you guys to watch me like I'm a five-year-old."

"We're just looking out for you."

"Seriously Jae Won, I don't need your protection or his protection for that matter. I'm a big girl."

"That's the thing," he said patiently, kneeling on one knee next to the edge of her bed. He regarded the dried blood on the side of her lips. "That's all that you are in this world. You're just a girl. A girl amongst a society of people trained to be Gods and killers. And not just any girl at that, but a girl who has seemingly become the King of Serpent's new girlfriend."

"I'm not his—"

"*Seemingly*," Jae Won stressed. "You have to understand that in this world, appearances matter. Tae Hyun has tremendous power over this society, but in the same sense, he also has a lot of enemies. Because of this, your life is in danger in more ways than one. He understands that. You need to as well."

"Seriously Jae Won. Out of all the positions you could've gotten within Tae Hyun's gang, you *voluntarily* chose to be my bodyguard? Are you thinking straight?"

What was wrong with him? From the looks of it, Jae Won could have very well become another sub-leader in Tae Hyun's gang. Instead, he chose to work under her?

Gazing at her, almost in reverence, he grabbed hold of her hand.

"I failed once before to protect her," he began, his eyes never leaving hers. "I'm not going to fail again. You're it, Yoori. You're my second chance at making things right. I failed once before, but it won't happen again. I won't let it happen again."

Yoori felt a torrent of admiration flow over her for Jae Won. Truthfully, she was touched by his loyalty, even if she knew it wasn't for her. In that instance, she found herself growing envious of this Soo Jin girl who had all the guys in her life so mesmerized. First it was Ji Hoon, who had a one-night stand with her and couldn't even forget her to the point where he had mistaken Yoori to be her. And now she met Jae Won and Kang Min, both of whom were still obviously loyal to her.

All of this is a mistake, she thought with frustration.

How similar did she look to this girl? It didn't take Ji Hoon long before he realized that she no longer resembled Soo Jin, but for Jae Won and Kang Min, even after realizing that she wasn't Soo Jin, they were still looking at her like she was. The boys told her she resembled Soo Jin almost perfectly, but Ji Hoon said that she actually bared little resemblance to her in broad daylight. But then again, Soo Jin was merely a one-night stand. Ji Hoon's opinion of the resemblance didn't have as much credibility as the brothers'.

Her curiosity was getting the best of her. She had to go further into it. She had to know more.

"Your boss. Is her name Soo Jin?" she asked, finally ready to say her name out loud. It didn't occur to her that it might've been a bad idea to get into this topic of conversation.

Jae Won gaped at her dubiously. "How do you know her name?"

"I've heard it in passing," she said, excluding the fact that she found out from Ji Hoon.

"Yeah, that's her name," he confirmed. His eyes grew noticeably warmer at the reminder of his boss's name.

"What if she comes back and sees you calling me boss? Aren't you afraid? Wouldn't she be pissed off?"

Jae Won smiled. "I highly doubt that."

"Why do you doubt it?"

He grew silent as he released his hold on her hand and stood up. She could tell by the sadness of his eyes that it was a touchy subject for him.

"She's dead," he said simply.

A chasm materialized in her stomach. Soo Jin...Ji Hoon's one-night stand...Jae Won and Kang Min's boss...was *dead*?

She gazed at Jae Won apologetically. She felt horrible. "I'm really sorry. I didn't know."

Way to go, dumbass, she thought angrily. If she could shoot herself for her own stupidity, then she probably would've been dead several times over. All this time, she had presumed that Soo Jin merely went missing. But of course Soo Jin was dead. All the conversations that she had with these people clearly indicated that she was dead. Why did it take Yoori so long to come to this conclusion?

He waved his hand as a gesture for her to let it go. "It's been a while, don't worry about it." He bent down and picked up the luggage from the floor. "We really should go. We shouldn't keep Tae Hyun waiting."

He stopped, reminded of something when he mentioned Tae Hyun's name.

"Yoori," he started grimly.

"Hmm?"

"It is safer," he started, "if you didn't mention to Tae Hyun who you resemble."

Yoori laughed wearily. "It's not something I would—"

"Just for future references," he interrupted, his voice never losing its severity. "Whatever happens, don't tell him that I had mistaken you to be her. In fact, don't tell anyone that Kang Min and I had mistaken you to be her. Our boss was very well known in this world. There aren't a lot of people who know what she looked like, but if word gets out that there's a lookalike walking around, your life will be in danger—more so than it is right now. It is safer to keep this between the three of us."

Yoori nodded fearfully. Could Jae Won make this sound any scarier? Her curiosity for Soo Jin grew to unprecedented heights. She was already interested in this boss of his, now she was fascinated.

"She must be something," commented Yoori.

Jae Won nodded distractedly. "You have no idea. An Soo Jin was one of a kind."

Yoori snapped her head up like she had been electrocuted.

An Soo Jin?

Why did that last name sound so familiar?

"An Soo Jin?" she asked to reconfirm.

Jae Won nodded again. He looked like he was really anxious to leave. "We shouldn't keep Tae Hyun waiting." A sour expression skewed his visage. "The guy doesn't seem to have much patience for anything."

Yoori didn't hear his remark. Her mind was preoccupied with something else.

An Soo Jin.

She repeated the name in her head like a mantra.

An Soo Jin...An Soo Jin...An Soo Jin...

Her heart jolted to a stop.

It was as though a light bulb illumed in her head.

An Soo Jin?

An Young Jae?

Her eyes gradually returned to Jae Won, who seemed unaware of the change in her stupefied eyes.

"What gang were you a part of again?" she inquired slowly, the pit forming deeper within her stomach. Why did she have the feeling that this Soo Jin girl was about to become someone Yoori didn't want her to be?

He smiled. "Anything I say stays between us?"

She nodded inattentively, more interested in the answer at hand.

"I formed the Dragons gang three years ago," he began. "Before that, Kang Min and I were part of the Scorpions gang, one of the three most powerful gangs in South Korea at that time. We were under the direct order of An Soo Jin. If you've heard her name in passing, then you must know her nickname."

He looked at her briefly before stepping out of her bedroom, utterly oblivious to the fact that Yoori froze like a block of ice.

"She was known as the Queen of the Underworld."

Walking out, Jae Won failed to see the state he left Choi Yoori in.

With her eyes nearly popping out of her sockets, she stared at the doorframe in complete disbelief. The truth was, this day in general had been downright confusing. Yet, this little piece of information, so casually conveyed by Jae Won, took the cake as the most mystifying.

She furrowed her brows, attempting to organize her frantic thoughts.

She was the lookalike of An Soo Jin.

An Soo Jin was the Scorpion girl.

The Scorpion girl was the Queen of the Underworld.

Therefore...Choi Yoori was the lookalike of the Queen of the Underworld?

Her world slowed to a stop.

Running her fingers through her hair, there were only three words to properly sum up Choi Yoori's feelings at that particular moment.

"Shit. Holy Shit."

"Notoriety is everything."

20: Less than Human

Yoori recalled the moment she woke up from her car accident three years ago.

She was in the hospital, in some city a couple of hours from her hometown. The first thing she remembered feeling when she woke up was soreness. There was a bandage wrapped around her head and bandages all over her body. The second thing she remembered feeling was confusion, complete and utter confusion as two strangers she didn't know, a middle-aged man and woman, leapt up from their seats and came running to her bed.

"Yoori!" they cried, hugging her with relief. "We were so worried! Are you okay? Where are you hurt?"

The entire time, as they slammed her with question after question, Yoori could only remember being overwhelmed. Her mind swirled and she tried to search her memories for their faces, their names – essentially any memory she had of them. All she could draw was a blank.

"Wh-who are you?" she asked them, causing them to cease with their screams.

Yoori swallowed, breathing roughly as they pulled away from her, stunned that she asked them such a question. Her lower lip quivering, she tried to recall her own name, her own identity, her own life. When she drew a blank again, her head began to throb.

Brokenly, she whispered, "Who's Yoori?"

Yoori would never forget the moment the woman broke into tears while the man ran out of the room to get the doctor. When the doctor and nurses came in, they took the man and woman out. After what felt like an eternity, the doctor explained to her that the car accident caused tremendous trauma to her head. For this reason, she had lost any memory she had of her previous life. He explained other things to her, but at this point, Yoori couldn't find the strength to listen. All she could focus on was the fact that her mind was blank. A complete and utter blank.

When she went home with her family weeks later, it worsened. She assumed her parents would do everything in their power to help her regain her memory, but it was the exact opposite. Reasoning that all of this was a blessing in disguise, they refused to help her. They only told her that God meant for this to happen because he wanted to give her another chance. She was such a disobedient daughter the years leading up to her accident that they were intent on making sure that she would never revert back to her old ways again. If that meant not helping to regain her memories, then so be it. The most they did when she pleaded for help was show her old family pictures of their happier times. Apart from that small mercy, they were of no help.

Disheartened, Yoori gave up.

If her parents were so disappointed in her the years leading to her amnesia, then Yoori herself reasoned that perhaps it was best for everyone if she became the obedient daughter they'd always wanted. No matter how little memories she had of them, she still respected them as her parents and because of this, she respected their wishes as well. If they didn't want her to regain her memories, then she would oblige. If she was such a horrible person in her "previous" life, then she did not want to remember either. She was given a second chance and Yoori was determined to make the most of it.

This was the memory that replayed in her mind after finding out that she was the lookalike of the most infamous Queen in the Underworld.

It took Yoori all the physical and psychological strength she had to not fall to her death as she descended down the long windy stairs of her apartment complex. Firmly gripping on the silver railing that curved into the stairs, each dreadful step she took played out as a reminder to the haunting words that churned in her congested mind.

I look like An Soo Jin, she thought while she walked down. Her pulse hammered, the vibrancy of life draining from her face. *And An Soo Jin is the Scorpion girl...Queen of the Underworld...*

Each word felt like daggers to her soul.

For Yoori, this revelation felt like it would be the equivalent of her finding out that she'd been diagnosed with some incurable disease.

How could she have been so dense? The answers were all right in front of her. It all made sense now. She now understood why some of Tae Hyun's men reacted the way that they did when they first saw her. She now fully understood the predicament Jae Won and Kang Min were in when they thought that their boss had returned from the dead. The gang leader of all gang leaders had seemingly returned from the grave to plague them once more. It all made sense now.

Well, everything made sense except for Ji Hoon.

His voice echoed in her mind as she took another step down the stairs.

A one-night stand.

He lied. He blatantly lied. An Soo Jin was obviously not a one-night stand.

Bastard lied like no other, Yoori thought with venom.

And if he lied about Soo Jin being a one-night stand, then she was sure that he lied when he told her that she no longer resembled Soo Jin to him. She couldn't understand his motives though. Why the hell would he lie?

When she took the final step off the stairwell, Yoori cast her attention to the biggest catalyst for her headache.

She'd be a fool if she didn't take her amnesia into consideration when thinking about the possibility that she so strongly (in the eyes of others) resembled that girl. In the same token, she'd be a fool if she considered the chances of her actually *being* the heartless gang leader. How could the spineless Choi Yoori ever be the Queen of the Underworld?

Yoori neglected to thank Jae Won when he held open the exiting door for her. She was still in the midst of trying to organize her thoughts – and her sanity. Thank God for Tae Hyun's hoodie for doing a wonderful job of concealing her face. It prevented Jae Won from seeing how flabbergasted she was.

This could just be a big fat coincidence, she rationalized with a smidgen of hope.

If she had woken up with no family, then she would've taken into account that she may be the Scorpion girl. But no, she woke up *with* a family who reminded her about her life prior to the car accident. It wasn't much of a life, but it was a life she lived with them regardless. They even showed her *pictures* for Heaven's sake! Photographic evidence of her existence as their daughter. In addition to that, An Soo Jin's brother verified that Soo Jin did indeed die. There was no possible chance that Yoori could be An Soo Jin. She was sure of it. No possible way.

Her heart grew heavy when the auburn streak of the setting sun ran over her. It could very well be the chill she got from the wind that flew by, but she could've sworn she felt a hint of doubt course through her. It was times like these when she hated that she had amnesia. Even when she was sure that she couldn't be An Soo Jin, there was still another part of her that doubted the verity of that statement.

All because of the amnesia.

She closed her eyes and stopped walking.

She couldn't let anyone know about her amnesia. If anyone found out, especially Jae Won or Kang Min, then they'd go back to believing that she was the Scorpion girl. If anyone found out, then only horrifying demons would frequent her future. Her life would essentially be sentenced to death if anyone in this society found out.

The knot in Yoori's stomach tightened.

She couldn't let that happen. She *wouldn't* let that happen. Even if there was the slightest possible chance that she was An Soo Jin, she wouldn't accept it. Unless there was foolproof evidence that she was An Soo Jin, she would not accept slight possibilities. Because, truth to God, fearing for her life aside, Yoori was disgusted with Soo Jin more so than anything. Call it naivety, call it stupidity or call it denial—Yoori didn't want to entertain the fact that she was a psychotic serial killer and she would be damned if she allowed anyone else to tell her otherwise. This was her life and she was going to do what she wanted with it.

Inhaling the fresh air, she swore that this issue wouldn't bother her any longer—at least for the moment. At least for the moment she would let it go. For tonight and the remaining days to come, she was Choi Yoori. The one who resembled An Soo Jin, but wasn't An Soo Jin. The one and only Choi Yoori.

"If you don't let your body rest soon, you'll be handicapped before you know it," a voice said briskly behind her.

Forgoing her headache ensuing thoughts, she scrunched her face at the new distraction at hand. "Huh?"

A strong arm laid itself behind her back while the other reached behind her legs and literally swept her off her feet.

"Ahh!" she cried, instinctively encircling her arms around Tae Hyun's neck as a preventative measure to avoid falling flat on the ground. By doing so, she had also inadvertently relinquished the remaining thoughts about her resemblance to a particular gang leader.

"Holding you like this is fast becoming a favorite hobby of mine," he said jokingly, a smile twinkling in his eyes.

When the initial shock left her that she was indeed fighting gravity, she looked at Tae Hyun with eyes wide open.

"What do you think you're doing?" she cried, her arms tight around his neck.

He smirked, very amused with her reaction. He bent close to her ear and whispered, "Being a good boyfriend."

His eyes traveled over hers as if hoping the little joke would lead her to crack a smile.

The gravity in her expression remained.

"Don't joke about something like that," she said crossly, even though her cheeks grew a deeper shade of pink.

He faked a wounded expression. "Some girls like this, you know?"

"I'm not like other girls."

He laughed. "No need to tell me twice."

She glared. She hated that he was trying to be nice again. He was making it harder for her to dislike him and she resented that.

Moments later, his laughter subsided and his expression gradually grew serious. "You shouldn't put anymore pressure on your legs. Do you know how frail you looked limping out of the door like that?" He eyed her with concern. "Just relax. I got your back."

"I can walk. I don't need you carrying me." She released her hold over his neck and attempted to remove herself from his grasp.

Tae Hyun repositioned himself just in time to keep her within his hold. His expression was uncompromising. "You're not walking. I'll throw you over my shoulder if I have to. It's either I carry you like this or I carry you caveman style. It's your choice."

Yoori gawked at him. She knew he wasn't bluffing. However, she had some fight left in her and she didn't feel like letting him win. With her right arm dangling freely, she held his gaze challengingly.

He tilted his head and looked at her tiredly. "Stop being so stubborn."

Her challenging eyes and free dangling hand remained.

Tae Hyun smirked, leaning in closer to her ear. "If you keep insisting, then cave man style it is..."

He could very well be bluffing, but as Tae Hyun made a move to reposition his hold on her, Yoori yelped in fear. She quickly encircled her hands around his neck, thereby forgoing any challenge or fight she had left. She didn't want to be carried caveman style and have her butt hanging in the air for the three guys to see.

She heard Tae Hyun laugh at her reaction. He steadied his hold on her. "To tell you the truth, I prefer to carry you like this. Bridal style. Much more romantic, don't you think?"

Yoori looked away instead of replying. All of this was pure torture. She hated him, but he was making it hard for her to *keep* hating him.

"Why are you being nice all of a sudden?" she voiced with frustration, hoping that he'd make it easier for her to give him the cold shoulder by being his usual hotheaded self. "This is so unlike you. Stop it. It's freaking me out."

His grasp on her tightened. "Let's just say," he began, staring down at her with a soft gaze, "I owe you for what happened in the warehouse." He smiled. "If my assistant can muster up the courage to attempt to save my life, then I can muster up the nerve to be a little bit nicer to her, if only for a couple of moments."

If there ever was a spare moment for Yoori to be touched by the sincerity of Tae Hyun's uncharacteristic words, this was that moment.

Closing her eyes, it took all the strength she had to block out Tae Hyun's words. She refused to be touched by what he said. She refused to allow him to make it harder for her to despise him. She couldn't let him get to her. She was determined about that.

"Put me down."

"Choi Yoori. Why are you acting like this—?"

"Maybe it'll be a better idea if I carry her," Jae Won spoke up, sensing Yoori's discomfort.

Tae Hyun turned to glare at Jae Won.

Unaware of the fury blazing in Tae Hyun's eyes (as Jae Won *did* interrupt him while he was speaking), Jae Won handed both of the suitcases he was holding to Kang Min. He took a step forward with his arms outstretched, ready to help take Yoori off of Tae Hyun's arms.

He only stalled when he saw the death glare Tae Hyun bestowed upon him.

"Don't. Touch. Her," Tae Hyun warned dangerously, taking a step away from Jae Won.

Jae Won gaped at Tae Hyun in dismay. He turned to Kang Min with a "what's-his-problem" look on his face.

Without so much as another word, Tae Hyun took off in the direction of the limo, leaving the brothers behind.

Kang Min merely shrugged, a broad grin curving on his face as he watched Tae Hyun carry Yoori in his arms. He patted Jae Won's shoulder. "I guess the new commandment is that no one touches Choi Yoori except Kwon Tae Hyun." He began to follow them. He threw another look at his older brother before quickening his pace after them. "And no one interrupts him while he's talking to her."

Jae Won scoffed in amusement after hearing Kang Min's interpretation. He took a moment to think it over himself. A small, knowing grin graced his face. Stifling a bout of laughter, he ran after his younger brother and his two bosses.

"Jesus, you're such a psycho!" Yoori cried, tightening her hold around his neck, forgetting for a moment about giving him the cold shoulder. The speed at which he carried her scared the hell out of Yoori. Who knew Tae Hyun could power walk this fast while carrying someone?

Ignoring her insult, he quickened his pace toward the limo.

"Jae Won," he called out once he reached the vehicle.

Jae Won swiftly opened the door. Carefully, Tae Hyun got in. Gently placing Yoori on her side of the seat, Tae Hyun reached for the door and pulled it closed.

"But what about Jae Won and Kang Min?" Yoori asked when they threw her luggage into the trunk of the limo.

Couldn't they come too? She didn't want to be alone with Tae Hyun.

"They have other things they need to get done tonight," Tae Hyun said simply, the engine of the limo igniting. Smoothly, it drove off.

"What other things?" she asked suspiciously.

"Confidential stuff." The limo picked up pace. "Stuff you shouldn't concern yourself with."

Yoori grimaced at his reply. He never fully answers her questions. Instead of picking at that point, she decided it was best to keep quiet and let it go.

She nodded absentmindedly as her reply to him. She was getting anxious. She hadn't been completely alone with Tae Hyun since their morning together when he cooked breakfast.

That episode felt like a lifetime ago, she thought with unexpected grief.

She turned her attention to the shifting scenery outside her window. So much had happened since that morning and the only thing that lingered in her mind were Ji Hoon's words about what Tae Hyun did.

She honestly didn't know how to act around Tae Hyun right now. What was she supposed to say to the guy?

I know that you told me that you're a monster, but I never believed you could be an actual monster and kill your own brother, she thought solemnly. That was what she wanted to say to him, but her mouth remained shut. She didn't have the courage—or the heart—to say it.

"You know," he finally uttered, breaking Yoori from her train of thoughts. "It's probably just me, but if I didn't know better, I'd say you were angry at me." He assessed her. "More so than you usually are."

"I'm just really tired." She felt his gaze on her, but she didn't turn to face him. She didn't want to. It was easier to give someone the cold shoulder when you didn't have to look at him directly. She wanted to tell him to get the hint and move on. Wasn't it obvious that she didn't want to have any further interaction with him?

To her surprise, Tae Hyun didn't say another word for the majority of the car ride. She didn't know what was running in his mind, but she could sense his growing irritation.

"Choi Yoori," he finally spoke out again.

No longer able to ignore him, Yoori drew her attention to Tae Hyun. She eyed him with anticipation, expecting him to say more than her name. For the first time since she had known him, she could've sworn there was an ounce of confusion within his eyes. It was as if he didn't know what to say to her either. The thick silence lengthened. After several more seconds, he parted his lips, finally ready to articulate his thoughts. Yet almost immediately, he stalled.

A sudden speck of life appeared in his blank eyes when they settled onto Yoori's lips. Whatever Tae Hyun had wanted to tell Yoori became second priority to the blood coating her lips. Distracted by the malady, Tae Hyun reached for a tissue box beside him. After pulling out several strips, he grabbed a water bottle and dabbed the tissues with it. Placing the water bottle aside, he moved closer to her.

"Stop," she breathed, knowing what he intended to do with the moist tissue. "I can do it myself." She reached for it, but he eased it away from her.

His eyes still gentle, he lifted her chin with his left hand. The touch caused tingling sensations to run over her body. For a nanosecond, all the pain within her body vanished.

"I can do it," he whispered, delicately wiping the dried blood off the side of her mouth.

Yoori flinched at the coolness exerted from the tissue. It was really cold.

As a response to her unpleasant reaction to the moist tissue, Tae Hyun leaned in closer. Stopping mere inches from her semi-quivering lips, he began to delicately blow warm air on the bloody corner of her mouth, a mechanism used to offset the coolness of the moist tissue.

"What am I going to do with you, assistant?" He lifted her chin a little higher, effectively leaving her with butterflies fluttering around in her stomach.

He continued to dab with care.

Her eyes became dazed as she sat rigid in her seat, her heart hammering at a rapid pace.

Why was he being like this? Did he really not realize how much she despised him? Didn't he realize that she hated him more than anything right now? She hated him for the simple fact that he was a monster and for the simple fact that he made it so much harder for her to hate him—especially when he exerted so much kindness to her.

Yet, she knew all of this was fabricated reality.

The truth was...he was a monster.

A monster that killed his own brother.

Resentment coiled inside her like a snake while she felt each careful dab. Her firm gaze narrowed onto his distracted eyes.

Her lips parted. She was finally ready to ask the most anticipated question of the day. "Did you really kill your own brother?"

If there had been music playing in the background, then it would have stopped when Yoori asked that dreaded question. The dabbing immediately ceased as a muscle worked in Tae Hyun's jaw.

He lifted his eyes up to meet with hers, his left hand drawing away from her chin.

She knew the answer from his reaction.

Guilty.

Without a doubt, Tae Hyun killed his own brother.

Every iota of vulnerability that was once present within his eyes vanished. He smirked knowingly. "This is what you and Ji Hoon talked about?"

Now it was Yoori's turn to stiffen her jaw. "How did you know—?"

"I ran into him while I was on my way to find you," he interrupted, his voice suppressing his obvious anger with her. He tossed the moist tissue on the floor and turned away from her. He focused his eyes on the changing scenery outside the limo window.

"Ran into him? You mean you saw him after the warehouse?"

He ignored her question.

"Tae Hyun." Her patience, the little amount she had left, was wearing thin. Now was not the time for him to ignore her.

"He told me that the two of you had an informative chat," he shared calmly, his back turned to her. "I should have known that bringing up my brother would've been in his bag of tricks."

Her mind was boggling. They talked. They *talked*? Right after she left Ji Hoon? What the hell? She wanted to know more about the content of their conversation. Obviously it concerned her, but to what degree? Though her curiosity about the two gang leaders' run-in was momentarily sparked, it didn't hold a candle to the confrontation that was about to ensue with Tae Hyun. She could care less what they talked about. The only thing that mattered now was Tae Hyun and his unforgivable sin.

"You didn't answer my question."

Tae Hyun laughed. He gazed back at her. "Why should I? You already know the answer."

"You're right, I do know the answer. But what I want to know is do you really have no remorse for what you did?" Her anger heightened. "He's your *brother*."

She resented that she still hoped that he could still be a better person. All Tae Hyun had to do was show some remorse. All he had to do was show a bit of regret and show that he wasn't hopeless after all. That was all he had to do.

"I know who he is," Tae Hyun snapped back, no longer able to hold his composure. His dark eyes narrowed onto hers. "And yes, to answer your question, I really have no remorse for what I did. If given the chance, I'd kill him again without a second thought."

168

That was all it took for Tae Hyun to annihilate any shred of hope that Yoori had for him and his humanity.

The limo came to a slow stop in that very same second.

He blinked down at her. "What else do you expect me to say?"

Yoori narrowed her cold eyes onto an equally frustrated Tae Hyun. She simply scoffed at him. To her, he said more than enough.

"Congratulations Kwon Tae Hyun," she said through gritted teeth. She shoved the limo door open. She no longer cared about making an effort to be civil with him. "You really are the bad guy in this story."

Stepping out of the limo, she slammed the door in disgust. She began to limp away to his apartment. She was bound and determined to never allow herself to get any closer to him. She may have to be his assistant for the next couple of months, but that didn't mean she had to talk to him.

"Yoori!" she heard him scream after her.

She ignored his call and picked up speed.

"Choi Yoori!" he shouted again before slamming the limo door closed. "Damn it! CHOI YOORI!"

Without an acknowledgment for his calls, her pace accelerated.

"What a way to end a horrible day," she muttered bitterly, stepping into Tae Hyun's apartment complex.

She just wanted to sleep. Her body needed to rest. Nothing else mattered anymore. Kwon Tae Hyun, that monster, no longer mattered.

She was done with him.

"Make sure they will never betray you again."

21: Trust

The next three days flew by without Yoori uttering so much as a word to Tae Hyun.

At the offset, it worked out well. Tae Hyun respected (more or less) the cold shoulder she was giving him and was even adamant on giving her the cold shoulder too. After the second day, however, he was overtly becoming displeased with the entire situation. The cold shoulder was starting to get to him.

Though her anger had subsided since that night, Yoori was still angry enough about the entire situation to keep the cold treatment going. Rational or not, Yoori hated being disappointed. Whether Tae Hyun realized that he disappointed her or not was not the issue. The only issue was that he disappointed her, and now she really didn't want to be around him. In addition to the disappointment, there was something else that she was angry about. Something about Tae Hyun's situation sparked a nerve within her – a guilt-filled nerve. A guilt-filled nerve that remained a question mark for her. A nerve that stupendously aggravated her. If she had it her way, she'd continue the cold shoulder for the rest of her time with him.

Unfortunately for Yoori, Tae Hyun had never been a fan of getting the cold shoulder and he was not intent on hiding that fact.

"We have to talk," he verbalized, grabbing her wrist and leading her into the bedroom after she walked out of the bathroom.

She bit her freshly washed lips in irritation as he tossed her onto the bed. She tipped slightly to the side when she made impact with the mattress. She had just woken up and was still feeling somewhat fatigued, but this assertive conversation starter really woke her up. She sat upright and glared at Tae Hyun.

"I don't have much to say to you," she replied bluntly, smoothing her pajamas before repositioning herself in her seat.

He cleared the distance between them and placed both of his hands on the bed, on either side of her body. Still standing, he leaned in closer to her, stopping only when his face was inches from hers. This particular action caused Yoori's heart to beat rapidly, a sensation that was becoming vastly common nowadays.

She swallowed slowly.

It baffled Yoori that even when he wore casual black pajamas, he still exuded so much power. Where could she bottle some of that power?

He studied her intently, his eyes leveling with hers.

"Choi Yoori," he began diplomatically, the minty freshness of his newly brushed breath assailing her nose. "It's been three days. I've been considerate enough to sleep in the living room because I knew you wanted to be left alone. I've been patient because I realize that you need to blow off steam from what happened the other day." His tone signaled the beginnings of an eroded patience. "But this is getting ridiculous. You of all people should know that I hate being ignored."

"I'm not ignoring you," she retorted. She manufactured a look of disinterest. "I'm giving you the cold shoulder. There's a big difference."

"Oh yeah," he replied sarcastically. "The difference does make me feel a whole lot better."

"I don't care about making you feel better," she snapped back at once.

A look of exasperation colored his countenance. He grew quiet for some time before his lips parted again. "What can I do to make things better?" It was evident in his demeanor that he never had to ask that question in his life. "Just tell me."

Yoori snorted. "Am I hearing right? Is the King of Serpents begging for forgiveness?"

"I'm not begging for forgiveness. I'm compromising. There's a big difference," he replied, mimicking Yoori's previous retort.

Her irritation with him intensified.

He closed his eyes as if to reprimand himself for accidentally mocking her. He opened his eyes once more. "I don't like that you're giving me the 'cold shoulder.' So whatever it is that I need to do to make things right, just tell me."

"There's nothing you can do." The verity of her statement disappointed her.

He tilted his head, suspicion rousing his expression. "Is all of this really about my brother? I get that you're upset about the news, but he's my brother, not yours. Why are you so upset?"

Tae Hyun really should've shoved her instead of asking her that question. How was she supposed to respond to that?

"I expected more from you. I thought you were a better person. So I'm sorry. Sorry for thinking that you were a better person than you really are. Sorry for not being able to see you for the scum that you truly are. Sorry for being stupid and having hope and disappointing myself in the end. And sorry for allowing the news to affect something deep within me—something I can't figure out. It's killing me. All of this is killing me."

No. She definitely wasn't going to tell him all of that. Absolutely not.

"No, this isn't just about your brother," she speedily lied. "I'm sick and tired of being handcuffed to you."

He looked at her incredulously, not believing her line of reasoning. "Are you serious? I've left you alone for the last couple of days. I haven't even taken out those cuffs."

"That's not the point," she argued, the factualness of her "lie" surprising her too.

Now that she had the nerve to bring it up, she realized that she was pissed off about the cuffs. She was frustrated with her *entire* situation with him in general. She looked at him harshly. She might as well let it all out now.

"I feel like a caged bird. I can't go anywhere without being by your side. I'm suffocating here."

Tae Hyun took a moment to process her words. He nodded in understanding. A charming smile kissed his lips as he leaned in closer to her. "You know, some girls count their blessings when they're around me as much as you have been."

Yoori inverted her brows in aversion. "I count my curses," she said, even though it was only half true.

He smirked. "Fair enough."

Perplexity milled into her eyes. Needless to say, she was taken aback as she watched him nod in understanding.

"Go," he said briskly.

Her bafflement escalated. "Huh?"

"Go," he repeated. "Go ahead and go out today. See whoever you need to see. Do whatever you want."

"You're joking," she spluttered, still surprised by the words emitting from his mouth.

"No, I'm serious. This is my compromise. Today is your day. Do whatever you want. I won't interfere."

She ogled him. This was so unlike him. "Are you completely serious?"

He simply nodded to confirm.

"So that's it?"

"That's it."

"It's not that easy, you know," she said warningly, a big part of her already set on still giving him the cold shoulder—even after her day off. "It's going to take more than one day of freedom to make all that's happened go away."

He smiled at her less than promising premise on what the future may hold. "The goal right now is to make my assistant happy. We'll worry about the rest of the compromises later."

Yoori nodded distractedly, perplexed as to why she wasn't as excited about her "day off" from work as she should be. She peered up guardedly. She was instantly reminded of her unfavorable position in the world now that she was associated with Tae Hyun.

"Should I bring Jae Won with me?"

"He's on assignment right now."

She blew a maddened breath. "So much for being my bodyguard."

His smile remained. "These next couple of days was supposed to be me by your side. He's not your only bodyguard, you know?" There was humor in his voice as he easily held her gaze. "I could always go out with you to watch over you today..."

She made a rude noise. "Won't that defeat the purpose of my 'day off' then?"

172

He shrugged, fabricating cluelessness. However good his acting skills were, she knew what he was trying to do.

She raised her chin up. "I'll be fine by myself."

He chuckled and straightened up. "If you insist on going out alone, I suggest you go somewhere that's packed with people. There will be less Underworld activities there."

He turned on his heels and set off for the door.

"I'm seriously going," she cried after him. It was more of an act to get confirmation than anything else. She still wasn't sure if he was really serious.

His next response gave her all the confirmation she needed. "Have fun out there."

With a wave of the hand, he turned the doorknob and left the room, leaving a dazed Yoori in his wake.

■ ■ ■

As pathetic as it may sound, Yoori was actually becoming bored with her "day off." Treading around the mall for about five hours without buying anything wasn't exactly her idea of a fun day.

The truth was, she'd much rather call up Chae Young and hang out with her. However, even though she missed her friend, Yoori was also cautious of the repercussions of her company. The last thing she wanted was to put Chae Young in any danger. Moreover, the road leading to the diner was infested with Underworld activities. Given what she had been put through with Jin Ae, she decided it was best if she stayed in an area where Underworld activities were scarce.

A heavy boredom surfaced over her when she stepped outside of the mall and into the busy streets. She consulted her watch. It was only 7:06 P.M. Surely she couldn't return to Tae Hyun's apartment as of yet, especially after making such a big deal about feeling like a "caged bird."

Her bored eyes wandered over the street she was slowly becoming cemented to. She was looking for a distraction, anything to keep her occupied.

As if on cue, a beautiful looking red convertible Mercedes manifested across the street. Yoori was gearing up to leave for her next unknown destination when it arrested her attention. It was a bad habit. You see a nice car and you have to see if the owner is as hot as the car.

This particular car and its owner both passed the test in terms of being easy on the eyes. Midway with continuing with her walk, Yoori spared another glance at the owner who was getting out of the car. He wore a dark blue dress shirt with a loose black tie, dark faded jeans and stylish looking aviator sunglasses. Yoori found herself feeling some familiarity toward the guy.

"Who is that?" she breathed, lost in a momentary trance. "That looks like Lee Ji Hoon," she said absentmindedly, the impact of her own observation not yet hitting her.

Her gaze lingered on him.

It was only after the guy took off his sunglasses that Yoori's eyes bloomed in recognition.

Shit!

It *was* Lee Ji Hoon!

Instinctively, Yoori flung herself into hiding behind a big pot of plants that embellished the sidewalk. She winced in pain when her left arm made impact with the unforgiving concrete. Brushing the pain away, she rolled up into a little ball and silently prayed that Ji Hoon didn't catch sight of her.

For the last several days, she had been so preoccupied with being angry at Tae Hyun that she neglected to focus a lot of time and energy into thinking about her strong resemblance to the Scorpion girl. Seeing Ji Hoon at that instance reminded her about the other areas of her fucked up life. She could only imagine how screwed up she'd be if she had to talk to the guy. He was always the bearer of bad news.

Her breath held in and her eyes glued shut, she was almost ready to nix the idea that Ji Hoon saw her. The street was pretty crowded and she *did* disappear out of sight pretty quickly. The guy could easily have bad vision and–

"Well, aren't you the prettiest little stray cat I've ever seen."

Aw, crap.

She knew the voice belonged to the one and only Skulls leader. She squeezed her eyes shut. Maybe if she continued to ignore him, he'd get the point and wander on.

"Yoori," he started, his voice suppressing the urge to laugh out loud. "Honestly, I'm this close to picking you up myself and taking you home if you don't stop ignoring me."

That was all he needed to say to convince Yoori to quit with the immature act. She didn't need another gang leader to hold her captive in his home. She opened her eyes. Peering up at the handsome Skulls leader, her fears were confirmed. She was going to have to talk to the guy.

"Funny seeing you here." She laughed uneasily, lamely trying to pretend that she didn't see him. She stood up awkwardly and crossed her arms, gazing at him cautiously. Oh how she wanted to make another quick exit.

A grin spread across his mouth. He stifled a laugh when his eyes ventured on to the top of her head.

She looked at him strangely. What was he laughing about?

"What?" she asked, offended that he found her to be so comical.

He raised his hand, his fingers approaching her hair.

She instinctively slapped his hand away and took a step to the side. "What the hell are you up to?"

"Yoori," he said, not in the least bit offended that she spoke to him with such hostility. "There's something in your hair."

She paused. "*What?*"

Was it a bug?

He reached his hand out again and picked out a stray leaf that fell onto her head during her little hideout session.

She gaped at the leaf in his hand. A spasm of guilt clawed at her. "Thanks," she muttered, feeling horrible for having such a short fuse with him.

It couldn't be helped though. Being around him reminded her of all his past actions that pissed her off. From sleeping with Tae Hyun's sister and chronicling the entire thing on voicemail, to threatening her and Tae Hyun in the warehouse, to sleeping with Jin Ae and finally, the one that pissed her off the most, lying to her about Soo Jin.

He flicked the stray leaf away. "Was it really necessary to hide from me?"

Of course, she wanted to shout out. Instead, she laughed uneasily. She didn't want the meeting to be more dramatic. "I wasn't hiding. I just tripped."

He nodded, clearly not wanting to call her out on her idiocy. "Ah, I see."

Her awkward stance persisted. Though his presence was obviously no threat to her, the simple fact that he stood there reminded her about her unfortunate resemblance to a particular evil gang leader. She didn't like the discomfort that came with being around him. She was adamant with making herself more comfortable.

"Anyway, um, I should go. Bye." Before even waiting for his response, Yoori managed to push past him.

"Yoori, wait."

Yoori made it exactly three steps past Ji Hoon before she felt him grab hold of her free hand, anchoring her from her exit. She tried unsuccessfully to keep her frustration at bay. The try-to-leave-but-someone-holds-on-to-your-hand trend was fast becoming an annoying occurrence.

She whirled around. She looked at his hand and then looked up at him with hardened eyes.

Sensing her irritation, Ji Hoon released her from his hold. "Sorry about that," he said, placing both of his hands in his pockets. His face grew almost angelic when he smiled at her. "It's just that we haven't seen each other in a while. We just ran into each other and I was just thinking about you. Do you really have to leave so soon?"

Her eyes softened. A pang of guilt speared into her when she heard the anxiety in his voice. God, she hated seeing his disappointment, especially when it came to conversing with her. "I—"

"At least give me another ten minutes," he compromised eagerly, desperation now present in his voice. He smiled hopefully at her.

She looked at him, dumbstruck. She was still reeling from their last round of ten minutes. Did he really think she'd go for another round?

She shook her head, caution clearly visible in her eyes. "To be honest, I think that's a really bad idea, for my own sake. I haven't fully recovered from our last ten minutes."

He crossed his arms. "I suppose bringing up Tae Hyun's dirty little secret could have been done with more grace on my part."

"There's no graceful way to share something like that." Her gaze on him became scrutinizing. "And you knew that."

Discontent molded on his face. "You're not pissed enough to stop seeing him, so I guess my plan for telling you didn't work out as well as I hoped."

Yoori opened her mouth to refute that statement. She was giving Tae Hyun the cold shoulder now, and if she weren't contractually bound to him, she probably would have left him already. She didn't allow the words of rebuttal to flow out of her mouth though. Ji Hoon didn't need the satisfaction of knowing that his plan worked out perfectly.

Instead she said, "Tae Hyun and I are working it out. So I'd appreciate it if you didn't throw anything else at me. I'm a bit overwhelmed at the moment."

He nodded. "I promise, I won't bring up Tae Hyun. I hate it when we talk about him anyway. This round of ten minutes will be solely dedicated to us. Me getting to know you."

She shook her head.

He took a step forward, reached for her hand and herded her to a nearby bench.

"Come on, Yoori." He sat down and gently tugged at her hand for her to sit down beside him. "We're just talking. There's no harm in that, right?"

Staggered by Ji Hoon's bold move, Yoori took a moment to steady her beating heart while staring at him with a dumbstruck expression. She had been holding back on these feelings for some time now, but she couldn't help but be flattered with the attention he bestowed on her. He was a master with getting people — particularly girls — to let their guards down.

Biting her lips as a way of chastising herself, she was abruptly reminded of Tae Hyun and the unfavorable situation she was put in. She pulled her hand away from him. "I really shouldn't be speaking to you."

Though his face remained as kind as ever, she could tell by the veins appearing on his forearms that he wasn't happy with her retort. It was no secret that Ji Hoon was not fond of Tae Hyun. Obviously any hesitation on Yoori's part *because* of Tae Hyun was a big annoyance for him.

"I see," he said carefully. "Going against Tae Hyun's commands really isn't ideal for you?" Though his question sounded understanding, Yoori knew he purposely posed it in a way that would make her jump up and attack.

Regardless of knowing his motive for posing the question in such a manner, it did not stop her from turning into her hotheaded self.

"Commands?" Fire brimmed in the edges of her eyes. She didn't like Ji Hoon insinuating that she was afraid of Tae Hyun. She was being considerate. There was a big difference. "No. He doesn't own me. I can talk to whoever I want."

"Then why is ten minutes like pulling teeth?"

She shot him a distrustful look. "Because you're hitting on me every time you open your mouth."

"I disagree with that."

"Oh yeah?"

"I'm hitting on you as I'm staring and smiling as well."

Yoori stifled a scoff. "You see the predicament we're in? Tae Hyun doesn't own me, but I'm still with him regardless. Talking to you is asking for trouble."

He smiled and rose from his seat. It took him less than two steps before his six-foot self towered before her. He raised his hand up to her and rested the back of his right index finger on her cheek, causing her to freeze while her cheeks tingled. The tingling sensation only worsened as Ji Hoon tenderly ran the back of his index finger down her cheek, and then to her jaw, chin, and neck. Bending his index finger to form a pointy curve, he ran it back up her neck and used it to prop up her chin so her lips were more visible for him.

"I'm only trouble," he started smoothly, his eyes resting on the fullness of her pink, pouty lips, "if you want me as much as I want you."

No longer able to resist the temptation of her mouth, Ji Hoon lowered his lips to meet with hers.

Yoori's eyes grew wide as she, with the quickest of reflexes, snapped her head back to avoid the collision with Ji Hoon's lips. He missed her by mere millimeters.

"I *don't* want you like that," she replied, faintly out of breath.

Clearly disappointed that he didn't get his kiss, Ji Hoon tried to appear composed. He straightened his back and crossed his arms in amusement.

"Good, then there's nothing to worry about here. You don't care and I'm chasing. I'm essentially harmless."

She gave him an "are-you-serious" look.

A harmless gang leader?

There was no such thing.

"Okay, just harmless to you," he corrected. "So, what do you say? Ten minutes?"

Yoori considered the proposition. If she gave him a few minutes, it would be over before she knew it. It would certainly be less of a headache than spending seven minutes not giving him his ten minutes.

She nodded, crossing her arms. It was just ten minutes. It couldn't hurt. Well, actually, she was sure seven minutes had passed since he last asked.

"Three minutes," she said decisively. "*Go.*"

He gave her an incredulous look. "Wait, what? Only three minutes?"

"Yes, we spent the last seven minutes deciding whether or not I should give you ten minutes."

"But I didn't—"

"Tick-tock," she said impatiently, tapping her watch.

He sighed in resignation. He paused to look around. "Can we talk somewhere else? It's really crowded here."

Yoori surveyed her surroundings. Go somewhere else and lose all of her witnesses and protectors? How about no?

"It's here or nowhere."

Ji Hoon tilted his head and smiled at her in disbelief. "Seriously Yoori, I'm not going to kidnap you or do anything bad."

"I don't know that."

A hearty laugh escaped from his lips. "I swear, sweetie. These low opinions you have of me are starting to break my heart. If this keeps going, I might actually turn into the bad guy and take you home for the heck of it."

Yoori scowled at his joke.

His smile only grew stronger. "Trust me. The last thing I want to do is get on your bad side."

"Trust me."

Ji Hoon really shouldn't have said those words to her.

The fact of the matter was that the entire ordeal relating to her resemblance to the Scorpion girl had been bubbling as soon as she saw Ji Hoon. It only took two simple words from him to finally release everything that she held captive – temptation for more knowledge about the Scorpion girl being one of them.

A one-night stand.

His previous lie to her about who Soo Jin was echoed profoundly in her head.

She really didn't want to get into this, but it couldn't be helped. Learning more about An Soo Jin was much like a heroin addiction for Yoori. She knew that learning more would equate to bad consequences for her, whether it meant more headaches or irrevocable evidence that she may actually be the infamous serial killer. Yet, in the same degree, learning more could also help provide her with more confidence that she really wasn't the heartless gang leader. Ultimately, as much as she didn't want to be associated with An Soo Jin, she wanted to know as much about this mysterious gang leader as she could. It wasn't healthy, but it was reality.

Anxiousness coated her features. "Will you tell me more about Soo Jin if I give you your ten minutes?"

She expected Ji Hoon's expression to grow despondent at the mention of his old love, much like his previous reaction when she first met him. To her surprise, he was better with his composure this time around. As if he practiced this countenance many times before, the amused expression on his face remained.

"Soo Jin?" he asked, pretending to be oblivious. He leisurely folded his arms across his chest. "I already told you, she was a one-night stand. I don't know anything abo – "

"Don't lie to me," Yoori said inflexibly, her eyes on him unblinking. "I know who An Soo Jin is. Or who she was."

He took a moment to gaze at her silently. Whether he was staring at her guardedly or staring at her with hilarity, she wasn't sure. His face was an assortment of composure and caution. He appeared to be debating about whether or not he should venture into this topic with her. After several seconds, life returned to the eyes of Lee Ji Hoon.

"Choi Yoori, what do you know about An Soo Jin?"

"I know that she was the Scorpion girl. And I know that you two were together before she died. That you loved – "

"Love," he corrected her at once. His eyes bore into hers. "I haven't stopped."

Yoori nodded, ruffled by his stern interjection. "That you love her," she continued. "And that I resemble her."

His brows creased together like her last statement was the most irrational thing he'd ever heard. "Haven't we already established the fact that you do not look like her? At least to me."

"There are others that—"

"No. No, there are subtle similarities, but you do not look like her. Whoever has been feeding you this crap is off their hinges. If you truly looked like her, do you think I'd stand by and watch as you run off with Tae Hyun?"

"Why do you keep insisting on talking to me then?" she voiced with anguish.

Things were more complicated now. So now there was only a subtle resemblance?

"Yoori," he intoned gently, sensing her anguish and confusion. "In all honesty, when it comes to getting girls, I have no trouble in that department. It takes a lot to impress me—to mesmerize me." He assessed her favorably. "There's something about you that fascinates me. I've taken an obvious liking to you. There's no more to it. I like you. I want to get to know you better. There's no harm in that, right?"

"There's so much more to what you're telling me right now," she stated confidently, feeling a migraine ensue. "You know that."

"The sole fact that you're Tae Hyun's girl may have sparked this interest," he admitted slowly. A muscle twitched in his jaw at the mention of Yoori being Tae Hyun's "girl." He shrugged. "I haven't figured it out yet, but does it really matter now?"

A small part of Yoori didn't believe his explanation, but the bigger part of her *liked* his explanation. She liked that he was interested in her solely because he wanted to compete with Tae Hyun. She liked that he said she didn't resemble An Soo Jin. She liked his explanations because they helped to further her belief that she couldn't be the Scorpion girl. With her desperation in hand and gut instinct in the backburner, she accepted Ji Hoon's explanation as the truth.

He smiled at her hopefully. "What do you say? Can't you give up another ten minutes?"

"I want to know more about An Soo Jin," she demanded, not giving up on her unhealthy addiction.

Ji Hoon sighed once more. He stared at her like she was a lost cause before a sudden twinkle appeared in his eyes. "Fine, Yoori. If you want to learn more about An Soo Jin, then I'm happy to oblige."

She beamed prematurely, thinking she was going to get her way right at that moment.

He raised a hand as his way to interrupt her. "But that conversation will take place at our next meeting, which would require an hour of your time."

Her jaw fell. "An *hour*?"

He lifted his shoulders to confirm.

"Wh-what happened to ten minutes?" she stammered, confounded with his proposition.

Ji Hoon exhaled dramatically. "If you're going to make me relive the pain of talking about my ex-girlfriend, then you'll have to spare enough time to comfort me in the end."

Another internal battle commenced inside her. She wanted to learn more about An Soo Jin, but an hour with Ji Hoon? No matter how tempting the proposal, this was a bad idea.

She peered at him silently, not knowing what answer to give him.

"Think about it," he coaxed, as if knowing that she'd give in sooner or later. "Have a good night, Yoori."

Without another word, he turned on his heels and walked toward his car.

She didn't like to admit it, but as she watched him drive off into the distance, she could almost swear that she felt her heart ache for him.

That was the problem with Choi Yoori.

She always had a tendency to get too easily attached to people – even if she only met them for a short time.

Kang Min, Jae Won and Ji Hoon were prime examples.

And, of course, Tae Hyun.

She squeezed her eyes shut when Tae Hyun came to mind.

Especially Tae Hyun.

She exerted a heavy sigh and began to drag her feet back to Tae Hyun's apartment. An upsurge of guilt prickled over her as she took one step after the other. Albeit the conversation with Ji Hoon was harmless, she felt like she betrayed Tae Hyun somehow. Even though she expressed strong feelings about being "done" with him, she felt guilty.

Remember what he did, she reminded herself as she descended down the street, the sun setting closely beside her. She hoped that this reminder would lessen the guilt that plagued her. She hoped it would strengthen her resolve before she saw him again.

Remember what he did to his own brother.

■ ■ ■

With substantial dread weighing her down, Yoori took out her card key and scanned it through the machine when she reached Tae Hyun's apartment. The metal door instantaneously clicked open, allotting her entry. She made it approximately two steps in before she heard the apartment owner's voice.

"How was life on the outside?" the soothing voice asked.

Yoori inhaled sharply, allowing the door to click shut before wandering further into the living room. Tae Hyun sat on the couch with his Blackberry in hand. She had hoped that he went to another one of his gang meetings so she wouldn't have to talk to him for the remainder of the night. She surveyed him. He wore a black suit with a loosened green tie. It was clear he just came home.

"It was good," she replied tiredly. She stood awkwardly behind the sofa, rubbing her left arm with her right hand as a mechanism to warm the cold chill she was experiencing (and to subtly ease her nervousness).

He glanced at her from his Blackberry screen. He took notice of her rubbing her own arm. "You should have brought a jacket with you," he said quietly, placing his Blackberry on the coffee table. He vested his full attention on her.

Yoori merely nodded as a response.

He smiled. "Did anything interesting?"

"Mall," she said simply.

And saw Lee Ji Hoon, she added in her head.

The rubbing of her arm grew more rapid. She debated about whether or not she should share this piece of information with Tae Hyun. It would be a bad idea to do that. She didn't know how he would react. Would he throw a tantrum and instruct her to never see Ji Hoon again? Would he care enough to throw a tantrum? Did he care period?

He assessed her empty hands in confusion. "Why didn't you get anything?"

"I've never been much of a shopper."

"A girl who's not much of a shopper," he marveled with a laugh. "Now I've really seen everything."

She felt the words bubble in her throat. She didn't understand her motive for telling Tae Hyun, but she had to let it out.

"I saw Lee Ji Hoon," she blurted.

The rubbing of her arm grew stagnant. She studied Tae Hyun expectantly. It was stupid, but a small part of her hoped that he'd react irrationally—angrily if anything. Anything just to show her how he felt about her and this entire situation.

Much to her unpleasant surprise, Tae Hyun did not even blink when he processed what she said.

His cool expression remained. "That's nice. And how was he doing?"

"F-fine," she stuttered. " I...you're not angry?"

An indifferent brow arched. "Should I be?"

"I don't know," she continued against her confusion. "Should you? You were angry when Jin Ae slept with him."

"Jin Ae and you are completely different to me," he said disinterestedly, his face blank. "I'm not concerned when it comes to you."

Yoori nodded with composure, hiding the fact that her stomach churned inwards from the statement Tae Hyun casually conveyed.

"That's good to know," said Yoori, not really knowing how to react to him basically telling her that he didn't care enough to be angry that she spoke to Ji Hoon. Oh how she wanted to disappear and stop talking to him. "I...I think I'm going to head back into the bedroom and get some rest."

She was ready to retreat backward when his next words stopped her. "Are you going to see him again?"

"Probably," she answered distractedly, not really listening to his question. She gazed at him with eyes wide open when she digested his question. "What? I mean no. Well, maybe. Actually, I'm not sure. I'm just—I—I'm glad you're not mad. Anyway, I'll see him when I see him. Glad you're okay with it. I'm going to get ready for bed now."

She wanted to hide in the bedroom. There was too much going on in her head, too much confusion, and too many headache-inducing thoughts.

"Yoori," she heard him call after her when she hurried into the hall.

Purposely accelerating her pace so she wouldn't have to talk to him, she ignored his calls.

Tae Hyun sped after her. Catching up with her, he snaked his arm around her waist and spun her around to face him.

"Tae Hyun, seriously. I'm not in the mood," she said wearily, thinking he wanted to speak about Ji Hoon. She pushed herself away from his grasp and moved away. She didn't even make it an inch away when she was blocked with the wall behind her back.

He took a step forward and placed each of his hands on either side of her, consequently locking her in. Leveraging his weight on each hand, he leaned in closer to her, successfully regaining her full attention and causing her breathing to become shallow.

He drew her gaze to him. "You never asked me why I killed him."

She closed her eyes in frustration, not really listening to what he was saying. "I said I don't want to talk about Ji—" She halted and gaped at him when she registered that he wasn't talking about Ji Hoon. "*What*?"

"My older brother," he clarified, his eyes on her. "You never asked me why I killed him."

"I..." She paused momentarily to think it over. Was there ever a good reason to kill your brother?

No, she answered in her mind. She eyed him critically. She was curious though. What possible reason could he have apart from stealing the Serpents throne?

"Are you going to tell me?"

"No."

"Why not?"

"Because you never asked me."

"Why did you kill your brother?" she asked, growing infinitely more curious.

"Why are you so angry with me?" he fired back, dissatisfaction prominent in his voice. "Did you talk to Ji Hoon to punish me?"

"What? *No*. I ran into—" She paused to regain her composure. This wasn't about her. She was not the one on trial here. "No, it doesn't matter. What's *your* reason?"

"You answer my question first."

"I asked you first."

"I care about your answer more. Just tell me—"

"I empathize with your guilt," she proclaimed thoughtlessly. Her gaze rounded when she realized what she said.

Frustration dissipated out of Tae Hyun's eyes. Stupefaction took its place. "What?"

Yoori bit her lip, berating herself for answering without thought. The answer also didn't make sense to her. What was she thinking giving him that nonsensical answer?

"Forget it," she voiced irritably, aggravation mounting over her flushed face. "I really don't care enough to delve deeper into this. Whatever your reason, I hope it was good enough to kill your own brother."

She made an effort to leave. She was once again stopped by Tae Hyun.

"Can't you trust that I had a good reason?" His voice was frosted with the same tone of indifference. Such a tone that didn't bother her before pissed her off like no other now. There was absolutely no guilt in his voice. None whatsoever.

Hate streamed inside her.

How dare he try to minimize his sinful actions with a question like that?

No, she couldn't trust him and she wouldn't trust him.

She released herself from his grasp. "Have a good night, Tae Hyun."

Her right foot leading the way, she drew away from a now quiet Tae Hyun. He slowly pushed himself off the wall and watched from the corner of his eyes as she went into the bedroom.

Closing the bedroom door, Yoori rested the back of her head against the door for support. She squeezed her eyes shut. She didn't know why, but it felt nice just standing there like that. It felt nice and safe standing there in silence as she attempted to organize her frantic thoughts.

She didn't understand why she shared with Tae Hyun her meeting with Ji Hoon, and she didn't understand why she cared about his reaction. She also couldn't comprehend why she told him she was angry with him because she "empathized" with his guilt. Nothing. *Nothing* made sense to her. All of her actions by far were a mystery to her.

She raked her fingers through her hair. If she could, she would have stood there longer. However, as a muscle twitched in pain in her right leg, she knew it was due time for her to rest. Finally opening her eyes, her fingers reached for the light switch. She flicked the lights off. She approached Tae Hyun's bed in total darkness and climbed onto the mattress. She laid her head on the pillow and threw the covers over her.

Finally, she closed her eyes.

She no longer wanted to organize her frantic thoughts. Her priority right now was to sleep and sleep quickly. If she fell asleep fast enough, then she wouldn't have to think about forgiving him. If she fell asleep fast enough, then she wouldn't have to think about Tae Hyun. If she fell asleep fast enough, then she wouldn't have to think about why Tae Hyun's guilt left such a big impression on her. If she fell asleep fast enough, then she wouldn't have to be consumed with this nonsensical guilt.

Drifting off to sleep, Yoori failed to realize that the big reason why she was upset with Tae Hyun was because his unforgivable guilt reminded her of her own, that his guilt reminded her of her own guilt that was buried deep in her subconscious. If she had realized all this, then she probably wouldn't have been so keen on falling asleep so fast. Because even in dreams, her unforgivable sins lived on.

Each in a deep slumber...waiting...just waiting to be reawakened.

"Finish them off."

22: Victims and Saviors

"Kneel," she whispered softly, crossing her arms. Her blank eyes fell onto her three captives.

With a kick to the legs from her men, the three shadow figures dropped to their knees.

The young woman stood before them with a smug look on her face.

"I'll never kneel before you, you heartless bitch!" one of the shadow figures screamed out as he stood up with full force.

Several of her men took out knives from behind their backs, ready and willing to put the standing man in his place.

The smug expression still cold on her face, she lifted her hand as a gesture for her men to put their knives away. Exchanging hesitant looks, they obliged with their boss's unspoken order.

"You have a daring mouth, don't you?" she asked serenely, her entertained eyes shifting from the two kneeling men to the one standing in the center.

It happened within a split second. The trace of amusement in her eyes vanished as darkness took its place.

"Kneel," she repeated once more, her voice composed, but coupled with an ominous pitch.

Though his hardened posture faltered after seeing the subtle change in her eyes, he remained standing. "Never," he uttered bravely, his voice strong, but his eyes filled with a sea of worry.

An annoyed smirk graced her pale face. Her dark eyes narrowed onto the disobedient man. Shaking her head, she turned away in disgust. "God, I hate it when dogs don't listen to their master."

Her icy eyes fell onto one of her men. Slowly approaching him, she shook her head in frustration.

Intense silence mounted over the dark warehouse once she stopped in front of one of her subordinates. Without notice, she reached for the gun of the faceless subordinate and fired two perfect shots into the kneecaps of the standing man.

The thunderous sound of roaring bullets echoed on to the walls of the warehouse. It was immediately followed by a blood-curdling scream.

Writhing in agony, the man fell to the floor. Surely enough, he fell into a kneeling position before his entire body collapsed face-first onto the floor. His head fell right beside the boots of the young woman.

She squatted beside him and traced the black gun along the side of his agonized face. "This is what happens when dogs don't listen to their master," she lectured softly, finding more hilarity with seeing him twitch his face in pain rather than the actual lesson that was being taught.

She withdrew her gun from his quivering face and stood up with a lethargic stretching of her right shoulder.

"I do hate getting my hands dirty when it comes to killing people," she whispered, her right hand firmly gripped on the gun. Her eyes sharpened onto the two kneeling men. Both were watching the entire scene in terror.

"I think it's time to let others play."

Her eyes focused on the faceless subordinates standing behind the three captives.

"Knives," she said to the faceless shadows.

The entire warehouse shook with roars of knives hitting the floor. One by one, they landed in front of the two kneeling men and the fallen man. When the last of the dozen knives fell onto the floor, the young woman parted her smiling lips.

"I'm feeling a bit altruistic today." She tossed the gun back to one of her men. "And I'm in the mood to be entertained."

Her dark eyes centered on the kneeling men. They stared at her in trepidation. They knew what they had to do with those knives.

"Do you guys want to live?"

They nodded quickly, staring desperately at the knives before them.

She smiled calculatingly. "The game is simple. One of the three of you will walk out of here alive. The other two will die by the hands of the survivor." She laughed when her gaze wandered on to the man she shot. "It seems," she voiced mockingly, feigning disappointment, "my favorite dog in this game lost the fight before it even began."

The two kneeling men stared at the knives on the floor, desperation foaming in their eyes. Each of the knives symbolized their gateway to freedom or gateway to hell. It was clear in their eyes that each was determined to be the one to walk out of the lion's den alive.

As she reached behind her back, each of the men held their breath. They knew what was to come.

"Ready," she started, her heart beating impatiently for the fun she was about to witness.

She pulled out her knife and threw it toward the floor.

It danced in the air...

"Set..."

The knife made a deafening sound, its slim figure making contact with the floor that was about to be polluted with blood.

A sadistic smile appeared on her face as her lips parted in pleasure.

"Go."

Waking up with a loud gasp, Yoori could've sworn her heart was ready to pop out of her chest. She placed her right hand over her rapidly beating heart and rubbed her face with her free hand.

Shit.

This was by far the most disturbing dream she'd ever had. She had been in this Underworld society for too long if unbearable violence was prominent, even within the parameters of her dreams.

She steadied her breathing and began to gently slap herself back to reality.

"Just a dream. Just a dream," she chanted as she repositioned herself in Tae Hyun's bed. Her heart beat like it was about to take its last breath. "Just a dream. Just a dream—"

She stopped chanting after turning to her side. A new, nightmarish distraction presented itself. Her pulse slowed to a stop when she looked down and spotted a pair of legs that loomed beside the bed. Running her eyes from the bottom up, she cast her petrified gaze onto a pale looking mystery girl. The girl stared at her with unblinking eyes.

What the fuck?

Her cold hands squeezed her comforter in desperation. She wanted to ask the girl who she was. She wanted to jump off the bed and run off. But she couldn't. She couldn't do any of the things she wanted to do.

Gulping in absolute fear, Yoori did the only thing a rational person could do at that moment. She screamed bloody murder.

With shaking instincts, she propelled up on the bed and stood upon it. Whilst holding her comforter against her chest, Yoori's own unblinking eyes stared down at the mystery girl.

The girl blinked at her in bewilderment.

Though Yoori stood more than a couple of inches higher on the bed, she could tell that the girl was tall. She was dressed in a short white halter dress and sported ridiculously high heels. The girl stood at about 5'7 or 5'8 with the heels on. Yoori really couldn't tell with her mind shaking from the shock and all. Needless to say, dressed in baggy white pajama pants with a simple white fitted tank, Yoori felt really "bummish" compared to the mystery girl.

Comparison of clothes aside, Yoori was more interested in finding out who the hell the girl was.

Yoori pointed a shaking finger at the mystery girl, who smiled at her like Yoori was the most entertaining thing on earth.

"W–who," Yoori panted loudly, placing her right hand over her heart as a way to steady her own breathing. "Who. The. Hell. Are. You?"

The mystery girl's smile grew wider. "I was planning on asking you the same thing," she said cheerfully, looking Yoori up and down approvingly.

Yoori inverted her brows when the girl "approved" her with her eyes. The hell? Fear vacated her body. In its place came bafflement. Who on earth was this chick?

The mystery girl opened her mouth to say something else. She was punctually interrupted when the door blasted open.

"Yoori!" came Tae Hyun's voice when he exploded into the bedroom like a bat out of hell.

Yoori and the mystery girl swerved their attention to the frantic gang leader.

Yoori's eyes bloomed at the sight of a noticeably underdressed Tae Hyun.
In the name of all that is Holy!

Unknowingly losing grip of the comforter she held against her chest, a soft gasp escaped from Yoori's lips. Her rounded eyes gaped at Tae Hyun's half-naked form. Standing at the doorway, bare from the top up whilst holding a meager white towel around his hyperventilating abs, the sheer masculinity of him aroused her womanly senses. He looked like he was made of muscles. Rivulets of water streamed from various parts of his body, gliding lovingly over the hard ridges of his statuesque form. Wet from head to toe, her stunned self could only surmise that he must've ran out of the shower when he heard her scream.

Whoa, Yoori thought, so entirely lost in the world of Tae Hyun's hot, wet body teasing her that she completely forgot about the strange girl in the bedroom. She also temporarily forgot that she was supposed to be "done" with him.

Oblivious to the unusually perverted stare Yoori bestowed upon him, Tae Hyun's frantic eyes ran from Yoori and then to the mystery girl. His own eyes grew wide when settling on the mystery girl.

"Hae Jin," he grounded out, his voice throbbing with rage. "How the hell did you get in?"

Hae Jin?

Yoori's eyes were fixated on his misty body while the girl's name rang in her head. Then, once she processed the familiarity of the name, she faced the girl.

Hae Jin?

The little sister?

"Oppa!" Hae Jin squeaked out, calling Tae Hyun the Korean endearment reserved for younger sisters to address their older brothers. Her right hand waved nervously at him. She obviously knew she was in trouble.

"I came in and you were in the shower...and I was wondering who was in the bedroom and—" She stopped and glanced at her scantily dressed brother and then at Yoori, who was still standing atop the bed with her eyes wide from shock. She gave out a knowing laugh and covered her mouth. "Oh my God! I'm so sorry! I didn't mean to interrupt!"

Yoori's jaw fell when she realized that Hae Jin misunderstood the content of their relationship. They were *not* getting ready to have sex!

"No, no, no!" Yoori cried desperately, jumping off the bed and running to her. Hae Jin covered her mouth in amusement.

"It's not what it seems!" Yoori shouted breathlessly.

Hae Jin wasn't listening. "I'm sorry," she muffled through her hands. Her eyes had a hint of a smile and an apologetic gaze as she eyed Yoori keenly.

"No," Yoori repeated frantically, getting exasperated. "It's not what it seems!"

How could this be happening? It was one thing to "seemingly" be Tae Hyun's girlfriend, but to be "seemingly" having sex with him? No matter how inappropriately tempting the thought, Yoori could never do that! She didn't even know *how* to have sex. She paused. Okay, that may not be true. She knew the mechanisms of how sex worked, but it wasn't like she had ever done it. She paused once more when she recalled her amnesia. Not that she knew of anyway.

"Hae Jin!" Tae Hyun roared, interrupting Yoori's disconcerting thoughts. "Get out, right now!"

Though he did grab their attention, neither of the girls jumped at his resounding voice. They were well accustomed to him elevating his voice to such a level.

Giving Yoori a slight bow, Hae Jin took her hands off her mouth and made her way to the door.

"Oppa," she called when she reached her older brother. "Is that your girlfriend?"

"No!" Yoori screamed, panicking once more.

"Hae Jin, that's enough," Tae Hyun said firmly, purposely ignoring her question.

Yoori expelled a breath as she watched Tae Hyun reach for the doorknob. At least he'd be able to clear up the misunderstanding.

His next words, however, strongly combated that reassurance.

"Sorry baby, go back to sleep."

"What?" she shrieked.

Having the forefront to sense the eruption of rage that was ready to emit from Yoori, Tae Hyun gave her an apologetic smile and instantly pulled the door closed.

"What did you call me?" she hollered, running to the closing door. Yoori stopped and gazed at the two siblings through the half-closed door. Was this seriously happening?

Looking over her brother's shoulder to steal another peek at Yoori, Hae Jin smiled favorably when the door finally closed shut. "Oh my God, she's so pretty!"

Even though she was reeling from the last five minutes, Yoori couldn't help but smile at the recent round of flattery imparted to her by Tae Hyun's sister. It may be because Hae Jin boosted Yoori's ego, but Yoori already liked Hae Jin. If you discounted the fact that she scared the hell out of Yoori a few minutes ago, the girl wasn't so bad.

"Hae Jin, please shut up," she heard Tae Hyun beg his younger sister from the other side of the closed door.

"Big bro," his little sister squealed teasingly. Laughter erupted from the other side of the door. "You're such a porn star right now."

Yoori snickered after hearing Hae Jin tease her older brother. How could one not be amused with this endearing conversation? She doubted it was an everyday occurrence that the King of Serpents got teased like this.

"Fuck. My. Life," said Tae Hyun when he processed that his half naked self should put some clothes on. "I have to change. *Don't* bother her."

"Aw, look at my big brother being overprotective of his precious new girlfriend. I just want to talk to her..."

"Hae Jin," he voiced sternly. Yoori was pretty sure that he must've given her another one of his death glares because Hae Jin's voice was instantly silenced.

Standing in front of the door, Yoori remained quiet, shadily hoping that she'd be able to overhear more. After a long period of silence, Yoori concluded that Tae Hyun must've gone back into the bathroom to change into appropriate clothing.

Her gaze on the white doorframe, the image of Tae Hyun running into the room with nothing but a towel on flashed in her mind. She couldn't deny that such a sight was definitely a nice picker upper to her strange morning.

"Ah, pervert, pervert," she mumbled, bringing her hands up to her face. She rubbed her eyes as an attempt to drown out all the perverted images she was having for her gang leader boss.

It took her a minute of staring at the doorframe to fully remember what her attitude toward Tae Hyun should be. All perversion aside, she hadn't forgotten their conversation from the night before. Her face grew solemn and her smile faded. Her heart grew heavier as recollections of the night before haunted her. She squeezed her eyes shut, allowing the illumination of the morning sun to graze her skin. It was a welcome feeling in face of the unpleasant memories from the previous night.

Then, another thought invaded her mind.

"Girlfriend?"

She groaned. Oh God, had it really come to this? At first, she thought their relationship as "boyfriend and girlfriend" was used strictly to get Jin Ae off Tae Hyun's back. But now he was lying to family too? What was she supposed to do? Play along? She scoffed. Like it mattered if she consented? If Tae Hyun wanted her to play along, then she would have to. It wasn't like he gave anyone much of a choice when he wanted something.

She muttered an incoherent cuss. You didn't have to be a rocket scientist to understand that being labeled as the official girlfriend of the infamous King of Serpents would merit a little bit more than a "congratulations" from his crime lord friends.

Say hello to an endless amount of death threats, Tae Hyun's new "official" girlfriend, she thought scornfully.

Her current of thoughts ceased when her ears perked up after hearing the sound of muffled laughter from the other side of the door. Her curiosity getting the best of her, Yoori approached the door and leaned her ear against it to get a clearer idea of what the two siblings were up to.

"Is she coming out?" she heard Hae Jin ask Tae Hyun. Loud clacking footsteps approached the door.

"Crap!" Yoori muttered frantically. She retreated several steps to prevent herself from getting caught eavesdropping.

The sound of footfalls running after Hae Jin's heels took over the hall.

"Don't bother her," came Tae Hyun's voice. He must've stopped and pulled his sister away from the door. "She's not in a good mood."

Footsteps descending away from the door soon followed.

"What did you do to make her mad?" Hae Jin asked as their voices became harder to hear.

"Why do you assume it was me who did something?"

"'Cause you're the one sleeping outside."

Yoori smiled approvingly. That Hae Jin was a smart cookie.

If Tae Hyun responded to his sister's observation, then Yoori couldn't hear it. Either they were whispering or they were done talking. Whatever the case, the conversation outside was no longer audible to a curious Yoori. She debated once more about sticking her ear against the door, but heavily fought against that. She shouldn't be nosy, especially when the door could slam into her at any moment.

There was a much safer way to quench her curiosity.

She exhaled deeply and approached the door with the intention of going outside to talk to Hae Jin. Regardless of her ill feelings for Tae Hyun, Hae Jin didn't do anything. Yoori couldn't be rude and stay inside Tae Hyun's room. Plus, it was better if she was outside so she could know exactly what was going on. She turned the knob. She didn't even make it out the door when she was unexpectedly greeted with a familiar face.

"Hi!" Hae Jin waved happily, standing right in front of the door. Right in front of Yoori's face.

"Holy shit!" Yoori screamed, jumping back. She gaped at Hae Jin, her eyes bitterly boring into the girl. It was the second time in a row where this girl scared the shit out of Yoori. "Is it your mission to give me a heart attack today?"

"Oh man," Hae Jin began wearily, briefly covering her mouth in disbelief. She smiled apologetically. "This is crazy. I swear, I'm not some creep who walks around with the intention of scaring the hell out of you." Her eyes flickered to the empty living room. "My brother is outside on a business call. I just wanted to take the time to get to know his new girlfriend before I leave."

Yoori regarded Hae Jin with open suspicion. In all honesty, it was freaking her out that Hae Jin was so nice. Could this really be a crime lord's sister?

She grew calmer at the sight of Hae Jin beaming at her. She slowly lowered her guard. Kwon Hae Jin definitely had a contagious energy. How could she be angry at someone who was so nice?

Feeling awkward that they weren't formally introduced, Yoori said, "I'm Choi—"

"Yoori," Hae Jin finished for her, the smile never leaving her face. "Already heard it in passing when my brother came in screaming your name."

"Yeah," Yoori uttered uncomfortably, attempting to block out perverted images upon being reminded of Tae Hyun running into the room with only a towel on.

"Anyway," started Hae Jin, "I'm—"

"Hae Jin," Yoori finished for her. Of course she knew who Hae Jin was. After what took place at the warehouse, who wouldn't know who Kwon Hae Jin was?

Hae Jin nodded, pleased that Yoori already knew her name. "Well, Yoori. What do you say? Do you have a few moments to talk? I don't get to meet my big brother's girlfriends very often, if ever."

"I'm not his girlfri—" Yoori stopped midway, realizing that she would have to play along with Tae Hyun no matter what. Mentally sighing at the lie she was about to embark on, she reluctantly parted her lips.

"It's complicated," she voiced instead, meaning every word of it.

Hae Jin nodded understandably. She strode into the bedroom and took a seat at the edge of Tae Hyun's bed. "It's always complicated with my brother." She placed a hand next to the side of her mouth and lightheartedly whispered, "Between me and you, I think he's a little weird."

Thrilled that someone finally understood her, Yoori laughed as she closed the door and ran over to sit on the edge of the bed beside Hae Jin. "Seriously, right?"

Hae Jin nodded again. She pulled up her legs and crossed them on the bed. "He has a good heart though. This brother of mine has never been too good with letting his feelings out. Sometimes it comes out a little rough around the edges. Look at it this way. At least he hasn't shot you in the head, right? Simple relationships with him usually involve him killing you."

Hae Jin's face lit up. She laughed at her own joke—or what Yoori presumed to be a joke.

Yoori strained to keep her weak smile in place. She awkwardly laughed with Hae Jin. "Heh...yeah...heh, heh, heh..."

"Anyway," Hae Jin said again, her laughter dying down. "Give me the 411. How did you and my brother meet?"

Yoori winced at Hae Jin's unexpected, but highly reasonable question. Although she knew she had to lie, who knew she would have to lie *this* much to someone she just met?

The uncensored version played like a movie in the backdrop of her mind.

"Apparently, I caught his eye at the diner where I worked," Yoori answered slowly, her voice suppressing the urge to blurt out the whole truth.

He blackmailed me into slavery, she desperately clarified in her mind.

Hae Jin's smile widened. "Wow, really? How did he ask you out?"

Yoori paused to nervously bite her lower lip, thinking up a good enough answer to give. She faked a laugh of joy. "Oh your brother...being the sly devil that he is, essentially told me that he wanted me by his side..."

As his assistant.

"And things just quickly rolled from then on. Next thing I knew, I was in his limo clinking that damn champagne glass with him and agreeing to always be by his side whenever he needs me."

Hae Jin's eyes grew huge. "Wow, you guys move fast. You weren't afraid of the commitment with a total stranger?"

Yoori laughed despairingly. "Yeah...heh, heh, heh...you know that brother of yours...definitely has that certain charm to put anyone under his spell..."

Crime Lord! Crime Lord! Crime Lord!

Hae Jin nodded before her face contorted in confusion. "So what are you guys arguing about? He looked pretty pathetic slumming on that couch while he was talking to me about you."

Yoori stopped emitting fake joy. "What did he say?"

"That you're mad at him about something. He didn't really get into it." Hae Jin eyed Yoori, her eyes faintly asking Yoori for the reason why she was giving her brother the cold shoulder. "To be perfectly honest, I don't think he really knows why you're mad at him either."

"It's complicated," Yoori replied softly but firmly.

Yoori fidgeted, feeling awkward. A big reason why she was angry with Tae Hyun was because he killed his older brother. Hae Jin's eldest brother to be exact. How was she supposed to tell Hae Jin that?

Hae Jin gave a small smile as her way of assuring Yoori that she wouldn't pry for any further details.

Yoori returned the small smile. She was surprised that Hae Jin was so much sweeter than she expected her to be. Before Yoori met her, she assumed that Hae Jin would be much like Jin Ae, especially given what she knew about her from the warehouse incident.

Yoori shuddered at the thought. Thankfully Hae Jin was nothing like Jin Ae.

"You're really different than how I imagined you to be," Yoori said in a matter-of-fact tone, crossing her legs on the bed. If it were anyone else, then Yoori probably would've thought twice before making such a bold statement. Yet, there was something about Hae Jin that made her comfortable.

Hae Jin looked at her, amused. "Good different or bad different?"

"Good," she reassured. "Definitely good."

Hae Jin nodded with a smile. "Good."

Yoori also nodded, her thoughts migrating back to the event that took place in the warehouse.

"Your brother was really worried about you the other day," she continued mindlessly, curious as to why Hae Jin would sleep with Ji Hoon and piss her brother off. The siblings seemed to get along incredibly well.

"Yeah, I heard about that," Hae Jin trailed off uncomfortably. Her eyes locked on the bed. She began to toy with the lining of the comforter. The sudden tautness in her demeanor made it appear that she felt guilty.

"Why did you—?"

"I was pissed off at the bitch Jin Ae for cheating on my brother with Lee Ji Hoon," Hae Jin answered without hesitation, already expecting Yoori to ask that question.

With her attention on the comforter, she continued. "I was mad at someone else too, and I had too much to drink." She swallowed tightly at the reminder of this "someone else." "Really, it was nothing. I was drunk and stupid that night."

Despite Yoori's attempt to conceal it, an incredulous gaze formed on her countenance. "*Really?* You slept with Ji Hoon just to piss off Jin Ae and piss off whoever you were mad at?"

Hae Jin scratched her left temple with frustration. "Like I said, I was really upset and drunk." Anger bubbled in her voice. "And Jin Ae has never been someone I favored." She took her eyes off the comforter and gazed at Yoori. "You've probably never met the girl, but she's the absolute worst thing on earth. Think of the worst bitch you can imagine and multiply that by a hundred and you'll get Jin Ae."

Yoori remained silent. Even though she did heavily agree with what Hae Jin said, she didn't want to interrupt Hae Jin as she continued with her line of reasoning.

"My brother never took her seriously, but it still left a sour taste in his mouth when he heard that she was sleeping with Ji Hoon. He was too nice to do anything about it, so I decided to take care of it myself."

Hae Jin sounded so proud of her one-sided reasoning. It would be a disservice if Yoori didn't shed some light on the hole in her reasoning. "You didn't think it'd be worse for your brother once he heard that you slept with Ji Hoon?"

She paused, regretting her boldness with speaking to Hae Jin in such an authoritative tone. Oh God, why did she suddenly feel like the equivalent of an older sister as she spoke to Hae Jin?

Hae Jin sighed. "Yeah, that thought did cross my mind in my drunken state." A smirk outlined her lips. "But I take bigger joy in knowing that Jin Ae must be throwing a tantrum right now, to know that she means absolutely nothing to the two crime lords she claimed as her own."

Seriously?

Yoori wanted to shake Hae Jin and ask her what the hell she was thinking. Her reasoning made sense. Yoori wasn't a big fan of Jin Ae either. Having said that, it baffled her as to how Hae Jin could use her body so freely like that. The girl couldn't be older than eighteen. It may have been an old enough age for someone to start having sex, but that didn't stop Yoori from feeling protective over Hae Jin.

Shortly thereafter, she felt a trace of jealousy rummage through her when an image of Ji Hoon and Hae Jin making out before they got intimate popped into her mind.

"You don't like Ji Hoon, do you?" she asked keenly, perhaps sounding a bit more envious and bitter than she should have.

Hae Jin gawked at Yoori. "What? No, of course not. Ji Hoon was a mistake. He used me and I used him. That was the beginning and end of our relationship."

"Okay," Yoori accepted, surprised that she was relieved by Hae Jin's answer. She had hostile reservations for Ji Hoon, but the thought of him being intimate with any other girl didn't sit well with her. It was a weird feeling. Though being jealous wasn't the word Yoori would like to use, she couldn't deny that she was feeling territorial.

Catching the discomfort in Yoori's eyes, Hae Jin said, "Lee Ji Hoon is a dog."

Yoori stilled, thrown off by her words.

Hae Jin continued. "No matter how charming he may be, plenty of girls that my brother dated fell victim to that charm of Ji Hoon's, only to be tossed aside after he was done using them."

"Why are you telling me this?" Yoori asked hesitantly, pretending to be clueless. She knew why Hae Jin was telling her that, but ignorance always sparked a more civil and less difficult conversation.

"Because Lee Ji Hoon is the type of person that would go for you, if he hasn't made various attempts already." A confident smile curved her lips. "I'm not worried about you though. Just be careful around him if you see him. He's trouble with a capital T."

Yoori nodded. "My guard will always be up." And she meant every word. Even with her small attachment toward Ji Hoon, she knew she had to be careful with him. She had to be careful with everyone in this world.

Hae Jin beamed. "I'm sure my brother would be happy to hear that."

Yoori smiled appreciatively at Hae Jin. Hae Jin's protectiveness over Tae Hyun reminded Yoori much of the protectiveness Kang Min had for Jae Won. She felt her heart grow warmer as the admiration for these siblings streamed through her. It was probably because she lacked such a strong bond in her own life, but she truly loved that the younger siblings had their older sibling's backs.

Loyalty within your bloodline—nothing beats that.

Just as that comforting realization warmed her, it soon became the bane of her emotions. Her stomach churned inwards when the impact of the statement purged through her. The unfortunate fact that Tae Hyun did not have the same protective loyalty over his older brother, like the one he possessed for his younger sister, unnerved her.

Yoori glanced at Hae Jin, her curiosity for how Hae Jin felt about her second older brother killing her eldest brother reaching its apex. Surely Hae Jin must harbor some negative feelings toward the whole situation, right? Hae Jin must know why Tae Hyun killed their eldest brother.

"You're very protective of your brother," Yoori voiced delicately, strategically steering the conversation to where she needed it to be.

"He's the only family I have," Hae Jin answered proudly. Her eyes warmed up. "I gotta watch out for family."

This was it.

This was where Yoori needed the conversation to be.

With the utmost velocity, Yoori voiced the one question she knew would give her all the answers she needed. "Were you not close to your eldest brother?"

As soon as the question poured from her lips, she regretted it.

The light in Hae Jin's eyes darkened. She regarded Yoori with unreadable eyes.

Shit.

Yoori regretfully watched as Hae Jin's vibrancy evaporated as soon as Yoori mentioned her eldest brother. If Yoori could take back what she said, she would. If it was possible, Hae Jin had grown even paler. It was as if all the life had been sucked out of her when Yoori mentioned Ho Young.

"Is this why you're angry at my brother?" she asked slowly, the sudden seriousness in her voice scaring Yoori. "Because he killed Ho Young?"

Something was wrong here. Hae Jin's reaction wasn't what Yoori anticipated.

Yoori opened her mouth. Nothing but a stutter came tumbling out. "I—"

"Kwon Ho Young was a bastard," Hae Jin said hotly, angry tears welling up in her eyes. Her breathing began to grow shallow. "He deserves to die a million times over."

"I..." Yoori was at a loss for words. Thunderstruck, she watched as tears started to flow down Hae Jin's cheeks.

Yoori couldn't be more confused. What did Kwon Ho Young do to have his younger siblings hate him so much?

Her dubious eyes lingered on Hae Jin.

She began to piece everything together.

No girl would react the way that Hae Jin did unless...

Tae Hyun's words from the previous night lingered in her mind.

"Can't you trust that I had a good reason?"

Comprehension finally dawned on Yoori. She covered her mouth when the answer finally hit her. That was when it *all* made terrible sense.

She gazed somberly at a quietly weeping Hae Jin. Yoori's own breathing grew heavy as her stomach began to tie itself in excruciating knots. There are certain situations when a girl can empathize with the unbearable pain of another. In this instance, as tears began to well up in her own eyes, Yoori felt Hae Jin's pain. The only difference being that she was only feeling a miniscule of the pain. Hae Jin was the one feeling all of it in its entirety.

"Hae Jin," Yoori said meekly, finding it difficult to find her own voice. She extended a hesitant hand toward Hae Jin's shoulder. Her throat became dry and she struggled with her next words. "I'm so sorry," she whispered. She was shaking as she spoke. "I'm so sorry. I didn't know..."

Shit. That was what Yoori felt like as the pit in her stomach worsened. She felt like shit.

Why? Why did she always have to be such a damn know-it-all and assume things? If she had just shut up, then Hae Jin wouldn't be crying right now. None of this would be happening right now. She hung her head in shame. She had never been more disgusted with herself.

Such guilt was relieved with Hae Jin's next set of actions.

Sensing the overbearing guilt on Yoori's part, Hae Jin slowly lifted her head. "I know," she said reassuringly, the quiet tears still present in her eyes. "I know that you didn't know."

She took another moment to close her eyes to regain her composure. Hae Jin's demeanor soon changed as a wave of vibrancy re-entered her body. An artificial smile adorning her lips, she gazed at Yoori with joyful eyes that still glistened with captive tears.

"I'm sorry about all of this," said Hae Jin, wiping her tears away. She laughed sadly while turning away. Her eyes lingered around the room for a distraction. "This is very awkward. I rarely cry, I swear."

Yoori shook her head. "Please don't apologize."

"Let's talk about something else," Hae Jin said abruptly, her eyes finally falling onto Yoori. Though her face shimmered with cheerfulness, her eyes told the truth. Yoori could see right through them. She could see the pain and desperation within them.

But she knew better now. If it was Hae Jin's wish to no longer venture on to that horrible topic, then Yoori would oblige. It was her duty to oblige. For the rest of their conversation, Yoori indulged in Hae Jin's wish. She never brought up that topic again—at least not with Hae Jin.

"Kindness is overrated."

23: Rumors

"It was so nice meeting you," Hae Jin said gently, pulling Yoori into an embrace after they proceeded into the living room.

"It was so nice meeting you too," said Yoori.

She embraced Hae Jin a little tighter than she should have. She could've sworn she heard Hae Jin yelp in pain. She couldn't help it though. Even though she obliged with Hae Jin's wish to not bring up the horrible incident, she still felt the need to apologize. Hugging Hae Jin tightly was her way of apologizing once more for her ignorance.

And, as if wordlessly saying, "don't worry about it," Hae Jin tightened her embrace as well.

"I'm happier knowing that my brother has a nice girlfriend to keep watch on him," she added happily. "I think he likes you a lot. Don't break his heart, alright?"

Yoori laughed wearily, unable to respond. After having such a great bonding session with Hae Jin, she felt especially guilty for lying to her about the content of her relationship with Tae Hyun. The topic also made her wary because she was sure that Tae Hyun didn't like her like that.

"Anyway," Hae Jin said tiredly, pulling out of the embrace. "Where is this brother of mine? I need to say bye to him before I leave."

Her eyes roamed the living room. Yoori did the same. She stopped when she saw Hae Jin's line of vision fall onto the balcony area.

"Ah," Hae Jin said happily, pointing at the window. "Oppa!"

Though there was a glass sliding door that stood between the balcony and the living room area, Hae Jin's voice successfully permeated through the barrier as Tae Hyun, who was leaning against the rail of the balcony with his Blackberry in hand, turned in the direction of the living room. Catching sight of Hae Jin, Tae Hyun, now fully dressed in a white buttoned up shirt and a black jacket with black pants to match, straightened his back. He slid the door open.

"I thought you left already," he said nonchalantly, striding in with his arms outstretched. He hugged Hae Jin.

"I couldn't leave without getting to know my brother's new girlfriend," Hae Jin said slyly. Behind her brother, she winked at Yoori.

"Oppa," Hae Jin whispered loud enough for both her brother and Yoori to hear. "She's a good catch. Don't be stupid and lose her. Okay?"

Tae Hyun's quiet eyes settled on Yoori. A sudden light flickered in his gaze. It was clear he didn't realize she was there until his sister mentioned her.

Yoori blushed at the comment as she leaned against the wall. Her arms were crossed uneasily in front of her. Though her eyes were on the siblings, her attention was mainly focused on Tae Hyun. Guilt began to wallow in her and she turned her gaze away from him in shame. She felt awful for how she treated him these past few days.

"Anyway," Hae Jin said, pulling out of the embrace. "Is Kang Min back yet? I want to see him before I go back to my apartment."

"Yeah, he's back," Tae Hyun answered distractedly, the bulk of his attention on Yoori.

She stood in the corner of the living room, still avoiding his gaze.

Hae Jin smiled. She knew her presence in the room was no longer required. "Okay, I'll see you lovebirds later." She grabbed her blue handbag from the couch and strode to the door.

"Bye Hae Jin." Yoori gave her another quick hug before she opened the door. Yoori pouted as Hae Jin brushed past her. Would it be unethical to steal Hae Jin from Tae Hyun and turn her into Yoori's baby sister instead?

"I'll see you soon!" Hae Jin screamed warmly before exiting into the elevator.

Closing the door, Yoori allowed it to click softly. Her mind was already running. She debated about whether or not she should talk to Tae Hyun now or later. She sighed. The guilt within her growing worse, she knew an apology on her part was needed right now.

She swiveled around, expecting Tae Hyun to be standing in the living room. Instead, her eyes found him outside on the balcony, leaning against the railing for support. He was still scrolling through his Blackberry.

Yoori breathed in carefully to prepare herself for the conversation to come. She went over to the sliding door. Her hands reached the lever and she slid it open. Chills ran through her when her bare feet made contact with the cold surface of the balcony.

Sliding the door closed, she was almost disappointed to see that Tae Hyun didn't even look up from his Blackberry. She folded her arms in a desperate attempt to warm herself from the gushing wind. Then, she approached him.

She stopped beside him and shared in the afternoon view of the breathtaking city before them.

"Came out here to scold me for lying to my sister about us?" he asked, his eyes off his Blackberry and fully vested on to her.

Yoori looked up at him. "No," she said quickly, her voice shaking from the cold wind. "Don't worry," she reassured. "I didn't tell her otherwise."

Tae Hyun nodded. "Good to know." He looked like he was about to say something else, but paused midway. As though uncertain if he should continue to converse with her, Tae Hyun returned his focus to the city vista.

Oh no. Awkward silence, Yoori brooded dreadfully. Her mind was churning. Determined to not allow the awkward silence to ensue, Yoori took the liberty of freeing the first thing on her mind.

"I like her a lot," she declared, her eyes skimming over the plethora of skyscrapers that stretched out before her.

Her reminder of Hae Jin made her feel more at ease. It was amazing considering how it had only been a few hours since she met Hae Jin. She was already so fond of her. Yoori didn't have a little sister and Hae Jin would be the perfect one to adopt as her own.

His attention focused on the view, a smile spread across his face.

"At first, I was worried that there might be some complications between the two of you. Hae Jin isn't normally too friendly with the girls I..." He trailed off his last words. "Let's just say, if I just use them for certain things, she doesn't think too highly of them either."

Yoori dubiously wrinkled her nose. Use them for certain things? What constituted as "certain things"?

Before she had the chance to fully process what he said, Tae Hyun broke her string of thoughts when he said, "I'm happy to hear that you two get along well."

Yoori smiled, nodding silently.

It was an understatement to say that she really wasn't absorbing much in regards to their current conversation. Her mind was clouded with uncertainty of how she should approach the conversation she wanted to have with him. Guilt suspended over her like a dark cloud. She had to apologize soon.

She drew in a deep, preparatory breath.

It was now or never.

"Tae Hyun," she started, looking up at him hesitantly.

She was finally ready.

He drew his concentration away from the view and locked his eyes with her.

She stood frozen in front of him. She didn't understand why it was difficult for her to let the words out of her lips.

An unbearable silence threatened to plague them.

Do it! Her angry conscience screamed out at her.

Shaking from anxiety, she finally said, "I'm *really* sorry."

The curiosity within Tae Hyun's eyes faded. He was clearly surprised by her apology. "You have nothing to be sorry about."

He didn't seem to understand what she was even apologizing for.

"Yes, I do," she insisted. She turned to get a better view of him. "I'm sorry for misunderstanding the situation with your older bro – "

She halted her words, realizing that she shouldn't bring up his brother when it wasn't her place to do so.

The damage was done though.

A light of understanding shined through Tae Hyun's eyes. Though his jaw tightened, the coolness in his voice remained. "Hae Jin told you?"

Yoori nodded apprehensively, not quite sure of what to say after that.

The sight of Tae Hyun taking his eyes off of her and returning his gaze to the city didn't inspire much comfort. If anything, it made her more anxious. Truthfully, Yoori had never been too good at offering her condolences to anyone. It had always been an awkward topic for her, but with Tae Hyun, the topic was especially more perturbing because the awkwardness was also coupled with unbearable guilt. She had been a certified ass to him, and she couldn't have regretted it more.

She opened her mouth, ready to say anything to break the progressing silence. She clamped her mouth shut when in place of her voice, Tae Hyun's voice began to permeate the balcony instead.

"Hae Jin was thirteen when she first told me that our older brother was acting weird around her."

His face was emotionless as his concentration on the city appeared to become stronger. He seemed lost in contemplation.

Yoori sensed by the tone of his voice that this was a secret that Tae Hyun had harbored for quite some time. She studied his profile, distress materializing in her sympathetic eyes. He didn't show any emotions, but she could feel his pain. And unlike her empathizing pain for Hae Jin, it was so much more difficult for Yoori to see Tae Hyun in pain.

"That happened five years ago, right after our father's death," he continued, pain and guilt prominent in his voice. He laughed bitterly. "I was lost in my own pain of mourning for my father's death that I didn't take what she said to heart. I basically told her to get over it and to never bother me with nonsense like that again."

Yoori's heart clenched as she continued to listen to his words—his grief.

At this point, the acceleration of the cold afternoon wind picked up. It was as though it was preparing Yoori for the painful story Tae Hyun was about to tell.

"I went back to the U.S. shortly after that to continue with my studies. I left the memory of our father and Hae Jin to fend for themselves as I ran off to another country to free myself from anymore pain."

He was quiet for several minutes before he inhaled deeply, preparing himself to relive the worst. Yoori waited with bated breath. She knew the worst was coming.

"Three years ago, I started to hear rumors—rumors that I found to be ludicrous, but they wrapped themselves around my mind nonetheless. It didn't take me long to pack up everything I had and return to Korea."

He laughed jadedly, bleakness inhabiting his eyes. "I remember it like it happened yesterday. The estate was eerily quiet when I walked in. I remember calling out each of their names, wondering if anyone was even home. I remember thinking to myself, 'Someone has to be home. All the lights are on. Someone has to be home.' I barely put my suitcase down when I heard Hae Jin's scream."

The gust of wind picked up so violently that Yoori's hair flew in just one direction. The sudden change in the force of the wind did not distract her from Tae Hyun though. Her eyes stared aimlessly at the city before them yet her full attention was irrevocably on him.

Tae Hyun rubbed his face in misery, the pain of his past distracting him from the violent wind as well. "Everything that happened after that was a blur," he continued, his misty eyes now set on the railing of the balcony. "I ran up the stairs and kicked her door open. Everything happened so fast, but the image I saw remains in my mind. I couldn't believe my eyes as the door swung open...there my brother was with his shirt off, his hands on Hae Jin, ready to rip her shirt open."

He took a moment to compose himself as his eyes glistened in rage. "I don't know how long I stood there frozen as I watched the scene before me. Kwon Ho Young was getting ready to rape Hae Jin. *My brother* was getting ready to rape *our sister*."

He exhaled sharply.

"I remember being so angry...so fucking angry that any conscience left within me vacated. I wanted to kill him. I was determined to kill him. I didn't care anymore. I just wanted to kill him. I didn't care about that bastard anymore."

Though the sternness of his voice acted as proof for the verity of his own statement, Yoori could tell from the tiny split in his voice that there was regret in what he said. She could tell that there was overwhelming guilt present within him that challenged his spoken words.

Tae Hyun went on, his eyes frantic as they relived the worst of his memories. "Next thing I knew, I pulled him off Hae Jin. She was crying and her face was bloody from all the punches he threw at her. Her entire body shook as her cries grew louder. My blood boiled as I slammed him against the wall. 'How could you do this?' I kept asking him as I slammed my fists into his stomach, his chest, and his face. 'My sister!' I kept screaming. 'Our sister!'"

Tae Hyun's glistening eyes soon dried up in revulsion. He went on, disgust and anger threading his voice.

"He laughed as I threw him onto the floor. 'I'm the King of Serpents, you stupid little prick. I can do whatever the hell I want.' He got up and charged at me. We fought for God knows how long. My energy was wearing thin as Hae Jin's cries were still prominent in the room. 'You should have stayed in the U.S. where you belong,' he whispered before removing a knife from his pocket. Taking countless jabs at me, he managed to cut my arm. It wasn't enough to kill me, but it was enough to cause me to lose focus. With a hard kick from him, I fell to the ground. I had been trained with the best of them, but I've never had a messier fight in my life. I've never been so unfocused, so stunned."

He swallowed past his trauma. "When I fell, I must have hit the counter because then, as fate would have it, his gun fell into my hands. He didn't seem to notice. He charged at me once more with his knife in hand, ready to slice my throat open."

His voice grew soft, almost with pent up remorse. "That was when I knew I had to act. That was when I knew he would kill me without even blinking an eye – that was when I knew that we were no longer brothers. We were enemies and I knew what I had to do with my enemies. So I pointed the gun at him. I pointed it at his heart."

Leaning his head back, Tae Hyun closed his eyes. The sudden anguish that hit him seemed to surprise him.

"I don't remember how many times I shot him. I couldn't stop as the image of him on top of Hae Jin replayed in my mind. All the rumors, all the horrible things he did kept replaying in my mind. I couldn't stop. I shot him until the anger left me, I shot him until the gun ran out of bullets, and I shot him until I couldn't shoot anymore."

He continued to stare at the railing of the balcony. Yoori couldn't tell what he was thinking. His breathing was so shallow that it broke her heart. He was in so much pain. She had never seen him look so vulnerable.

She wanted desperately to reach out to him and comfort him. But her arms remained frozen as they lay folded in front of her chest. She didn't know why she was hesitant, but she was. There was something about his silence. It wasn't the right time to talk to him. He was in the process of regaining his full composure. He was probably shaking with regret for telling her the story and making himself appear more vulnerable than he ever should. She couldn't bring herself to make it worse by extending her hand out to him—even though she wanted to.

After what felt like eternity, he finally lifted his eyes up to face her. He looked more composed, but only slightly. "That's why I told you that, if I could, I'd kill him again without any hesitation." He sighed, his voice becoming its steady self again. "I don't expect you to understand my hatred towards my older brother, why I showed no remorse for killing him. But you have to understand that—"

"I would've killed him too," Yoori interrupted thoughtlessly, her unblinking eyes on Tae Hyun.

The gust of wind stopped at this point.

He faced her. It was evident he was surprised by her violent statement.

"If it was me, I would have killed him as well," she repeated, gazing at him with understanding eyes. "I would have killed him a million times over."

She returned her attention to the distant city ahead of them. She was unsure of the verity of her own angry words. It perturbed her briefly, how much she meant what she said, but only briefly.

"You shouldn't have to feel any remorse," she went on, her eyes focusing on the distant blue sky. "He doesn't deserve any remorse."

She hated Tae Hyun's older brother. She hated him for the simple fact that he ruined Hae Jin's life, and she hated him for the simple fact that he left Tae Hyun with the inescapable guilt of killing his own brother.

Tae Hyun's face became unreadable as he processed what she said. Returning his gaze to the view of the city as well, his only reply was silence.

Even though he didn't say anything, and even though they weren't looking at each other, Yoori could sense his relief. Relief that he was finally able to let this secret off his chest and relief that she finally understood why he had to kill his brother.

The wind became more unforgiving as they remained on the balcony. The sound of the howling wind was the only spoken voice falling between them. What do you say to one another after a conversation like that?

Finally taking notice of the icy chill attacking her bare shoulders, Yoori flinched from the cold. The pain of freezing only lasted for a couple of seconds when a black jacket was carefully draped over her shoulders. She gazed appreciatively up at Tae Hyun, who was staring at her quietly, his eyes gentle since he last gazed at her.

Then finally, the silence was broken.

"Choi Yoori," he began cautiously, returning his eyes to the view ahead of them. "What we talked about out here today...is to never be spoken about again."

Yoori nodded in understanding. She returned her gaze to the view ahead. She understood that everything he told her out here was spoken in confidence. Just like that, Yoori promised herself that although she'd always remember what occurred here, she would never bring up the topic again. She would never bring up the pain for Tae Hyun to relive again. Never again.

Nodding silently, he began to step away from the railing of the balcony.

"I'm sorry for everything," he said suddenly.

Astonished with the words emitting out of him, Yoori gaped at Tae Hyun. The guilt looming in his voice took her by surprise. Had Tae Hyun really just apologized for everything that happened since they first met? A small part of her felt that there was more to what he was apologizing for. Yet, the bigger part of her challenged that belief with the obvious. Of course he was apologizing for what had happened so far. What else could he be apologizing for?

After mentally scolding herself for not acknowledging the obvious, a tiny smile edged her lips. Though she was sure that Tae Hyun understood that her smile was her gesture of accepting his apology, she was surprised to see that his eyes were still imbued with guilt. If anything, he looked guiltier.

She didn't have the opportunity to think more of it. Tae Hyun, seemingly sensing her alertness, wore a smile on his own face. In a split second, he obliterated any trace of pained guilt.

"It's cold out here." He made his way back to the warm apartment. Sliding the door open, he stepped in halfway, his left leg in the apartment as his right leg stood on the foundation of the balcony.

"Choi Yoori." He raised his hand up, creating an open invitation for her to take it. "We both haven't eaten all day. Let's go out. What are you in the mood for?"

Her right hand still holding on to his jacket to keep it from falling off her shoulders, Yoori smiled and took a step forward. She took his hand and allowed him to help her in.

"Italian," she answered happily.

She stepped into the apartment, releasing her hold on his hand. The warmness of the apartment embraced her. Standing before Tae Hyun with her back to him, a measure of peace came over her. She was glad that they were finally going to return to their previous form of interaction—the light-hearted one.

"Italian it is." Hunching forward, his warm breath lingered near her ear. "Now hurry and get dressed before I leave without you."

Yoori shivered with butterflies.

Luckily, there was humor present in his voice. One that thankfully calmed Yoori's excited nerves. Though their relationship was complicated, she was sure that he didn't think of her as anything more than a good friend/assistant.

Regardless, Tae Hyun was undoubtedly a handsome guy and actions such as whispering into her ear always left her with tingling sensations that she had grown wary of having. It also didn't help that she caught another whiff of that intoxicating cologne of his. Needless to say, the humor in his voice definitely aided in helping her to function normally, reminding her that their complicated relationship was actually a simple one—they were just good company for each other. Nothing more, nothing less.

As she digested his words, Yoori laughed incredulously, knowing fairly well that he would never leave without her. It would definitely be a pitiful sight for Tae Hyun to dine at an Italian restaurant alone. Moreover, she was sure he was relieved that she was no longer giving him the cold shoulder. The last thing he would endeavor to do was piss her off so soon.

Rather than retorting with the usual smart-ass comment, Yoori merely nodded, the smile never leaving her face as she rushed into the bedroom.

Why the rush? Was she afraid Tae Hyun would leave her?

No, it wasn't that.

She was excited to finally eat. And of course, as much as she hated to admit it, she was also excited to talk to Tae Hyun again—even if their conversations would consist of nothing but useless bickering. She was surprised to admit that she actually missed their bantering and was happier knowing that they'd be able to put everything behind them and get back to normal.

Whatever "normal" was for a crime lord and his personal assistant.

"You have to kill people like they are worth nothing."

24: Shop 'till You Drop

It had been more than several days since their Italian dinner and it didn't take long for things to quickly return to "normal" for Yoori and Tae Hyun. Yoori went back to being the bitter, "blackmailed-into-slavery" assistant and Tae Hyun went straight back to being the demanding, "cold-hearted" crime boss.

Bickering became the equivalent of breathing for them.

All "normalcy" aside though, something was off about their relationship—something that Yoori, for the life of her, couldn't quite figure out. Tae Hyun was acting more abnormal than usual, and to a certain degree, she was acting abnormal too.

A prime example of all these abnormalities occurred when they went to the supermarket to restock their food supply. Apparently, even with the simple task of shopping for food, Tae Hyun and Yoori never failed to leave a lasting impression on everything around them...

"Choi Yoori, are you seriously buying that much instant noodle?" Tae Hyun asked, watching as she reached for her second box of instant noodles.

"Shut up. I can't cook," she replied stiffly, emphasizing the last bit.

She glared at Tae Hyun. Could she help that they were out of edible food and the only thing she could "cook" were instant noodles? Although her unhealthy choice of food bothered Tae Hyun, she didn't really care too much. At the end of the day, it was her choice to eat unhealthily, not his.

She lugged another big box of instant noodles from the grocery aisle with her un-cuffed hand and struggled to throw it into the shopping cart.

"You've got to be kidding me," Tae Hyun commented when the box she threw into the shopping cart doubled over. Displaying impressive speed, Tae Hyun managed to catch the falling box with his free hand. He held it against his chest and chucked it back into the aisle from where Yoori first fished it.

"No! What are you doing?" she cried dramatically, struggling to retrieve the box. Her efforts were futile when he held her back.

"You act like instant noodles are the only food out there. Come on, let's get actual food," he said tiredly. His cuffed hand finding hers, their fingers became casually intertwined as he continued to push the cart down the aisle.

They agreed, due to Tae Hyun's continual insistence, that holding hands in public would be a good thing to do to mask the fact that she was handcuffed to him. Though it had never occurred to Yoori that Tae Hyun would be the type to be afraid of getting in trouble, she didn't think too much of it and agreed to such a gesture. It wasn't like holding hands with Kwon Tae Hyun was the most horrible thing to happen to her.

No. At the moment, the worst thing that could happen to her was being denied her unhealthy choice of food.

"You're so cheap," Yoori muttered, unknowingly tightening her grasp on his hand. She kept her bitter gaze on the ever-changing products on the aisle.

He gazed down at her, not believing her line of reasoning.

"What the hell are you talking about? I'm getting ready to spend *more* money so we can actually eat healthy food," he defended as they strolled into the vegetables and fruits section.

When Yoori didn't respond or return his gaze, Tae Hyun sighed as if she was a lost cause and immediately changed the subject. He seemed to do that a lot whenever a silent treatment became imminent on her part.

"So what's your favorite dish?" he asked nonchalantly, his hand reaching out to inspect a couple of tomatoes for their firmness.

Yoori rolled her eyes. Of course Tae Hyun would bring up food to get her to start talking to him again. Though catching on to his tactics, Yoori turned to face him anyway.

"Oh, like you're going to let me eat what you cooked this time?" She hadn't forgotten about that fateful morning where he enjoyed a decadent breakfast while she ate dry cereal.

He grabbed a plastic bag and placed four firm tomatoes in it.

"Yeah, of course," he replied, feigning innocence to the events of that morning.

Yoori scoffed at his answer.

He gazed at her questioningly. He was offended she didn't believe his sincerity. "What?"

"Why are you being nice?" she finally asked.

Yes, all normalcies in their bickering aside, she had also noticed that Tae Hyun had grown a wee bit nicer to her. He wasn't being entirely nice, but just the small ounce was enough for her to take notice. Naturally, it was enough to freak her out.

She inspected the tomatoes in the bag. "Are these the equivalents of poisonous apples or something?"

She was half-joking and half-serious. Though she leaned a bit further to being serious.

He peeled the bag from her and placed it in the shopping cart. He was visibly offended. "What? You'd rather I be mean?"

"No, that's not what I'm saying. It's just weird." She held out her arm as evidence for her observation. "See? I'm getting goose bumps."

He was outraged. "I can be nice."

"Oh yeah," she began sarcastically, holding up her cuffed wrist. "Yes, Mr. Crime Lord. You are definitely kind beyond words."

He eyed her cuffed wrist and chuckled like a kid caught with a lie. Walking over to the salad section, he used the opportunity to change the subject once more. "Anyway, you didn't answer me. What's your favorite dish?"

She hesitated to answer. What was the point? He wouldn't be able to make it anyway.

"Um, you probably can't make it."

"Try me."

Her hesitation remained.

"Stop being such a baby," he incited, knowing well that name-calling would get Yoori fired up.

Yoori grimaced at his comment. Closing her eyes as a means to calm herself before she flipped the bird at him, she took in a deep breath. She relaxed when she thought about her favorite dish. A big smile crept on her face. Her mouth watered. Oh, he really shouldn't have asked.

"I really like sushi," she said dreamily, her eyes twinkling with excitement as she spoke. "There was this really good sushi dish at this restaurant near where I lived. They had this special roll called the 'Tiger Roll.'" She paused and closed her eyes like she was savoring the taste in her hungry mouth. "Oh man, it was the most delicious thing ever." She sighed when she opened her eyes. She slumped her shoulders and pouted. "Too bad it closed down."

Tae Hyun suppressed a chuckle and shook his head at her.

"What?" Yoori asked, thrown as to why he laughed. She smacked his shoulder when he didn't answer her right away. "What's so funny?"

Tae Hyun sighed, ending his abrupt laughing stint. "It makes sense that you would like something that I have no talent in making."

His attention transferred to the destination ahead. He began to push the cart to the frozen meat section.

Yoori followed him, perturbed with his behavior. Seriously, what had gotten into him?

"Gosh, you're being so...*nice*. Is everything okay?" Yoori found herself asking. She craned her neck, watching as Tae Hyun threw a couple of frozen chicken thighs into the shopping cart.

His hand firmly gripping on the rail of the shopping cart, Tae Hyun turned to Yoori with an exasperated look on his face. "Suddenly being civil is considered 'nice'?"

"Maybe..."

"Shouldn't you be milking this for all it's worth?"

"Yeah, I suppose I should be milking it. But I'm just being careful."

"Why are you so paranoid?"

"I don't know. You get weird mood swings. One minute you're nice and the next, it's almost guaranteed that you'll snap." She shrugged. "Like I said, it's weird."

He scrutinized her harshly. "Haven't you ever considered that I only get angry when you make it hard for me to be civil? No, let me rephrase that, when you make it hard for me to be 'nice' to you?"

She was baffled with what he was insinuating. "When have I done that?"

"*Oh look, see I'm getting goose bumps*," he mocked in a falsetto tone, holding his arm up just like she did earlier.

She stared at him dryly. "And you wonder why I'm being careful?"

Stifling a smile at her comment, he lowered his arm with amusement. "I suppose you have a point."

She smiled. "You think?"

He laughed at her widening grin. "Come on, let's hurry up and finish up here. I'm tired."

With their eyes scanning for anything and everything they were going to need for the apartment, Yoori couldn't help but sigh happily.

"Do you know what we are?" she asked cheerily, gazing at the assortment of canned foods that lined the aisle.

"What?" he responded, his voice bored, but his eyes interested as he peered down at her.

"We're friends," Yoori said proudly, her eyes on the various items lined up on the aisles.

She kept walking, unaware that her statement caused Tae Hyun to stop dead in his tracks. She registered his action when her cuffed hand only allowed her to move so far.

She whirled around. She came face to face with a confused looking Tae Hyun.

"What?" she asked, stepping closer to him.

What had gotten into him?

The mystification on his face evolved into a somewhat thwarted one. His hand firmly gripped the railing of the shopping cart.

"You see me as a friend?"

"Uh, yeah," she replied, perplexed with his question. "Is there something wrong with that?"

"I don't have girls who are friends," he replied sharply. His tone of voice made it seem as if he couldn't believe she said something like that.

This! This was the prime example of the "abnormal" way Tae Hyun had been behaving as of late. He always seemed to get frustrated at her for the most stupid things. Why couldn't they be friends? They might as well be friends. They were around each other enough.

"I have girlfriends, but not girls who are friends," he added upon seeing the bafflement on her face.

"Well, I can be your first," Yoori replied adamantly, offended that he wouldn't even call her a friend. She knew she was the "assistant" and all, but come on! The guy could at least play along so she didn't have to feel inferior.

"My first girlfriend?"

Her eyes swelled up. "What? No. No. The first girl who's your friend."

Tae Hyun scoffed as if Yoori had posed the most ridiculous proposition he'd ever heard. "Why would I want you as a friend?"

Her mouth fell open. How rude could this guy be?

"Why can't we be friends?" she asked, trying to conceal the hurt she felt with how he was treating her.

"Because guys and girls can't be friends."

Now it was Yoori's turn to scoff as she glared at Tae Hyun. He still had a look of disbelief on his face. "Says who?"

"Me," he answered without hesitation.

It took all of Yoori's self-control not to smack Tae Hyun right across the head for his arrogant reply. Biting her bottom lip as a gesture to remind herself to not get physically violent with him, she merely released the hold he held on her cuffed hand. She began to take huge strides down the aisle.

"Oh yes, since you are the Almighty King of Serpents who knows and controls everything, right?"

Tae Hyun followed closely behind her. Still pushing the cart, he leaned forward and placed his whole weight on the shopping vehicle. He was amused with her reaction to everything.

"Choi Yoori, your sarcasm is not appreciated." He muttered something under his breath before saying, "You're such a hothead. Can't you take a joke?"

Her blood simmered. Joke? *Joke*? How was she supposed to know that he was joking? His damn face was serious as hell when he talked to her. She cursed when she realized that he called her a hothead. Who was Kwon Tae Hyun to call anyone a hothead? He was the *king* of all hotheads.

She couldn't let that insult go unanswered. She just couldn't.

"Oh yeah," she launched grouchily. "You're definitely the right person to call someone a hothead. Let me tell you something, buddy. You are the king of all hothe—Ahhh!"

Distracted by Tae Hyun, she didn't pay attention to the spilled bottle of juice sprawled across the tile. With no suction in the bottom of her cheap flip-flops, Yoori's balance was compromised when her left leg went flying up in the air. Soon, both of her legs lost their hold on gravity and her butt was ready to meet the hard surface of the supermarket tiles.

"Yoori!"

In a flash, Tae Hyun strategically positioned himself behind her, allowing her to fall onto the cushion of his lap as opposed to the unforgiving tiles.

She yelped in pain when they both fell to the floor. She probably should have saved the yelp for a split second later though, because right after she fell, a couple of canned food from the shelves above decided to join her and Tae Hyun on the floor.

"Ow!" Yoori howled after five heavy cans tumbled onto her left leg.

Tae Hyun groaned behind her.

Yoori turned her head after hearing Tae Hyun's groan. Her eyes grew wide when she saw that he was in serious pain.

"Tae Hyun?" she asked urgently, her anger subsiding as concern took its place. "Where are you hurt?"

Turning a full circle, she only stopped to reposition herself when she noted that the cuffs prevented her from being able to properly face him. After readjusting in a position where they were face to face, she craned her neck over his shoulder. She winced in empathizing agony. It didn't take long for her to conclude that Tae Hyun must have hit his hip against the sharp edge of the metal aisle when he cushioned her fall.

"Are you okay?" she asked again, touching the area of his hip that must've had the most impact from the collision.

"Yoori, don't—" he groaned hoarsely.

She retracted her fingers. "I'm sorry!" she cried, watching him inhale sharply.

"It's alright," he tried to reassure her once he noticed the guilt on her face. "I'm fine."

Yoori mentally berated herself for touching him where it obviously hurt. Why do people have that bad habit of touching someone in the area where the pain is worst? Yoori shook her head. That was certainly not a question she wanted to dwell on.

Determined to help make things right, she grabbed one of the shelves and used it to prop herself up. Standing up, she extended her hand out to Tae Hyun, who stared at her strangely.

He looked determined to not appear helpless.

As Yoori anticipated, Tae Hyun allowed his pride to get the best of him. He shook his head, rejecting her help.

"No, I can get up myself," he replied, trying to sound strong when it was obvious he was in pain.

He groaned when he fully sat upright.

Yoori sighed at the pathetic scene before her. Boys and their stupid pride.

Her eyes remained on Tae Hyun, who tried to grab hold on to one of the shelves to get up.

She extended her hand further for him. "Come on, Tae Hyun," she coaxed, taking another step forward. "Stop being so stubborn—Ahhhh!"

As it became apparent that there was still leftover juice attached to Yoori's flip-flops, she slipped face-forward. Falling down, her legs awkwardly spread across each side of Tae Hyun's stomach. She fell into a sitting position onto his hard abs. With no control of her stance, the impact of the fall caused her to lunge her upper body forward onto Tae Hyun, causing his head to slam against the tiles.

Once again, his body broke her fall.

"Fucking hell, Yoori," Tae Hyun uttered with frustration.

"I'm so sorry," she whispered breathlessly. Yoori couldn't have felt crappier for causing him more physical pain. How clumsy could she be?

Gently placing both of her hands on Tae Hyun's shoulders, she sat herself up, unbeknownst to herself how scandalous they looked. You know, with him lying beneath her and her legs spread apart while she sat on his abs and all...

Being the first to notice the provocative position they were in, a happy grin spread across Tae Hyun's handsome face. Any shred of anguish was obliterated from his countenance. It was evident he had found the remedy for his pain.

"What are you smiling about?" Yoori asked worriedly, afraid that this sudden attack on Tae Hyun's body had paralyzed his brain.

"You know," he began silkily, staring at the lower half of her body that was still situated on his hard abs. "If you slid just a little further south, this would be the perfect position to make all my pain go away."

Yoori gaped at him in dismay.

She looked past her blue top and settled her eyes on her pajama pants – or more specifically, her legs. It took Yoori less than a millisecond to finally realize where she was actually sitting.

Shit!

She yelped and struggled to grab hold of the shopping cart to help prop her petrified self up.

"Yoori, no!" Tae Hyun screamed when she rested her full body weight on one side of the shopping cart.

Too late.

Before Yoori could react, the shopping cart was already falling toward them. Collapsing back down in the same sitting position she was in moments before, the gargantuan weight of the shopping cart soon collided with Yoori's left leg and the right side of Tae Hyun's body. A monstrous thud thundered across the aisle as everything in the shopping cart came sprawling out.

"Ow!" they both howled when the contents landed on them.

Silence collapsed onto the aisle where the commotion once took place.

With her hands reaching out to push the chicken thighs out of her way, Yoori immediately reached for the empty shopping cart. It laid on her leg and the right side of Tae Hyun's body.

"I think," she groaned pathetically, picking up the shopping cart and pushing it off of them. "I think I need to be un-cuffed now."

"Yeah," Tae Hyun replied breathlessly. He took in another sharp, painful breath and cursed to himself. "Definitely."

"Even when you know for a fact that it's not true."

25: Instincts and Distractions

"Tae Hyun! Seriously just put me down!"

"Just slide the damn card!"

"Ugh!"

After Yoori crankily slid the card through the reader, the metal door to Tae Hyun's apartment flew open. Running in like a racecar with Yoori in his arms, Tae Hyun kicked the door closed behind him and made a beeline for the bedroom.

"Slow down!" Yoori screamed in a panic, feeling herself slip out of Tae Hyun's hold. "We're here, we're here!"

His pace only quickened when he felt her sliding off. Upon entering his bedroom, he ran straight for his bed. Dropping Yoori on the bed with the utmost care, it was clear that Tae Hyun couldn't find the energy to stand up anymore. Spent, he threw himself onto the bed.

"Shit," he whispered. He was visibly surprised with the amount of energy he had to exert to carry Yoori home, especially considering that his own body was in pain. "Shit, that was really painful."

Yoori watched Tae Hyun with guilt splashing over her. After the hazing affair they received at the supermarket, Tae Hyun was insistent, regardless of the fact that his own body suffered more damage than hers, that Yoori should not exert more pressure on her legs. Before she even had a chance to refute that proposition, Tae Hyun had already un-cuffed her and lifted her off the floor. The next thing she knew, he was zooming out of the supermarket like a speeding bullet.

She reached for a water bottle on the bedside table. She unscrewed the cap and handed the bottle to Tae Hyun. He took it without hesitation.

"I told you I could've walked." She watched him lift his head up to drink the water. "Why did you run so fast?"

"I..." He stopped midway and began to drink furiously from the water bottle. He wiped his mouth after he was done and handed the half-full bottle back to Yoori. "I was about to drop you."

His face red from fatigue, he lowered his head back onto the mattress and continued to pant in exhaustion.

Yoori freed the water bottle from his grasp. "I would have been fine if you dropped me," she said quietly, before drinking from the water bottle. Wanting to help ease Tae Hyun's bout of exhaustion, she lifted her free hand and began to wave it back and forth, hoping the fanning motion would help cool him down.

I would have been fine if you dropped me? Her inner self asked critically upon further inspection. Okay sure, she would not have been fine, but she would have felt less guilty. That was for sure. How was it possible that the guy could be such a jerk one moment and be so considerate the next?

She placed the water bottle back on the counter. The fanning motion of her hand accelerated. "How are you doing?"

"I'm a crime lord who got hurt because of his assistant's clumsiness in a supermarket." He stifled a chuckle after he thought the situation over. He gently grabbed her wrist to stop her fanning motion. He regarded her with an entertained smirk on his face. "How do you think I'm doing?"

She smiled ruefully, blushing at the feel of his warm hand around her wrist. "For what it's worth, I think you're a really good friend for propping yourself underneath me and carrying me home, even when you're in pain too."

His smirk grew when he released his hold on her. He lifted himself up and leaned on both his elbows for support. His eyes locked on her with much interest. "Is that what friends do?"

Yoori nodded, her blood growing hot at the sight of him staring at her like she was the most interesting thing on earth.

"Good friends...yeah," she replied mindlessly, as if also trying to convince herself.

Tae Hyun nodded.

She wasn't too sure if he actually processed what she said though. His unusual silence made her think that he was distracted with something else.

"Choi Yoori, I think it's time for us to renegotiate our terms."

Yoori's eyes bulged. She sat closer to Tae Hyun in excitement.

"Seriously, buddy?" she asked happily, emphasizing the word "buddy." She knew calling Tae Hyun a "friend" to his face would merit her some points.

Tae Hyun nodded to confirm, his eyes visibly pleased with the excitement exuding out of Yoori. Apparently, at that moment, neither of them felt the spasm of pain that their bodies should've been experiencing.

Yoori squealed in delight. She clapped her hands together and cleared her throat, staring at him seriously. She was ready for the renegotiation exchange to begin. They would start with the most uncivilized of terms.

"Handcuffs?" she prompted swiftly. Surely, she must get rid of the one thing that anchored her from actual freedom.

He pondered the proposal.

"Still necessary," he said slowly, his eyes on her apologetic.

"What? Oh, come on!" This negotiation exchange was already starting to look pretty gloomy for Yoori. So much for being friends.

"I'm not done," he supplied. "The cuffs will stay on, but only at night when we're sleeping. Anytime else, when we go out or do whatever, we won't be handcuffed."

214

Though she was secretly happy that the severity of the punishment had been lessened, she knew she shouldn't settle. Yoori had to negotiate until she received the best deal she could get.

"Do you realize how difficult it is for one of us to sleep on the floor with the cuffs on?" she asked, silently praying for the handcuffs to be gone – permanently.

"Which brings me to my next point. Let's talk about the sleeping arrangements."

Yoori folded her arms and stared at him suspiciously. "Okay..." She already had a bad feeling about this part of the negotiation.

"We'll both have to compromise," he said suggestively, looking at her with a hint of a smile in his eyes.

Her mouth dropped open.

You know you've been around someone for too long if you know what he's thinking just by looking at him. And in Yoori's case, she had been around Tae Hyun for too long. She already knew what he was suggesting.

She shook her head, hoping she misunderstood his intentions. "You're not suggesting..."

He eased himself up into a sitting position. He faced her with a virtuous expression on his perfectly crafted face. Casually, he said, "Let's be mature adults here and share the same bed."

By this time, Yoori had already backed to the further end of the bed in fear.

"No, no, no," she said frantically, shaking her head. "Isn't this like sexual harassment or something?" she found herself asking.

"What?" He looked at her incredulously. "Sexual harassment is 'unwanted sexual advances.'" He regarded her with a smile of disbelief. "Are you insinuating that I'm making sexual advances on you?"

"Maybe," she replied quickly, though she was completely unsure. At times, she couldn't tell if Tae Hyun was teasing or if he was actually flirting. Players are like that. They sometimes flirt without even realizing it. It was in their nature.

"Choi Yoori," he began, his twitching mouth holding back a round of laughter. "Trust me, if I was making sexual advances on you, you'd know." He inched closer to her. "Come on, what's the big deal? This compromise is supposed to be good for both of us.

"Seriously, I can sleep on the floor or the couch," she said, desperation present on her scarlet face. "I don't mind."

"No, I'd feel bad," he said, his voice sincere. "I'll sleep on the further end of my side of the bed and you can sleep on the further end of yours. We'd never know that the other was there."

Yoori continued to shake her head at his ridiculous suggestion. How could a guy and a girl not know that the other was in the same bed?

Kwon Tae Hyun, you moron! Your reasoning has a big hole in it! She wanted to scream out at him as she moved further away.

"Come on, *buddy*," he coaxed. "I'm not going to do anything to you and you're not going to do anything to me. It's no big deal. We *are* friends?"

"I thought you didn't have girls who are friends?" she asked with a perplexed expression.

He grinned sheepishly at her. "There's a first time for everything, right?"

She continued to shake her head. This was so inappropriate on so many levels.

When it looked like Tae Hyun was about to say more to convince her to see things his way, he abruptly stalled.

"Huh..." he said unexpectedly, scrutinizing her frightened appearance. A sly, perceptive smile appeared on his face. All of a sudden, he began to back away from her. "Ah crap, why didn't I see this before?"

"Wh–what are you doing?" Yoori asked, confused. "Why are you looking at me like that?"

"Choi Yoori…" He inspected her fearful demeanor more closely. "If I didn't know better, I'd seriously think you're really attracted to mc."

That was all it took for Yoori to snap out of her fearful stupor. "*What*?" What the hell?

"It makes sense now." He dramatically got off the bed and shook his head. "I thought it was strange how your eyes are *always* swelling up whenever you see me come out of the shower. Now, I know why."

Her face grew a darker shade of red. That was not true!

She thought about it further.

Well, it was true, but he shouldn't point it out like that! Acting like she was some pervert who stalks around the room, waiting for him to come sauntering out of the shower with his sexy naked upper body distracting her eyes. Yoori stopped when she realized that he might have a point. However, being the prideful fighter that she was, Yoori certainly wasn't going to let Tae Hyun win this game. She was *not* going to be labeled as some perverted fan girl!

"Look, we gotta get a couple of things straight," she said tightly, preparing to get off the bed as well. She only stalled when Tae Hyun theatrically placed both of his hands up in midair.

"No. It's okay, assistant. I understand now. Of course casually sleeping beside each other is a bad idea. If it doesn't help your obsession with me, then it's definitely a better idea if I slept on the floor."

Bending his knees, he prepared to lie down on the floor. Such a gesture, however, was foiled when Yoori grabbed him roughly by the arm.

"No!" she shouted heatedly. With all the strength she had, she pulled him back to the bed. "You get your ass in bed!"

Yoori's hold wasn't strong enough to pull Tae Hyun, but with a secret grin on his face, he dutifully followed her pull and hopped onto the mattress.

Yoori couldn't be more irate and offended. She grumpily placed her legs under the comforter. At this point, sleeping was her best option of ending this terrible negotiation exchange.

"Saying I like you...yeah right!" she huffed crankily, pulling the covers over herself. She rested on the pillow, not done articulating her outrage. "You have some nerve saying that. God, you're such an arrogant piece of—OH MY GOD! WHAT ARE YOU DOING?" she shrieked when she glanced up and saw that Tae Hyun was not only *not* paying attention to what she was saying, but he was also *not* wearing a shirt to cover that flaming hot body of his.

In the name of all that is Holy, why was he torturing her like this?

"It's a relief we're such good friends that I can sleep like this," he said breathlessly, discarding his black shirt aside. "I don't have to worry about you sexually harassing me at night."

He ran to the corner with only black pants to cover all those beautiful muscles and switched off the light. When the room swam in darkness, he sped back to the bed. Yoori bounced in frozen horror when the bed adjusted to his powerful frame. She could smell that sexy cologne of his as he situated himself underneath the covers. Through the darkness, she gaped at him in dismay.

He repositioned his pillow underneath his head and stared back at her.

"What is it, *buddy*?" he asked innocently. Even in the looming darkness, she could tell his eyes were twinkling. He knew *exactly* why she was staring at him with such horror.

Tae Hyun. Tae Hyun that damn, teasing bastard had more than polluted the true meaning of friendship!

Y—you friendship abuser, she wanted to say to him for turning the innocence of her friendship into this. Yet, her face remained stoned as she lay on the other side of the bed. With her heart beating at an alarming rate and her face turning bright red, she couldn't have been more thankful that the room was dark.

"Nothing, buddy," she muttered resentfully. She slyly scooted a little bit further to avoid being close to Tae Hyun's promiscuous body.

See no evil. See no evil. See no evil. The phrase repeated like a mantra in her head. She tried desperately to erase the tempting image of a shirtless Tae Hyun.

"Good," he answered before nuzzling the right side of his face onto his pillow. "Sweet dreams, Choi Yoori."

Silence befell the room when he closed his eyes.

Yoori rolled over onto the right side of her body. She strategically positioned herself so that her back would be facing Tae Hyun. It was a tactical strategy employed to not only decrease the acceleration of her heart rate, but also to prevent her from staring at Tae Hyun's sleeping countenance.

She closed her eyes and pulled the comforter tightly around her. She tried her best to fall asleep so she didn't have to think about her half-naked, "friendship abusing" buddy on the other side of the bed.

Such an attempt was stymied when he called out to her.

"Choi Yoori," she heard him say as she attempted to drift off to sleep.

"Hmm?" she answered instinctively.

She mentally slapped herself for answering so fast.

What was she thinking? Did she really want the night to progress with Tae Hyun, whether directly or indirectly, teasing her womanly senses? Maybe it would have been a better idea if she pretended to be asleep. She could only imagine that he must have wanted to torture her some more before he called it a night.

His next words took her by complete surprise. "Tell me a little bit more about yourself."

Wow, she really didn't expect to hear that.

She rolled back and faced Tae Hyun. The side of his face rested on the palm of his hand while he gazed at her with a small smile.

She initially hesitated to say anything, but when she reasoned how comfortable she had grown around Tae Hyun, she decided to open up. They were friends after all.

"What do you want to know?"

"Where is your family?" he asked. "I've never heard you talk about them."

Yoori smiled sadly. "They died in a fire a while back."

It felt strange to say this out loud, but in the same token, it felt like this burden had been lifted off her chest. She thought that it would've been harder to open up, yet Tae Hyun made it easy for her. Instead of stiffening up and becoming uncomfortable, as most people do when they find out about the death of your loved ones, he remained as warm as ever.

"I'm sorry," he said sincerely.

Yoori nodded. "Thank you."

"Was it just you and your parents?"

"I had a cousin who lived with us. She died too. I don't have anyone left."

He eased a loose bang that fell over her eyes. "Were you close to them?"

"I don't know." When he gave her a questioning look, she said, "I...I was a really bad daughter. I did a lot of wrong things and I disappointed them a lot. I even ran away a couple of times." She inhaled slowly. "I only became a good daughter after I got into a car accident. After that, I had a new outlook on life and I guess I just...changed." She strained to smile. "Hopefully for the better."

His warm smile lifted her spirits. "Too bad they can't see you now."

She laughed. "I'm sure they wouldn't be too impressed with me being the personal assistant of a crime lord. No offense."

"You didn't do it for money," he said quietly, holding her gaze. "You did it because I used your moral obligations against you."

She stared into his eyes. She hadn't noticed it before, but he really had beautiful eyes. They were the kind that melted you with a simple stare – they were the kind that made you feel like the whole world revolved around you simply because he was giving you his full attention.

Now that she had shared her story, she was infinitely curious about his. "What about you? Were you close to your family?"

He nodded. "Growing up, I was close to all of them."

"What happened to your mom?"

Grief rippled in his gaze. "My father's death really hit her hard. After he died, she couldn't take it." He swallowed softly. "She committed suicide."

Yoori shifted uncomfortably. "I'm sorry."

"And I'm sorry for yours," he said gently. He reached out and reassuringly caressed her cheek. "I lost three of my family members during separate occasions. I can't imagine losing them all at once."

Another sad smile outlined her lips. "I lost them all at one time, but the shock from it only happened once. Your pain was prolonged. I can't imagine going through it three separate times." Yoori readjusted her head on the pillow, unknowingly moving closer to him and those caressing fingers. "Do you miss them?"

"Everyday."

Another stream of silence spilled over them like a waterfall.

Tae Hyun stared at her for the longest time, his fingers stroking her cheek. Hypnotized by how nice it felt to be caressed by his gentle touch, she let him stroke her cheek as he pleased. He was too captivating to resist.

A few minutes passed before he suddenly said, "How are you holding up in this world?"

Yoori looked at him. She knew he was referring to the Underworld. "I can't believe it existed right under my nose. It's hard to believe how big this world is."

He nodded before grimly saying, "This world is nothing compared to the real thing."

She knitted her brows. "What do you mean?"

"What you see so far is the little that the public knows. When you get deeper down, this society becomes more...complex."

"How so?"

"It's more dangerous."

"Why haven't I seen all that the Underworld has to offer?"

"Because I've been keeping it from you."

She laughed. "And why have you been doing that?"

He looked at her seriously. "It's not a good world to be welcomed into."

"If it's so dangerous, why are you still in it?"

He smirked. "I was born into it. It's different."

"Do you sometimes wish you were in another world? A more normal and safe one?"

He chuckled, pulling his hand away. He edged closer to her, so close that the heat from his body felt like a furnace next to hers.

His brown eyes holding hers captive, he almost seductively said, "I am revered like a King in this world. Why would I ever want to leave it?"

Yoori shrugged, struggling to maintain poise amid the longing inside her. It took all her strength to not draw any closer to Tae Hyun, to get lost in the heat of his tempting body.

Keep calm and carry on as though he wasn't teasing you, she instructed herself.

"You hold a lot of lives in your hand when you're a King," she said. "When you're just another human, you have more time to enjoy the simpler things in life."

Tae Hyun smiled. After a long, pondering moment, he showed mercy by relinquishing with his subtle teasing of Yoori and her womanly senses.

"Thanks for coming back," he said unexpectedly.

She tilted her head in confusion. She didn't understand what he was referring to. "Come back?"

His smile widened marginally. "The warehouse," he clarified.

"Oh," Yoori finally recalled, the events of that day returning to her. "Oh that."

"Why'd you come back?"

Even in the darkness, Yoori could swear that there was a hint of vulnerability in Tae Hyun's eyes when he asked this. When he saw that she was finally on the same page as him, his interest grew. He sounded nonchalant, but she could sense he really wanted to know her answer.

She didn't know why, but at that second, her stomach churned when he asked that question. It didn't churn because of disgust. It churned because of caution. Whatever the reason for her sudden state of alertness, her gut instinct told her to be careful. That caution heeded, she answered with the first bullshit answer that popped into her mind.

"Because we're friends," she said promptly, her eyes never leaving his.

His composure was challenged with her unforeseen answer.

"Because we're friends?" Tae Hyun repeated after her, the tone of his voice now unreadable. He didn't seem to believe her.

She nodded as guarded silence fell upon them.

The sting she felt after those words poured from her mouth surprised her. She wasn't too sure why she came back to the warehouse. She only knew that the reason she gave Tae Hyun wasn't a hundred-percent true. Whatever the case was though, she didn't delve deeper into it. Her gut told her that it was a better idea to leave things as they were. And, for tonight, she was happy to oblige.

After taking a few moments to inspect her face for some form of bluff, a small and somewhat thwarted smile appeared on his face.

"That's a pretty stupid reason," he finally concluded. Before Yoori could retort, he went on. "You're a smart girl, but you better not do anything stupid like that again. When your life is in danger, you run. Don't try to save anyone else. You'll do well to remember that, alright? You might have been lucky at the warehouse, but you have to understand that the Underworld is an unforgiving place. It is unlikely you'll get lucky the second time around."

Yoori pursed her lips in annoyance. She wasn't the only stupid one that day.

"Why did you have me leave the warehouse before Ji Hoon appeared?" she found herself asking.

Judging by the perplexed expression on his face, she could surmise that he wasn't sure of his answer either. However, being an expert with hiding his bluff, the uncertainty on Tae Hyun's face vanished as quickly as it appeared.

"Because we're friends," he said firmly, his composure reappearing. With a mischievous smirk, his eyes challenged her to find his bluff.

Yoori sighed at his answer. A part of her was glad that he offered her that simple answer. A simple answer for the simple relationship they had with one another. A larger part of her felt disappointed. It would have been nice to hear something else. She couldn't deny that.

Tired of the serious atmosphere that cloaked them, Yoori took it upon herself to take the conversation into another direction—a more lighthearted direction.

"Anyway, it was also stupid of you to put yourself in front of me when that guy was pointing the gun at us. What's wrong with you?" she asked, hoping Tae Hyun would follow her lead and start to bicker with her so the intensity of their conversation would lessen.

He took the hint. "What is it about us smart people that makes us do stupid things?" he asked, faking a tone of disbelief.

Yoori shrugged, happy that he was following along with the lighthearted conversation she wanted.

"I don't know," she answered blithely. "I guess we were both distracted by everything that was going on. I wasn't thinking. I followed my instincts that day. So don't be flattered or anything that I came to 'save' you. Sometimes my own stupidity gets the best of me."

"Yeah, mine too," he agreed, lost in contemplation as he played with the fabric of his comforter.

When she watched his fingers tug on the loose string of the fabric, it finally occurred to Yoori why Tae Hyun had been acting abnormal lately.

"You know," she ventured timidly, making it a point to get his attention. She went on when he lifted his eyes off the comforter to meet hers. "It hadn't occurred to me until now that you've been acting especially strange lately because you've had something on your mind." She hesitated before saying, "What's bothering you?"

He studied her with a raised brow. "Do I look bothered?"

Yoori shook her head. "You don't look it. But I just have a feeling you are."

A broad smile danced on Tae Hyun's lips. Amused, he briefly turned away. Though he didn't look bothered, she knew he was. She was so confident that she was even willing to challenge his smile.

"I'm following my instincts tonight," she stated confidently. "And I think I'm right when I say that something's been bothering you these past few days."

Poor Tae Hyun. He truly did try to keep the smile firmly solidified on his face. However, when it was apparent that he was caught, he merely exhaled with exhaustion. "If you must know, I've been feeling a bit conflicted."

"About what?"

"Choosing between two things I want," he answered carefully, his eyes refusing to meet hers. The internal battle ensuing within him was evident in his somber state. The air of arrogance that typically frequented his personality dissipated when he admitted this.

"Oh?"

"Well," he amended, his eyes staring at the outlining of the comforter. "I'm not sure if I actually want the second one."

Perplexity flooded over Yoori's face as he continued, "I mean...I'm feeling conflicted because I'm still unsure of *why* I'd want the second thing. For the first thing I want, I've wanted it all my life. But for this second thing, it just occurred to me that I *might* want it. But I don't know if I just want it for the sake of wanting it or if I really want it. Having said that, I honestly don't know what I'd do with it if I did get it. So essentially right now, I'm not only deciding between two things I want...but I'm also confused. I don't know if the second thing is even worth wanting."

After finishing his puzzling reply, his eyes returned to Yoori. "That is what's bothering me. I can't decide what I want."

Yoori returned his gaze with a blank stare.

"Wow," she began sarcastically. "Could you *be* anymore specific?"

He chuckled at her sarcasm. "If it makes you feel any better, you're not the only one confused around here."

Apparently. She wanted to ask him for specifics as to what exactly those two things were, but she hesitated. She knew the limitations of Tae Hyun's secretive nature; she knew this sum of information from him was as good as it was going to get—at least for now.

She favored him with an empathizing smile. "You don't strike me as an indecisive person."

The King of Serpents troubled because he doesn't know what he wants? This was an entirely new development.

"I've been taken aback by this abnormality myself." He playfully regarded her. "So, Choi Yoori, any suggestions for a remedy to help me sort out my internal conflicts?"

"You really can't have both?" she suggested hopefully, not understanding why the decision was so difficult for him. If it were Yoori, she would fight to keep both. She wasn't afraid to admit that she was selfish and greedy like that—just like all human beings.

He shook his head. "It's one or the other."

"I see," she said, instantly understanding this special predicament. It was one of those situations where the choices played out like divided forks on a road, each a roadblock for the other and each leading the decision maker down two separate paths. If you choose one, you must give up the other. If you're undecided and choose both, then you end up going nowhere with either.

Smiling sympathetically, she gave Tae Hyun the one, perfect universal answer that would help to resolve anything.

"Follow your instincts," she advised simply, truly believing in her pearl of wisdom. "Whatever you want more, your instincts will go after that in the end."

Yoori observed the light of indecision in his eyes. She immediately understood that the decision was a much tougher one than she originally assumed it to be.

Tae Hyun nodded inattentively. He allowed his eyes to draw away from her. The air of concentration that emitted from Tae Hyun told Yoori that he was actually taking her advice into consideration. She watched him carefully, curiosity gleaming like diamonds in her gaze. Was he actually choosing right now? Her internal question was answered by the progressing silence.

Yes, he was indeed making his decision.

The hushed breathing between Yoori and Tae Hyun became the only vocalization that graced the dark bedroom. Tae Hyun grew lost in the internal battle within himself. Yoori blinked quietly and waited with bated breath. She watched as his long fingers played with the fabric of the bed, as if peeling away at his reasoning. His eyes were locked on an undetected area of the comforter like he was trying to figure out which decision was the true apple of his eyes. His contemplative breathing grew more intense, hinting to her that he was almost done with his decision.

Throughout the duration of this, Yoori was so curious. She wondered what his string of reasoning was and, more importantly, what his final decision was. Did he choose the first one or the second one?

"Have you made your decision?" she finally inquired, curiosity ripping off the last shred of her patience.

His eyes locked with hers. "I think so."

"What'd you pick?"

"The first one," he answered carefully, the cautious tone in his voice making it appear as if he was also trying to convince himself that it was the right choice.

Taking inventory of his doubt, Yoori grimaced in disappointment. To her, it seemed that Tae Hyun, rather than following his instincts like she had suggested, instead took it upon himself to follow his rationale—two completely separate and conflicting entities.

Unable to restrain her observant nature, Yoori threw all reservations out the window and called him out on that. "You don't seem so sure."

"Choi Yoori," Tae Hyun began, ignoring her remark. The subtle urgency in his voice caught Yoori's undivided attention. It scared her, how truly conflicted he appeared. "Do you remember when I told you that to get in a position of power...some actions are unavoidable?"

"I remember," she confirmed. Her concern for him heightened. Why was he bringing that up?

He smiled bleakly. "Good. Every now and then, make sure you remind me, alright?"

However much she was puzzled by how they ventured on to the discussion at hand, she decided to go along with the conversation. Though he didn't show it, she could feel his desperation. Whatever his reason, Tae Hyun really wanted to have this conversation with her. She could feel it.

"When will I know you'll need a reminder?"

"When I look distracted."

Yoori looked at him uncertainly. Thoughts of her amnesia came into play. "To be perfectly honest, I don't have a good track record of remembering stuff. I might fail you."

Tae Hyun's smile indicated to her that he was confident she'd do well to remind him when it was necessary.

He remained quiet for a couple of seconds after, eyeing her keenly. It was like there was something else bothering him. In place of voicing it, he simply closed his eyes and pulled the cover to his neck.

"Good night, Yoori." He followed that statement with a big yawn before he nuzzled his face into his fluffy white pillow.

Closing his eyes, Tae Hyun's breathing became light as he drifted off to sleep. The confliction that once hounded him was no longer present in his relaxed visage.

Dread coursed through Yoori. Her eyes flicked over a sleeping Tae Hyun. This time, she was sure that he wasn't going to wake up to chat with her again.

"'Night," she whispered back, disappointed that their conversation was once again cut short.

Sleeping there, engulfed in the darkness and stillness, Yoori was tempted to dig deeper into their conversation. She wanted to poke at Tae Hyun and wake him up so they could continue talking.

Yoori was introduced to a different side of Tae Hyun tonight – a side that although despondent upon introduction, was a side that she desperately wanted to interact with again. He didn't behave as a revered King in the Underworld. No, he simply behaved like any other human being. A human being who was not only vulnerable, but a human being who was also relatable.

Yoori sighed at her absurd desire.

After fighting off the temptation to wake him up, Yoori nuzzled the left side of her face into her pillow. Her initial plan was to close her eyes and drift off to sleep. She instead found herself staring at Tae Hyun's sleeping countenance. The illumination from the moon touched his face perfectly, making it appear like he was glowing.

Yoori was mesmerized.

As her gaze on him remained, she found herself aching when she recalled the desperation in his voice when he spoke to her about his internal conflict. Whatever it was that bothered him, Yoori truly hoped that he would get all of that sorted out soon.

Though a part of her didn't understand why she cared about him and his internal conflict so much, her mind reasoned that it was probably because Tae Hyun was the first person she had ever spent so much time around and the first person she formed a bond with. Even though the usual contents of their conversations revolved around them going at each other's throats, Yoori knew that it didn't overshadow the strong bond she felt with him. Tae Hyun was someone that she truly cared about and even his secretive nature wasn't enough to deter her from empathizing with him when he was troubled.

She exhaled, clenching her hands together when a bout of longing tingled through them.

She wanted to lift her fingers up and trace the outlining of his perfectly sculpted jaw. It glowed underneath the moonlight, beckoning for her to touch him. It was a strange moment for Yoori. All she wanted to do was reach out and touch him, comfort him. But when she heard a soft murmur escape from his sleeping lips, all temptation flew out of the window and rationale returned.

Yawning quietly and finally convincing herself that it was due time to stop staring at Tae Hyun, she closed her tired eyes in preparation for a much needed slumber. After pulling the comforter over herself, Yoori slowly fell out of consciousness. As she drifted off to sleep, Yoori failed to consciously realize that she was actually replaying a significant part of their earlier conversation in her head. A part of the conversation that may have sounded trivial at the moment, but would have a significant meaning in the future...

"Do you remember when I told you that to get in a position of power...some actions are unavoidable?"

"I remember."

"Good. Every now and then, make sure you remind me, alright?"

"When will I know you'll need a reminder?"

"When I look distracted."

Finally losing consciousness, it didn't occur to Yoori that the next time she verbalized those words, it wouldn't only be to serve as a reminder to Tae Hyun about the necessary things he would have to do to become the Lord of the Underworld—it would also serve as a reminder about the necessary things she would have to do as well.

"You have to show no remorse."

26: An Hour with Skulls and Scorpions

It was the slight touch of the mid-afternoon rays that woke Yoori up from her dream about the two lovers—the one about the girl wanting to kill herself and her lover trying to convince her not to. Murmuring quietly, she tugged the covers over her head. She attempted to drown out the rays and steal a couple more minutes of sleep. But as she tossed and turned, the content of the dream becoming slowly forgotten in her head, she knew stealing a few more moments of sleep was impossible—especially when she realized that she was tossing and turning diagonally, essentially invading someone else's side of the bed.

Crap!

With all this tossing and turning, how close was she to Tae Hyun and that naked chest of his?

She frightfully opened her eyes and anticipated one of two things: she expected to wake up to see Tae Hyun sleeping soundly beside her, completely oblivious to her tossing and turning (this would be the ideal option), or if he wasn't sleeping, then she anticipated to open her eyes to see him smirking at her as he makes a comment about knowing that she wants him, even when they're sleeping (this was obviously the less ideal option).

As luck would have it, Yoori quickly realized that there was a third option she didn't anticipate seeing.

Apparently, Tae Hyun wasn't even in bed.

Wide-awake, Yoori sat up on the bed. Perplexity presided over her. Although she was relieved that she didn't wake up in Tae Hyun's arms, it was disconcerting to see that he was missing. Her eyes wandered the room in worry. Where was he?

Throwing the covers off of herself, Yoori was prepared to go out to the living room to find him when she noticed a piece of white paper fluttering off the counter. Still situated in bed, she placed one hand on the mattress for balance. She reached her right hand out to lift the piece of paper off the floor. Upon retrieving it, she pulled herself back up and held the paper in front of her. Her eyes shook off the last of its sleepiness when she saw that it was a note from Tae Hyun.

A mentor is in town.

I'll be out all day.

You probably didn't remember and

I didn't want to wake you

but have fun on your day off.

Don't do anything I would do.

— TH

"Day off?"

She reread the note.

Still sleepy, her brief disorientation remained for a couple more seconds before she finally recalled that her day off from Tae Hyun was apparently a weekly thing. As her alertness returned, it didn't take her too long to figure out the implications of her day off and what she needed to accomplish today.

One hour.

Ji Hoon's proposition sprang into her mind.

A new spell of internal conflict engulfed her. *It was probably terrible*, she mused, staring at the note. It was probably terrible that even though she was happy to learn that her "day off" was a weekly occurrence, she found herself missing Tae Hyun's company. She never took it into account before, but this was actually the first morning, since the night Tae Hyun first took out the cuffs, that she spent a morning without him. Not that she was attached to him or anything! It was just weird for her because she was so used to him being around.

The awfulness didn't end there. Her internal conflicts lingered on to someone else. It was also probably really bad that as she reread the part where Tae Hyun wrote, "Don't do anything I would do," the face of Lee Ji Hoon popped into her mind.

Along with the image of Ji Hoon came the memory of their last meeting and what he promised her.

She knew that when Tae Hyun wrote, "Don't do anything I would do," it was his subtle way of requesting that she doesn't meet up with Ji Hoon. Although she felt more loyalty toward Tae Hyun than Ji Hoon, she still wanted to be selfish and put Tae Hyun's needs behind her own.

How could she abandon the one opportunity to learn more about the infamous An Soo Jin from the one source that mattered? How could she abandon the one opportunity to gather evidence to further prove that she wasn't the Scorpion girl?

She inhaled with anticipation.

The unquenchable addiction to learn more about An Soo Jin gushed over her in the early afternoon. In that instant, Yoori knew what she had to do.

Jumping out of bed, she knew it was horrible that she couldn't control her desire to learn more about An Soo Jin. It was also awful that, even though she had already missed Tae Hyun's company, a small part of her was also excited to see Ji Hoon. This was such a bad idea, but a tempting one nonetheless, and for today, even though her gut was telling her not to go, Yoori decided to give into temptation.

As she grabbed a towel and ran straight for the bathroom, Yoori decided to abandon all internal conflicts that pertained to Tae Hyun and Ji Hoon.

Today was her day off.

And the only thing that mattered was her and An Soo Jin.

■ ■ ■

Sitting outside on one of the mall benches, excitement streamed over Yoori whenever she heard a car zoom past. Because with every passing car, Yoori would think that it was Lee Ji Hoon stopping by for their "date." Unfortunately for Yoori, as she watched the thousandth car pass by, she couldn't help but conclude that she was probably getting stood up.

The truth was, it definitely would've helped if she had actually scheduled a meeting with the guy before coming to the mall and waiting outside for the past five hours like a fool.

It was an understatement to say that her excitement to learn about the Scorpion girl had since died down. She shivered from the cold.

This is what I get for giving into temptation, she thought scornfully. The sun began to set and the air around her became chillier.

This was what she got for going against Tae Hyun's note and doing something he would do. This was what she got for thinking that she meant that much to Ji Hoon for him to remember that he was supposed to meet her here this week. He probably moved on to another girl already.

She took out her phone and glanced tiredly at the screen. 6:47 P.M. Looking around, she observed that there were less and less people on the streets. She deduced it must've been because of the cold.

Though her black jeans and white zip up jacket did a wonderful job of protecting her body from the evening breeze, she really didn't have any protection for her face. Her teeth chattered loudly.

"Goddamn, it's cold!" she finally screamed irritably.

She folded her arms and brought them closer to her chest. She began to mutter her infamous incoherent cuss. Pissed off, Yoori concluded that Ji Hoon must have really lost interest in her if he hadn't arrived by now.

"So much for learning more about An Soo Jin," she grumbled.

Indignant that her ego was bruised (and extremely disappointed that she couldn't learn more about An Soo Jin), Yoori decided that enough was enough. It was time for her to go home.

Decision set, she got up from her seat and began to make her way back to Tae Hyun's apartment.

For Yoori, the only good thing about going home this early was that Tae Hyun might be home. And if anything, he could cheer her up and make her laugh. Or make himself laugh by making fun of her – whichever came first. Regardless, she was excited to see Tae Hyun again. It had only been half a day, but she was ashamed to admit that she really missed him already. At least it was always entertaining when she was around him. That was for sure.

She walked for a good minute when a voice called out to her.

"Have you been waiting for a while?"

She whipped her head around, already knowing who the voice belonged to. A mental smirk formed in her head. It was indeed Lee Ji Hoon.

Sitting comfortably in his car, Ji Hoon wore a white dress shirt and light grey pants that more than complimented his tan skin. He couldn't have looked more comely while driving his Mercedes at the slowest of speeds.

"No," she lied. She turned around and began to walk again. Though she was vaguely happy that he actually appeared, the guy was already really late and she was already really pissed off. There was no way in hell she was going to give him the satisfaction of knowing that she waited for him.

As she quickened her pace, Ji Hoon continued to trail his car along the sidewalk.

He pouted at both her reply and her cold treatment toward him. "Aw really? I really thought you waited. My heart was ready to leap out of my chest in joy."

Her silence lengthened.

Ji Hoon laughed. He glanced quickly at the road to make sure he wouldn't accidentally run something—or someone—over. When the coast was clear, he returned his attention to her.

"I'm sorry you had to wait. I had an important meeting before this. Then after that meeting, I stopped by a teashop to get us something warm to drink. You wouldn't believe the line. I had to beg the couple in front of me to let me past them because my girl was waiting for me in the cold."

Your girl? She wanted to shout out at him. However much she wanted to, she fought the urge to scream at him and just kept the silence going. She knew better. He was just trying to make her mad so she would talk to him.

When it became clear that his tactic of calling her "his girl" didn't work, Ji Hoon moved on to something else. "Would it make you feel better if I told you I've been waiting for you all week?"

Sighing as if knowing that he couldn't be effective with getting her to talk to him while he was still behind the wheel, Ji Hoon went from driving five miles per hour to fifty miles per hour. After speeding forward, he managed to stop a couple of feet away from Yoori. Without delay, Ji Hoon got out of the car and rushed right over to her. Upon reaching her, he stood frozen in front of her, effectively blocking her path.

She glared threateningly at him. "You're in my way."

He slanted his head. "I was excited to see you all day and now you're giving me the cold treatment?"

"Yes!" she said angrily, unable to control herself. She held up her entire hand with her five fingers in view. "Because I spent five hours waiting in the cold and—" She stopped abruptly when she saw a small grin appear before Ji Hoon's face.

Damn. He just tricked her. He got her to admit that she waited for him.

He nodded apologetically, his grin fading. He placed both of his hands into his pockets and said, "I'm sorry, Yoori. For what it's worth, I feel really bad."

Yoori nodded sullenly and turned away. "Whatever."

Yet the truth was, her cold heart was already thawing. As good of an actress Choi Yoori was when it came to giving the cold shoulder, she always had a tendency to forgive easily as well, especially when she felt that the other person was sincerely sorry.

"If you don't mind, I'd like to make you feel better," he said upon observing that she was still angry with him. He caught her hand and easily led her to his car. "Should we start our hour now?"

"In the car? Can't we just talk out here?"

She knew he wouldn't do anything to her, but it would be more appropriate if they just stood outside and talked.

"It's freezing out here," he answered. He scrutinized the hesitation on her part. "Come on, Yoori. I won't take you anywhere. We'll just stay here. It's just warmer in my car. Plus, I bought you tea. You'd enjoy it more sitting in the car."

Yoori nibbled her bottom lip, still unsure.

Ji Hoon smirked as he opened the passenger door and casually ran to the other side of the car where he opened the driver's side. Once he got in, he looked at her mischievously. "The hour starts now. If you want to make good use of this hour, I suggest you get in so we can start talking. As I recall, you're a pretty unforgiving timekeeper. It's been seven minutes since we first spoke and time is quickly ticking away."

Yoori gaped at him disbelievingly. Was he really doing this to her?

His smile remained. He dramatically consulted his watch. "Oh look, now it's eight minutes..."

Muttering a curse, she flung her bag into the car. Yoori got in and closed the door behind her. "Start," she instructed sourly.

"Well, first off," he said coolly, picking up a foam cup that had a white lid over it. "Here's your drink."

She took it with caution. "What is it?"

"Queen of babylon white tea with a mix of rooibos rose garden tea and a touch of German rock cane sugar," he answered easily, ignoring the "what-the-hell" look on Yoori's face.

His smile broadened when he picked up his cup and began to sip from it. He closed his eyes with delight. It was as if the tea was the most wonderful thing to ever grace his tongue. His eyes urged her to give it a chance. "It's my favorite and it might become yours as well. Try it."

Curious as to how good this tea would taste, Yoori brought the tip of the lid to her lips. She sampled it. The synapses in her brain burst to life.

As the euphoric taste of this foreign tea wafted on her tongue and glided down her throat, her eyes expanded in astonishment.

She glanced at Ji Hoon, whose smile was already wider from witnessing Yoori's obvious enjoyment of the drink he introduced to her.

"This tastes like heaven!" she couldn't help but exclaim. She blew into the cup and took a couple more sips from it. She closed her eyes to savor its heavenly taste. She was already in a better mood.

Ji Hoon chuckled. "This is why I was late. Do you forgive me now?"

Yoori opened her eyes and shrugged, taking another sip. "Depends how you use the rest of the allotted time."

"Don't worry," he reassured her, gazing at her with much adulation. "I know why we're here, why *you're* here. I'll do my best to give you the hour you want."

Nodding at his answer, she was quiet as she took another sip.

"Did you really wait all week?" she found herself asking inaudibly. She avoided eye contact by staring at the smoke emitting from her cup. She hated the warm sensation that always appeared whenever he looked at her like that.

Although her eyes were still on her cup, she could hear Ji Hoon move. Reaching his hand out, he laid a finger beneath her chin and lifted her face up to meet his. The touch of his finger brought heat to her body.

He took a moment to gaze at her with smiling eyes. "I'm really happy you made it."

Yoori nodded dubiously.

Though he didn't respond to her question with a direct answer, she already knew the meaning of his actions.

It was a yes.

Yes, he really did wait all week.

A new layer of blush waltzed on her cheeks. *Be still my thawing heart...*

"Before we start," he began delicately, as if knowing he shouldn't prolong what she was really here for. "Have you been well since the last time I saw you?"

Yoori nodded again. "Yeah. It's been a good week. How was yours?"

He laughed wearily. "I had an okay week." He glanced at her. Though his eyes were smiling at her, she could see hints of fatigue in them. "I gotta tell you...I couldn't be happier right now though."

To say that it took all her self-control to not melt was an understatement. She was pretty sure she resembled a bobble head with all the nodding she was doing, but she didn't care. Baffled as to how to respond to the charm Ji Hoon was throwing at her, she did the only thing she could do to keep her mouth shut at the moment: she drank tea.

Sensing the awkwardness on her part, Ji Hoon shrewdly changed the topic so she didn't have to reply to what he just said. "Although I'd like to believe that your interest for me precedes other needs, we both know why you're here."

Yoori was about to weakly combat that statement with some bullshit answer like she didn't mind getting to know him too, but Ji Hoon had already stopped her.

"Don't worry," he said with a reassuring smile. "The main objective tonight is to merely get on your good side. I'll worry about making you interested in me later."

"Will you be okay talking about her?" she asked hesitantly. As much as she wanted to learn more about An Soo Jin, she didn't want to make Ji Hoon do something he wasn't ready to do. God knows she made that mistake too many times in the past with other people. E.g. Tae Hyun.

He smiled. "That's why it's great that you're here. You'll take good care of me, right?"

Yoori smiled wearily. Albeit the words were there, they refused to come out. Her heart began to beat faster under his gaze. He was extremely good at making her feel like she was the most amazing thing on earth.

"Anyway," she said loudly, a gesture for her and Ji Hoon to break out of their trance.

He smirked at her actions, but said no more. He straightened up in his seat. "So what do you want to know about An Soo Jin?"

"I don't know. You pick where you want to begin. I mean, who exactly was she?"

Ji Hoon smiled. "The first thing you should know about An Soo Jin is that she was amazing beyond words." The fondness never left his eyes as he thought back to the past. "In my life, there have been countless girls who came and went, but Soo Jin was the only one who ever made a lasting impression on me."

He stared at his cup, running his eyes over the outlining.

"We met at an opening for one of my father's clubs. I was being groomed to become the King of the Skulls at that time, so naturally it was my night to watch over the club to make sure everything went according to plan." He laughed reminiscently. "Someone should have warned me that night that I was going to meet the love of my life because if someone had warned me, then I probably wouldn't have looked like such an idiot in front of the entire Underworld when I met her."

Yoori laughed at the sheepish smile on Ji Hoon's face.

She was already sucked into the story. "What happened?"

He told the story and Yoori didn't once interrupt. "It all started a little over five years ago, when one of my men came running into the VIP lounge I was in..."

"If you show just an ounce of weakness..."

27: The Meeting of Skulls and Scorpions

Five Years Ago...

"Boss!" one of the Skulls members screamed out as he came running into the VIP lounge.

Lee Ji Hoon, who was enjoying himself in a private lounge with two scantily dressed girls sitting to either side of him, looked up at the uninvited gang member with distaste.

"You better have a good reason for interrupting me," he said coolly, planting a kiss on the neck of one of the girls. She giggled drunkenly upon feeling his warm lips.

"Boss! Outside!" the Skulls member panted. He pointed at the door. "There are Scorpions outside causing trouble!"

"*What?*"

That was all it took for Ji Hoon to snap out of his cool state.

Ji Hoon peeled his arms off the two girls and ran out of the room. Music blared into his ears once he made his way out of the VIP lounge. He muttered under his breath, ready to kill the bastard who dared to disturb the first club opening that his father left him in charge of. Didn't these Scorpions realize that they were messing with the future King of Skulls?

Marching onto the main floor, Ji Hoon searched for the source of the commotion. His eyes narrowed onto the crowd that formed a circle on the dance floor. He took huge strides toward the commotion. Ji Hoon pushed his way through the crowd. When he reached the spacious center of the circle, his eyes grew wide at the sight before him.

On the floor were five of his patrons, kneeling side by side. Their bloodied faces hung low in shame. Their hands were raised up with big bottles of Smirnoff vodka in their possession. They looked like five children who were being punished for skipping school.

If his blood wasn't boiling before, it was definitely boiling right now. Who the fuck would have the balls to do this?

He ran his fiery eyes from his customers to the Scorpion sitting before them. Ji Hoon was determined to kill whoever was in charge.

His determination was fleeting when his eyes snagged onto an unexpected Scorpion. Needless to say, as his focus rested on the beautiful gang leader, his anger had more than subsided.

She wore a short black dress that complimented every inch of her body. Her dark heels brought out the length of her long silky legs and the jewelry she wore brought attention to her gorgeous skin. Ji Hoon was unquestionably mesmerized. It was a shame that time didn't freeze for Ji Hoon because if he had it his way, he'd spend another five minutes checking out the gorgeous creature before him. Yet when her bored gaze finally settled on him, Ji Hoon was instantly slapped out of his stupor. It took him less than a second to finally realize the complications of the situation before him.

His patrons were kneeling before her.

She was the one in charge.

He muttered a series of curses in his head. His biggest weakness had always been beautiful women. It would make sense that the most beautiful woman he'd ever seen would be in charge of creating a scene at his club. How the hell was he going to go about dealing with this situation?

As if hearing his question, the kneeling patrons began to call out to him.

"Ji Hoon!" the five men cried desperately. Some of the men attempted to get up from their kneeling positions. They were immediately kicked back to the ground.

Clearing his throat, Ji Hoon was ready to deal with the situation as best as he could: he was just going to wing it.

"What seems to be the problem here?" Ji Hoon asked diplomatically, his voice a bit more serene than it should have been. He was still too entranced by the nameless beauty to function. He wanted to resolve whatever the hell was going on, but he also wanted to charm the pants—or the dress—off a particular girl.

When all she did was stare at him blankly, Ji Hoon took out his best defense and flashed her one of his charismatic smiles.

Screw beating people up tonight, he concluded as he felt his lust for this girl grow with the passing seconds. If he had it his way, he'd be fucking someone in a particular short black dress and dark heels tonight.

Her bored gaze on him remained.

"Let me guess," she observed, looking at him up and down. Unimpressed, she took her eyes off him and studied her nails in boredom. "The heir to the Skulls throne, right?"

Unaffected by her cold attitude, the smile on Ji Hoon's face persevered. Even that voice of hers was driving him crazy. "I'd be honored if you told me who you are."

Satisfaction entered him when he saw that she actually smiled at his response.

Uncrossing her legs, the nameless beauty stood up from her seat and approached him.

He gazed at the whole scene with bated breath.

It took Ji Hoon all of his self-control to not reach out, grab her, and throw her into one of the VIP rooms and do what came naturally.

234

When she reached him, her bored gaze evolved into a somewhat teasing one.

"How about you take a wild guess?" she asked coyly, tilting her head to the side.

He didn't answer. He was too distracted by that sweet smelling perfume of hers and the temptation to grab her by the waist and kiss her like no tomorrow.

She smirked at his lack of response. It appeared as though she knew he was more than enchanted and she didn't mind playing with him.

Upon seeing that alluring smirk of hers, Ji Hoon found himself a bit more amused. He didn't give a damn that the girl was intending to play him for a fool. It didn't matter what her intention was; the only intention that mattered was his.

As a gesture to remind himself to keep his hands off her, Ji Hoon folded his arms.

Her teasing nature faded as her impatience grew. Clearly annoyed with his lack of response, she scoffed rudely. "Didn't your parents tell you it's rude to stare?"

"Isn't that smoking body of yours telling you that you should be in my arms right now?" he found himself asking, his eyes landing briefly on her chest. Now this girl was in for it. He was going to give her everything. All of his charm. He was ready to turn it all on for her.

She laughed disbelievingly. "You're seriously hitting on me right now?" She looked around. "At a time like this?"

Apparently the entire club agreed with her as they murmured in disbelief.

He shrugged, not caring about who was watching. The only thing that mattered was her. "All rationale aside, I like to follow the commands of my heart."

"Or your penis," she corrected sharply. She was clearly unimpressed.

Unfazed by the harsh reply, Ji Hoon took it as an open invitation for more flirtatious lines on his part. "We'll both follow your command as well," he whispered huskily, his eyes already admiring the fullness of her pink lips.

Hiding back a smile, she shook her head at his answer. It may have been pure amusement on her part, but it seemed to him that she was already warming up to him.

"Ji Hoon!" one of the patrons finally screamed out, reminding him that the nameless beauty in front of him wasn't the only witness to his charm. "What the fuck are you doing?"

Remembering the patrons who were being punished, rationale returned to Ji Hoon. He cleared his throat again and turned back to his nameless beauty with apprehensiveness.

"Why are they kneeling?" he asked carefully, straddling between sounding serious and still being charming. He wanted to address the situation, but he also didn't want to piss off his gorgeous new eye candy.

"They had a lot of horrible things to say about my father," she answered with no indication of regret. "They deserve the punishment I gave them."

His brows drew together. "Father?"

In a flash, it all clicked together for him.

Of course.

Why didn't the obviousness occur to him before?

He gazed at her warily.

"An Soo Jin?" he asked carefully, already knowing the answer to his question.

She blinked as a gesture of her confirmation.

He shook his head, his affectionate gaze on her remaining. One would think that Lee Ji Hoon would lose interest in the girl after finding out that she was the daughter of the enemy, but as his lustful gaze on her grew stronger, Ji Hoon was more than surprised that he wasn't repulsed. He was actually much more turned on that she was not only a beautiful eye candy, but also a forbidden one at that.

"Fuck, Ji Hoon!" the patron yelled again. "Why are you spending so much time talking to that little bitch? Help us!"

Ji Hoon and Soo Jin whipped their heads to the direction of the screaming patron. Soo Jin closed the distance and approached the kneeling men. There was murder in her eyes. Her palm held out, she pointed it at the direction of one of the Scorpions. On cue, one of her men took out a gold gun from behind his back and threw it at her. With impressive skills, she caught the gun in the perfect shooting position. She aimed in the direction of the now petrified patron.

Soo Jin was ready to put a bullet through his head. As her fingers made contact with the trigger, Ji Hoon's sudden appearance between her gun and the patron caused her to think twice. Waiting with bated interest, Soo Jin lowered her gun and watched Ji Hoon's every move. She appeared more than curious at Ji Hoon's motives.

A frown firmly solidified on his face, Ji Hoon advanced toward the patron with fire in his own eyes. As he brushed past two of the kneeling patrons, he grabbed the vodka bottle one of the other patrons was holding up.

What happened next took everyone in the club by surprise.

Ji Hoon didn't rush to his patron's side to save them. He rushed over to punish them.

Demonstrating impressive alacrity, Ji Hoon gave the standing patron a powerful kick to the gut that left him with no hold on gravity. As an added complement to the powerful assault, Ji Hoon then slammed the vodka bottle into his skull before he fell to the ground. The bottle shattered and various ounce of Smirnoff overflowed onto the writhing body of the patron. He was now bleeding incessantly from the head. As blood from the patron's head began to mix with the vodka, the atmosphere of the club became disbelieving.

The expressions on the club patrons said it all: what had gotten into Lee Ji Hoon?

The broken tip of the bottle still in hand, Ji Hoon pointed threateningly at the four kneeling patrons. "If anyone dares to talk to her that way again, I'll make sure that you will not only have the same fate, but I'll be sure to rip all your tongues out as well. Do you understand?"

The remaining four patrons nodded in fear.

Satisfied with their quick understanding, Ji Hoon threw the broken bottle to the ground.

The crowd churned with endless whispers as they all watched Lee Ji Hoon make his return to An Soo Jin. The Scorpion princess was eyeing the scene before her in complete disbelief as well.

"They're all yours," he said almost triumphantly.

"Was that really necessary?" she questioned, gazing up at his now smiling face.

"No one will ever get away with talking to you like that. I'll make sure of it." The sincerity in his words surprised him. Though he had only known the girl for a short time, she made enough impact on him to make him want to rip anyone who dared to disrespect her to shreds.

"I could've taken care of him myself," she replied thanklessly.

"I know, but you shouldn't have to get those pretty little hands of yours dirty."

"Well, aren't you a hero in disguise?" she asked sarcastically. Though her critical gaze on him remained, he could tell from her eyes that she was more than amused with him.

"Not a hero, just a guy who's infatuated."

"I bet you that infatuation will fade if I put a bullet through that cocky head of yours," she replied nonchalantly, casually folding her arms so her gold gun was in plain view.

Exhibiting no fear, he leaned in. "You can do anything you want because as of this second, it seems that I'm yours as well."

Soo Jin took a step back and moved away from Ji Hoon. Though she didn't say anything, Ji Hoon could see by how Soo Jin was staring at him that she may have developed a certain infatuation toward him too.

"You're lucky I find you to be amusing, pretty boy." She turned away and nodded at her men. After seeing her nod, her men grabbed the vodka bottle from each of the patrons' hands and proceeded to smash the bottle into each of their heads.

After sounds of breaking glass and screams of agony permeated the club, Soo Jin returned her gaze to Ji Hoon. He was unaffected by what had just happened.

"Thank you for an entertaining evening, Lee Ji Hoon," she said warmly, already making her way toward the exit.

Stopping suddenly in her tracks, she maneuvered around and steadily trained her gun at the patron who Ji Hoon assaulted for disrespecting her.

"This," she began, her eyes cold, "is for disrespecting me." Without even blinking an eye, she fired three perfect shots into his abdomen, chest, and head.

The roaring bullets echoed in the now quiet club. Soo Jin shook her head at the dead patron's body and begun toward the exit once more. With her Scorpions, and Ji Hoon's eyes, trailing closely behind her, she threw her gold gun back at one of her men and made her way out the door. As one of the Scorpions held the door opened for her, Soo Jin spun around to steal a quick glance at Ji Hoon. He was still gazing at her with unrivaled interest.

"See you around, Lee Ji Hoon," she whispered, flashing him a seductive smile of her own.

Ji Hoon's smile grew wider as he watched her leave. She couldn't have appeared more beautiful to him. "See you soon, babe," he whispered as he watched the door close.

"Just one ounce..."

28: Massacre

"I think you know what eventually happened after that," Ji Hoon concluded pensively.

"She sounded like she was one heck of a chase," Yoori prompted a little too enthusiastically. Now that she knew how they met, she also wanted to know how the courting between them progressed. She knew she should've taken Ji Hoon's pain into account, but it was really the last priority for Yoori. She just wanted to learn more about their relationship. "How did you eventually get her?"

"Ah, that part is a secret," he said wistfully. "Sorry Yoori. As much as I would love to share, I don't kiss and tell."

Yoori frowned at his answer, but didn't push him. No matter. She was interested in the other stuff anyway. "What was it about her that made her so special to you?"

From how he spoke about meeting her, he sounded more interested in bedding her than anything else. How did An Soo Jin turn this player into a lovesick puppy? His exterior charm aside, Yoori could tell that he truly loved Soo Jin.

His eyes rested on his steering wheel. "An Soo Jin began merely as a means of entertainment for me. She was the coveted trophy in our world. Though she had just made her debut, her name was fast becoming infamous in our society. Everyone was fascinated with the Princess of Scorpions whose knowledge of weaponry and martial arts exceeded those around her."

His distracted gaze on the steering wheel remained.

"Her beauty was what attracted me in the beginning. I wanted the glory of catching her, the glory of making her mine. As the chase went on though, I began to find myself entrenched in just being around her." He laughed wearily. "The funny thing was that I didn't realize that I had already fallen for her—hard. She was the first and the only woman I've ever truly given my heart to. There was not a day that went by that I didn't count my blessings when I was around her. She made me feel like there was a bigger purpose to this type of life, like there was more to me than just being a crime lord. It was such a simple, yet powerful thing. She made me feel like I was—"

"Human," Yoori absentmindedly finished for him.

She smirked to herself. It was ironic to her, crime lords embracing the vulnerability that came with being "human."

Ji Hoon turned to Yoori. "I know what you're thinking. How could one ruthless killer fall for another ruthless killer, right?"

She remained quiet. That was exactly what she was thinking.

"Choi Yoori, if there's only one thing you need to know about our world, it is that everyone is trained to be a killer, especially the ones born into it. It's a terrible thing, but from birth, we were all raised to not only desire power, but also yearn for it. In this world, if you have no power, then you'll die a pitiful death." He stared off into the distance. "Soo Jin did what she had to do to keep her reputation alive in the Underworld. She was ruthless and cruel when she needed to be. In the same token, she was also loyal and caring when she needed to be. It really depends on which side of the coin you fell on for her. But then again, that's the case for anyone who holds any form of power in the Underworld. For people involved in our world, they know what they got themselves into when they made this their lifestyle. The rest from then on is fair game. You kill to stay alive, to get to the top. That's how it works in this society."

Yoori shook her head at his explanation. He made it all seem so simple, so black and white. "You say that people who involve themselves into this world know what they're getting into, so it's fair game from that point on. But what about the ones thrown into it?"

Tense lines formed on Ji Hoon's face. He knew where she was headed with this question. Before he could utter anything to stop her from finishing her thoughts, Yoori had already ventured into dangerous territory.

"What about that family in the club who were killed that night?"

"Yoori," he said warningly, making it clear that he didn't want to discuss this.

"What about them, Ji Hoon?" she continued, ignoring his overt distaste to where she wanted to take their conversation. Why was he being so secretive about this? What did he have to hide? "You said it wasn't her fault. It wasn't her fault – so was it yours? Were you the one who killed them?"

"No!" he answered, turning back to her. "It's not what you think. I didn't kill them. Those were all rumors."

"Then why won't you set it straight?" she asked, annoyance mounting in her voice. "Do you realize how difficult it is for me to even try to be civil with you when I have thoughts of you killing that poor family running around in my head?" Ignoring the distress on his face, she continued. She was going to get to the bottom of this once and for all. "Just tell me."

There was a long silence before he said, "I can only tell you what happened afterwards."

Yoori shook her head. She was becoming more frustrated by the second. "Why won't you tell me what happened?"

"Because I can't."

"Why?"

"I just can't."

"Why not?" she screamed.

"Because I wasn't there when it happened!"

That was all it took for Yoori to choke on the remaining words that were ready to escape from her lips. Her mouth agape, she fell back into her seat in shock. She was uncertain of how long she stared at Ji Hoon in stricken silence. It must have been a while, she concluded dimly. It must have been a while because her eyes were beginning to ache from not blinking for so long.

"What?" she finally stammered. She couldn't be hearing right. She must be going crazy. There was no way she could've heard right. How could Ji Hoon not be there when the family was murdered?

"That night," he said again, his breathing now painfully shallow, "when that family was killed, I wasn't there."

She was thunderstruck. All this time, she had thought Ji Hoon was either there helping Soo Jin kill that family or standing by and watching it all happen. But this...this new piece of development was a shocking one for her. It changed everything.

Yoori felt so ashamed to admit that she had a small hope that An Soo Jin would have no part in the killing of the family. She was ashamed to admit that a small part of her would rather have Ji Hoon admit to her that he was the one behind the massacre that night. If it were just Ji Hoon, then it would've been easier for Yoori to hate him. It would've been easier to hate him as opposed to hating An Soo Jin. Nausea engulfing her body, her tired eyes went back on to Ji Hoon. She was so disappointed. Not in Ji Hoon, but in An Soo Jin and herself.

"Why didn't you tell me this from the beginning?" Yoori asked, her voice trembling as she kept her gaze on him.

His silence remained.

Curiosity eating away at her, her probing continued. It didn't matter if he was having a hard time with this. All that mattered to her were the answers. She seized his shoulder and shook his attention back to her.

"Did you do all of this just to protect her? You said that it wasn't her fault, but it was, wasn't it?"

"Yoori, don't—"

"It was all her fault," Yoori found herself saying when it all began to make sense to her. The nausea and pit in her stomach expanded as she went on. "She killed them and you allowed people to think that you were in on it because you wanted to lessen her fault in all of this. But it was really her. All of this was her fault."

Yoori couldn't help but wince when it all hit her.

The truth.

Finally the truth.

She closed her eyes in resignation. Every time...every time she thought that there was hope for An Soo Jin to appear more human, something like this occurs to show her that Soo Jin truly was a monster.

"She wasn't that type of person," he began, facing Yoori with desperation. "You have to understand that Yoori. What happened that night was out of character for Soo Jin."

"Tell me what happened afterward then."

He shook his head. It was clear he wanted to take the time to talk about the type of person Soo Jin was first. "Just let me — "

"Stop trying to lessen her guilt," Yoori said sternly. "Just tell me what happened afterward."

She was too immersed in all of this. She couldn't waste anymore time listening to useless stuff. Here was finally the truth about the Scorpion girl, the one that people have been telling her that she resembled. All Yoori needed to know was the truth so she could further validate her belief that she couldn't be An Soo Jin.

Her head began to ache.

God, she desperately needed that validation right now.

When it looked like Ji Hoon was about to continue with trying to lessen Soo Jin's guilt, he stopped. It was palpable on Yoori's face that she didn't want to hear him stand up for Soo Jin anymore. It was clear on her face and she knew he saw that.

Yoori knew it was reprehensible that she was forcing him to relive something that obviously pained him to relive. He was only doing it to satisfy her need. It was also appalling on Yoori's part that she was feeding on all of this. Now that she had come to terms with how coldhearted An Soo Jin was, she felt...validated.

In a strange way, she *wanted* Soo Jin to be a monster. If Soo Jin was a monster, then it further supported Yoori's stance that she couldn't be the Scorpion girl. The more horrible An Soo Jin was, the more validated Yoori would feel about herself. Rationality no longer mattered. All that mattered was that she hated An Soo Jin with all her might. She couldn't be someone she hated, she just couldn't.

Her desperate gaze on Ji Hoon grew stronger.

All he had to do was keep feeding her all of this.

All he had to do was give her what she was yearning for: validation.

"Ji Hoon," she whispered when he didn't say anything. They've come too far. If he was going to share this much, then he was going to have to finish it. "Please..." she added. Her unblinking eyes began to well up. Her breathing was becoming so rapid that it was beginning to hurt her. She was that desperate to know. "Please tell me."

Leaning against the window, Ji Hoon's face had grown so pale that she was sure he was more likely to kick her out of the car than proceed with telling her what happened. But as she watched him part his lips, his eyes staring off into the dark street ahead, she knew Ji Hoon was ready to bear the pain just for her. He was ready to share his side of the story.

"I still remember how broken her voice was when I listened to the voicemail," he said brokenly. He kept his eyes away from Yoori. "She was so distraught. I remember it like it was yesterday..."

■ ■ ■

"Ji Hoon," Soo Jin cried over the voicemail. "Please. Please come...please help me. I need your help..."

242

Closing his cellphone lid, Ji Hoon muttered a string of curses as he floored the acceleration on his Mercedes and sped through the night. He ran past several red lights, nearly getting into several accidents in the process, but none of it mattered to him. Soo Jin's helpless voice replayed itself in his mind. His heart ripped apart as his concern for her grew. Soo Jin had never been the type of girl to ask anyone for help and if she asked for help now, then it must mean that something horrific had happened.

Parking his car in the no parking zone, Ji Hoon turned off his engine and fled out of his car. He flew toward the club entrance. When he opened the door, the horrific smell of death invaded his nostrils. His concern for Soo Jin's safety heightened, he ran into the pitched dark club screaming out her name.

"Soo Jin!" he shouted, stepping into the center of the dance floor. With the aid of the light from his cellphone, his eyes quickly adjusted to the darkness.

His face contorted with disgust when his eyes finally made out the dozens of dead bodies laying on the floor of the club. There was blood seeping out of the bullet holes in each of their heads. Though the light from his cellphone was dim, there was enough illumination to show him that a massacre took place here.

Men and women alike, their lifeless eyes watched him as he took cautious strides over them. His stomach churned as he glanced at the pool of blood that was beginning to mix together.

"Shit!" he shouted when he almost slipped over amputated fingers that laid beside the dead bodies. Though it disgusted him to no end, what Ji Hoon was seeing was nothing new to him. Death was something that Ji Hoon saw everyday.

But the next thing he saw threw him through a whirlwind.

"Oh fuck," he uttered, covering his mouth to prevent himself from throwing up when he made eye contact with two lifeless kids, both of whom stared blankly at him. Laying side by side, their blood became mixed with the blood of a woman. Ji Hoon could only guess that she was their mother.

"Shit, Soo Jin." His eyes scoured the room for her. "What did you get yourself into?"

Finally, out of the silence and darkness, Ji Hoon heard soft sniffles that captured his attention. His eyes found Soo Jin sitting in the far corner of the club, her head buried in her knees.

Blood.

Even in the darkness, he could see that there was blood on her. Blood on her black jacket. Blood on her jeans. Blood on her boots. Blood on her hands. Even bloody fingerprints were present on the gold gun laying beside her sobbing body. Blood was everywhere.

"Soo Jin." He rushed to her. He jumped over the dead bodies in his way. When he reached her, he extended his arms out to her.

"Baby, are you alright?" he asked, pulling her close to him.

He cupped her face with his hands and brought her face into view.

"What happened?" he inquired, his heart breaking at the sight of her tear filled eyes. His thumb wiped away the small splatter of dried blood that was on her face.

The blood wasn't hers, he knew that much.

Soo Jin's lips quivered uncontrollably. She looked around the room. Her eyes glossed over with more tears when she laid her desperate gaze on him.

"This is all my fault," she said painfully, her face growing paler by the second.

"Soo Jin, what happened?" he asked again, hoping she'd answer him. He watched her eyes dance around the room in confusion, his concern for her more than magnified. What happened to her? What the hell happened tonight?

"I went too far," she started frantically, her eyes glistening even more. She took in a deep breath and grew lost in her frantic thoughts. "But they wouldn't stop crying. I told them to stop crying, but they wouldn't stop!" Her voice elevated to an abnormal level. It appeared to Ji Hoon that she was actually reliving what happened. "I told them to shut up or they'll all get a bullet to the head, but they wouldn't stop crying. I tried. I tried so hard to tell them to be quiet or they'll die, but they *didn't* listen. They wouldn't listen! They began to cry even louder."

She pounded her head against the wall and closed her eyes in anguish. Her breathing became heavier, her chest moving up and down at a rapid pace.

"God, they just wouldn't shut up," she repeated again, her eyes filled with trauma. "Next thing I knew…the bullets started going off from my gun…" She covered her mouth with her bloody hands. Pained guilt teemed on her face. "This wasn't supposed to happen," she cried through muffled hands. "This wasn't supposed to happen."

Ji Hoon was confused. He was more than confused as he listened to Soo Jin. She didn't make sense at all. And if being confused wasn't enough, he was also worried that she'd end up hurting herself. From the looks of it, if he didn't get her out of the club soon, her condition would worsen. His concern for her at its apex, Ji Hoon immediately grabbed Soo Jin by the shoulder and carefully pulled her up. It didn't matter what happened. The best thing to do now was to get her out.

"Baby, look at me. Look at me," he said firmly, his hands cupping her cheeks again. He looked her dead in the eyes. "It'll be okay. I promise. Go wait in the car. I'll take care of this."

Fresh tears formed in her eyes. She shook her head in protest. Knowing fairly well that leaving her in the club would worsen her trauma, Ji Hoon decided that it was best if he left with her. Pulling her cold body close to him, he sped toward the exit. As he held on to her with one hand, he held up his cellphone with the other. He scanned through his phone and dialed the number of one of the higher-ranking members in his gang.

Pushing the exit door open with his shoulder, Ji Hoon pulled Soo Jin closer to him. They proceeded out of the club. His phone to his ear, it only took one ring before someone picked up on the other end.

"Boss?" the voice asked over the receiver.

"Club Pure," Ji Hoon said without pretense. "Bring whoever is with you and bring several cars. There are bodies I need you to get rid of."

He struggled to hold on to Soo Jin, who was having a hard time holding herself up.

"We'll be there," the voice answered dutifully before hanging up.

Ji Hoon hung up and threw all of his attention back to Soo Jin. When he reached his car, Ji Hoon sped to the passenger side and opened the door for her.

She was now staring lifelessly at the ground.

He cupped his hands against her face and stared reassuringly into her blank eyes. "Baby, it'll be okay. I'll make sure it's okay, alright?"

All she did was nod absently.

Though she was gazing into his eyes, he could tell from the blankness in her expression that she was already lost in contemplation about something else. Coming to terms with the fact that there wasn't much more he could say or do, Ji Hoon gave a worried sigh and helped her into the car.

He ran to the driver's side and got in. Speeding off into the night, the Mercedes squealed in the silent streets, leaving behind the unimaginable massacre that would eventually leave its notorious mark in the Underworld.

■ ■ ■

The truth was, Yoori had never known uncomfortable silence like the one she and Ji Hoon was sharing. She knew that Soo Jin was a troubled person, but she couldn't have anticipated how troubled Soo Jin was.

An Soo Jin completely lost her mind that night.

Both leaning lifelessly against their respective doors, it took Yoori all of her self-control to not allow tears to flow out of her own eyes. An Soo Jin was alone when she killed the family that night. She was completely and utterly alone when she killed them.

It was just her that night.

There was the validation Yoori needed to convince herself that she couldn't be the monstrous Scorpion girl.

Fuck amnesia, she brooded angrily. She couldn't believe she even allowed herself to remotely believe that she could be the Scorpion girl. So what if she had amnesia? So what if people told her she resembled An Soo Jin? Fuck that. *All* of that.

How could she let all of that get in the way of the fact that she had a life in her hometown? She had a family by her side when she woke up in the hospital that day. They not only reminded her of her life prior to the car accident, but they also took care of her from then on. She was almost sure she was a burden to her parents, but they took care of her regardless because she was their daughter. Who would put up with taking care of someone if they weren't related?

She shuddered as she recalled the part of the story where Ji Hoon almost slipped on the amputated fingers. It didn't take Yoori long to surmise what Soo Jin was doing in there. Soo Jin really did torture that family for hours before she killed them, she concluded with disgust.

An Soo Jin was not just a monster; she was a monster that lost her mind.

Ji Hoon finally broke the silence when he took stock of the disgust on her face. "Before you begin to judge Soo Jin for her mistake that night, you should know that she died that night as well."

At that moment, she really didn't want to say anything to him. Yet as the vagueness of his words penetrated her psyche, she knew she couldn't go on with the silence. Yoori looked up at him with frustration present in her face.

"What?" she finally uttered softly.

"Her soul," he clarified. "It died that night. Soo Jin was never the same after all that happened." He breathed in painfully. "Soo Jin changed after that night, immensely. She became more distant and aloof. Though she didn't speak of it much, I knew that every night, she thought about what happened and entertained the idea of ending her own life. It killed me to see her so miserable, it killed me that I couldn't do anything to help her. An Soo Jin was merely living on borrowed time as I tried desperately to hold on to what was left of her."

Yoori was barely listening.

Ignoring this, Ji Hoon continued. "That night, when I heard that someone had killed her, I knew..."

"Knew what?" she asked absentmindedly. It was obvious that she no longer wanted to be part of that conversation, but she continued because she felt obligated to still be in it.

"I knew that she died without fighting. There are few people who could've touched Soo Jin, let alone kill her. The only way she could've died that night was if she went obediently. The only way she could have died was if she *allowed* someone to kill her."

Yoori knew she should've listened more carefully to what he was saying, but she couldn't bring herself to. There was just so much in her mind.

She knew that Ji Hoon was trying to make Soo Jin sound better than she ever was. So what if Soo Jin regretted what she did in the end? So what if God punished her by giving her a soul in the end, only to have it torn up before she died? She still ruthlessly murdered an entire family. Soo Jin deserved every inch of that pain and more.

As far as Yoori was concerned, Soo Jin was let off too easily.

Returning her gaze to Ji Hoon, Yoori brushed off what he just said and focused on asking something that she was also still curious about.

"She didn't tell you what actually happened in the club, did she?" Yoori asked instinctively. She couldn't let that part go. What happened in the club, she couldn't let it go.

Clearly disappointed that Yoori purposely ignored what he just said about Soo Jin, Ji Hoon just shook his head at her new question. "She never spoke about it and I never brought it up."

When he spoke, Yoori heard it again—that pain in his voice. It was there again. And it was so much stronger this time. So much stronger that it was enough for Yoori to allow another avalanche of guilt to engulf her.

All this time, she had misunderstood Ji Hoon. All this time, he only took part in the blame because he wanted to lessen Soo Jin's guilt. He allowed the rumors to flow free because he wanted to protect her, even after her death.

Yoori gazed at Ji Hoon with remorse. All disappointment in Soo Jin aside, at least there was one good thing that derived from it. Yoori no longer had a valid reason to dislike Ji Hoon.

"I'm sorry for misunderstanding," she began quietly, avoiding eye contact with him. She stared at her shaking fingers. She mentally scoffed at herself. She seemed to be doing a lot of misunderstandings lately. First it was Tae Hyun and now it was Ji Hoon. Boy, she was definitely on a roll.

Before Ji Hoon could utter another word, his phone started beeping relentlessly. Yoori knew that it was his alarm.

Their hour was up.

Turning off his alarm, he smiled at Yoori. "I normally wouldn't care too much if our hour is up. However, I have some people to meet and stuff to take care of so—"

"How can I make this up to you?" she found herself asking abruptly. She felt awful for what she did to him. She hated Soo Jin, but Ji Hoon did nothing wrong. The only thing he did wrong was love Soo Jin, despite her inhumane flaws.

He pondered her offer. "Let's meet again. This time, it will be just you and me. We won't talk about Tae Hyun or Soo Jin. It'll just be about us."

It was probably too premature of her, but in light of what she put him through, it was truly the least she could do. So with a small smile on her face, Yoori nodded in agreement.

It didn't help that, as soon as she nodded, Tae Hyun's face popped into her mind. She flinched. She wasn't dating Tae Hyun or Ji Hoon, but she was already feeling like a two-timing hussy. She may not be dating Tae Hyun, but to others, she was still his girlfriend. Even though it was a false thing, she didn't want Tae Hyun to deal with unnecessary gossip, especially one pertaining to Ji Hoon. She couldn't do that to him.

"On our next meeting though, you can't take me anywhere where we'll be seen," she stipulated, trying to minimize the catastrophe that may occur if someone caught "Tae Hyun's girlfriend" on a little outing with Ji Hoon. "Cause you know, I'm still Tae Hyun's girlfriend and it just looks bad."

Though she knew the mention of Tae Hyun had more than rubbed Ji Hoon the wrong way, he managed to keep his composure. "Don't worry. I understand."

Grateful for his reassurance, Yoori then decided it was time to leave. She grabbed her handbag and pushed the door opened. "Good. I'll see you later then."

As she pulled herself onto the cold street, Yoori knew she had to do something to lessen the intensity of the atmosphere that formed between them. She had to leave Ji Hoon on a somewhat carefree note.

She turned back around with a smile on her face. She handed the empty foam cup to Ji Hoon. "Thanks for the heavenly tea," she said warmly. "I demand another one next time."

She didn't know why she gave the guy an empty foam cup and demanded something for their future date. It was the most random thing to come out of her mouth. However, when she saw his smile grow a little wider, she knew that her odd tactic worked.

"As you wish, beautiful," he said, grabbing the foam cup and placing it in the cup holder. There was a hint of charm present in his voice again.

Yoori rolled her eyes at his cheesy line. At least it made her feel better to see the flirtatious Lee Ji Hoon make his return before their night ended.

"Be good, Lee Ji Hoon," she said, closing his door with much amusement.

"I'll see you soon," she heard him say as his engine started.

She threw one last wave at him and proceeded down the curb. As she descended into the dim lighting of the streets, Yoori was besieged with thoughts about An Soo Jin and the information Ji Hoon disclosed with her.

She was hoping that the hour with Ji Hoon would help to ease her confusion about who An Soo Jin was, but as fate would have it, Yoori only emerged from the meeting much more puzzled. She weighed the different pieces of information that Ji Hoon shared with her. An Soo Jin was a horrible person, she knew that much for sure. But what about the rest of the details that Ji Hoon left out because he wasn't there when it happened?

Questions that will never be answered by anyone but Soo Jin ran through Yoori's mind at a relentless rate.

Why was Soo Jin the only one in the club that night?

What exactly happened to Soo Jin that night? Did she really lose her mind?

How did Soo Jin torture and execute all of them by herself?

And finally, the one question that started the chain of events of that night and the most important question of all: out of everyone, why did Soo Jin choose that particular family?

"Then you're done in this world."

29: Hold on Tight

Walking into Tae Hyun's apartment complex, it was no surprise that Yoori still found herself consumed with what happened with Ji Hoon. She was still so mixed with emotions.

She was relieved to learn more about An Soo Jin, but in the same token, she was also angry about what she learned. Every now and then, images of two faceless kids with bullets to their head would invade her mind and haunt her as her hatred for An Soo Jin lived on. Her stomach churned. Recollection of the story continued to repulse her to no end.

In addition to being angry, Yoori was also feeling guilty with how inconsiderate she was to Ji Hoon. Now that she had time to think over their conversation in his car, she felt worse for being such a bitch and treating him so horribly. Apart from his bad relationship with Tae Hyun, Ji Hoon had been nothing but kind to her. He didn't deserve to be treated with such hostility, *especially* when one of the primary reasons why she deemed him to be the "bad guy" was because she assumed he was part of that club massacre. Obviously that proved to be no longer valid.

Frustration escalating within her, she sighed dramatically. The elevator button lit up after Yoori tiredly pressed it down. As she waited for the elevator doors to slide open, it became natural for Yoori's thoughts to swing back to the set of questions she asked before she reached Tae Hyun's apartment.

Was that family chosen at random or were they chosen for a reason? And if there was a reason, then what was that reason?

She desperately wanted to find out the answers to these questions. But how would she? Even Ji Hoon didn't know and he was the only valid link to the inner workings of An Soo Jin. The only one who would know was Soo Jin herself and unfortunately, Soo Jin took those secrets to her grave.

Though the elevator door had dinged open, its call did little to rouse Yoori from her stupor. She was so preoccupied with her feverish curiosity that she didn't even notice the elevator was waiting for her. She also didn't realize that someone was standing beside her, waiting with her in silence as well.

It only became clear to Yoori that there was another in her company when she heard a recognizable voice and felt a familiar hand intertwined its fingers with her own.

"So, what's gotten my little party animal so lost in contemplation?"

It happened so naturally that she didn't even catch it. When Yoori peered up at the handsome face of the Serpents leader beside her, her frustration subsided along with her thoughts about An Soo Jin.

A new distraction had presented itself and this much-needed distraction was named Kwon Tae Hyun.

Dressed in a simple black hoodie and black jeans, Yoori was surprised that Tae Hyun still looked slick and stylish in such casual clothing. She concluded that it must be that particular air of confidence he always strutted around with. He looked good in whatever he chose to wear and he damn well knew it.

Purposely ignoring his question, Yoori hid a bashful smile. Did it get warmer in this building or was it just her?

"Hey stranger," she said composedly, concealing the fact that she was more than happy to see him again. It had only been a day, but it felt like it had been forever since she last saw him.

"Missed me?" he teased, a mischievous smile already forming on his face. His hold on her hand tightened. He seemed pretty happy to see her as well.

Yes!

"Didn't even know you were gone," she replied coyly.

Tae Hyun laughed. He took a moment to study any bluff on her face. Shaking his head with hilarity, he boldly said, "You're such a bad liar."

Like a rose wilting under the scorching sun, her hidden smile gradually condensed into a frown. Challenging his bold (and unfortunately true statement) she gazed at him in amazement. How could he just see through her like that?

"I can tell you're really happy," he added, his smile broadening when he saw the disbelief on her blushing face.

"Don't flatter yourself," Yoori quipped, unable to think of a better retort.

Without warning, he reached his free hand out and curled it around her waist. Yoori's eyes widened at his bold actions. It not only scandalized her that she didn't mind it so much with how he was holding her, but it also surprised her that her heart was racing like crazy. All of this was happening too fast and none of it was making sense to her. What was he doing?

His hand resting on the small of her back, he effortlessly pulled her closer to him. "How can I not be flattered when you flatter me, babe?" he asked serenely, pulling her petrified self just a little bit closer so that their bodies were almost touching.

Yoori was confounded. Was he really hitting on her right now?

"Wh-what's going on? Did you drink alcohol today?" she squeaked lamely. She felt herself turn to mush with the precarious position Tae Hyun placed them in. How did playful teasing on Tae Hyun's part turn into a full-on mating fest? Did he get drunk when he met up with his mentor or something? What had gotten into him?

In lieu of answering, he simply lifted their intertwined hands and waved it in the air.

Baffled, Yoori turned to the direction in which Tae Hyun was waving their hands. There she saw the doorman waving happily at them.

That was when it all made sense to her.

Apparently, Tae Hyun was only acting that way because they had an audience. Yoori grimaced. She suddenly felt offended that he was only acting.

"Next time, let me know when there's a show that I need to perform for," she whispered through gritted teeth. She wore a warm smile for the doorman as well.

The disappointment that came over her unnerved Yoori. Their intertwining fingers now appeared less genuine than she had anticipated it to be. As shocking as it may be that she thought Tae Hyun was purposely hitting on her, she couldn't deny that she was also a tad bit flattered and excited at the thought that he may have been interested in her in that manner. Finding out that he was merely doing it for appearances left a bad taste in her mouth. A bad taste she couldn't ignore.

"Who said I was performing?" Tae Hyun asked, returning his smiling gaze to her.

Yoori rolled her eyes at the unprecedented charm he threw at her. There was a subtle light that shined through his eyes that led Yoori to believe that he may have caught on to the fact that she misunderstood his actions.

"You're not upset, are you?" he asked, verifying her speculations.

Yes.

Yoori deceitfully shook her head, making an effort to avoid eye contact. She took newfound interest in staring at the lobby tiles. She knew how transparent she could be at times and she didn't want him to see through her.

He tilted his head down, successfully claiming her gaze and attention. "Well then let's wipe that frown off that pretty little face of yours, alright?" He chuckled. "Cause God knows I spend so much time with you that I find myself frowning too if you're in a bad mood."

Despite telling herself not to, Yoori laughed at his comment. It was odd how simple, yet impactful, that sentence was. That selfish Tae Hyun was always thinking about number one. Credit must be given to him for his abnormal charisma though. All selfishness and egotism aside, his charm had an endearing quality to it. It was enough to alleviate her disappointment and enough to bring a smile to her face.

Tae Hyun grinned when the frown thawed from her countenance.

After waving goodbye to the doorman they were so ardently performing for, Tae Hyun led the way as they stepped into the elevator.

"So, you didn't answer me," Tae Hyun noted when the elevator ascended. Interestingly enough, they were still unknowingly holding hands in the elevator. "What were you so lost in contemplation about?"

"Nothing," she replied quietly, embitterment returning to her upon being subtly reminded of An Soo Jin. She kept her eyes glued down on the floor. She didn't want to talk about it, especially with Tae Hyun.

He scrutinized her with a raised eyebrow. Bluntly, he said, "What the hell did you do on your day off? You look like you just came back from a funeral."

"Nothing," she muttered again, unknowingly tightening her grasp on his hand for comfort.

"So, how was your day off?" she asked meekly, wanting desperately to change the subject.

However awkward it was becoming, she continued to avoid his gaze. She was sure of it. If she allowed him access to the gloomy state her eyes were in, Tae Hyun would be able to read her mind. Well, maybe not read her mind, but something close to that.

Taking note of her unusual behavior, Tae Hyun merely smiled tiredly. His eyes found interest in the closed elevator doors. It appeared that he might have gotten himself lost in somber contemplation as well.

"I had a pretty busy day. I'm pretty worn out right now."

Yoori tilted her gaze up when she heard the genuine strain in his voice. "Did something happen at your meeting with your mentor?"

"I just find myself a bit more conflicted than I'd like to be." This time, he purposely hid the strain once present in his voice. The acknowledgement in Tae Hyun's eyes hinted to Yoori that he knew she caught the fatigue in his voice. He was careful to not give anymore away.

Yoori snorted at his broad answer. As talkative as he may be, the guy could be pretty damn secretive as well. It was fast becoming an annoying trait for her.

"You're always conflicted," she critiqued. She gave him the evil eye and looked away.

The meeting with Ji Hoon was probably the straw that broke the camel's back. She certainly wasn't in the mood to deal with anymore secrecy. If Tae Hyun wasn't keen on divulging confidential information then she was not going to bug him about it. There was already too much on her mind.

Tae Hyun leveled his gaze on her. Astonishment reveled on his face. He appeared taken aback by her indignant demeanor toward him.

"Wow, assistant," he began blandly, unable to conceal his newfound observation of her. "You usually show a bit more patience before you proceed with the evil eye."

The silence from her lips was all that Tae Hyun needed to realize that she was more conflicted than he originally assumed.

"What's on your mind?" he asked again. When she didn't answer, he charmingly added, "I might be able to help make it all better."

Yoori concluded that it was a rare gift that Tae Hyun had, the innate ability to thaw her emotions with just mere warmness in his voice. Out of everyone to have such a gift, she couldn't for the life of her figure out why it was Tae Hyun who had it. *Go figure.* Though Yoori heavily doubted that he would be able to make it all better, there was enough charm in his voice to cause her to at least crack a smile.

"I guess I'm feeling pretty conflicted too," she finally admitted. A pause before she grudgingly added, "Internal conflicts suck."

Tae Hyun nodded thoughtfully.

He pondered the thought. After a short period of silence, his eyes lit up. He unexpectedly pressed the "L" button for the choices of floors the elevator would descend to.

"What are you doing?" She eyed him warily. What was he up to?

He only answered when the elevator doors slid open, revealing the view of the lobby again. "I need to go somewhere where I can think things over."

He gently tugged her out of the elevator with him.

"And you need an assistant to accompany you there?" she asked pointedly. She was excited to hang out with her friend again, but Yoori was not amused. It had been a tiring day. She just wanted to go to bed.

"I was actually planning on going by myself," he said, his pace quickening. He beamed at her, purposely disregarding the blatant disinterest on her face. "But since you're conflicted as well, I might as well take you too."

"Wait, wait! Tae Hyun, stop!" she protested feebly.

He wasn't listening.

She attempted to pry her hand from his. The slippery lobby tiles and his unmatched strength did little to help her efforts. She pouted as he continued to effortlessly pull her toward the exit.

"It's too cold outside!" she continued dreadfully. She suppressed the urge to bite his hand and free herself. *And I'm sleepy*, she wanted to petulantly scream out.

Yoori abruptly stopped struggling when they approached the doorman. She couldn't have the doorman be suspicious of their relationship (or lack thereof). Damn keeping up appearances!

"Going out for a late night walk?" the stout, bubbly old man asked merrily. His grin was wide upon seeing the big smiles on their faces. Well, a genuine smile on Tae Hyun's part and a manufactured smile on Yoori's part anyway.

"Yeah," Tae Hyun confirmed, still holding Yoori's hand. He turned and gazed at her affectionately, "I just want us to spend some quality time together. I haven't seen her all day, I've missed her."

As the doorman chuckled in understanding, Yoori too found herself lost in Tae Hyun's affectionate gaze. How did those eyes of his become so spellbinding?

It could very well be that he was a very good actor, yet despite knowing better, she gave a small smile in return. She felt her heart race while this rush of exhilaration hummed in her body. Whatever this feeling was, she didn't mind it so much. Now that she thought about it, there shouldn't be too much harm with hanging out with Tae Hyun.

"Well, we'll see you later," they both found themselves saying. They waved goodbye to the doorman and descended out of the apartment complex.

"So, where are we heading to, mister?" Yoori asked. Chills crawled up her skin when they ran into the coolness of the night. She looked around. The street was absolutely free of people because of the frigid weather.

"You'll know when we get there," he answered subtly, the lighthearted smile never leaving his face.

"Is it far?" she found herself asking. The extreme coldness of the night was making her think twice about their little outing.

"It's a pretty far walk."

Yoori made a face. She had to succumb to the cold a second time tonight? Damn her luck. Her lips quivered. "You've got to be kidding me."

She was still mindlessly walking when she crashed into him. He had slowed down without warning. She scrunched her face in annoyance. What did he slow down for? She followed his gaze. Yoori froze at the sight before her.

The whining in her head ceased as they drew closer to a stunning looking Yamaha motorcycle.

Forest green embellishments adorned the shiny black exterior of the motorcycle, making it appear as if it was glowing in the night. It didn't take long for Yoori to surmise who the bike must've belonged too. The mascot color of the Serpents was a big hint to her—that and the fact that Tae Hyun was getting on the bike also played a huge part in helping her guess who the owner was.

She pointed at it.

"This is *yours*?" she blurted dubiously. A disbelieving smile was solidified on her lips. Unable to restrain herself, Yoori began to graze the smooth surface of the motorcycle with her frozen hands.

"Well, I *am* a crime lord," Tae Hyun remarked with suppressed amusement. "Driving a motorcycle is part of the job description."

Yoori nodded inattentively, discounting the humor in his voice. She continued to graze her fingers across the surface of the beautiful bike. She realized that all this grazing could easily be viewed as an act of molestation on Tae Hyun's bike, but she didn't care. Motorcycles are hot. And as much as she hated to admit it, guys who ride motorcycles are even hotter.

Tae Hyun chuckled. He took out black gloves and placed each of his hands through them. "I didn't realize you were such a fan of motorcycles."

She leaned down to admire the impressive tires. "They're hot!"

"Me and my bike?" he asked roguishly, a big grin already outlining his face. He obviously knew she was too distracted to hear what he actually asked.

Yoori sauntered right into that trap.

"Yeah!" she agreed dreamily.

She paused after digesting her words. After realizing what she just answered to, Yoori bestowed Tae Hyun with a small glare.

"Wait, no," she promptly corrected, ceasing with the molestation of the hot bike. "Not you. Just your bike."

He smirked, raising his hands in a "whatever-you-say" manner.

Sure. Yoori would confess that Tae Hyun's usual hotness already did enough to take her breath away. She would also admit that the image of him sitting on a hot bike was more than enough to make her want to jump his bones. However, admitting all of this would only occur in the inner sanctum of her mind. She refused to give Tae Hyun the satisfaction of having his ego stroked.

"Anyway," she said to veer the topic away from Tae Hyun's attractiveness. "You've had a motorcycle all along? Why did we walk around town for all those weeks then?"

He shrugged. "I don't know. Probably because it gave me an excuse to hold your hand as I show you off around town?"

Yoori scowled after taking what he said as a way of mocking her.

He chuckled at her reaction and started the motorcycle. "Hurry up and get on. The night is young and cold. Let's go before our asses freeze to death."

Kwon Tae Hyun, master at pillow talk, Yoori thought sarcastically as she made a move to take her seat behind him.

She stopped when a disturbing thought occurred to her.

Yoori gaped apprehensively at the empty seat behind Tae Hyun. If she sat there, then that mean she was going to have to...

She gasped.

She blinked warily, her shyness for touching the opposite sex rearing its ugly head.

Then that would mean she was going to have to wrap her arms around those chiseled abs of his! Before she could contain it, there were already sprinkles of blush appearing on her cheeks.

Grow up, Choi Yoori, her inner self scolded. *If you don't get on, he's going to insinuate that it's because you like him!*

And she definitely couldn't have him thinking that.

After the internal pep talk, Yoori abandoned all unnecessary hesitation and quickly got onto the seat behind Tae Hyun.

Touching isn't touching unless you touch, she reminded herself.

She carefully wrapped her arms around him. She made sure the enclosures of her arms were as loose as possible. She had to hold on to the guy, but she didn't have to hold on to him that tightly.

Unfortunately for Choi Yoori, the gentleman in front of her didn't agree with her prerogative.

"Choi Yoori," she heard him say as he prepped his motorcycle for take off.

"Hmm?" she answered distractedly, already getting lost in that cologne that she had grown to adore so much.

"Hold on tight," he whispered.

With the blast of cool air nibbling her face as her guide, she did what Tae Hyun advised: she held on tight. She rested the side of her cheek against his back and closed her eyes. She reveled in the gliding sensation as the night's wind blew through her hair. It made her feel like she was flying.

Lost in the moment, she sighed blissfully. She didn't know it then, but it truly was going to be a long and eye opening night. And the fact of the matter was, all throughout this long and eye opening night, Yoori won't be the only one holding on tight.

"That's why I'm one of the best."

30: Sitting Positions

"Are you serious?" she spluttered in disbelief.

Distractedly unwrapping her arms from around his waist, Yoori took a moment to survey her surroundings while Tae Hyun turned off the motorcycle.

Yoori couldn't believe it.

She would never in a million years think that Tae Hyun was capable of bringing her to a place like this. She got off his motorcycle. Lost in a daze, it became clear to Yoori that the impossible had occurred: the slide, monkey bars, and swings…they were all truly there in front of her.

Excitedly, she smacked Tae Hyun's arm just as he was getting off his bike. "Wow, the playground? Really?"

Goddamn, her inner child was excited already. She could feel it. It was going to be a great night!

Tae Hyun looked at her regretfully as he took off his gloves.

"Not tonight, assistant," he said apologetically, effectively ruining her excitement. He placed both hands on her shoulders and herded her in the opposite direction, away from the playground that was seemingly beckoning her to come play in it.

Her heart dropped when Tae Hyun gently pushed her in the direction of a wide-open lawn. What a disappointment. "That was such a tease."

"We'll go in the other direction another night. Tonight, I need to clear my head on the other side of the park."

Normally Yoori would refute what Tae Hyun said with words of protest, just because she had a naturally combative personality like that. But, when she took into account the strain in his voice, she knew that he really needed to go to the other side of the park. Whatever his specific reason for it was, Yoori didn't want to ask him at that point. She just knew it was best if she obliged.

When it was evident that she wasn't going to take off in the other direction, Tae Hyun took his hands off her shoulders and took it upon himself to walk beside her as they ventured up the grassy green hill. Though his composure remained, Yoori could tell that he was feeling really anxious. She wasn't sure if it was a good anxious or a bad anxious, she just knew he was anxious.

After reaching the top of the hill, Yoori marveled at the scenery. Twinkling stars and dancing trees surrounded them.

The only view of the modern world was evident in the traffic headlights passing through the various spaces between the trees. Yoori sighed pleasantly. She could see why Tae Hyun would choose to come to this place when there was a lot on his mind. It was undeniably a lovely place to gather your thoughts.

"Finally," Tae Hyun said with a breath of relief.

He sat down on the sleeping grass with his knees bent up and his hands behind his back. He smiled upward at Yoori and patted the reserved spot beside him, a gesture for her to sit down as well.

She obliged. Yoori crossed her legs and carefully settled beside Tae Hyun. He had already begun to stare blankly at the passing cars in the distance. She mirrored the position of her legs by crossing her arms and bringing them closer to her chest. She hugged herself to fight against the late evening chill.

It wasn't working out very well.

Desperate to distract herself from the threat of pneumonia, Yoori followed the direction of Tae Hyun's gaze. Within seconds, Yoori was also entranced by the multitude of changing car lights in the distance.

Companionable silence floated between them as the chilly wind nibbled away any warmth left in Yoori's face. Not wanting to interrupt the serene silence they had going, it took all of Yoori's strength to keep herself from visibly shaking. Early winter was definitely upon them.

Her attention was taken off the cold when she felt his touch. She stiffened from the unexpected electricity that zinged through her body. She sat still as Tae Hyun tucked her loose bangs behind her ear so the wind wouldn't be able to get them in her eyes.

She faced him. "You're a lot less social right now," she said, observing the hint of sadness shown within his stare on her.

At her observation, he nodded. His eyes gazed into hers with fatigue milling in them. "I've got a lot on my mind right now."

Overtly shuddering at a whiff of cold air that brushed past them, Yoori's voice shook when she replied, "You're still not conflicted about those two things from last night, are you?"

It was truly a careless question. She didn't know why she asked it. It just came out of her mouth. As the fates would have it, that particular question was the best question Yoori could've asked.

A smirk quirked on Tae Hyun's lips. His thoughtful expression on her remained. He seemed more attentive to the fact that she was shivering in the cold than wanting to answer her question.

He stood up. "Damn it, Choi Yoori. Even when you're sporting a jacket, you always seem to be so cold."

Yoori creased her face at his remark.

Thinking that Tae Hyun standing up meant that they were getting ready to leave, she prepared to get up as well. So much for clearing her head. She flattened her hands on the cold grass to give herself a boost.

What happened next caused her to freeze in her seat again. Apparently, when Tae Hyun stood up, it wasn't with the intention to leave; it was to reposition their seating arrangement.

It became clear to Yoori what the new seating arrangement was when she saw that Tae Hyun had just positioned himself behind her. His sitting position mirrored that of how he sat earlier. His knees were still propped up and his legs were still spread slightly apart. The only difference in this new sitting position was that Yoori was occupying the space between his propped up knees and—oh yeah—he was embracing her from behind!

Yoori's face became reminiscent of a deer caught in headlights. She questioned the verity of the reality she was in. Was this really happening? Was he really hugging her? She pinched herself. She flinched at the pain. It was definitely real. She looked around frantically. There was no audience in sight. He couldn't be acting for the wind, right? Her pulse raced at the possibilities. Oh dear Lord, what was Tae Hyun doing to her?

This is a test, she told herself, trying very hard to make sense of what was going on.

Tae Hyun, that big bully, was testing her to see if she was obsessed with him, she reasoned. Regardless of her obvious attraction to his handsome physique, Yoori knew she couldn't let herself fail "the test." She could only imagine the torment Tae Hyun would put her through if she gave him a reason to believe that he had been right all along, that she was just like the other girls who became putty in his hand.

No.

She couldn't let that happen. No matter how hard it may be, she refused to be seen like any other girls.

"You know," she floundered, not wanting the silence to reflect the shock on her face.

She struggled to find the right word vomit to release from her confused mouth. "You know, your hoodie would have done a great job of warming me up too!"

She grimaced. Could she sound more like a weakling?

Chuckling, Tae Hyun rested his chin on her right shoulder. A mischievous grin graced his mouth as he tilted his head toward her ear. He leaned his lips close enough to her earlobe. There was a microscopic space between his parting lips and her skin.

"If I give you my hoodie," he whispered softly, his hot breath teasing every sense within her. "Then wouldn't I be cold too?"

Yoori closed her eyes in agony when she heard it, that seductive tone in his voice. He was teasing her. The sexy crime lord was teasing her. Oh man, why was he doing this to her?

"Boss, this is completely inappropriate," she croaked. It may have given her a nice bubbly feeling, but Yoori knew sitting like this with Tae Hyun was just a bad idea.

"Isn't this what friends do?" he inquired innocently, his embrace seemingly becoming just a bit tighter.

Yoori frantically shook her head. "No. No, this isn't what friends do."

"This is what I do for girls who are my friends." He laughed at the tenseness exerting from Yoori's rigid body. "Don't think too much of it, assistant," he teased in an even tone. "I just need to sit here for a bit longer to clear my mind. Then, after that, we can leave. Until then, just relax. I can't have my assistant freezing her ass off. Can you imagine the crap I'd have to deal with if you're sick?"

Yoori was no longer listening.

"No, no, no! I can't do this!"

She struggled for a moment before managing to pull herself out of Tae Hyun's embrace. She propped herself up and took a couple steps away from Tae Hyun. She shuddered at the frigidness that attacked her after leaving his embrace.

Still seated in the same position, Tae Hyun merely smiled upward at her. He extended his hand out to her. "Hurry up and come back here. You're going to get sick soon."

Stop tempting me, she wanted to say. Instead, she shook her head.

Tae Hyun lowered his hand and rested it on his kneecap. He held a steady gaze on her. Then, that knowing smirk made its appearance.

Yoori's eyes rounded when she saw it. It wasn't so long ago (last night to be exact) that she saw that particular knowing smile of his. She knew he was going to do this!

Outraged, she pointed a trembling finger at him. "Don't you dare say that I'm being like this because I want you and I don't want to be tempted."

Even though it may be slightly true, she couldn't have Tae Hyun thinking that.

He faked an innocent expression. "I didn't say anything!"

"That stupid smile of yours is saying it all."

He shook his head. "Actually, the way you're acting right now is saying it all." He sighed dramatically before tipping his head back. A long pause before he quietly said, "I knew it."

While voicing this, he made sure to stare at the night's sky, making it appear as if he was now too shy to make eye contact with someone who clearly had an obsession with him.

Yoori screamed in her head. She screamed so loudly that she was surprised her head didn't explode. Contorting her face in aversion, Yoori muttered a string of curses as she thought about her less than favorable position. Damn this Kwon Tae Hyun. He sure knew what buttons to push.

Angered by his cocky attitude and persuaded by her strong desire to salvage her pride, Yoori did the only thing she knew she could do at that moment: she was going to have to act like it was no big deal and sit there with him hugging her from behind.

"Make room," she voiced angrily, stomping back to him.

She slapped his kneecap as a gesture for him to know that she was getting ready to sit in the space between his legs. When he made room, Yoori sat down with pure bitterness. She was instantly reminded of the night before where Tae Hyun "convinced" her to share the same bed with him.

A victorious smile on his face, Tae Hyun wrapped his arms around her as she situated herself in front of him.

Yoori felt renewed fire in her blood. She mentally prepped herself to act as normally as she could. *Don't let him know he got to you or he'll tease you forever,* Yoori reminded herself, feeling her body naturally lean itself against Tae Hyun's breathing chest.

Tae Hyun gave a deep sigh when he rested his chin on the crown of her head. His embrace on her tightened just a bit more. It may have been too bold of a thought on her part, but Yoori was almost sure that Tae Hyun really enjoyed the position they were sitting in.

As awkwardness poured in, Yoori felt the unbearable need to spark a conversation before her insides turned to mush and she actually became putty under Tae Hyun's hold. Before she had the chance to say anything, Tae Hyun had already broken the peace.

"Just relax, will ya?" he whispered offhandedly. "You'll have a hard time clearing your mind if you're tense like this."

Not wanting to seem too affected by what was happening, she listened to him. A muted curse escaped her lips as Yoori allowed her body to relax under Tae Hyun's hold. As her back rested heedlessly against his breathing chest, Yoori felt the last remaining chill leave her body.

And at that moment, something happened that Yoori didn't want to happen.

The foreign bolts of electricity glided through her small frame and she knew she couldn't deny it anymore. She couldn't deny how nice it felt to be in his arms like that, she couldn't deny how natural it was that she somehow fit into his hold so perfectly and she couldn't deny how blissful she felt.

As the last of the rigidness left her muscles, a sense of safety, warmth, and contentment reigned over her. Slowly, Yoori allowed herself to get lost in Tae Hyun's hold. But, just like anything else in the fated world, it would make sense that Tae Hyun would be the one to kill the nice moment they had going on.

"You know," he began carefully, cutting through the wave of her thoughts. "I've been thinking about this since I first met you." He paused for a second before continuing. "You always get really awkward when you're close to me. It never occurred to me until now, but have you ever had a boyfriend?"

If it was even possible, she froze even more.

It was a good thing that Yoori's back was turned to Tae Hyun because the look on her face would've given him the obvious answer. Stiffening up at his question, Yoori's mouth dropped open.

No, she never had a boyfriend; none that she could recall anyway. Amnesia had a tendency to do that to you. Resolved to not get into the messy details of her love life – or lack thereof – she did the only thing she was comfortable with doing: she lied.

"Of course," she replied in an even tone. Though her voice was confident, her blushing and terrified face more than gave away her true answer. She counted her blessings that her back was still turned to him.

He chuckled into her ear. He couldn't see her face, but Yoori somehow knew that Tae Hyun sensed she was lying.

He verified her suspicions without a moment's hesitation. "Liar."

As her eyes shifted around in fear, Yoori did her best to keep her poise. She defended herself at once. "How dare you call me a liar?"

"'Cause you are."

She was flabbergasted at this point. How could he be so sure?

"Why are you so sure I'm lying?"

Due to the fact that his chin was still rested on top of her head, Yoori could feel Tae Hyun smile when he gave her his answer. Tightening his embrace on her, he said, "Because you stiffen up every time you lie."

Yoori sputtered with embarrassment. She twisted around and faced an angelic looking Tae Hyun. The "angel" had a devilish smile on his countenance. "Is that why we're sitting like this? So you can be a human lie detector?"

The nerve of this guy!

Well, she wouldn't have it!

As she made a move to leave, she felt Tae Hyun gently pull her back down. "Stop, you're going to get sick."

"I don't care," she argued, still making an effort to rise up. Blood rushed to her face. "I don't want to talk about my personal life."

"Okay!" he conceded. "Geez, assistant. I was just trying to have a nice bonding moment."

Bonding moment? Her mind was going haywire. What was he doing to her? Did she misunderstand? Wasn't this supposed to be a test? He wasn't really hitting on her, was he?

"Tae Hyun," she began breathlessly, unable to conceal her confusion. "I gotta ask. You're not hitting on me right now, are you?"

He regarded her with humor in his eyes. That cunning smile of his never left his face. Though he didn't seem surprised with her question, he did well to fabricate ignorance. "Do you think I'm hitting on you right now?"

"I...I honestly don't know," she stuttered with an embarrassed expression on her face. "I...I mean I usually know if a guy is hitting on me or not, but I can't tell with you. I don't know if this is just how you are or if you're actually hitting on me."

His smile remained as he shook his head with pure amusement. Exerting a sigh of fatigue, he blithely said, "Choi Yoori, don't flatter yourself. The only reason why I'm keeping you warm is because I don't want you to get sick. Do you know how much I hate being around sick people?"

What the?

Hate being around sick people?

She was dumbfounded.

Her doubtful gaze remained. "Are you serious?"

He nodded seriously. "Yeah. I hate hearing people sneeze and cough. It's truly a sickening sound."

Yoori was ready to call Tae Hyun a liar until she took a moment to mull over what he just said. However ridiculous his answer sounded, it did make sense if it came from him.

She made a frustrated sound when she concluded that he was indeed telling the truth. "You are a terrible person."

Who in their right mind gets annoyed with sick people?

Apparently, her crime lord boss.

"I'd be worse if you got sick," he replied. "Now can we just get back to relaxing and clearing our conflicted minds?"

"Fine," she replied, whirling around. Wanting to punish him for being mean, she purposely threw all her weight backward. Her back made a big thud sound when it collided with Tae Hyun's chest.

"Ugh!"

She smirked in satisfaction after hearing him gasp for air.

That'll teach him to mess with her and sick people.

Clearing his throat after the unexpected attack, Tae Hyun heedlessly wrapped his arms around her and repositioned his chin over her head.

"Well, aren't you the little devil right now?" he asked frostily.

"Sorry, I was just relaxing. Just like you wanted, right?"

"Maybe it's not such a bad idea to let you get sick."

Yoori laughed, her eyes running over all the tree leaves that were dancing in the night.

"So do you come here to clear your head often?" she asked, gradually getting comfortable with how they were sitting.

"I used to. When I was younger, I came here almost every other night." He took in his surroundings. "I always come here when I need to organize my thoughts. It's always so nice and peaceful here."

Yoori nodded automatically. "You said you used to come often when you were younger. What made you stop?"

There was a slight pause on Tae Hyun's part before he answered this. "I stopped after I became the King of Serpents," he replied coolly. A trace of fatigue was present in his voice when he said this. He didn't elaborate, and Yoori didn't ask him to elaborate. She already knew why he no longer wanted to come here.

"To get in a position of power...some actions are unavoidable."

Tae Hyun's previous words replayed in her mind. It was amazing how quickly, even though he didn't directly give her a straight answer, she understood his predicament. She could only imagine the monsters looming in Tae Hyun's conscience since he succeeded the Serpents throne. It made sense that he would avoid coming to the one place that would make him feel human.

"Why is tonight different?" she asked carelessly. Her focus locked on a bright car light that flashed by and disappeared in the distance.

Tae Hyun lifted his chin from the top of her head. Resting his hot lips against her ear, he delicately whispered, "Because you're here."

Yoori giggled like a geek at his goodwill attempt to give her a bullshit answer. "Good answer."

He laughed softly, now resting his chin on her shoulder. "I thought you would like it."

And she did. However insincere it might sound, she liked his answer a lot.

Not wanting to think too much about how nice he made her feel, Yoori inhaled the fresh night's air and said, "So how was your day? You saw your mentor, right?"

"Yeah." His mood became a bit more serious at the reminder.

"How was that?"

"It was productive. I was reminded of stuff I needed to take care of."

"Productive and stressful, I imagine."

"It was an unexpected meeting. He just arrived in town today."

"I can't see you being forced into a meeting you don't want to go to."

"I respect this mentor immensely. If he asks for a meeting, then I cancel everything else and I go."

She nodded. For reasons she didn't entirely understand, Ji Hoon's face cascaded into her mind as Tae Hyun spoke about his day. Guilt started to heave through her.

"I saw Lee Ji Hoon again," she blurted out. She knew that Tae Hyun had clearly expressed that he wasn't concerned with what she does with Ji Hoon, but she just wanted him to find out from her. It was always better that way.

Though she felt his hold on her stiffen slightly, the composure in his voice remained. "I see."

She smirked to herself when his reaction reminded her of his careless attitude toward her. She didn't even know why she bothered to tell him. He obviously didn't care—

"You don't like him, do you?" he asked out of the blue.

Huh? She struggled to remain composed. She uncomfortably cleared her throat. "Does the answer matter?"

His tone became indecipherable. "It might."

"It shouldn't," she countered. He had no right to be acting like this.

He laughed dryly, regarding her like she was a lost cause. "Don't tell me he's another one of your friends."

"No, of course not. Are you kidding me? I don't consider him to be a friend."

Tae Hyun smiled prematurely at her reply.

"He's more like a suitor," she amended.

"*What?*" he shouted, suddenly standing up in outrage.

Yoori jumped at the unexpected outburst from Tae Hyun.

She rose to her feet and backed away from him in disbelief. "What is your problem?"

He had a thunderstruck look on his face. He also looked taken aback with his reaction to all of this.

He glowered at her incredulously. "I thought you had higher standards than that."

She grimaced at his nonsensical reply. "What the eff are you talking about?"

"I didn't think you were the type that would fall *that* easily," he elaborated, the expression of disbelief growing stronger on his face. This was the first time that Yoori had ever seen Tae Hyun lose his cool in this manner.

Was he jealous?

He had no right to be jealous.

"What's the big deal?" She folded her arms in annoyance. "I thought you didn't care."

He looked at her like she was high on drugs. "When did I say I didn't care?"

She faked ignorance as she brought a finger up to her chin and looked aimlessly at the sky. "Oh gee, hmm let me think...How about when you said, 'You and Jin Ae are completely different to me...I'm not concerned when it comes to you.'"

"That's not what I meant. I mean I—"

He stopped what he was saying.

With his mouth hung open and his eyes enlarged, he stared at her in open shock. His stunned eyes had a light to them. It was one of those lights that went off when you realize something. It was one of those lights that went off when you finally have an epiphany.

"Shit," he finally whispered, raking his hands through his hair. His breathing grew vaguely heavier as his gaze on her remained. "Holy fucking shit," he added in complete and utter disbelief.

Yoori also found herself breathing heavier. Tae Hyun's strange behavior was bewildering to her. What had gotten into him? He wasn't acting like himself.

Worry began to set in for her. "What's wrong?" she inquired uneasily, approaching him with concern. Did he catch something?

Stopping in front of his stunned self, Yoori reached out for his forehead to gauge if he was feeling sick. Yoori didn't take it into account, but as her hand made contact with his forehead, Tae Hyun actually held in his breath as he watched her silently.

Tae Hyun's hot forehead thawed her cold hand.

"You're burning up!" she observed worriedly. No wonder he was acting so strange. Poor guy caught something.

After hearing the distress in her voice, Tae Hyun snapped out of his stupor. "Huh? What?"

"I think you caught a fever," she proclaimed. She reached up to feel his forehead once more.

"No. No, I'm fine," he assured, grabbing her wrist to keep her from touching him.

She gave him a strange look. Was it just Yoori or did Tae Hyun seem a bit *shyer* around her? She couldn't tell if it was the fever or not, but was he blushing?

"Okay, okay," she conceded. She lowered her hand. She wasn't too inclined to touch a sick person anyway. Whatever it was that he caught, she hoped she wouldn't catch it too.

A stampede of wind gusted pass them. Distracted by the strong chills, she averted her full attention back to Tae Hyun. He now seemed lost in thought.

"Seriously, can we please leave?" she asked desperately. Her lower lip quivered. "I really think you caught something. And if we don't leave soon, I think I might catch something too. I mean I waited five hours for Ji Hoon because he was busy with some meeting. All this cold is getting to me. I think I can feel something in my throat and—"

Tae Hyun's brows drew together after hearing the word "meeting."

"He had a meeting?"

The lost stupor that was present on Tae Hyun's countenance vanquished. Whatever it was that arrested his interest, it was enough to bring him back to life—with full force.

Yoori's brows inverted in confusion as well. She didn't understand why that part of her statement interested Tae Hyun so much. "Uh yeah. He said he was at an important meeting all day and that he—"

She paused. That was when it all aligned for her. The sudden realization on her face mirrored that of Tae Hyun's. The only true difference was that his was more ominous.

"Wait a second. This doesn't have anything to do with your mentor, does it?"

"Yoori," Tae Hyun said sternly, ignoring her question. The expression on his face said it all: he was more than concerned. "What else did Ji Hoon say about this meeting?"

At this point, Yoori's pulse was already racing in fear. Tae Hyun was scaring her with his behavior.

"I…uh…" she strained to remember. The disoriented fear was blurring her senses.

"Yoori," Tae Hyun prompted again, urgency booming in his voice. "What else did Ji Hoon say about this meeting?"

She bit her bottom lip.

She finally recalled what Ji Hoon said. "That he was going back to it later tonight."

Tae Hyun's eyes enlarged.

"Fuck." He whipped out his Blackberry in record pace, an action that left Yoori more than bewildered. Speed-dialing the number of the person he was trying to reach, Tae Hyun brought the Blackberry to his ear.

"Tae Hyun, you're scaring me," Yoori uttered. She was numb from head to toe. Why did she have such a bad feeling all of a sudden?

"One second, Yoori," he said before muttering a curse under his breath. Whoever it was that he was calling, they weren't picking up. He closed his eyes in frustration. It was clear that he was being directed to a voicemail.

"*Kang Min*," Tae Hyun started anxiously, preparing to leave his message.

Yoori's eyes swelled when she heard Kang Min's name. What was going on?

"Shin Jung Min is back in Korea. Kang Min, you and Jae Won – *both of you*—call me back right away when you get this."

Jae Won? Yoori grew frantic as she watched Tae Hyun pull his Blackberry away from his ear. *Shin Jung Min?* The acceleration of her heart quickened when she registered that both Kang Min and Jae Won could be in danger. Whoever this Shin Jung Min was, she could infer from the tone in Tae Hyun's voice that he was trouble.

"What the hell is going on?" she asked, gazing at Tae Hyun with worried eyes.

"I'm taking you home," he said, ignoring her question.

As he reached for her hand, Yoori instinctively pulled it away from his grasp.

"Kang Min and Jae Won," she inquired again. "Are they ok?"

Her heart was racing so fast that she was sure she was going to have a heart attack soon. Why wasn't Tae Hyun telling her anything?

"Yoori."

"I'm not going anywhere with you until you tell me what's going on! Where are Jae Won and Kang Min? What are you having them do? Who's Shin Jung Min? Is he the mentor you met earlier?"

"He's *not* my mentor," he replied firmly.

"Then who's your mentor?"

"Shin *Dong* Min," he answered quickly. Probably too quick. The regret in his eyes shined through as he briefly closed them in frustration. It was obviously too late for him to take it back.

"Shin..." she looked at Tae Hyun in the purest of confusion. "Then who is Shin Jung Min?"

Why did he have the same surname as Tae Hyun's mentor?

Questions after questions churned in her mind. Without holding back, it all came flowing out of her lips. "And what's the big deal with all these meetings that you and Ji Hoon have been going to today? What's happening?" Realization dawned on her. "Does this have anything to do with that man that everyone has been mentioning? Ju Won?"

Tae Hyun muttered a string of expletives at the situation he was thrown in. He reached his hand out to her again. "All these questions, I'll answer them...but only if you take my hand and leave with me now."

Yoori grabbed Tae Hyun's hand without hesitation and followed him as they descended down the hill. Moving away from the peacefulness of the sleeping grass and dancing trees, the pit in Yoori's stomach had already formed to warn her against the new set of information she was about to receive. Prior to listening to the answers Tae Hyun was about to enlighten her with, Yoori had already ascertained that this long night was about to become longer.

She could sense it.

For the next few hours, she was about to embark on one hell of a night.

The foundational knowledge for the Underworld had been set. Now, it was not only time for Yoori to find out how this society worked, but it was also time for her to find out who the other powerful players of the Underworld were.

"That's why people kneel before me."

31: Hold on Tight – There's Layers

In states of urgency, there are certain characteristics that you forgo in the interest of encouraging productivity and effectiveness. In the case of Kwon Tae Hyun, the one characteristic trait he relinquished in the interest of getting Choi Yoori home so he could quickly deal with helping Kang Min and Jae Won was his secretive nature.

Even though Yoori had always known that when the time called for it, Tae Hyun wouldn't disappoint in terms of "getting down to business," she honestly thought he would've been a bit more reticent before he decided to give her any answers. It goes without saying that, as they migrated back to his motorcycle, she was more than surprised at the efficiency Tae Hyun displayed. He wasted no time in getting down to the specifics and telling her what she needed to know.

"One of the more important things you should learn before anything else," Tae Hyun began, pulling her with him as they descended down the grassy slope. "Is that there are different layers in our world."

"Layers?" Yoori asked, staggered that he was so quick to address her questions.

Even though she had since deduced the seriousness of the situation, the simple fact that Tae Hyun was so anxious to get the answers out of the way only further validated her fears. Something big was happening and it was serious enough that he just wanted to get her home as quickly as possible so he could start "taking care" of stuff.

He nodded at her question, the efficiency in his voice still intact. "There are three different layers to the Underworld and different groups of people who rule over them."

He took a moment to survey their surroundings. When it appeared as if he was satisfied with the silence in the empty park, he continued, his pace quickening slightly.

"The 1st layer is the one open to public scrutiny. The ones who control the inner workings of this layer are known as the 'Corporate Crime Lords'. The corrupt businessmen, politicians, and influential public figures – all the ones you see on TV—they are the ones who make the law *flexible* for those in their inner circle."

"Inner circle?"

He nodded. "The individuals in each layer work interchangeably. If you want any type of power in your own layer, you have to make your alliances with certain groups from each layer."

She gave him the gaze that pretty much said: "Go into more detail."

He obliged. "I grew up and went to school with two of the more powerful heirs to the 1st layer. The Serpents family and those two corporate families pretty much watch each other's backs. When they need me to 'take care' of certain people or make 'certain things' happen, I make it happen. It is in my best interest to help them rise to the top because that would ultimately mean –"

"You will gain as much power as them," Yoori provided in understanding, her gaze never leaving his profile. Another big gust of wind flew past their mobile bodies. "So what do these Corporate Crime Lords help you with?"

"Confidentiality," Tae Hyun answered simply, his pace quickening when the distant view of his Yamaha motorcycle was in sight.

"Unlike regular rankings, the different layers have a different set of statuses in the Underworld. For our world, the crime lords of the 3rd layer are more powerful than the rest. We oversee everything. Murders, weapons smuggling, extortion, counterfeit money, assassinations, blackmailing, illegal gambling, and finally every gang's bread winner—drug trafficking. The 3rd layer essentially controls how the entire outside world works. It's just that our layer has come to learn that ruling a country is best done in the shadows. This is the reason why confidentiality is crucial. Our brothers in the 1st layer understand this and helps support that endeavor."

Yoori was reminded of the story Chae Young told her about the Underworld, how no pictures were taken and that only the ones active in the Underworld would know the face of each gang leader. So there was the importance of confidentiality.

They went over the 1st and 3rd layer, yet she still hadn't heard the citation of the three names from earlier. "What about the 2nd layer?" she verbalized, knowing this was the layer that would be of importance for the night.

"The rulers of the 2nd layer are the ones we in the 1st and 3rd call 'The Advisors.'"

"The Advisors?"

Tae Hyun nodded. "They are the ones who have ruled both layers and have since retired from both worlds." He locked eyes with her. "And there's only three that hold any real power in that layer."

"Just three?"

"Just three," he confirmed. He didn't seem to like that it was such a small and exclusive number as well.

"Shin Dong Min is your Advisor," Yoori thought out loud. "That means Shin Jung Min is Ji Hoon's advisor." She peered up at him. "So Ju Won is the 3rd Advisor?"

"The eldest and most influential Advisor," Tae Hyun corrected.

He backtracked upon seeing the confusion on Yoori's face. "Seo Ju Won, Shin Dong Min and Shin Jung Min were the top crime lords of their time. Their affairs had them ruling in both the 1st and 3rd layer. During their reign, Seo Ju Won was the appointed high crime lord of their era and was the one calling the shots."

"What about the other two?"

"Shin Dong Min and Shin Jung Min are brothers, Jung Min being the elder one. The brothers first started out as bodyguards for Ju Won. As Ju Won grew into power, so did they. Though the brothers had since formed their own successful crime syndicates and held reputable positions as corporate crime lords, their loyalties never strayed too far from Ju Won."

"So is that the reason why Ju Won has that much power over you and Ji Hoon? That's why you couldn't kill each other at the warehouse? Because of Ju Won's orders?"

It didn't make much sense to Yoori. Logic would dictate that from Tae Hyun's explanations, the 2nd layer had little power in comparison to the 3rd layer.

"*Request*," Tae Hyun emphasized upon hearing her use the term "order." "The 2nd layer, however influential they are, doesn't get fear, but respect from me. I imagine this is the case for Ji Hoon as well. At their age, the only silver lining in their survival is the fact that they've since retired from active Underworld life. At the end of the day, everyone in all three layers know that the true Lords of the Underworld are the ones who preside over the 3rd layer. Seo Ju Won and the Shins know this, which is why they are picking their alliances and investing in that alliance. The one reason why their 'requests' holds any power in the 3rd layer is because of the monetary value they bring to us."

"Their fortunes," Yoori supplied mindlessly.

Tae Hyun forged on as a subtle way of telling Yoori that so far her understanding was correct.

"Shin Dong Min has been like a father to me. He has been my mentor before my inauguration as the King of Serpents and he continues to be my mentor today. Because of the absence of my own father, he taught me everything I needed to know to be an effective crime lord in the Underworld. From his expertise in martial arts, weaponry, and the connection to his vast inner circles, everything was bestowed to me and bestowed only to me. And, much like a father, he trusts that I would be the one who rules the Underworld in the end. So as a token of his confidence, I was given the one thing that would aid in all of that."

"You're the heir to his empire," Yoori said instinctively.

Tae Hyun nodded, taking another look around once they stepped off the grass and onto the pavement that led the way to his motorcycle.

"And Shin Jung Min favors Ji Hoon?" Yoori asked, struggling to keep up with Tae Hyun. His pace rivaled even the speed of light.

"The Shin brothers, although they grew into power together, are infamous for always butting heads. There was probably only one thing in their lives that they didn't butt heads about, but they do not disappoint with other aspects. It makes sense that each of them would choose to support two opposing Kings."

He flicked a glance at Yoori to make sure she was okay with the quick pace. Yoori adopted a reassuring smile, hiding the fact that she was actually panting relentlessly. Damn being out of shape!

When he was satisfied that she could manage, he proceeded with the enlightenment. "Shin Dong Min hates Ji Hoon and Shin Jung Min hates me. There's a breakeven effect to the rivalry between Ji Hoon and myself because both brothers' empires are roughly worth the same. So as of now, Ji Hoon and I are going after the one thing that would tip the pendulum of power in our direction."

"The only one left to sway the support is Ju Won," Yoori responded, understanding more and more about how things worked now.

Tae Hyun gave a stiff nod.

"Seo Ju Won has absolutely no power," he said with an agitated voice. It was evident he had never been too fond of Ju Won either. "He does, however, hold a lot of influence. His fortune is endless. The one who inherits his empire is almost guaranteed the Underworld on a silver platter. Ju Won knows this and has been dangling it in front of us. His public request to have the Serpents and the Skulls halt in killing one another until his 65th birthday was a power play on his part. Ju Won is by no means a peaceful crime lord. He couldn't care less who dies and who survives. He just wants it known that although he has no direct power, he does have influence. And being the greedy crime lords that we have become, the prospect of getting an old man's fortune is enough to instill some patience within us—me at least."

Yoori could see that Tae Hyun was already losing his patience with the old man.

"That's why the two of you have been following his 'requests.' He's still in the midst of choosing one of you to become his heir," said Yoori breathlessly.

All this accelerated walking was getting to her. Why did it feel so short when they were headed toward the hill, and now, when they were heading back to the motorcycle, it felt like an odyssey?

Unaware of the continual panting on Yoori's part, Tae Hyun hurried to finish up his explanation of how the 2nd layer worked. "Right now, it's just a matter of expanding our respective gangs and creating a stronger name for ourselves. Ju Won is a businessman at heart. He would only invest in the King he sees as having the highest potential to ruling all three layers."

"Who's winning so far?"

"My favor has picked up since the recruitment of Jae Won's gang."

"Okay, now I know who everyone is. So where's Jae Won and Kang Min?" she asked, watching as he threw one leg over the motorcycle. "What have they been doing for the past week?"

There was a short pause as he situated himself on the bike. "Do you remember what I said I'll do for you when I found out that Jin Ae's men attacked you?"

In light of all that had happened to Yoori, getting assaulted from Jin Ae's men was the last thing that crossed her mind. Yet, as she recalled Tae Hyun saying to Kang Min that he wanted those responsible for the assault to kneel before him, dread seeped into the marrow of her bones.

"You had Jae Won and Kang Min go after Jin Ae?"

"It shouldn't have taken more than a week, but it did," he began, frustration brewing in his voice. "It took more than a week because Jin Ae and her men went into hiding. It never occurred to me that she was stupid enough to hide out in her uncle's mansion while he was out of the country. Everyone knows that Ju Won goes crazy when anyone enters that precious mansion of his without him there as a host."

"So that's where Jae Won and Kang Min are? At Ju Won's mansion retrieving Jin Ae?" Her words scrutinized his impulsive decision. "Why would you have them go through all of that? Just to have Jin Ae and her men kneel before you?"

"I told you I'll have them kneeling before *you*," he retorted, as if the specifics of his reasoning would make him seem less reckless.

"At the expense of Jae Won and Kang Min's safety?"

Though Yoori wouldn't go as far as saying that she had since forgiven Jin Ae and her men, this wasn't an issue that she wanted Jae Won, Kang Min, or Tae Hyun, for that matter, to actually deal with; *especially* if it meant that it'll put them in danger.

"It wasn't supposed to be dangerous," Tae Hyun clarified, reading her mind. "Jae Won had to prove himself to me. Ju Won was out of the country with Shin Jung Min. They were not supposed to be back for another week. I didn't know they were back until you told me that Ji Hoon has been in a meeting all day as well."

Her throat growing dry with the passing seconds, Yoori gazed at Tae Hyun. Reluctant hope lit in her eyes. "Even if they're caught, they'll be okay, right?"

She had hoped that he would nod in agreement. She was disappointed when she saw the uncertainty on Tae Hyun's expression.

"Ju Won is a retired crime lord, but a crime lord nonetheless." His eyes brimmed with concern. His own explanation was making an impact on him as well. "He highly values respect. If he catches them, he'd more than likely go on a power trip and execute them before everyone as an example."

A paralyzing horror overcame Yoori.

Execute Jae Won and Kang Min?

"That's why I'm taking you home now," he continued, his eyes urging her to get on the bike. "If all three of the Advisors are back, then they'd likely call a meeting for Ji Hoon and I. The Advisors would be at that mansion. I have to get to Jae Won and Kang Min's side before Ju Won catches them or does anything to them. But, before that, I have to take you home. It'll be safer there."

Though lost in a stupor, Yoori had enough hold on reality to know that she still wanted to go with Tae Hyun. "But—"

"No arguments," he cut off. "It's safer for you to be home. Now get on."

Yoori breathed quietly, her eyes practically gleaming with fear. Acknowledging that any more arguments with Tae Hyun would be futile, Yoori obediently got onto the bike and wrapped her arms around him.

The truth was she was afraid.

Tae Hyun had given her so much new information to register that she was now sincerely afraid. Though Tae Hyun didn't view Ju Won as much of a threat, Yoori somehow just had a bad feeling about the man. There was something about him that made her uneasy, something about Seo Ju Won that made her think he was much more of a threat than Tae Hyun gave him credit for.

Moreover, the fact of the matter was that she had no more strength or bravery left within her. A big part of her knew that going home would be the best option and she was willing to listen to Tae Hyun. Tightening her arms around him, her fears of the unknown plagued her. There was no more combative personality left. In times of urgency, she relinquished her curious and hardheaded traits. The only important trait left to hold on to was self-preservation.

As Tae Hyun was getting ready to drive off, his Blackberry sounded, catching the immediate attention of Yoori.

She somehow already knew who it was.

The grave expression on Tae Hyun's countenance when he glanced at his Blackberry screen confirmed Yoori's suspicions as to who the person on the other line could be.

It was indeed the eldest Advisor.

"Ju Won," Tae Hyun answered punctually, holding the phone extremely close to his ear. He was attempting to block out any residual sound that may allot Yoori the opportunity to hear the other side of the conversation.

"Tae Hyun, my boy," the hoarse voice said clearly from the other line.

Curiosity got the best of Yoori when she heard Ju Won's voice. The ticking clock of a long life swam in his rasp, but strong voice. Though his voice didn't sound too intimidating, the amused and ominous echo within it led Yoori to conclude that Ju Won was no ordinary man enjoying retirement. If the tone of his voice gave any indication, Ju Won was not only a power hungry old man, but he was also a scheming one at that.

She purposely rested her head on Tae Hyun's slouching back. Very closely, she listened to the phone conversation.

"How are you?" Tae Hyun asked coolly, straightening his back to get Yoori off so she wouldn't be able to eavesdrop.

Annoyed, Yoori made sure to wrap her arms tighter around him. She continued to rest her head against his back. She didn't care if he didn't want her to hear the conversation. The temptation to know what was happening was just too strong for her to resist.

Ju Won got straight to the point. "It seems that I have a couple of unexpected visitors tonight—your men to be exact. Kang Min and Jae Won." He chuckled. "From the sounds of it from Jin Ae, I believe you've ordered them to find her and have her kneel before someone?"

Though Ju Won's voice was calm when he asked this, Yoori could hear the subtle scowl in it. Ju Won was pissed. He may have been pissed at Tae Hyun, but he was more pissed at whomever Tae Hyun wanted Jin Ae to kneel before.

"My girlfriend," Tae Hyun answered without reservations.

Her heart expanded. Though it was sweet of him to announce it so proudly, she wished that Tae Hyun would keep the specifics about her intact. It was such a rash thing to do, and Ju Won didn't have to know the specifics. It scared Yoori. She didn't want the man to know anything about her.

Ju Won laughed at Tae Hyun's answer. "Bring her here," he said at once. "I, along with the rest of the Advisors, would love to meet her."

The intonation of his voice was one of those nice pitches that had mockery clearly wrapped within it. Sensing the insulting tone, Tae Hyun's eyes sharpened. Even in the face of losing one of his potential "investors," Tae Hyun's pride will never fail to get into the mix.

"Do *not* tell me what to do," he growled.

The humor in Ju Won's voice did not cease. "My boy, it was not an order, but a request from an old man's part."

As if looking at something, Ju Won continued. "Kang Min and Jae Won are a little tied up right now. I'm sure they'll be happy to see you and your girlfriend. Plus, I've already invited Ji Hoon to come. We'll have our impromptu meeting since everyone is in town."

Tae Hyun had already stiffened up upon the mention of Kang Min and Jae Won being tied up.

"Let them go, Ju Won," he ordered gravely. "I'm not in the mood for anymore meetings."

Ju Won refused to let up. He had something Tae Hyun wanted, and he wasn't afraid to dangle it in Tae Hyun's face. "This meeting will only prove beneficial to you, especially after finding out that you've somehow managed to get Jae Won to merge into your gang. It's impressive and we must celebrate."

The fire in Tae Hyun's eyes cooled.

He was reminded of a particular empire that he had been after for quite some time. As his senses came back to him, so did the diplomatic tone in Tae Hyun's voice.

"Another night—"

"You're already standing on higher ground than Ji Hoon," Ju Won interrupted before Tae Hyun could suggest an alternative. "Are you really going to compromise that position because of an attendance problem?"

Tae Hyun fell silent.

Satisfied with Tae Hyun's silence, the smiling voice of Ju Won barreled on. "I'll see you soon. And please, bring your new girlfriend. I'd love to meet the girl you want Jin Ae to kneel before."

The mention of Yoori was the only thing that brought combative fire back to Tae Hyun. "Ju Won," he gritted firmly, "I'm *not* bringing her."

"See you soon, young King," Ju Won said clearly, feigning ignorance to Tae Hyun's retort before hanging up.

Muttering a muted curse that he couldn't get a word in edgewise, Tae Hyun angrily placed his Blackberry back into his pocket. When Tae Hyun made no comment to Yoori about the content of the conversation, she concluded that he was still set on taking her home.

Too bad for Tae Hyun.

Yoori had already made up her mind when Ju Won abruptly hung up on him.

"I'm going with you," she said resolutely, her voice struggling to remain strong when she said this.

She was still afraid, really afraid; however, the thought of Kang Min and Jae Won getting hurt because of her was clawing at her. She was terrified, but Yoori wanted to do all that she could to help them—even if that meant she would have to show her face to the Advisors, all of whom she could only imagine were waiting to punish her for being the "troublemaker." Her fears, as overbearing as it had become, was no match to the protective nature she had for both Kang Min and Jae Won. Under her watch, nothing will happen to them. She was determined to make sure of that.

Tae Hyun looked at Yoori like she was now the one being reckless. He made no effort to appear diplomatic. "Are you crazy? There's no way in hell you're going with me."

"Yes, I am!" she shouted back. "You heard the tone of his voice. He's not going to let them go unless I show up."

"Don't be stupid. I can take care of Ju Won. I'm not letting you go in there."

"You have to take me with you."

"Why do I have to take you with me?" Tae Hyun asked, his voice tight with anxiety.

"Because you can't go alone."

"Are you kidding me? This is *me* we're talking about. I can handle Ju Won and the rest of them. It's you who can't handle them."

Yoori held on to her stubbornness. "I have to go help Jae Won and Kang Min."

At that moment, both had lost their patience – Tae Hyun being the first contender. "What did I tell you about doing stupid things?"

"Tae Hyun," she said inflexibly, her mind already set on going with him. Now it was Yoori's turn to lose her patience. She knew what she had to say to end this senseless argument. "You're taking me. If you don't take me with you, then I swear to God I'm going to run off. The moment you take me back to the apartment and take off, I'll run without any hesitation. And this time, trust me. I'll go so fucking far that I'll make sure you will *never* find me again."

A pause collapsed over Tae Hyun as his disbelieving gaze met her decisive and threatening face.

After taking a moment to seemingly search for any bluff within her fiery eyes, Tae Hyun shook his head. Irrefutable anxiety flooded over his visage.

"Choi Yoori," he began, his voice graver than she had ever heard it. "Do you realize that the world that you've been exposed to so far is nothing compared to the world you're about to enter if you officially meet the Advisors?"

Yoori nodded, unabashed fear seeping out of her once stubborn gaze. If Tae Hyun was trying to make her think twice about going, it worked pretty well.

"Tae Hyun," she said again, her voice trembling. Despite Tae Hyun's grave warning, she still had to go. "You'll watch over me, right?"

Yoori knew that the decision to go was a stupid and reckless one on her part. Even though she knew that her safety would be guaranteed at home, the stubborn part of her felt the unbearable obligation to go. At this rate, all that she needed to compartmentalize her fears were the reassuring words from Tae Hyun. That was *all* she needed.

With his last thoughtful glance on her, Tae Hyun offered her a quiet sigh as a confirmation of his response that he would still watch over her. Turning around, he had already started the motorcycle.

"Stick close to me," he said before taking his foot off the ground and steadying them on his bike.

Her heart feeling a bit lighter than before, Yoori tightened the enclosures of her arms around him. She rested her face on his back as they sped off into the night. While this occurred, Yoori did her best to maintain the last vestige of strength and bravery she had left.

She wasn't sure how fast her heart was beating as they raced through the empty streets. She wasn't sure how pale her face had become as they whizzed past several stoplights. She wasn't even sure how long it took them to get there once Tae Hyun parked his motorcycle in front of the massive silhouette before them. Yet, as she gazed up at the infrastructure that towered over her, Yoori couldn't help but bite her lower lip in awe.

Standing enormously in the silence of the night, enveloped in shadows cast by the full moon behind it, the white mansion couldn't have appeared more magnificent—or intimidating—for Yoori.

It was probably fear.

It was probably fear that was eating at her as Tae Hyun helped her off the motorcycle. It was probably fear that clawed its way out of her terrified eyes, and it was probably fear that made her think twice about coming here. Now that she saw what she had gotten herself into, Yoori couldn't help but regret the fact that it was too late to change her mind.

They were at Ju Won's mansion and there was no turning back.

As though sensing her overwhelming fear, Tae Hyun cupped his hands on her cold cheeks and lifted her face up to meet his. "When you speak to them, make sure to look them dead in the eyes. Do not let them know that you're afraid. You got that?"

Yoori nodded meekly, feeling marginally better that she at least had Tae Hyun by her side. Though the feminist within her would kill her for thinking this, she did feel better going into this knowing that Tae Hyun was around to protect her if anything were to happen.

Hopefully nothing too deadly happens.

He released his hands from her cheeks. His left hand then managed to find her right hand. Interlocking their fingers together, his reassuring smile on her remained. "Whatever happens in there, remember to hold on tight."

Though her throat was almost too rigid to speak, Yoori nodded. "Alright."

She tightened her grip on his hand. Her fears, although still present, subsided for the time being. However deluded it was of her, having Tae Hyun there made her feel safer than she ever could with anyone else.

Hand in hand, they descended toward the mansion.

While striding toward it, it felt strange for Yoori to feel that her senses had suddenly heightened. She took inventory of her surroundings.

She took note of the six cars that were in the driveway. Six cars that looked empty, but she was sure was occupied by at least four men in each car. She took inventory of the subtle breathing in the shadows of Ju Won's enormous gardens. She couldn't see them, but she knew there were at least eight men patrolling the area. And finally, she also took notice of the five individual silhouettes hiding on the roof of the mansion. It was hard to see, especially in the blinding darkness. At second glance, she no longer saw the subtle silhouettes. However, she knew they were there. Bodyguards or intruders, whoever these people were, she doubted they would be on her side if anything were to go down in that mansion.

She inhaled deeply at all of the new anxiety her heightened senses brought her. She silently prayed to come out of this long night alive and with all of her limbs intact. She glanced quickly at the brick walkway that had smears of fresh blood on it. She shook harder. Yoori was beginning to think that such a prayer was probably far-fetched in this place.

When Tae Hyun rang the doorbell, Yoori found herself biting her lower lip in worry for what was to come. The truth of the matter was it had *just* occurred to her that the path she had been on had only been the bridge leading her into the depths of the Underworld.

With uncertainty deluging within her, Yoori knew that this night was a marked night.

This particular evening was not only the night where she will finally meet the crime lords of the 2nd layer, but it was also the night where she will officially enter the world she's had her curious eyes on for so long.

"Choi Yoori..." she whispered warily when the door swung open, the unknown contents of a long night staring at her dead in the eyes. "Welcome to the Underworld."

"It's truly a terrible thing."

32: Blood In

The instant they stepped into the estate, Yoori felt a tsunami of chills ram against the fortress of her skin. The artificial odor of an icy coolness filled her nostrils while her lungs struggled for breath upon the unsuspecting attack that left her with no feeling of warmth.

Seo Ju Won's mansion was unexpectedly and painfully cold.

Reeling from a temperature that would do the North Pole proud, Yoori shivered as one of Ju Won's men, whom Yoori suspected to be one of Ju Won's many bodyguards, spoke to them—or to Tae Hyun to be precise.

"They're waiting for you in the meeting room," the man, who was dressed in a sleek black suit, voiced politely. His tone was embedded with every ounce of respect for Tae Hyun. Seemingly afraid that a direct line of sight with Tae Hyun would merit him an early grave, his gaze was lowered the entire time as he spoke to him.

Tae Hyun, whose sole attention was still focused on Yoori, gave a careless nod.

Taking Tae Hyun's response as a nod of dismissal, the bodyguard bequeathed a distracted Tae Hyun with a respectful bow before closing the door and disappearing into the abyss that lined the corridor of Ju Won's spacious mansion.

Yoori looked around.

The mansion itself was an unusual one.

Its gargantuan size was more defined indoors than its outer appearance. It lacked everything a proper home would require. To start off, it had no stairs, no living rooms, and no bedrooms—none of the likes. The vicinity was merely a rectangular shaped infrastructure that housed a second rectangular room implanted in the center of the "home." Four separate corridors surrounded the space between the two separate chambers.

The mansion was reminiscent of an arena more than anything.

To the further right hand corner of the corridor they were in, Yoori spotted two oak doors that led into the entrance to what she could observe as the meeting room. To the side of it, her eyes caught sight of two silhouettes.

Before being allotted the chance to get a better glimpse at them, her attention was swayed by Tae Hyun.

"You're freezing," he observed, barely noticing the bodyguard bidding him goodbye. He faced Yoori and placed his hand on her pale cheek. His face lit with alarm when he noticed that her body temperature had dropped dramatically.

"Why is it so cold in here?" she stuttered, forgetting about the silhouettes when she felt his touch. Albeit his hand was just as cold, it made her feel faintly warmer.

"Your body is much more alert under the freezing temperature," he explained, paying more interest to the chattering of her teeth. He sighed at the sight of her quivering lips and extracted his free hand away. "Your body, if and when an unexpected fight occurs, will react with more instincts than thought. This cold temperature can only be more favorable to you."

As Yoori thoughtlessly nodded at his explanation, Tae Hyun was already pulling her into the far corner of the left corridor. They moved behind a small wall that led to the coat closet. Tae Hyun only stopped to place her in the triangular corner, right beside the closet door.

He lifted his arms up.

"Wh-what are you doing?" Yoori uttered, even though it was quite obvious to her what he was doing.

She watched Tae Hyun pull his black hoodie up over his head. She was surprised to find that he was also wearing a black track jacket underneath the hoodie.

He handed her the hoodie. "Here."

"You're so prepared," Yoori marveled, grabbing the hoodie without hesitation. Normally she would show more apprehension with taking someone's article of clothing, but desperate times call for desperate measures. She was freezing her ass off and if Tae Hyun was willing to offer his jacket, then she was going to accept it; it was that simple.

When her hand made contact with the fabric, Yoori heard a distant giggle that made her ears perk up in vigilance. She knew the giggle could only belong to one person: Jin Ae.

So that was who one of those two silhouettes were...

"Hurry and put it on," Tae Hyun urged. He was also reminded of the quandary they were in with the announcement of Jin Ae's presence.

Stepping out of the corner as Yoori prepared to slip her arms through his hoodie, Tae Hyun thoughtlessly added, "And make sure to pull that hood up."

Yoori quickly slid herself into the hoodie. Her hands were in preparation of pulling up the black hood when she heard a familiar voice address Tae Hyun. Tae Hyun's back was still in view as he stood under the dim corridor lighting. Although Yoori remained unseen, Tae Hyun was clearly visible to the two people at the other side of the corridor.

Yoori listened closely.

"Tae Hyun," the warm voice of Lee Ji Hoon greeted, his tone embellished with taunt and arrogance.

Even in the absence of his face, Yoori could tell from her visually impaired corner that Ji Hoon was more than likely shooting daggered glares at Tae Hyun.

"It's wonderful that you made it. Jin Ae and I were placing bets as to whether or not you'd dare show your face here." Ji Hoon paused as if to play with something. "Obviously Jin Ae here won because you did show up."

A blast of indignation spiked through her when she registered that he didn't pause to play with something—he paused to play with *someone*. She scowled internally. Wasn't it just a couple hours ago that she was with him? This guy was unbelievable.

"Tae Hyun," she heard Jin Ae's sickeningly sweet voice.

It could very well be that she hated Jin Ae immensely, but the sound of Jin Ae's flirtatious tone of voice with Tae Hyun made Yoori sick to her stomach. Who did this girl think she was talking to Tae Hyun like that?

Her bitterness was short-lived at the sound of Tae Hyun's cold voice. "It's a shame that Ju Won would spend money on two worthless guard dogs." She could hear the smug smirk in his voice when he stated this.

Yoori couldn't be happier with his insult. It did well to temper the anger mounting inside her. Yeah! Go Kwon Tae Hyunnie!

Not that she wanted Ji Hoon to be insulted. Even though he unknowingly disappointed her tonight, she only wanted Jin Ae to get insulted. Ji Hoon was merely the necessary casualty of war.

"Tae Hyun," Jin Ae voiced meekly. She was hurt with Tae Hyun's blunt insult.

Her pouty voice became overshadowed by Ji Hoon's angry voice. "Tae Hyun, you piece of shit!" he barked irately, his patience with Tae Hyun never lasting too long. "Do you have a fucking death wish?"

Satisfied with the reactions he received, Tae Hyun smiled to himself. He turned his gaze back to Yoori.

"Ready?" he mouthed quietly, pleased that Yoori got an unfiltered performance of what Ji Hoon was like when she wasn't around. It was a bold assumption on Yoori's part, but she was convinced that Tae Hyun was still bitter when she called Ji Hoon her "suitor."

Extending his hand out, Tae Hyun's smile remained as he waited for her.

Albeit she was content with Tae Hyun's cold interaction toward Jin Ae, Yoori also found herself simultaneously disappointed with Ji Hoon's behavior when she wasn't around. Apparently the "womanizer" in him was very much alive with other girls as well. Though it was difficult to deny her feelings, Yoori also knew that she had no right to be territorial. It wasn't like Ji Hoon was her boyfriend or anything.

No longer keen on prolonging the internal conflicts milling inside her, Yoori lifted the hood up and took Tae Hyun's outstretched hand. She followed his lead and took her first step into the dimly lit corridor.

Clearly bothered with Tae Hyun's show of disrespect with his inattentiveness, Ji Hoon's furious voice saturated the room as Yoori came out of the corner. "What are you—?"

Ji Hoon halted mid-sentence when Yoori slid out of the corner and into view.

Caught.

At the unexpected sighting of Yoori, Ji Hoon quickly jumped to his feet and hastily pushed a smug looking Jin Ae off his lap. Though Yoori didn't catch the entire view of Jin Ae sitting on Ji Hoon's lap, she could surmise that was what occurred, especially considering Ji Hoon's quick reaction to push her off.

"Ji Hoon!" Jin Ae screamed, nearly doubling over. She repositioned her black high heels just in time to balance herself. She muttered a curse while she straightened her little red dress.

Ji Hoon gaped at Yoori. "Yoori…"

Jin Ae's voice shadowed after his. "What the hell are you doing here?"

Feigning ignorance to the more than dramatic reactions of the people standing parallel from him, Tae Hyun simply gazed at Yoori.

"Better?" he inquired, referring to the nature of her warmth. He didn't have to say anything else, but Yoori knew what Tae Hyun was doing. It was his subtle way of throwing another insult toward Ji Hoon and Jin Ae by ignoring them. The King of Serpents loved making people feel like shit.

Yoori nodded distractedly, the hood of the jacket bouncing with her head. "Much better," she replied wryly, a bit uncomfortable knowing that all eyes were now solely on her.

"Yoori," Ji Hoon said loudly, trying once more to get her attention. He appeared to have regained his composure. His face was now pale with uncertainty. He had the guilt filled eyes of a kid who got caught red-handed.

At the call of his voice, Yoori turned to him. She didn't miss the death glare Jin Ae, who was standing off to the side with her arms folded before her, shot her way.

"Wh-why are you here?" Ji Hoon asked, his voice actually shaking. He looked frantic with concern. When Yoori didn't answer him immediately, Ji Hoon then turned to Tae Hyun. His pale face colored with anger. "Why the fuck did you bring her here?"

Tae Hyun clenched his jaw. He was reminded of his own stupidity for bringing her to the mansion and he wasn't happy. He glimpsed at Yoori, his eyes conveying to her that he wasn't joking when he said that it was dangerous for her to come. Ji Hoon's outraged question only further validated his point.

"I wanted to come," Yoori answered at once, knowing that Tae Hyun was probably entertaining the idea of throwing her back onto the motorcycle and driving her back to the apartment.

Ji Hoon fell silent at her answer, his eyes becoming unreadable.

Jin Ae, however, was less graceful with her reaction.

"You stupid twit," she started wrathfully, snarling at Yoori like she was the biggest airhead in the world. "We're in this mess because of you. You think my uncle and the Shins will forgive you for ruining the peace before his birthday party? You have some fucking nerv—"

Jin Ae ceased with her words when she saw Tae Hyun's foreboding glare. Biting her lower lip to keep from saying anything else, she pulled her folded arms closer to her chest and looked away. Her demeanor said it all: she would've definitely hurled more poisonous insults at Yoori had Tae Hyun not been there.

Yoori scowled at Jin Ae's words.

Having the type of combative personality that she does, Yoori had to bite her own lips to keep from uttering a series of damning curses at Jin Ae. She could feel the insults pulsating in her mouth. Mentally, she calmed herself down. If this were any other occasion, Jin Ae would've gotten a mouthful from her already. Yet from the experience of being Kwon Tae Hyun's personal assistant, Yoori had become a bitter expert at keeping things boiled in. She would deal with Jin Ae later.

"Are we just going to stand here and stare at each other all night or are we going to do something productive?" Tae Hyun asked curtly.

Yoori hid a smile and subconsciously tightened her hand on his in approval. Ah yes, it was definitely more amusing to see Tae Hyun be mean to anyone other than to her, especially when that person was Jin Ae. She felt less angry already.

After breaking out of their trance, Ji Hoon and Jin Ae straightened up, their smugness completely gone: Jin Ae's gone from being reprimanded by Tae Hyun and Ji Hoon's gone after being caught off guard with Yoori's unforeseen attendance.

Pushing the two oak doors opened, Ji Hoon turned to Yoori apprehensively. His face was still full of unspoken concern. His eyes briefly raked over her before he made his way into the dark room.

With her arms still crossed, Jin Ae followed closely behind Ji Hoon. Before going in, she turned and stole a quick glance at Yoori.

"Good luck," she mouthed, a taunting smirk firmly solidified on her face as she made her way in. The sound of her heels clicked away in the darkness.

"Pull your hood a little further down," Tae Hyun instructed quietly. "The less the Advisors see your face, the better. They're not known to be forgiving and I don't imagine that you're on their good side tonight."

Yoori heeded his advice. Her body humming in anticipation of finally being able to meet the Advisors, Yoori drew the hood down just a little bit more, her fears already reaching its apex at his chilling warning. If she had her way, she'd wear a mask as well.

Tae Hyun tightened his hold on her hand. Yoori knew this was his non-verbal way of making her feel safer and it was a gesture that served its purpose. She inhaled deeply and followed Tae Hyun as he approached the opened doorframe. Their fingers were still tightly intertwined as the darkness of the meeting room swallowed them whole.

Yoori marveled at the room ahead of her.

She knew upon walking in that Ju Won's "mansion" was not a mansion built for a crime lord to get some shut-eye. Absolutely not. This particular mansion was built for a crime lord who wanted to have secure meetings with his affiliates in the Underworld. Having the vicinity masked as a "homely" mansion was just part of that plan to camouflage what was really in here.

When they drew further into the meeting room, Yoori's eyes continued to survey the space.

The dim illumination of light coming from the center of the room helped her to ascertain that the confined space was big enough to be called an arena. And of course, it was an arena big enough to fit the entire Underworld of Seoul. The front entrance from which they walked in was dark, a characteristic trait that matched all four corners of the abnormally large room. Distinct sounds of breathing could be heard ricocheting off the high ceilings.

At the call of her instincts, Yoori twisted her neck upward. Still walking, her eyes struggled to find something in the darkness. The high ceilings. There was something going on up there…When the darkness that veiled the ceiling left her vision with nothing but a blank canvas, Yoori lowered her gaze, dismissing her paranoid instincts and paying attention to more important things at hand.

Straight ahead at the source of the lighting, Yoori could see that there were five figures standing off to the left side of the room. It was Jin Ae, Woo, Jin Ae's two other bodyguards and Ji Hoon. Ji Hoon stood closer to the light than the rest. He was facing something—or someone.

Yoori followed the direction of Ji Hoon's gaze.

At the sight before her, Yoori suddenly found herself tightening her grasp on Tae Hyun's hand. A sinking feeling forced its way down her stomach. At the further end of the room, where another source of lighting glowed from above, sat three older gentlemen. They were sitting on chairs so majestic and enormous that it could only be fit for kings. It didn't take long for Yoori to infer that the one sitting in the middle, his chair being noticeably higher than the other two, was none other than the infamous Seo Ju Won.

Though he was the oldest of the three, Ju Won looked utterly fit for a man of his age. With the faint light glowing hazily on the bald surface of his head, his mustache was the only indicator of his old age. It was lined more by the tone of gray than black.

"Tae Hyun," he spoke, his voice resonating across the high ceilings when his eyes spotted the two figures emerging out of the darkness.

His gray suit rustled when he repositioned himself on the seat to get a better view of Tae Hyun. Tae Hyun had just stopped right unto the rectangular light, leaving Yoori to stand a couple of feet beside him in the cloak of darkness. Yoori understood then that Tae Hyun was still determined to do everything in his power to make sure the Advisors didn't get a good visual of her face. If it meant hiding underneath the hood of his jacket and standing in the blinding darkness for the entire night, then so be it.

"Wonderful that you two made it," Ju Won continued, staring directly at the darkness that shrouded over Yoori. She could see a smirk form wrinkles on his face. He knew what Tae Hyun was trying to do.

"Ju Won," Tae Hyun voiced politely, giving a slight bow to Ju Won.

The old man nodded approvingly, his eyes flickering toward Yoori's abyss covered direction every so often.

Though it was subtle on his part, she was sure she saw Ji Hoon steal a quick glimpse in her direction as well. He looked uneasy.

Tae Hyun continued with his salutations.

He turned to the man dressed in a long sleeve black buttoned up shirt and light gray pants. He was sitting to the right of Ju Won.

"Uncle," he greeted with a smile and a bow. His voice was more genuine with respect.

The middle-aged man, whose short black hair continued to layer his head, nodded at Tae Hyun, his face lighting up into a smile. It was clear to Yoori that this was Shin Dong Min, Tae Hyun's mentor.

To the man on the left, who appeared a couple of years older than Dong Min, Tae Hyun gave the same bow of respect. His voice was the only thing that faltered in terms of respect.

"Jung Min," he voiced softly. Noticeable disdain waltzed in his voice.

Shin Jung Min, whose face mirrored a matching disdain, merely blinked his eyes in response. He clearly did not favor Tae Hyun. He dusted imaginary dust off of his white dress shirt and his dark gray pants, his blonde and gray hair glowing in the dim lighting. A tense sigh issued from his mouth, the upper portion embellished with a gray mustache that matched his hair. He turned away from Tae Hyun like it was too difficult for him to stare at something so unworthy.

"What a surprise that you're all here tonight," Tae Hyun began, paying no mind to the fact that Jung Min was pretty much dismissing his existence. His attention slid from Jung Min to Ju Won. "I was under the impression that both of you were going to be in China for a couple more days."

"We got the business we needed from the Lords of the Chinese Underworld," Ju Won answered coolly, the smile never leaving his face. "There's no point in furthering our stay there when I have potential heirs who are looking to be enlightened."

At identical times, Tae Hyun and Ji Hoon forced a smile to appear on their faces.

"Which reminds me," said Ju Won. He turned to his right and snapped his fingers. Sounds of shuffling emanated from the darkness.

Tae Hyun's expression fell.

"I bumped into your men tonight, Tae Hyun," Ju Won voiced soothingly. At the call of his snapping fingers, two bodyguards emerged out of the darkness.

Yoori tensed when she saw that they were pulling two tied up shadows with them. Both sporting dried up bloody lips and a combination of cuts and bruises on their bodies, the brothers looked like they had just been through hell and back. Their leather jackets were nearly ripped to shreds and their pants were tattooed with footprints. They were being led out, their wrists bound together in ropes. They could barely keep themselves balanced. Her chest tightened at such a heartbreaking sight. It took all her strength to restrain herself from speeding over to help Jae Won and Kang Min. Though she hated that they were being treated with such callousness, she also knew it wasn't the right time to do anything drastic. For now, she had to trust that Tae Hyun would make everything better.

Her heart grew heavier when she noticed that the brothers were now staring straight at her. Though she was enveloped in darkness, she knew they could sense her presence.

Unable to restrain his bewilderment, Jae Won whipped his horror-filled eyes to Tae Hyun. "Why did you bring her here?"

"Shit," Kang Min whispered through his bloody mouth. His worried eyes peered in her direction. He wasn't afraid for himself; he was afraid for her.

Like a tidal wave, Yoori was rapidly washed with a terrifying enlightenment. She knew that Tae Hyun was determined to keep her face hidden from the Advisors because she wasn't on their good side. Considering all that had happened with Jin Ae, that part didn't surprise her. But in the short amount of time that she had, Yoori hadn't once thought about another possibility that might inspire more fear and terror from her. A pang of uneasiness burst through her when she replayed the horror in Jae Won's voice and the fear in Kang Min's eyes.

Shit.

Why didn't she take into account that she resembled someone important in this world? She gazed fearfully at the Advisors.

Was it possible? Was it possible that the Advisors also hated An Soo Jin?

"Interesting reactions," Ju Won observed blithely, looking at her and the brothers.

The two bodyguards kicked Jae Won and Kang Min into kneeling positions, their backs facing the Advisors and their faces directly in front of Tae Hyun and Ji Hoon. Throughout this entire exchange, the two gang leaders remained silent.

Tae Hyun, who had a look of anger plastered over his face this entire time, returned his gaze to Ju Won. A storm rolled into his eyes.

"Let them go," he ordered simply. Though he hid it well, Yoori discerned from his voice that Tae Hyun was beyond the boundaries of patience.

"In a minute," said Ju Won, his big smile and gaze slithering from Tae Hyun to Ji Hoon. "Ji Hoon," he launched blearily. "Do you realize that Tae Hyun managed to recruit the leader of the Dragons?" He jutted his chin in Jae Won's direction. "Quite impressive, wouldn't you say?"

Ji Hoon's once opaque expression became transparent. "A small-time gang is nothing," he answered without delay. His eyes landed on to Jae Won before he returned his focus to Ju Won. He didn't seem the least bit impressed.

"An up and coming gang that gained much recognition from our world," Ju Won corrected. "And as I fondly recall, Jae Won here was trained by someone very revered in our world. Doesn't that alone merit your respect?"

Something shadowed over his expression and a bitter looking Ji Hoon said nothing.

Satisfied, Ju Won returned his focus to Tae Hyun.

The King of Serpents was looking more and more impatient by the second.

"I would like to commend you, Tae Hyun," he started warmly. "A couple of weeks ago, Ji Hoon managed to secure more than a couple of recruits when he had his men murder those rival gang members in Echo district."

Yoori instantly recalled the news segment she saw long ago. Goose bumps ran through her when she remembered that the corpses were found with their cheeks carved into the shape of a skull.

Seconds later, it also became clear that Yoori wasn't the only one remembering such a signature.

"His only mistake was showcasing this to the media." Ju Won averted his disapproving eyes to Ji Hoon. "You know how much our world values secrecy. You being the head of one of the more powerful crime families should know that."

Before Ji Hoon could reply, another voice had already spoken for him. "Ji Hoon secured more than ten dozen new recruits after that news segment hit the waves," proclaimed a proud Jung Min. "His methods, though dissimilar with our idea of confidentiality, shows the outside world how powerful we are."

"It goes against our unwritten laws," Dong Min chimed in. His voice teemed with disapproval.

"It caused an updraft of talent for our world," continued Jung Min, who looked amused with his brother. "One measly little news segment will do little to threaten our livelihood."

When Dong Min was about to say something as a retort, he was silenced by Ju Won's raising hand.

"Quite distasteful in my book, but impressive nonetheless," Ju Won concluded. Sighing, he then turned to Tae Hyun. "But of course, not as impressive as our King of Serpents here." He gave another dramatic sigh, a theatric prelude to his disapproval of Tae Hyun's actions by far. "Tae Hyun, you would be in a much better standing if you didn't have people barging into my home every night."

Ah yes, Yoori knew he was going to bring up Jae Won and Kang Min sooner or later.

"Jin Ae and her men need to be punished," Tae Hyun answered purposely, his expression never faltering from the anger that was writhing through him.

The sound of Jin Ae and her men shuffling uncomfortably could be heard after his bold statement.

Ji Hoon scoffed. He couldn't believe how stupid Tae Hyun was being. "I'm sure whatever it is, you can get over it, Tae Hyun."

"I'm sure you're the master of getting over things right, Ji Hoon?"

Yoori didn't understand what the double meaning of that question might be. Yet when she saw Ji Hoon clench his fists, she knew it was something that hit a sensitive nerve.

"What did Jin Ae do?" Ju Won asked, bringing them back on topic. When he asked this, the eyes of the three Advisors fell on to Yoori for a quick second.

Though it was subtle and short, Yoori knew they were *dying* to meet her. Everything they were doing, all the things they were taking care of—they wanted to resolve everything quickly so they could finally deal with her.

Ji Hoon smirked at Ju Won's inquiry about what Jin Ae did. It seemed as though he had mistaken Tae Hyun's wrath toward Jin Ae as pertaining to her cheating on Tae Hyun with him.

"I gave her what she deserved," Jin Ae reasoned, her eyes glaring in Yoori's direction.

As Tae Hyun bestowed another intimidating glare at Jin Ae, Ji Hoon had already begun to furrow his brows in confusion. He glanced at Yoori, quickly realizing that Jin Ae was referring to Yoori as "her." It took him a couple of seconds yet as his eyes enlarged in comprehension, he returned his gaze to Jin Ae. His expression hardened.

"What did you do to her?" he asked, his demeanor losing all composure. He already looked livid.

At Ji Hoon's unexpected reaction, the Advisors gazed at one another, thrown off balance by the situation before them.

Kang Min, who had the same glaze forming over his eyes, instantly parted his lips, understanding what he needed to do to turn the situation in their favor. "She had her men attack Yoori while she was walking home."

Yoori's chest constricted at the terrible reminder.

Responding the same way at Kang Min's reminder, Tae Hyun shut his eyes in anger. It was reminiscent of the calm before the storm. He was tempering his anger and saving it for the opportune time. Once that time came, all hell was going to break loose.

At the precise second Tae Hyun closed his eyes, Ji Hoon's eyes had enlarged even more from disbelief. Everyone in the room saw it. Both of the gang leaders were at the brink of their tolerance.

Jae Won's eyes lit up at what his younger brother was doing. Adding gasoline to the fire, he shrewdly added, "Jin Ae had also instructed her men to rape Yoori once they were done assaulting her. It was luck that Kang Min and I arrived on time before they got to tear her clothes apart."

That was what did it.

Opening his eyes with incredulity, Tae Hyun's unblinking eyes fell on to Jin Ae and her men, all of whom had already begun to shrink away in fear. It appeared as though that Tae Hyun was only informed about the assault, not the attempted rape.

At the same instant, a rage of fire burned in Ji Hoon's eyes.

There was no more bottling of their anger.

"Fuck kneeling…" Ji Hoon began severely, his breathing growing heavier.

"I am going to rip all of you to shreds," Tae Hyun finished dangerously, already inching closer to Jin Ae and her men.

Terror in their eyes, Jin Ae and her bodyguards were already inching closer to Ju Won. It was a well-known fact in the Underworld that the two Kings were a force to be reckoned with when they were alone, but when they both agree that they want your head, you know you're a breath away from death unless you had some serious protection.

"Ji Hoon," Jung Min spoke warningly as Ji Hoon and Tae Hyun advanced toward Jin Ae and her men. Bloodlust brimmed in their eyes.

After hearing his mentor's voice, Ji Hoon stopped in his tracks, his breathing still heavy from relentless anger.

Tae Hyun, whose legs were still taking off, only halted in his tracks at Dong Min's voice.

"Tae Hyun," he called sternly. "All will be resolved. Please calm down."

Tae Hyun laughed disbelievingly. He stood in the center of the room, in between Ji Hoon and the Advisors. His patience had long vacated the room.

"If Jin Ae was someone else's niece, I would've had her head already. She should've died the moment I heard she had her minions assault my girlfriend." He gazed irately at Ju Won. "But because she's your niece, I lessened the punishment to merely having Jin Ae and her men kneel before her." He scoffed again, biting his lower lip and recalling Jae Won's words about the attempted rape. "But as we all heard, the intentions of their assault went further than merely beating her. I have the utmost respect for you." He glanced at Dong Min and Jung Min. "All of you." His face then grew stern. "But I have more respect for myself and my girlfriend."

A warm feeling ran over Yoori when she heard this.

Tae Hyun continued. "So with that said, how do all of *you* plan on resolving this little conflict?

Before Ju Won, who was seemingly impressed with Tae Hyun's speech, could answer, Jung Min had already interjected with an unimpressed observation.

"It is not the brightest tactic to reveal your weakness, Tae Hyun," he stated frostily. "Girlfriends...as entertaining as they may be, are just as disposable as the minions that kneel at your feet. I'd advise you to watch your mouth in the future. Bad relations in our world are a bit more unforgiving than other worlds."

"What an interesting observation, my dear brother," Dong Min commented before Tae Hyun could reply with what Yoori could only guess as angry retorts.

Dong Min's voice was rife with sarcasm as he went on. His eyes landed on Ji Hoon. "It seems that Ji Hoon here has taken a liking to Tae Hyun's girlfriend." Dong Min smirked upon seeing Ji Hoon stiffen up at this observation. "If I didn't know better, I'd think he was ready to embark on some bad relations with hopes of impressing her as well."

And that was what ended the interjections from the elder brothers.

Unable to respond to his brother's retort, Jung Min merely bequeathed him a bitter glare before turning away, his resentment still very much intact.

"It's funny," Ju Won finally begun, ignoring all "observations" between the two brothers. His eyes latched on to Yoori. It was a gaze that caused the fine hairs on the back of her neck to stand on end. "Every time we request to meet someone new, they always end up hiding in the further corners of the meeting room. What is it about us that attract such behaviors?"

"We don't have a good track record of keeping people alive when they step into the light," Jung Min joked. Or what Yoori presumed to be a joke.

"Perhaps it's the fact that we have the wrists of Tae Hyun's men bound together," Dong Min stated carelessly. "I think that may be what's making her uneasy."

Ju Won nodded, leaning closer to speak to her in the distance, finally acknowledging her existence.

"We've been rude. Thank you for politely waiting as we address some business. Now that everything is more or less on the table, I would love to finally meet you so I can start resolving the matters at hand." He gestured her with his hand. "Please come forward."

"Stay there," Tae Hyun ordered, holding his hand out to prevent her from stepping into the light. Not that she was about to step into it anyway. She was perfectly content with hiding in the shadows.

"You requested that I bring her here and I did. But for her own protection, I'd like for her to remain in the shadows."

Jung Min scoffed as if Tae Hyun had just said the most idiotic thing he'd ever heard.

Though the smile on Ju Won's face remained, there was clear distaste reveling in his eyes. "We may have misunderstood each other Tae Hyun, but I'm pretty sure I requested we *meet* her in exchange for Kang Min and Jae Won."

Tae Hyun raised a challenging brow. "Have we reached a point where threats are presented?"

Ju Won casually shook his head at the insinuation. "As you said, Jin Ae needs to be punished for what she did to your girlfriend. In the same token, Kang Min and Jae Won should also be punished for what they did *for* your girlfriend."

Tae Hyun, along with Dong Min and the tied up brothers, tensed at Ju Won's reasoning. Yoori herself felt the air escape her when she heard him.

Ju Won went on. "My priority is resolving things tonight so we can move forward to more important matters. I need the common denominator of these conflicts and your girlfriend is it. So I think it would be beneficial for everyone involved if we get to meet her face to face. I'd definitely be more informed about the appropriate punishments once we get introductions out of the way."

When it looked as though Tae Hyun was prepared to combat that request, Yoori had already stepped foot into the light. She had had it. There was no more point in prolonging the inevitable. She wanted to help Kang Min and Jae Won as quickly as possible and that was her only goal. Whatever happened after that, she would let fate take the reins.

"No, don't—" were words that Jae Won and Kang Min were ready to finish until they saw that she had already stepped into the light.

It was too late.

An air of anticipatory stillness hung over the meeting room as Yoori took each dreadful step, closer and closer into the center of the room where Ji Hoon and Tae Hyun stood.

Only four more strides until she reached them, she thought, her breathing growing unsteady. Her heart was beating violently. She didn't know if it was from fear, or anticipation of her own.

For that split moment in time, everyone breathed in unison while they waited for her.

Stride one.

She could hear Jin Ae scoff in disgust.

Stride two.

She could hear sounds of shuffling from the high ceilings above her.

Stride three.

At the sight of her, two of the bodyguards standing behind Jae Won and Kang Min had already stiffened up in their stance. Several fingers were missing from their shaking hands as their eyes grew wide in shock.

Stride four.

Complete silence.

Naturally filling in the gap that separated Tae Hyun and Ji Hoon, Yoori's eyes were lowered the entire time as she stood a bit closer to Tae Hyun. Judging by his demeanor, he was already regretting bringing her to Ju Won's mansion.

Shaking in her stance, she tucked in the loose bangs of her hair behind her ear and with much apprehensiveness, pulled down the hood that lay above her.

The last group to be affected by her presence was the Advisors.

With their eyes gradually becoming enlarged, the elder brothers furrowed their brows in overt confusion. Leaning in to get a better view of her, the intensity of the silence surrounding them elevated to the extremes. Though this act of bewilderment was a big change for the brothers, the drastic change in facial expression went toward Ju Won.

His haughty smile faded into oblivion upon the full disclosure of Yoori's face.

It was then that Yoori knew she was screwed.

They all *definitely* saw her as An Soo Jin.

Their mouths hanging slightly open, Jung Min and Dong Min gaped hesitantly at Ju Won.

The eldest Advisor still had his full attention on Yoori.

The thick air of silence was becoming suffocating. It was becoming unbearable until...

"Come closer," said Ju Won, effectively breaking the thick silence. His unblinking gaze remained on her in the distance. The confusion in his eyes said it all. He didn't believe what he saw.

At his command, Yoori found herself instinctively obeying. Her legs took off, only to be stopped when she felt hands wrap around her wrists. Twisting her neck around, she realized that it was Tae Hyun and Ji Hoon who stopped her. Each had taken possession of her wrists to keep her from inching closer to the Advisors. Neither said anything when they did this.

Tae Hyun, Ji Hoon, Kang Min, and Jae Won—all four were paled with worry.

Unaffected by Tae Hyun and Ji Hoon's outright objection to Yoori coming closer to him, Ju Won, who no longer had the patience to sit around and wait, stood up and made his way down to Yoori. The eyes of the elder brothers locked on to him as he walked past Kang Min and Jae Won. He slowly approached her.

Yoori shook as she watched him approach her, his eyes poignant and his face blank.

Each step he took, her heartbeat escalated.

Each step he took, her fears multiplied.

After this, there was no turning back.

After he saw her, she would never get out of the Underworld.

Stopping approximately three foot away from Yoori, Ju Won's eyes gazed at her up and down. After what felt like years of inspection, he returned his eyes to meet hers.

"What did you say your name was?" he asked softly. Though his question was purposeful, Yoori had the innate feeling that he really didn't need to hear her answer. He had already arrived at his own conclusion.

Despite knowing this, she answered because she feared him so. "Ch-Choi Yoori."

"Choi Yoori," Ju Won repeated, his eyes now becoming indecipherable. He took a moment to think things over and then just like that, a crooked smile of comprehension curved his lips.

His discerning eyes were still gazing into her—inspecting her.

Yoori twitched uncomfortably. It was clear he was now inspecting her for a bluff—for a lie. She was unsure of the conclusion he came to when he suddenly turned and went back to his seat, leaving her in a tornado of confusion.

Upon reaching his seat, he sat down. His signature smile returning to him, he regarded Tae Hyun and Ji Hoon. They were both still quiet with severe expressions on their own faces.

"Choi Yoori, step forward," Ju Won said firmly.

At his orders, Yoori felt a strange outpouring of energy run through her. In that split of a second, she was no longer afraid of him. For that brief moment, she knew he wasn't going to hurt her. No longer wanting to spend her time shaking in fear, Yoori released herself from Tae Hyun and Ji Hoon's hold.

They both tried to reach for her again, but were unsuccessful.

She strode quickly to the center of the room, approximately three foot away from Jae Won and Kang Min and approximately six foot away from the Advisors.

"Jin Ae," Ju Won called.

"Uncle?" Jin Ae asked sweetly, her face still smug as she noted Yoori's shaking figure. She had mistaken her anticipation for fear.

"Kneel," Ju Won commanded at once.

Jin Ae's eyes flared. "What?" she screamed, her voice bouncing across the room. She was beside herself. She couldn't believe what the fuck was her uncle doing.

"I SAID, 'KNEEL!'" Ju Won hollered at the top of his lungs, his voice equally as loud and much more intimidating. He wasn't a man accustomed to disobedience and he wouldn't stand for it even from his own niece.

Though his scream was directed at Jin Ae, it was enough to cause every breathing entity in the room to harden in fear. If people didn't understand how he became such a powerful crime lord before, then they understood perfectly after hearing his thunderous voice. His authority, even through retirement, continued to exude out of him.

Once a crime lord, always a crime lord.

At his scream, the drooping sound of four pair of knees thrashed against the floor. Jin Ae led the pack as her bodyguards kneeled beside her. Her face was shaking with anger. She wasn't happy with what she had to do, but she feared the repercussions from her uncle even more to combat the kneeling.

As all of this occurred, Yoori's own eyes widened. Jin Ae wasn't the only one staggered by what was happening.

"Choi Yoori," Ju Won started diplomatically, his tone of voice returning to the cool tempo he always employed. "My deepest apologies for my niece's stupidity. Jin Ae, Woo, Tony, and Ken are young and inexperienced. They do not know any better. They will be punished accordingly under the family bylaws, but until then, I hope that having them kneel before you would merit your forgiveness?"

"Uh…" Yoori nodded stupidly at his request. She was honestly at a loss for words. Contrary to popular belief, it didn't feel good to see people kneeling before you—at least it didn't feel good for Yoori. She actually found herself feeling bad for Jin Ae and her men. But only slightly.

Ju Won smiled at her fervent nod of agreement. "Good."

With a simple gesture of freedom from his hand, the bodyguards standing behind Jae Won and Kang Min took out knives and freed the brothers from the ropes that bound them. As Kang Min and Jae Won prepared to make their way to Yoori, Ju Won reached behind his chair and pulled out a gun.

"Kang Min," he said clearly.

Kang Min, as well as everyone else in the room, instinctively turned toward Ju Won. He was now standing in front of his seat. Yoori froze when she saw that Ju Won had Jae Won's gold gun in hand.

"I believe this is yours," he said casually. Before giving Kang Min a chance to absorb the content of his words, he tossed the gun in the air. It landed squarely in Kang Min's outstretched palm.

Gazing at the gun and then to his brother with uncertainty, Kang Min only placed the gun behind his back after Jae Won gave him a stiff nod of approval. It seemed to Yoori that Jae Won didn't want to deal with saying the gun was his until they left the room. It was a desperation that Yoori empathized with; she couldn't wait to get out of the room either.

She looked around surprisingly. She couldn't believe it. Was it going to be this easy for her just because she resembled Soo Jin?

As if hearing her silent question, Ju Won had already begun to speak. "Now that Jin Ae's, Kang Min's and Jae Won's punishment has been resolved, it's time to deal with the common denominator."

The air was knocked out of her after she heard Ju Won's menacing words. He wore a serious countenance as he spoke to her, his eyes suddenly breeding an unforgiving fire that she had never seen before.

"Tell me, Choi Yoori. You weren't properly initiated into the Underworld, were you?"

"Wha—?" Yoori could scarcely utter a word when she was distracted with the widening fear in Kang Min and Jae Won's eyes.

"Boss—" they whispered urgently, staring at her with abrupt horror.

It was then that she sensed that there was something—or a couple of things—on her head. Holding in her breath, she slowly turned around. She caught sight of the same horror written over Tae Hyun and Ji Hoon's pale faces.

She gasped when she caught it as she turned, the glimpse of a red laser light being pointed in her direction.

Yoori understood now why the meeting room was so huge and so dark. It wasn't for show or for Ju Won's guests to be intimidated by him. It was built for his bodyguards, or his snipers to be precise. Just in case he ever needed their assistance, they would be there to deal with whatever it was that he needed resolution for.

Yoori thought back to the uneasy feeling she had when she walked in, the constant need of gazing up into the darkness. She wasn't paranoid or crazy. She gazed up because she could sense that the snipers were up there, breathing as they watched her in the darkness. Fear swallowing her whole, her body became more alert under the scrutinizing cold. She knew that there were at least six snipers. Six snipers who all had their guns pointed on her, the laser red dots of their aim forming a halo around her head.

Shit.

What a horrible way to die.

"Ju Won" Tae Hyun began unsteadily, his focus still on Yoori, whose eyes were now welling up with heightening fear. "Take those lasers off of her." To her, he reassuringly said, "Yoori, it's okay. I'll take care of this. Just don't move. They are trained to shoot if you move."

Yoori bit her lower lip and blinked in confirmation, her breathing growing heavy with anxiety.

"You know the bylaws of the initiation in our world," Ju Won said sternly.

"She is *not* a gang member," Ji Hoon found himself blurting out as he gazed at her, his face filled with the same worry that Tae Hyun possessed.

Ju Won laughed. "Regardless, she's heard enough standing there. If she's not 'in' our world then she's an intruder. We spoke about the importance of confidentiality. If she's privy to our secrets then we must initiate her. It's part of the bylaws that govern our world."

"Fuck the bylaws," Tae Hyun growled angrily.

"Don't be rash, Tae Hyun," scolded Jung Min. "The bylaws are what got you to where you are today."

Tae Hyun fell silent at the comment.

"How do you plan on initiating her into the Underworld?" Ji Hoon asked, fear dancing in his voice.

"Blood in," Ju Won said purposefully.

The boys froze at the term.

Ju Won went on. "You're either born into this world, forced your way in by killing another gang member or spilt your own blood to get in." He lowered his stare onto her. "Tonight, Choi Yoori will meet the third criteria."

Tae Hyun darted his eyes to Ju Won in disbelief. "And you think I'll stand by and watch as you beat her senseless?"

"Of course not," Jung Min answered. His face now just as unreadable as Ju Won and his brother's.

"You're all leaving," Dong Min added, his stare firmly placed on Tae Hyun. "It will just be us and Choi Yoori."

Tae Hyun glowered at Dong Min, his expression burning from the betrayal on his mentor's part.

"Five minutes," said Ju Won. "All she needs to do is spend five minutes with us. She can run around the meeting room throughout the allotted time for all I care, but she *will* go through with this initiation or we'll fill her head with bullets right now."

"It is better this way, Tae Hyun," Dong Min said softly, interrupting Tae Hyun who was about to utter words of retort. "With us, it is guaranteed she'll make it out alive. If anyone else conducted the initiation, you know that she'll die within the first two minutes."

And again, before Tae Hyun could utter words of retort, another softer voice had already interrupted him.

"I'll do it," Yoori found herself stating, her hope for survival appearing more viable with going through five minutes worth of initiation rather than chancing it with the snipers and their bullets.

"Yoori," the boys stated at the same time, their faces fearing for her survival. "You don't—"

"Five minutes," Yoori stated, ignoring their cautious call.

"Five minutes," Ju Won confirmed. He sat down, his face pleased with her decision.

Tae Hyun was outraged. "You don't know what you're getting into!"

"I'll do it," she repeated firmly, staring at Tae Hyun dead in the eyes. She shook at his last statement. "Just trust me. I can do this. Five minutes. I'll...I'll just make sure to keep running."

"You know there's no other way for her to come into our world than this," Dong Min added upon seeing the uncertainty on Tae Hyun's face.

Tae Hyun closed his eyes when it was evident to him that they have been backed into a corner. Then, as if realizing something, Tae Hyun advanced to Yoori, the back of his body taking half of the red lasers that were still being pointed at her.

"Tae Hyun! What are you—?"

Cupping her face, he leaned in, effectively interrupting her. His eyes were still rife with concern. "There's weapons hidden in the further right corner, behind their chairs," he said in a hushed whisper. "When you run, run in that direction and get one of those weapons. Don't be afraid to hurt them."

Yoori nodded in understanding, the heaviness of her heart lifting just fractionally with his near presence.

"And for the love of God," Tae Hyun added earnestly. "*Run fast.*"

He withdrew his hands from her cheeks and averted his attention to his mentor. He gazed up at Dong Min. He didn't say anything, but she could tell from his eyes that Tae Hyun wanted validation from Dong Min that Yoori will be alright. Dong Min took a few seconds to gaze back before giving a stiff nod of affirmation. At his nod the red laser encircling Yoori and Tae Hyun vanished.

At the disappearance of the lasers, a gesture that was good enough for Tae Hyun, he breathed a quiet sigh. Giving Yoori one last look, he speedily took off toward the exit. The impatience in Tae Hyun was evident: he wanted to end the inevitable as soon as possible. Surmising that having Yoori wait any longer for her five minutes will only screw her up in the end, he left without another word.

Heeding Tae Hyun's lead, Jae Won and Kang Min had also begun toward the exit, but not before stopping beside her. Their faces were shrouded with nothing but fear for her life.

"Boss, are you sure?"

"I'm sure," she reassured with a small smile. Then, she said, "Please go so I can get this over with."

With a slight push from Yoori, the brothers limped out of the meeting room, worry still set in their faces.

"Jin Ae, get the hell out," ordered Ju Won.

Still kneeling, Jin Ae's eyes teemed with hatred as she glared at Yoori. At her uncle's order, an indignant Jin Ae clambered up and flew toward the door, a string of curses and her bodyguards following her as they exited the left side of the meeting room.

This left Ji Hoon as the final one in the room.

"Be careful, Yoori," he said faintly before heading toward the exit in which Tae Hyun left. His eyes avoided hers. It was then that Yoori deduced that Ji Hoon was afraid. He was afraid of showing the Advisors that he cared about her. She didn't know if he was afraid of being seen as weak or if it was for another reason. All that she knew was that he didn't want to show that he cared for her – even though it was quite obvious.

After Ji Hoon disappeared into the hallway, both doors slammed shut, leaving only Yoori and the Advisors. A deafening silence crawled above them as Yoori stood before the Advisors, their eyes on her like hawks.

"The rules are simple," Ju Won began, very much entertained. "All you have to do is spend five minutes with us. You can run around the room, you can fight us, or get attacked by us. How you want to try to spend those five minutes is up to you."

"Okay," Yoori said nodding, her legs itching to take off already. She was pretty sure she could outrun three old men.

Ju Won smiled at her reply. He placed his elbow on the armchair of his seat and rested his chin on his right knuckle.

"You know," he prompted, his eyes inspecting her. "You remind me of someone." He smirked at the reminder. "Which is too bad because she didn't leave being on my good side."

Yoori's eyes grew huge at his insinuation. Before she could think anymore of it, she was distracted when both Dong Min and Jung Min rose from their seats. Rolling up their sleeves, they cracked their knuckles in preparation for the things to come.

"I forgot to mention," Ju Won added with a whimsical tone. "In the course of these next five minutes, my snipers will be firing at you as well."

Yoori's spine stiffened at the unexpected condition.

When she was about to respond with horror, she felt something flaming hot fly past her ear. Her heart plunging into her stomach, she jumped at the deafening sound of the bullet hitting the hard pavement of the meeting room.

Shit, was the only thing going through her mind as she gazed up at the various red lasers that were being pointed at her once more.

Ju Won smirked, his eyes promising blood. He was ready to enjoy the show to come.

With a simple wave of his hand several things happened: the elder brothers had raced toward Yoori, more than several bullets were shot in her direction and with her survival instincts alive and well, Yoori's legs had taken off in a frenzy.

As she dodged a bullet that flew past her right shoulder, Yoori knew then that this five minutes was going to be a lot tougher than she gave it credit for—*especially* when Jung Min caught her by surprise and served her with a powerful kick to the stomach. The assault stole every breath of air from her body, leaving her to violently slam against the wall.

She gasped for air as she slid down, pain present in every fiber of her shaking body.

No doubt, she thought in horror, catching sight of the laser beam that was being pointed straight at her heart, a bullet ready to follow its lead.

Her blood would definitely be spilled tonight.

"Terrible how unjust this world can be."

33: Five Minutes

Her stomach writhed in agony from the unsuspecting attack. In this bout of pain, pandemonium found her. Her heart panicking at the prospect of impending doom, Yoori, amidst all the chaos, subconsciously found herself lunging straight for the floor before the bullet befriended her heart.

When she landed on the ground, Yoori heard the swiping sound of the bullet entering the wall behind her. It landed in the exact same place her heart would've been if she had not slid out of the way in time.

That bullet could've blasted her heart apart!

Knowing well that being a fast runner was her ticket to survival tonight, Yoori, wanting to waste no more time with tending to her traumatized heart, scrambled back up from the floor and made an unsteady sprint to the further end of the wall to avoid anymore collision with the Shin brothers and the incoming bullets.

When she did this, she glimpsed at another red laser that was being pointed in her direction.

She threw herself into a nearby corner in a panic. The fiery bullet came flying past her, missing her by mere centimeters as it grazed her jacket. Steam flowed out as it embedded itself into the white walls. Yoori gazed at it in horror and made another run for it.

Crap! Crap, crap, crap!

Through the dark corners of the room she ran, her legs stopping, bending, crouching and taking off by itself as it pulled her away from bullets and further away from Jung Min and Dong Min, both of whom she knew were still chasing after her in the darkness.

Her breathing became heavy with shrill. Each inhalation and exhalation acted as a catalyst to give more alertness to her body as she fought against deadly bullets and terrifying crime lords. Essentially anything that was out for her blood.

Yoori couldn't have been more thankful with how cold Ju Won's mansion was. The heat exhausting from her running and the rigidness of the cold air had more than helped her become more alert under the blinding darkness.

Tae Hyun's words repeated in her mind while she ran, crisscrossing her way into the center of the room: *"There's weapons hidden in the further right corner, behind their chairs. When you run, run in that direction and get one of those weapons. Don't be afraid to hurt them."*

In the direction of Ju Won, that was where she needed to go.

Despite acknowledging the importance of that tip, Yoori also knew that she couldn't head in that direction yet, especially when snipers were watching to anticipate her moves. She intended to run every which way, revealing herself briefly in the light and camouflaging herself in the darkness. She had to be confusing. This tactic was not only used to throw the snipers off, but it was also used to throw Jung Min and Dong Mi—

Though she had anticipated the attack when her heart leapt in worry, there was not much Yoori could do to avoid it as a strong arm emerged out of the darkness, pummeling itself against the core of her throat.

Yoori gasped for air. The pain confined in the core of her throat pounded fervently after the sudden attack. Unable to retain her balance, she fell backward, one hand clutching on to her assaulted throat and the other one pulled out to break her fall.

She was seeing stars because she was in so much pain.

"Ugh..." She rubbed her throbbing neck, trying to swallow her saliva to judge the magnitude of the attack. She twitched in excruciating pain. It even hurt to swallow.

Out of the darkness, she heard soft chuckling.

Gazing up, her acclimated eyes found the tall silhouette that was staring down at her. Judging by the sound of the chuckle, she was pretty sure it was Shin Jung Min who not only kicked her stomach like she was a ragged doll, but also delivered the attack that left her unable to use her throat.

"Get up," Dong Min's voice ordered from behind her, stealing her attention.

She craned her neck backward. He was standing behind her with his arms behind his back. Although she couldn't make out his facial expression in the darkness, she was pretty sure he was frowning.

"Get up!" he shouted again when she didn't obey the first time.

Alarmed by the snarl of his voice, Yoori scrambled to her feet, her stomach and throat now rippling in pain. Unknowingly standing as the center point of an elongated triangle, Yoori eyed both elder brothers hesitantly. What were they planning to do with her now that they had her cornered?

"Block," Jung Min suddenly commanded.

"Huh?"

Without notice, the hand of Dong Min's that was holding a long block of unshaven stick came crashing down onto Yoori, its aim for her head.

Instinctively following Jung Min's command, she brought up her hands, crisscrossing her wrists above one another and shielded the top of her head with it, successfully blocking the stick from slamming into her skull.

After burying its splinters into the flesh of her hand, the stick broke apart, falling lifelessly to the floor.

"Fuck!" Yoori shouted, jumping in pain.

She shook the pain off the hand that was most impacted from the attack. Though she was glad the splinters from the stick was buried against the flesh of her skin rather than that of her head, she couldn't help but count her curses that she somehow found herself in this predicament to begin with.

Without allotting her any time to tend to her wounds, Dong Min's voice speared through the room. "Duck."

"Wh—*ah!*"

Her hair flew up as her legs immediately listened to his command. As she ducked, a sniper bullet flew past, its flaring heat intruding the confined space that Yoori once inhabited. She gasped, staring at the two Advisors whose silhouettes continued to tower over her. What the hell were they doing?

"Get up," commanded Jung Min.

Recalling that his and Dong Min's commands had saved her from death several times tonight, she was more than happy to oblige. When she was fully upright, Dong Min threw something in her direction. She caught it clumsily. Her eyebrows drew together. It was a...pool stick? Holding on to the stick, she peered at the brothers expectantly. She had already anticipated that even though she really didn't want to, she was going to have to use it against one of them. She groaned inwardly. How on earth was she supposed to attack them with it if they could block her every move?

"Break it apart with your knee," Jung Min ordered.

Afraid of hurting more of her body parts, Yoori hesitated, a move that angered Jung Min. He was ready to scream at her when Dong Min interrupted and said, "Take a step back."

Wasting no time in following his command, Yoori rocked backward. In a split of a very fast second, a sniper bullet flew past her from the side, its aim the side of her head had she not moved in time.

Damn these snipers!

She was ready to thank Dong Min when he threw his leg up in the air and delivered a spin kick that slammed into her left shoulder and had her staggering for the floor. One would think that kicking her like that was enough, but not for Dong Min. He followed after her and right before she fell to the floor, Dong Min bestowed her with another kick to the stomach and a final kick across the face, an action that left Yoori to spit coagulated blood into the air. Out of breath, she fell with a deafening thud. She was still holding the pool stick when she hit the floor.

It was then that she knew why Jung Min ordered her to break the pool stick. It was for her own protection against Dong Min.

She didn't know why they were doing this to her – taking turns attacking and mentoring her, but she no longer cared. The only thing that mattered was keeping them from attacking her any further.

Struggling to stand up, the blood still dripping from her mouth and the pain still prominent in her body, she lifted her right knee and used it to break the stick. The pool stick broke into two equal parts, the jagged edge of each stick appearing now like stakes.

"Hold them up and stick your right leg out behind you – in a fighting stance," Jung Min ordered, drawing a few steps backward and leaving Yoori and Dong Min to face one another. "Anticipate his attack with the sight of his movements. Pay close attention to the areas in which he leaves unshielded. Don't be gentle."

Yoori shook. She knew what was to come when she saw Dong Min pick up the broken stick that he attacked her with.

He wasted no time in coming in for the first attack.

Yoori moved to strike, but failed when she raised her arm to hit him, missed, and was caught off guard when he slammed the head of the stick into her right hip, causing her to scream in agony. The broken pool sticks fell from her grasp and she collapsed to her knees, nearly blacking out from the pain.

"You're kneeling before him already?" Jung Min shouted furiously, staring down at her with disgust. "We just got started! GET UP!"

Clutching on to her hip that was beginning to bleed from the attack, Yoori glared up at Jung Min and Dong Min. Rage rummaged through her. Hungry for revenge, she reached her shaking hands out and retrieved her two fallen sticks. She stood up, her breathing heavy as her eyes fixated on Dong Min.

Fire burned within her gaze.

This time...she was ready.

Dong Min smirked at the sudden change in Yoori's demeanor. Ready for a second round, he charged at her like a ferocious bull.

She slowly crouched her legs in preparation. Her hands sticking out with the broken pool sticks, she easily leaned sideway to avoid an attack from Dong Min when he attempted to slam the stick against her neck.

When he missed, Yoori saw her chance for an attack.

Using all the energy she had, she jumped up and aimed the dull head of the stick upward. The dull edge slammed against his jaw with a loud crack, causing Dong Min to lose balance as he wavered about. To finish the attack, she jabbed the second stick into Dong Min's stomach before finishing that assault off with a blow to the neck.

Just like that, the powerful Advisor collapsed to the floor.

She watched, her bloody mouth gaping open as Dong Min struggled to get up from her triple attack. She couldn't believe it. Did she really just successfully attack a revered crime lord?

"Fast learner," Dong Min commented, his voice hoarse from the attack. Strangely enough, he seemed proud as well when he stood up and dusted his shirt, acting like her attack was nothing but child's play.

Yoori gave him an incredulous gaze when she saw that he actually looked fine. What the hell? She would've blacked out from an attack like that.

At Dong Min's comment, Jung Min laughed in agreement.

Dong Min cleared his throat. He stretched his neck out before saying, "Now listen to the silence." Sensing her hesitation, he added, "Your life depends on it."

And that was what squashed any hesitation left within her.

Holding on to the two pool sticks, she lowered her head and listened. At first she couldn't understand why she was listening to silence. The only thing she felt was the convulsing pain within her body. But then…as a stream of enlightenment poured over her, faint sounds began to whisper itself into her ears — faint sounds of breathing and subtle rustling in the distance.

She could hear Jung Min and Dong Min breathe as they gazed at her. She could hear Ju Won, who was more than likely still sitting in his seat and watching the entire thing, breathing in the illuminated distance.

As her heightened sense of sound elevated, it shocked Yoori that she could now hear breathing from the high corners of the ceilings. It was the same heightened sense she had when she was approaching the mansion, the same heightened sense that allotted her the knowledge to know how many men were hidden in each part of the ceiling.

Only this time, she was able to control this heightened sense.

At first, when she wasn't really paying attention, she thought there were six snipers. Now as she continued to focus the breadth of her attention on to the "silence," she concluded that there were a couple more snipers who were unaccounted for. They have yet to shoot yet she could hear them breathing — she could hear their anticipation. They were getting ready to shoot.

"How many?" Dong Min finally asked.

She answered without hesitation. "Nine."

"Can you hear what they are getting ready to do?" Jung Min asked, his voice just as soft.

"Yes."

In that instant, two things happened: Jung Min and Dong Min had both spun backward, stopping at the same time as they stood nine inches away from where they once stood. In the same breath, Yoori found herself performing a triple backflip that gave her the opportunity to dodge nine rounds of sniper bullets that followed her in a straight sequential line.

She landed on her feet, her eyes wider than it had ever been.

What the hell did she just do?

She straightened her back to gawk at the scene before her. The nine bullets buried itself against the tiled floors and shortly thereafter, silence fell upon the room like nothing had occurred.

The sound of clapping then saturated the room, interrupting her disconcerting train of thoughts.

Ju Won had appeared behind her, a big smile on his face as he stood on the center floor.

"Very impressive," he commented, the smile growing wider than ever. "You have a minute and a half left. We've been easy on you. Let's see how you hold up against two Advisors and bullets that are not pre-warned for you."

Terror ignited in Yoori's eyes.

"Oh shit!"

Losing all the fighting instincts she had seconds prior, Yoori panicked at the advancement from the elder brothers and the sound of triggers being pulled from the snipers. She hastily threw the broken pool sticks toward the elder brothers as a diversion and made a run for it. She ran in the direction of the weapons area behind Ju Won's chair.

Oh God, oh God, oh God!

It was becoming harder and harder for her to breathe as she ran. Her hip, stomach, face, and legs—her entire body was aching and merely surviving off the adrenaline pumping through her.

When she inched closer to the throne-like chairs, Yoori whispered words of thanks, thinking it was going to be an easy task to retrieve the weapons. Her hopes were dashed when a round of bullets fired pass her, causing her to come to an abrupt stop.

Though she had only stopped for a moment, the brief second was enough for Dong Min and Jung Min to catch up to her. She turned around and she was met with two different legs that simultaneously kicked her stomach. The force caused her to stumble beside Ju Won's chair, gasping for air as the agonizing pain engulfed her senses once more.

"Get up and fight," Ju Won ordered, glaring at Yoori as he stood nearby and watched.

When she didn't immediately stand up, Jung Min snatched her by the hood of Tae Hyun's jacket and forcefully picked her up. He hurled her like a ragged doll onto the chairs behind her. She felt her back spasm in pain at the collision, her lower lip bleeding from accidentally biting herself.

She sucked in a pained breath, nearly wavering off her chair. She fought to stay conscious.

"You don't need the weapons behind the chairs." Ju Won advised, crossing his arms as he continued to watch the scene. "The things around you are just as effective, if not more effective."

At the advisement from Ju Won, she found herself more awake with energy. It was a foreign instinct that Yoori didn't recognize.

Her eyes narrowed onto the chair beside her. Reaching for the leg of Jung Min's chair, just when the brothers were ready to advance toward her, she used all the might she had and whipped the chair in their direction. The leg of the chair hit their faces as it flew. This move not only guaranteed a successful attack on the brothers, but it also acted as a shield for another fired bullet that she didn't even see coming.

"Now get up!" Ju Won roared. Beside him, Dong Min and Jung Min were still recovering from her recent attack. "Every time you sit there not attacking, you're a second closer to losing! Your initiation ends in twenty seconds. End it being victorious!"

It was an out of body experience for Yoori.

When Ju Won's roaring voice entered her, her body leapt up like it had been doused with life. Taking several steps back, she ran toward Ju Won's chair at full speed, jumped onto it and while using the back rest as a boost, she delivered a powerful spin kick that connected with the cheeks of Jung Min and Dong Min, leaving them to stagger to the floor. When she landed on the floor, not in the least bit finished with her attack, she served both with a prevailing kick that had the heels of her boots pressing into their noses.

The sound of beeping commenced as blood streamed down their noses and they fell to the floor.

Her five minutes…were up.

When Yoori fell to the floor, exhaustion riding her, her head bumped against the edge of Ju Won's chair. Paying no mind to it, for it seemed so small compared to the rest of the pain she was enduring, she merely leaned against it and closed her eyes. Her breathing was heavy, but the pain wallowing through her was heavier.

Once she regained her steady breathing, Yoori cautiously opened her eyes. She stilled. She observed that both Dong Min and Jung Min had just wiped the blood from their noses and were actually standing up. With dots of their own blood marring their expensive dress shirts, they casually cracked their necks and stretched their arms as they stood straighter. From how they were standing and behaving, it didn't even appear like her attack did that much damage to them.

Ju Won laughed at the stupefaction on her face. He kneeled on one knee beside her, his smirk graduating into a smile. He watched her, his eyes warmer than she had ever seen it.

"What do you guys think?" he asked the elder brothers, his full attention never leaving Yoori's.

"Her fighting skills are nonexistent," Jung Min critiqued with a sigh.

"Yet her heightened instincts are alive and well." Dong Min smirked, wiping some blood that was slipping out of his nose with his sleeve. "Not to mention her ability to quickly learn is impressive as well."

Ju Won nodded. "Your survival instincts are a force to be reckoned with." His smile morphed into a scolding frown. "But your killer instincts are very much lacking. There were more than several occasions where you could've stabbed them with the jagged edges of your pool stick. Not to mention, you missed the prime opportunity to snap their necks apart after your spin kick." He took an indrawn breath and stared at her reprovingly. "You refuse to be a killer in this world, Choi Yoori? Is that it?"

She wanted to answer him with a "yes," but she was too afraid to. Her mind was still too preoccupied with everything—fear and confusion being the dominant emotions. The only word that dared to slither out of her bloody lips was silence.

Ju Won shook his head at her.

"There's still unfinished business left on the table…" he murmured, turning his gaze to the side.

Yoori didn't know if he was just murmuring to himself or murmuring to her. Her instincts told her it had something to do with her lookalike. Afraid of the sudden intensity that reveled in Ju Won's firm gaze when he returned his eyes to her, Yoori felt the overwhelming need to save herself from any trouble with Ju Won. She began by distancing herself from the one person she was sure she reminded him of.

"I'm n–not her."

Ju Won raised his hand as a way of interrupting her. "It doesn't matter," he hushed sternly, his voice very entertained. "It doesn't matter who you are. At this point, it doesn't matter." His eyes lit up. "But just know that as a spectator, I'll be watching everything with much interest."

As he prepared to stand up, he then squatted down again and added, "And as a pearl of wisdom, you should know that Kwon Tae Hyun and Lee Ji Hoon didn't get to the position they are in today by being fools. They are both selfish, arrogant, power-hungry and calculating little bastards." He laughed dryly. "This in turn makes them ideal candidates for being the first true Lord of the Underworld."

Yoori gaped at him dubiously. "Why are you telling me this?"

Ju Won shrugged mildly. "It's just for your own personal reference and a fair warning. They will do whatever it takes to get what they want in the end. And you, my child, shouldn't be afraid of extending the same courtesy."

Without allowing Yoori time to absorb his words, Ju Won stood up, ending their interaction with a statement of dismissal. "Now please leave. I'd like to meet with Tae Hyun and Ji Hoon privately."

Not having to be told twice, for she had been ready to leave since she entered this building, Yoori used Ju Won's chair as a means to prop herself up.

As a courtesy, she smiled wryly at the three Advisors. They were watching her with their arms folded, their faces expressionless. She limped past them, pain rippling throughout her body. She grimaced. It felt like she had just been through a war. Hard to believe that it was only five minutes of beating—five minutes worth of beating that left five years worth of toll on her now broken body.

Before leaving, Yoori stopped in her tracks. Tilting her head back, she found herself doing a gradual 360-degree turn. She stared up at the darkness that inhabited the ceilings. Then she listened. Her eyes became vigilant as she listened to the snipers' breathing. She could sense it. They were *terrified* of her.

Yoori almost found herself lost in another stupor when she felt her body twitch in pain, begging her to go lay down somewhere. Ceasing her impromptu staring, Yoori began toward the door once more. The brown oak doors creaked open when she neared it. She pulled at the knob, ready to walk out when she heard something that made her stop in her tracks.

She turned like a snake, locking eyes with Ju Won.

He did not repeat himself and she did not need him to. She heard every word he conveyed—she just didn't understand the meaning behind it.

"It is only unjust for the people who kneel before you."

34: The Heir to the Throne

Emerging out of the darkness and into the dim lighting of the corridor, a traumatized Yoori was met by an anxious Tae Hyun. He was waiting impatiently by the door, his arms folded in anticipation. An equally anxious Ji Hoon, crouched on the opposite side of the door, was next to him.

"Where are you hurt?" they both asked at the same time, each advancing to her with the swiftest of speeds.

By the manner in which they paused, it was clear that both gang leaders concluded that it was a stupid question to ask. It was obvious she was hurting everywhere.

Surprised by the genuine worry in each of their voices, Yoori, still flabbergasted by what occurred in the meeting room, just stared at both of them awkwardly, unable to part her bloody lips to answer.

In response to her uncomfortable silence, Tae Hyun and Ji Hoon merely glared at one another without muttering a word.

Yoori thought it was interesting and out of character how they didn't exchange words of insults. However, she concluded that they must've spent enough time talking—or arguing—with one another while she was "initiated" in that five minutes timeframe.

"I'm okay," she said when she found her voice.

Even though the statement was far from the truth, she didn't want them to worry. Given that they were about to go into the meeting with the Advisors, they didn't need to be distracted.

"They want to have a private meeting with the two of you."

Despite her assurance, the worry had already started.

Cupping her face with his hands, Tae Hyun delicately scoured her face for all the maladies present. Apparently he found a big one.

"Who the fuck kicked your face?" he inquired, his voice vexed as he wiped the blood off of her mouth.

She grimaced. Oh, he should see the bloody hip...

"Who the hell hit you with a stick?" Ji Hoon asked, inspecting the splinters buried in her skin as he held her hand up.

Yoori was past listening at that second. She was too busy replaying a significant pearl of wisdom that Ju Won gave to her: *"They will do whatever it takes to get what they want in the end. And you, my child, shouldn't be afraid of extending the same courtesy."*

Yoori wasn't too sure if Ju Won voiced that "pearl of wisdom" to her because he wanted to inflict mistrust between her and the two gang leaders, but as the genuine concern of their voices flowed through her mind, Yoori decided then to merely place that pearl of wisdom in the back of her head. She would refer to it for reference, not for truth.

"I'm okay," she repeated, mustering up a smile that quickly wilted under her wounded lips. She crinkled her face, unable to hide the pain. She regarded them wearily. "I just want to go home," she added, her voice barely above a whisper.

She felt really discombobulated. There was so much on her mind and so much pain dancing up and down her body. At this rate, going to sleep was the only remedy she wanted.

When it looked like Tae Hyun was ready to nod in understanding, his eyes flashed red when he saw that Ji Hoon was holding Yoori's hand.

"Don't touch her," he ordered ominously. He pulled Yoori away from Ji Hoon. His eyes were hard as steel. "Haven't we established that she's my girlfriend and not yours?"

Ji Hoon's face turned grim at the unpleasant reminder. "Clearly," he said through gritted teeth.

"And you will do well to remember that."

Yoori's mouth was gaping open the entire time. Was this another one of Tae Hyun's "performances" or was he serious? He wasn't really jealous, was he?

"I'm glad you're okay, Yoori," Ji Hoon said quietly, the tenseness in his countenance loosening upon addressing her. He gave her a small smile before he flashed Tae Hyun a quick glare and proceeded into the meeting room.

When Ji Hoon was out of sight, Tae Hyun found the back of Yoori's hand smacking him across the chest.

"What the fu—?"

"That was so insensitive of you!" Yoori whispered crossly, feeling a bit of her spunky personality return in face of Tae Hyun's behavior. Even though she didn't like that he was being so terrible with Ji Hoon, she found herself secretly flattered with the jealousy he publicly displayed. Even if there was a strong possibility it was all for show, it pleased her nonetheless.

Tae Hyun laughed, purposely ignoring her disapproving comment. He had other things he wanted to address. He lifted his hand to her face and begun to help wipe the remaining dried blood off of it.

Regret in his voice, he said, "Didn't I tell you that you shouldn't have come?"

"Rub it in, will you?" she muttered drily, staying still as he continued to delicately wipe against her skin.

He hid a smile. "Apparently that's what I'm doing right now."

Yoori laughed quietly. Only with Tae Hyun could she genuinely smile after getting hazed senseless by three crime lords and nine snipers.

He continued to rub the dried blood away with his thumb. "Kang Min and Jae Won are waiting in the limo. You go to the hospital and then go home first. I'm going to be in late tonight so don't miss me too much."

Yoori rolled her eyes at the tail end of his comment.

He gazed sharply at the splinters buried inside the skin of her hand. "Dong Min was the one who hit you with the unshaven stick, wasn't he?"

"How'd you figure?"

Tae Hyun smirked knowingly. Bitterness resonated in his voice. "It was his favorite weapon of choice when he trained me."

"Oh I see—*oww*!" Yoori yelped when he accidentally applied pressure on the sensitive part of her face.

Tae Hyun sighed at her reaction, his eyes full of regret that he brought her to Ju Won's mansion. He withdrew his hands from her face.

"I'm going to kill them," he muttered to himself, backing away from her. His eyes raged with a deadly storm. "Get some rest. I'll see you at home."

Without another word or a wave of goodbye, an angry Tae Hyun stormed into the meeting room. The doors to the entrance closed behind him, leaving Yoori with the muffled sounds of Tae Hyun's irate voice screaming at the Advisors before the brown oak doors completely clicked shut.

■ ■ ■

"Ah," Yoori cried when she stumbled into the limo, her back hitting the leather seat closest to the door with a soft thud. Before allowing herself time to acclimate with the comfortable seating, Yoori took it upon herself to pull the door closed as the limo began to take off.

She heaved a breath before turning her attention to the two pairs of familiar eyes that were already locked on her.

"Hey boss."

"Hey Yoori."

The brothers greeted her in unison, each sitting at opposite ends of the limo. Their faces and bodies were as beaten up as hers. Between the three of them, it was hard to figure out who was in the most pain—and who was the ugliest.

"Hey," Yoori croaked. She readjusted her seating to make it more comfortable for the ride ahead.

It was probably because they were each in pain and had a lot on their minds, but as the limo picked up speed, a companionable stillness fell between Yoori and the boys. The only sound was the whirring of the limo moving against the windy streets.

Though they didn't say anything to one another, their eyes were more than active.

Darting their eyes from one person to the next, their lips remained sealed under the looming cloud of silence. Each stared at the bloody lips, the various cuts and bruises, the footprint embedded clothes, ragged hair, injured hands – all the maladies that the other individuals wore almost identically.

And then, just as the anticipatory stillness became too intense to handle, a common sound broke out from each of their lips.

"...Hehehehe."

Suppressed snickering illuminated the dark limo.

With one last glance at one another, the final action that acted as the last straw that broke the happy camel's back, the sound of guffawing roared through the vicinity of the limo. In one smooth action, Yoori and the boys pointed at one another and exploded in silliness.

"Hahaha! Look at your face!"

"*Hello* Yoda! Puhahahaha!"

"You—you—ahahaha—you guys look like the personification of shit!"

No longer able to sit straight from the explosion of laughter, they each fell to the side, the tickling escape of their laughter erupting with more intensity.

"Oww! Oww!"

Then came the punishment from the damaged fibers within their assaulted bodies.

Yoori began to cough relentlessly, her throat clogging up in pain. Jae Won clutched his stomach as he wheezed in agony while Kang Min placed a trembling finger over his cut lip that had extended too far from laughter. The unexpected pain, as agonizing as it was, wasn't enough to dampen their spirits. Quiet laughs continued to radiate from their lips.

Yoori smiled, fondly eyeing the brothers. Yes. Even under dire circumstances, Yoori and the boys continued to have that unspoken connection that made being around each other the best remedy they could ask for after the round of beatings they endured.

Having calmed down since the eruption of laughter, they sat upright once more.

"Who did that to you guys?" Yoori asked breathlessly, laying the back of her head against the seat.

"The same people who initiated you," Jae Won answered hoarsely.

Yoori groaned painfully. "It's like they took out all their anger on me."

"Yeah," concurred Jae Won. "Ju Won and the Shins aren't known to be very forgiving."

"If it makes you feel better, you came out looking better than Jae Won and I did when we were initiated." Kang Min smiled wryly, a move he regretted when he felt the pain from the cut on his lips. He shook his head again. "Dude, I couldn't see for two weeks after my initiation."

Yoori gaped at him. Couldn't see for two weeks? *Two weeks*?

Jae Won nodded, still clutching on to his stomach. "I broke several bones."

Broken bones?

"Oh, the curse of not being born an Underworld baby," Kang Min muttered sullenly, briefly closing his eyes to control his breathing. He then opened his eyes and gazed at Yoori. The same concern that brimmed within his eyes inside Ju Won's mansion appeared again. "How do you feel?"

"Scared shitless," she answered bluntly, finding it unnecessary to lie to Kang Min and Jae Won.

The brothers nodded in understanding, a serious air floating between them. The carefree icebreaker, as wonderful as it was, didn't blind them from the importance of venturing on to the much somber conversation at hand.

Once the air changed, the inevitable topic came up.

"Did they bring her up?" Jae Won asked.

He didn't need to specify who "her" was.

Yoori's warmth obliterated at the reminder.

Composing herself, she nodded slowly. "Ju Won said, 'You remind me of someone. Which is too bad because she didn't leave being on my good side.' Then they started the initiation."

The muscles in their jaws tightened. It was as if their fears were confirmed.

"Why did your jaws tighten?" Yoori asked suspiciously.

She observed that they were also twitching uncomfortably.

Now they avoided eye contact.

Yoori was beside herself with their silence. How dare they withhold information when she just shared something important?

"Jae Won?" she asked purposely, knowing he was the blabbermouth of the two.

His eyes remained strangely interested in the red carpet of the limo instead of on her. He bit his lower lip uneasily.

She grimaced, holding in an emission of anger before turning to Kang Min. He was finding interest in staring at the rope burns on his wrist. So apparently it was taboo to talk to her now?

She glowered at the two brothers. The overwhelming urge to smack them across the heads burned in her splinter filled hands.

"Are you kidding me?" She shook her head in disappointment. "Is this how it is?" she asked, unable to mask the melancholy in her voice.

Her somber voice acted as a trigger that caused the boys to drag their eyes away from their visual distractions and on to her. Both then heaved a loud sigh as a non-verbal way of consenting to one another about the conversation they were about to embark on.

Kang Min parted his lips, being the first to start the much-anticipated conversation.

Or so Yoori thought until she saw that he reached behind his back to retrieve something instead.

She was surprised to see him pull out the gold gun that belonged to Jae Won. Yoori stared at the gun that rested on the palm of his hand. He chose this moment to return it to Jae Won? Would it kill the kid to do it *after* he told her what she wanted to know?

She silently watched Jae Won lean forward to retrieve the gun—or so she thought until she saw him reach behind his own back.

Yoori's eyes enlarged when Jae Won pulled out a gold gun of his own. "There's...there's *two*?"

Questions started swarming her head like bees to honey. Yoori then realized the complexities of the conversation she was about to embark on with the brothers.

"Two identical gold guns were gifted to our boss from her father," Jae Won enlightened.

"As two of her most trusted Scorpions, we were each given a gun to look after," Kang Min supplied, touching the gold surface of the gun he held.

Yoori wanted to ask how Ju Won came into possession of the gun when Jae Won continued. "Guns are important to gang members like badges are to cops," he explained, staring at his own gun. "Our boss revered her guns like pets that she spent her life growing up with. She loved them."

"A gun can be used for many things. Some more obvious than others," Kang Min pressed on, lifting his eyes off his gun and on to Yoori. "Some revere their guns so much that it slowly begins to symbolize their honor—their word."

The dawn of comprehension brightened in Yoori's eyes.

It was all becoming clearer.

She parted her quaking lips, anxiety and anticipation reveling within it. "An Soo Jin promised Seo Ju Won something?"

Jae Won lifted his eyes to meet hers. "A favor."

"What favor?" she asked earnestly.

When Jae Won didn't answer immediately, she turned to Kang Min. "What favor?" she asked again, curiosity drenched in her voice.

Kang Min shook his head at her. "I honestly don't know." He paused, as if debating about sharing anymore. After taking a second to ponder the matter, he forged on. "I remember her saying that she was going to take care of some rival crime syndicates. I asked if she wanted me to accompany her, but she told me that this was a delicate meeting and that it had to be just her. 'I just need my gun.' I didn't think twice about it and handed it to her."

"How did she tell you she lost it?" asked Yoori, understanding it was the likely excuse An Soo Jin would give as to how the gun went missing.

"In a brawl with rival gang members," answered Kang Min.

"Now that I think about it," Jae Won mused. "She didn't seem too upset by it."

"Yeah, do you remember? She started acting strange. Like completely different. It was weird because it all happened right before the club—" Kang Min halted with his thoughts when he realized that Yoori was listening intently. Regretting his slip of a tongue, Yoori could sense that Kang Min was mentally scolding himself.

"The 'Club Massacre,'" prompted Yoori, dead-set on prying this information from him. "That's what you were about to say, right?"

Anxiousness undulated in her eyes. What a fool she had been to only depend on Ji Hoon for the knowledge of what happened that night. Of course An Soo Jin's two right hand men would have some knowledge pertaining to what occurred that night.

"Wh–what exactly happened that night?" she asked, trying to suppress the zeal in her voice.

Her heartbeat quickened, every part of her body fascinated by what really occurred that night. For the split moment in time, nothing mattered. It didn't matter that her body was throbbing. It didn't matter that she despised Soo Jin and didn't want to be associated with her. It didn't matter how uncomfortable Jae Won and Kang Min were when it was clear they didn't want to talk to her about this. None of that mattered. Consumed, all Yoori cared about was finding out more about what happened.

The brothers glanced uncertainly at each other. When they received confirmation from one another that since they'd ventured this far already, they might as well take Yoori all the way, Jae Won began to speak.

"The first thing you should know about our relationship with our boss is that the three of us were really close. We confided in one another and told each other everything."

"That was until the night after she 'lost' her gun," Kang Min added. "After that night, she started acting distant—secretive even. She was troubled with something. Something she couldn't talk to anyone about."

"Kang Min and I tried to ask her what was going on, but she kept insisting that everything was fine, that she was just exhausted from working too hard."

Kang Min spoke. "We heard about the killings in the club just like everyone else. Some lowly gang members were hanging out in a nearby alley when they spotted her and Lee Ji Hoon coming out of the club. They said she was covered in blood. Curious, they snuck into the club and were horrified to find the tiles covered with blood and various dead bodies with their fingers cut off."

"An infamous trademark that our boss employed to torture or to interrogate people she needed to get information out of," Jae Won enlightened, sending unnatural chills through Yoori.

Kang Min barreled on. "Shortly after finding the bodies, they heard cars approaching the club. They ran out, but not before catching glimpses of Ji Hoon's men infiltrating the club, gathering up all the bodies, and disposing of them."

"Did you guys ask her what happ—?"

Yoori didn't get to finish when Jae Won cut her off.

"She didn't want to talk about it and we were smart enough not to push our luck. When our boss was set on something, she was set for life. If she didn't want to talk, then you ended the conversation there."

"I heard her crying the nights following that event though," Kang Min supplied, his voice soft as he recollected the final memories of his boss.

Jae Won's face became melancholic. "Yeah, I heard it too..."

"Didn't one of the other Scorpions find the bloody clothes she dumped in the garbage?"

"Yeah," confirmed Jae Won.

Yoori's eyes fell on to the guns Jae Won and Kang Min held. Her eyes fixated on Kang Min's. She recalled the conversation she had with Ji Hoon about Soo Jin never being the same after the night in the club. What he said never really touched a nerve within her.

Yet, with Jae Won and Kang Min's information, Yoori actually felt her heart go out to Soo Jin. It seemed that the guilt ate Soo Jin up.

She shook her head.

Now was not the time to be distracted.

She measured the guns once more, the wheels of her mind running wildly. She began to put the puzzle pieces together.

"An Soo Jin met up with Ju Won and gave him her gun as collateral. And then you said she started to act distant shortly thereafter, like she was conflicted about something she promised she'd do for him. After that, the murders in the club took place and she was mum about that."

The question, "Why did An Soo Jin choose that particular family?" popped into Yoori's already swirling mind and she gasped, gaping at the brothers horrorstruck.

"Do you think Soo Jin interrogated and killed those people for Ju Won? What information did she want from them?"

The brothers shook their heads, harboring the same unanswered questions.

"We have no idea," said Jae Won. "But we think she never gave the information to him."

Kang Min nodded, lifting up his gold gun. "Ju Won returning this gun wasn't a gracious act. It was his subtle way of reminding you that a favor is still owed to him."

Yoori breathed heavily, her heart nearly stopping in fear. "Because he thinks I'm An Soo Jin."

She understood now why Ju Won said, "*There's still unfinished business left on the table.*" He wasn't done with Soo Jin, not by a long shot.

"Ju Won immediately recognized Jae Won as a former Scorpion," Kang Min continued at once. "But he didn't recognize me—not at first. No one ever really does because I looked much different when I was fifteen. But when he saw you in the meeting room, I guess everything fit together for him. Jae Won and I going after Jin Ae to make sure she kneels before you and us being overprotective—I can't imagine him viewing you as anyone else but An Soo Jin."

Having understood why Ju Won said Soo Jin left being on his bad side, Yoori wondered about their history. "What was his relationship with Soo Jin?"

"Seo Ju Won had very close ties to the Scorpion family," said Jae Won. "He only had one student that he mentored."

"And that student was Soo Jin?"

Jae Won nodded. "That's the reason why her status in the Underworld was elevated to such high levels even before she made her first official appearance into the Underworld society. Everyone knew about the Princess of Scorpions who was trained, not only by Seo Ju Won, but also the Shin Brothers—the most infamous and revered crime lords in the history of the Underworld. The Advisors revered her and that meant that the Underworld revered her as well."

"And now you think Ju Won is coming after me for the information he thinks I have because of my resemblance to Soo Jin..."

"That's why we were worried for you when we saw you walking in," said Jae Won. "Ju Won, as kind and friendly as he may appear, is calculating and scheming beyond words. If he wants something, he'll do whatever it takes to get it. He has no qualms about using others and pitting them against one another. In the end, all that matters is that he gets what he wants."

Taking note of her shivering state, Kang Min added, "Aside from a select few in this world, there is no one you can trust. Chances are, Ju Won already has them wrapped around his fingers, ready and willing to do his bidding."

"We're the only ones you can trust, Yoori," said Jae Won, his expression severe.

In that second, Ju Won's pearl of wisdom appeared in her mind concerning Tae Hyun and Ji Hoon.

"But what about Tae Hyun and Ji Hoon?" She recalled the scene where they both rushed over to her after she exited the meeting room. "I mean, they both have been looking out for me and—"

"We're still not sure about Tae Hyun. That's why you can't tell him about your resemblance," Jae Won replied candidly. "But right now, we trust that he's the best one to take care of you. He's the only one who doesn't seem whipped by Ju Won."

"But you can't trust Ji Hoon at all," Kang Min emphasized, staring at her dead in the eyes.

She gazed at him in amazement. She couldn't trust Ji Hoon *at all*?

"Why would you say that?" she inquired. "Wasn't he Soo Jin's boyfriend? They were in love."

"We never trusted him," said Kang Min. "Even when he was with her, we never trusted him."

Yoori was lost in a fog of confusion. "Has he done something to make you think he's not trustworthy?"

"It's more of a gut instinct," Jae Won provided. "We're unsure of Tae Hyun, but we don't trust Ji Hoon. There's no evidence or proof, just human gut instinct."

"What does your gut instinct tell you, Yoori?" Kang Min asked patiently, noting the uncertainty in her eyes.

The limo came to a slow stop in front of the hospital, a prelude to the curtains falling on to their conversation for the night.

She spoke without hesitation. "That I can trust both of them."

The brothers nodded in silence, offering no outright objections to her prerogative.

As the limo came to a complete stop beside the curb, Yoori's head bounced slightly forward. Like an ocean wave had collided against her, she recalled the last thing Ju Won said to her before she left the meeting room. They were simple words that held a world of meaning now.

Coldness seeped into her at the realization.

"Before I left the room," Yoori began quietly, claiming Jae Won and Kang Min's attention. Her eyes were lost in an unblinking stupor as she stared into space. "Ju Won said to me, *'I had always favored you.'*"

An upsurge of shock and understanding flickered in the brothers' gaze as she continued, their breathing growing slow in unison with hers.

"I didn't think much of it until now, but I think that for their deal, in exchange for what happened in the club that night…Ju Won promised An Soo Jin the Underworld."

"But just like all things in life ..."

35: Disappearing Act

Breathe in.
Breathe out.
Breathe in.
Breathe out.

As Yoori laid in the enveloping darkness of Tae Hyun's bedroom, she found herself completely and utterly consumed with thoughts of what occurred before Tae Hyun's personal physician treated her at the hospital.

Her mind raced.

Ju Won now saw her as An Soo Jin—as did everyone else who knew Soo Jin (with the exception of Ji Hoon of course, whom Jae Won and Kang Min adamantly informed her that she couldn't trust).

Soo Jin gave up her gun as a promise of a favor to Ju Won.

Ju Won returned the gun as a gesture of reminding her (Yoori) that she still needed to return the favor.

"There's still unfinished business left on the table..."

Ju Won now expected her to take care of the unfinished business. The information Soo Jin gathered from the night she tortured and killed an entire family...Ju Won still expected Yoori to give it to him. And finally the most troubling recollection of all, the one that occurred seconds before she walked out of the door after her initiation.

"You should know that..." Ju Won had begun softly, sitting on his chair as she came to a halt. "I had always favored you."

Ju Won groomed An Soo Jin to become the Lord of the Underworld, but before he gave her the Underworld, he needed her to perform a favor. He needed her to torture and kill the family in the club to gather information for him— information that Soo Jin never gave to him because she was supposedly too plagued with guilt from torturing and killing the family.

Yoori closed her eyes in agony, her heart pounding against her chest. The pit in her stomach grew deeper as every image came into her mind like a movie.

Her initiation...The fights...Her heightened sense of hearing...Her quick instincts when it came to avoiding bullets...Her agility to perform backflips and spin kicks that she had never done before in her life...

As she laid in silence, her eyes welling up with tears, Yoori couldn't help but finally gasp softly, the sound of her voice ricocheting into the darkness. With her heavy heart as her guide, Yoori knew then that she could no longer ignore it. The impending flood of wretchedness thrashed against the walls she had built. Biting her lower lip as a teardrop slipped down from her eye and onto the pillow, she knew that the evidence was becoming irrefutable…

She…She was really An Soo—

No!

Yoori shook her head stubbornly. No, she would not think it. It was a damning acceptance that terrified every fiber of her body. She thought about the hatred she would have for herself if she really were An Soo Jin. She thought about the overwhelming guilt that would rain over her if she had to accept Soo Jin's unforgivable sins as her own. She thought about all the misery and pain she would experience if this possibility became true.

The tears of desperation in her eyes said it all: if there should ever come a time where she had to truly admit she was someone so awful, then Yoori didn't know how she would be able to live with herself. Would she even be able to live?

Deep in the subconscious crevices of her mind, Yoori knew it was foolish of her to continue to believe that there was a *slight* chance that her resemblance to An Soo Jin was a mere coincidence. All the evidence pointed to the contrary.

She knew it was foolish.

It was a foolish desperation in a foolish girl's heart to fight something that was so obvious—to fight the fact that she truly was An Soo Jin. Despite her acceptance of her foolishness, she continued to fight—she continued to avoid the inevitable.

Would it be so wrong to kneel in front of that dam and block out the flood of truth for just a bit longer? Would it be so wrong to lie to herself and try to hold on to the slight chance that she wasn't An Soo Jin? Would it be so wrong to *try* and save herself from the pain and misery that came with being An Soo Jin?

Her chin wobbled.

It was wrong.

It was so wrong, but Yoori didn't care.

Someone once told her that denial was a human being's best friend and she couldn't have embraced that fact more now, when she was at her lowest point in life. She was too agonized to care if she was being foolish. She was too desperate to care if she was only delaying the inevitable.

So there she continued to fight, kneeling as she pressed her hands against the dam that kept away the wretched waters. The water fought to break through. *She could hear it.* She could hear it calling out to her. It wanted to drown her, to swallow her whole. But she wouldn't let it—not if she could be in denial for a little bit longer, not if she could hold out and save herself from the pain for a little bit longer. *Just a little bit longer…*

Finally closing her tear-filled eyes, she decided to seal this prerogative by embarking on to a long slumber. *Yes.* If she slept, then she could forget about all of this and start anew in the morning. She'd continue to live as she was living now, clueless, but happy with herself.

And that was what she did.

As Yoori drifted off, she vehemently decided that denial was going to be her best friend for as long as she could keep it. The truth would come when it needed to come, but for now, she would escape into her dream world where she was still the innocent Choi Yoori...

She dreamt about Tae Hyun as she slept. She dreamt that she heard him open the door. She dreamt that he came and kneeled beside her. She dreamt that he wiped her tears away while gingerly stroking her hair. She dreamt that he kissed her in her sleep.

"...Tae Hyun?" she whispered, looking at him through heavily lidded eyes. She was so exhausted.

Tae Hyun appeared in her field of vision, sitting on the other side of the bed. The sky outside was pitch dark, making it appear as if the world around them was sleeping with her. If he wasn't stroking her hair, making her feel good all over, then she would've deduced that she was actually awake.

She decided it was better to be safe and ask.

"Is this a dream?" she asked sleepily, blinking at him lethargically.

Tae Hyun nodded, his smile so breathtaking even in dreams.

He lowered himself and then scooped her up in his arms. While still sitting up, he was careful not to aggravate the pain in her body as he gently laid her on his hard chest.

Taking advantage of the dream, Yoori laid her chin on his chest and gazed up at him.

For a long moment they laid there like that, Tae Hyun stroking her hair while Yoori gazed up at him. His fingers gradually slid from her hair to the cut and bruises near her lips.

"How long have you been crying?" he finally whispered, wiping away the residual tears.

"Since I got home," she murmured distractedly, so sleepy that she couldn't even focus on staying alert for her dream.

He nodded, staring somberly at her for a couple more seconds.

After what felt like an eternity, he whispered, "I'm sorry for everything." He held her gaze, his finger lightly caressing the bruises on her face. "I didn't know anything like this would happen. If I knew, I would've never dragged you into this world."

"Not...not your fault..." she simply whispered, slowly finding that this dream was about to come to an end. She was about to leave for another dream.

"Everything is my fault," he responded softly. A resolve unlike any other filled his eyes. "But I promise you—I will never let this happen to you again."

"How can you make such a promise?" Yoori smiled sleepily before answering her own question. "Because you're a King in this world?"

Tae Hyun smiled. "Because I am a God in this world—because they will all kneel before me soon. And when they kneel before me, I will have them fall to their knees for you as well."

"Why do you care about protecting me?"

Tae Hyun's smile remained—if not warmer and more doting than ever. Rather than answering, he stroked her cheek, watching knowingly as she drifted further away.

"Are you leaving me for another dream already, assistant?"

"I don't want to go."

"I know you don't," he said soothingly.

"...Hold me until I go," she said softly.

He obliged. He held her close to him and lifted the covers over them as Yoori drifted further into her next dream.

"I will make it up to you," he whispered, his lips caressing her ear. "Starting tomorrow, I will make it up to you."

"How?"

"We're going to pull a disappearing act."

Yoori smiled at the simple statement before closing her eyes. As she left for another dream, she relished in the sensation of how beautiful this dream was—how incredible it felt to be held by someone like Tae Hyun—even if he was only a figment of her dream.

"I will see you tomorrow then," she murmured before drifting away, her subconscious completely forgetting about Tae Hyun's promise, completely forgetting about this beautiful moment and completely forgetting that this dream ever occurred.

"See you tomorrow," said Tae Hyun before she left him for another dream world. "Sweet dreams, Sleeping Beauty."

"You should know that what goes around comes around."

36: Clash of the Gods

The meeting room was quiet after an unusually busy night.

The "guests" had left, the Kings were gone, and the snipers had vacated. Other than the scent of blood, one would not have surmised that the room hosted a vicious five-minute initiation that would've killed hundreds of others in a heartbeat.

In the midst of this stillness stood Ju Won.

He lingered at the center of the floor, leisurely staring at a large projector that was split into three screens. The center screen showed a video of Ji Hoon fighting six men and using his kendo stick every so often to knock the life out of them. The screen to the right showed Tae Hyun fighting with dozens of men. Holding a sword, he swung at the masses with enviable agility. The screen to the left was grainier. It showed a clip of a third figure standing on a stage with two guns in hand. Before that third figure kneeled hundreds of people.

"I never thought I'd live to see the day where An Soo Jin would be standing across from me again," Ju Won finally said when the two elder brothers stepped in the room behind him. They had cleaned themselves up.

"Why did you return her gun?" Dong Min asked, wiping his hand with a tissue. His eyes were on the projector.

"I did not want her to forget what she promised me."

"She doesn't remember anything," stated Jung Min, staring transfixed at the projector as well.

Ju Won smiled, watching as the third figure in the video clip stepped into the light, revealing the face of An Soo Jin.

A face that looked just like Choi Yoori's.

"Her past is littered across this city. She may have found solace in blocking out the truth, but she cannot escape from the legend of her existence."

Ju Won smirked, watching as the scene changed to a clip where the infamous Queen beheaded three fully-grown men. There was a satisfied smile on her angelic face as she kicked the heads away, demanding another round of executions.

Ju Won's eyes then slid over to the scene where Tae Hyun was fighting with a sword, displaying unmatched skills as he sparred with his enemies. There was no question that he would emerge from the battle alive and victorious.

"What an interesting turn of events. The favored King and the infamous Queen." He turned to the other Advisors. "Between the two, who do you think will win if they fight to the death for the Underworld throne?"

They remained quiet and Ju Won smiled. He turned back to the projector. On the screens, the favored King and the infamous Queen were both wiping blood from their faces, looking like young Gods walking the earth.

Ju Won laughed.

His smile turned merciless as the clip of Yoori and Tae Hyun together just moments prior came on, overtaking Ji Hoon's screen. The video clip displayed Tae Hyun cupping Yoori's face, whispering something to her before her initiation commenced. The video was a polar opposite to the violent clips on either side of it. Whereas on the left and right screens, the King and Queen looked like living Gods, the center screen showed them as, oddly enough, humans.

"I do not know either..." Ju Won said, amused. His anticipation for their inevitable war further lit up the cruel smile on his face.

"All I know is that it will be the battle of a lifetime...and I cannot wait to witness every moment of it."

ABOUT THE AUTHOR

Con Template currently resides in California. When she is not occupied with daydreaming about traveling around the world, she relishes in being able to enjoy one of her greatest passions in life: conning realities.

Welcome to the Underworld is her first novel.

The Fall of Gods, Book 2 of the Welcome to the Underworld novels, was released on August 31st, 2013.

You can follow her at *contemplate13.wordpress.com* or *twitter.com/contemplate13*.

Printed in Great Britain
by Amazon